Shattered Shells

Francene Stanley

Cover Art:
Michelle Crocker

http://mlcdesigns4you.weebly.com/

Publisher's Note:

This is a work of fiction. All names, characters, places, and
events are the work of the author's imagination.

Any resemblance to real persons, places, or events is
coincidental.

Solstice Publishing - www.solsticepublishing.com

Shattered Shells

Francene Stanley

Dedication:

To all the experiences in my life, good and bad, I owe balance and understanding. Each person I meet has their own memories to carry. This knowledge allows me to see deep down and find a way to redeem the wonderful, rich characters in my novels.

Prologue

The buzz of conversation and steam hit George with the strength of an open furnace. The outer door swung shut behind him, cutting off any hope of fresh air. A bell tinkled, straight out of a kiddy's story about Santa's sleigh.

Women laughed and chatted beside occasional bored men while George approached the counter.

Despite gloomy reports, business was booming in the tearooms. A grin tugged the corners of his mouth. They needed protection.

George studied his custom-made pointy-toed boots to hide his glee. He wasn't buying into their fairy story. But they might be interested in his.

The young waitress placed a pot of tea beside a couple of women and glanced up. "I'll be with you in a minute."

"Take your time, love." Tea wasn't on his agenda. He leaned against the counter and tuned into nearby conversation.

"Have you visited Liliha since ...?"

"It's hit her pretty hard. Lucky her daughters were staying with her."

"I can't believe Beatrice left him to bleed to death in that old shed."

"What a horrible way to go."

George recollected the local murder a couple of weeks ago. A mentally disturbed woman took revenge on a former lover, the papers said. George tuned into their words again.

"... together." A cup rattled onto the saucer. "She'd sold a song, she'd married her love—"

"And moved into a wonderful home. Then, she lost it all."

"She never got a driver's license, did she?"

"She couldn't risk driving, what with the moonstone ring and everything."

The flushed waitress approached the counter with a handful of cash. George filed his speculation about the ring and straightened, ready to pitch his opening line. He should take on a partner. 'Hopkins and Co. Local Protection Specialists for St. Ives.'

Chapter One

Despite her pledge not to dwell on events, Liliha's stinging eyes promised a flow of tears. She missed Oliver so much. The train's table separated her swaying body from two passengers on the other side. She dipped her head so a curtain of hair shielded her.

The seat vibrated while she gained control, straightened and took note of her surroundings. Miles of suburbia flashed past the window on the return journey to St. Ives. She'd said goodbye to her daughters at the airport in London—Alissa off to boarding school and Kaelyn to begin a new job. *So lonely.*

To stave off a further outburst, Liliha tilted the moonstone ring on her right hand. The asterism, an optical effect inside the crystal, caught the flash of the star imprisoned at the beginning of creation. Although unbelievable in the present day, the ring contained hidden power. In ways she had yet to understand, the ring let her have visions of another place.

She glanced from the men reading their paper close by to the passengers across the aisle. A stranger's eyes flashed before he looked away.

How unprotected she must appear. Wearing the jewel on the train had been foolhardy, especially during her grief.

A hint of something sweet hovered in the air. In the next breath, the fragrance of lily flooded over her—the usual forerunner to a change of location. Heartbeats pounded in her ears. Would a vision pull her mind away right now on the train? With her fingers losing strength, an attempt to jerk the ring off did no good.

How could she help someone in trouble or avert harm

in her present state of mind?

Surroundings faded while a yawning aperture opened inside her mind. After a rumble and crack, hot wind stung her cheeks and hinted at danger. A sucking sensation dragged her consciousness into the familiar churning, twisting tunnel.

Red and gray pulsed on the outer perimeter. Her stomach tightened. No turning away. Be strong.

***

Without a body, ethereal as a spirit, I surrender to the freedom of the void between locations. My intuition rages amongst flashes and whirring sounds.

While the cloud which obscures my sight lifts in patches, I brace to confront whatever task faces me. I float in the air with no sensation of movement.

In a sudden rush, my experience of floating in a hot-air balloon changes to a plunge down the steep incline of a roller-coaster without the stomach contraction.

My psyche penetrates a roof, in a similar way to someone disregarding atoms of glass so they can see. I arrive inside a room containing toys, two youngsters, and a sleeping baby.

In an incredible way, I merge with a woman approaching the doorway and see the children with her eyes, my movement and sight constricted by the confines of her body. The hands gripping a doctor's letter are delicate with almond-shaped fingernails. I note her name, Nasheen, and her address in Northern England.

Worry about her husband's behavior drags at her inner core. I strengthen myself to help her handle whatever problem brought me here.

But something's wrong.

A third presence floods Nasheen's mind with dark

thoughts sent in waves, dragging her attitude into a spiral track—malevolence personified in the thoughts of doom.

I exert full force to stabilize Nasheen's mind and issue the suggestion: 'Calm and still.'

Her tempestuous beliefs override mine. 'How many women has he been with? How many extra babies has he fathered'?

The other personality inside her murmurs, 'Your husband is away too often. He's having an affair.'

Nasheen nods.

She accepts voices as normal? I grope with sensitivity and discern positive memories. I whisper, 'Remember times when he was good to you.'

A bunch of flowers last Mother's Day flashes into her memory.

Doom whispers, 'That wasn't for you. It was for any mother.'

A childish scream rips the air. The young boy snatches a doll from his sister.

I murmur, 'Love the children. They need you.'

Nasheen pacifies the girl with a kiss while she focuses on an idea. 'When my husband leaves, I'll have no money to feed them.'

Doom suggests, 'Put them out of their misery, now, before they suffer.'

'The little ones are innocent,' I counter. 'Don't think that way.'

The dreadful concept takes hold inside Nasheen. They'll be unprotected without her husband.

I'm aghast. 'Wait until you've spoken to him. This may never happen.' When she sighs, I experience the movement as my own released breath.

'He'll lie to you,' Doom quips. 'Don't waste your

time.'

I urge rethinking, but Nasheen, with me confined within her, wanders to the kitchen. We approach the work surface cluttered with pans and implements. A knife glints in the light.

She thinks, 'I've got to save us all from a life of poverty.'

'If he leaves,' I counter, 'you will be looked after. Nobody would let you starve. Don't do this dreadful thing.'

We rub our forehead.

Dooms voice erupts. 'The fiend is deceiving you. He'll make sure you never get help.'

I push with a thrust of energy to block off the contradictory message.

'I'll kill them quickly,' Nasheen reasons. 'They don't have to suffer.' Despite my wishes, our hand reaches for the weapon.

The little ones are innocent.' As well as voices inside her head, one of which is me, Nasheen must be locked in the grip of depressive illness. I use every ounce of intensity to bombard her with a powerful flow of calm to prevent her from taking action. I whisper an urgent plea. 'Put the knife down.'

Despite my effort, we carry the weapon into the children's room. Our dull stare lingers on each child. The children lean away, eyes open wide.

My stunned reaction breaks free like a mother whose baby is about to do something dangerous. 'No. No.'

Doom wavers, and then relaxes the malevolent hold.

I surge in and control Nasheen's thoughts. 'Take the knife back to the kitchen. Smile at the little ones. They're scared.'

In a daze, she complies.

A high moan escapes our swollen lips. 'I'll kill myself.'

'Wait.' Compassion and sorrow ooze from me. 'No killing. You're sick. Let someone help you. Call the emergency services.'

'I deserve to suffer.' Her hands shake as she opens the cupboard beneath the sink. When she grasps an open packet of rat pellets, I shriek into her mind, 'Stop!'

I send a stronger message, using strength I didn't know I possessed. 'Pick up the phone and ... call ... for ... help.'

We struggle to our feet with a closed fist. One hand reaches for a glass before she grips and turns the tap. We fill our mouth with tablets and gulp the water.

Numb yet retaining the prompt of an emergency call, we reach for the phone, wait for the operator to answer, and then speak in a dull tone. "I want to die." Our slurred voice slows. "I've taken poison."

The phone crashes to the floor.

With an intense thirst, we fill the glass again. Our hands quiver while we lift it, gulp the contents, and then slump.

I sooth with words of comfort and love, in an effort to combat the searing pain.

The ambulance arrives with a clamor of sirens.

Released from the meld with my contact, I lift off, sending compassionate concepts to the attendants.

***

Perfume. Flashing colors. Seated in the train after her tumbling return, stuffy air and muffled talk grounded Liliha. She leaned forward over the table to ease her spine and flashed a glance at the other passengers. Nobody paid her any attention.

Her watch revealed less than three minutes had gone by. She'd been elsewhere in the world in the same time-frame. She shook her head at the crazy concept, yet it had happened.

While settling into a more comfortable position, regret blurred her sight. This vision had not been satisfying at all. *Too much sorrow in the world. Too much pain.* For her entire life, she'd suffered with Scoliosis, and her back became even more painful with a low mood. What had she achieved during the last vision? With the swiftness of a sea eagle, the memory of Nasheen's writhing body swooped into the depths of Liliha's mind. The woman was sick, warped by illness, alone in her own mind, but not evil. She hoped the ambulance had reached the poor mother in time. At least the children were safe.

The last-minute decision to accompany her own daughters to the airport in London had been right. Loved-ones had kept her from collapsing with grief. However, while they got on with their lives, she faced life alone and must deal with forthcoming visions.

The malicious force had appeared when the bracelet trapped Kaelyn. Now, the power in the bracelet must be influencing someone else—in the opposite way to the ring.

The scarab decoration sucked any person who touched the bracelet into a moral lure which caused dark thoughts. Just as the ring sent visions to allow her to correct a problem, the bracelet must have directed an unknown person to harm Nasheen. Liliha cursed the day the evil bracelet was stolen from her shed.

She'd struck a major problem. By keeping her promise to Kaelyn about wearing the ring, she risked more contact with the malevolence. Why subject herself to extra psychological torture?

A glance at the beautiful ring brought the quandary into focus. Good visions gave her a sense of purpose after Oliver's death.

She hoped the thief would tuck the bracelet out of harm's way rather than give in to a desire to participate in further evil.

Chapter Two

How long could she keep up this pretense of composure during the never-ending train trip? During the last two hours, mumbled conversation had surrounded Liliha from two dozen people seated close by. Three more hours to go before they reached Cornwall. Low rays of sunlight streamed in from the west. Motion from the train jolted her body sideways, and then returned her to the original position. Trees blurred outside the window ahead of open fields which extended to the horizon like the spread of the ocean.

"That's lovely."

At a woman's American accent, Liliha glanced to her left.

The stranger bumped Liliha's arm to peer at her hand. "I hope you don't mind me bothering you, but I love antiques and your ring looks old."

Pleased about the nudge into reality, Liliha twisted to face a speaker about the same age as herself. The lift of the woman's mouth and her gentle expression radiated good humor.

"You're right." Liliha's sigh resembled a released bird eager for freedom. A pleasant chat would lift her mood. "The museum told me this comes from ancient Egypt." The pride in her blurted words pricked her conscience. She glanced away to regroup her thoughts.

Seated at the window on the other side of the aisle, the man with dark hair picked at ragged fingernails. He released a drawn-out grunt in his yawn before he stared up at the luggage rack.

Liliha averted her gaze.

The woman lowered her crochet work, grasped

14

Liliha's hand and tilted it. "That's a hefty chunk of gold. Looks pure too."

"Twenty-four carat."

"It lifts the stone a fair way up. The deep blue stone's nearly as wide as your finger too. I've read tons of books on ancient Egypt. How did those cuts get on the shaft at the side?" She leaned closer, sending hair over her cheeks and a spicy fragrance into the air. "My name's Alana, by the way."

"Liliha. It's spelled L-i-l-i-h-a but pronounced Lilia like Celia." She glanced about in case anyone could overhear.

Passengers studied their papers, books or magazines. Two teenagers stared at screens, and the man with dark hair across the aisle faced the window again.

"Better lower our voices," Liliha murmured. "The cuts have been there for centuries. Apparently, someone severed a finger to remove this ring."

"Why did you think that?"

"The experts at the London Museum seemed to think so."

"They were cruel back then."

"Has anything changed? People can be so greedy and violent."

"You're right." Accent heightened, Alana used a conspiratorial whisper. "Tell me all about the ring. Is it worth a fortune?"

Liliha murmured, "Could be. The men I spoke to at the museum wanted to buy it. But I wouldn't part with it."

The man seated at the far window held his neck too stiff. Had he listened into their discussion? *Better test him.* What could she say to pique his interest? She spoke at the same level as before. "What's on the floor in the aisle? A fifty pound note?"

"Where." Alana glanced up from her crochet and leaned across.

The man didn't turn his head and neither did the kids or the other passengers.

They couldn't have eavesdropped. Liliha chuckled. "It's just an advertising flier. So much rubbish nowadays."

"Wasted paper." Alana sighed. "When will they stop cutting trees and clearing forests?"

Relieved to have changed the subject, Liliha passed her time in pleasant company until the train slowed.

Alana searched her bag and pulled out a ticket. "Do you live here in Penzance? I could give you a lift home if you like. My car's parked up the road."

"No need." Liliha donned her coat and clasped her purse. "I live close to a farm outside St. Ives."

"Which one?"

"The Peters' farm."

"I live at Zennor." Alana's brows lowered. "I pass right by. You must come with me."

"I planned to ring a friend of mine. He can get here in fifteen minutes. No need for you to bother." Liliha's chest tightened. Perhaps she'd been too friendly, too naive.

"You don't have to wait. Anyway, this way, he doesn't need to make the trip. That's settled."

"Very kind of you." Liliha squirmed about accepting a ride with a stranger. But local people were a friendly bunch on the whole—nothing like the people in London, who rushed along the street as if nobody else existed.

When the train jerked to a halt and the doors slid open, they emerged onto the breezy platform. People spewed out the gate and headed for the half mile of car park. Clutching her coat against her neck, Liliha squinted.

Pale gold rays from the sunset glinted over the harbor where boats rode choppy waves. Sparked by the beauty, fresh sorrow welled up inside her.

"This way," Alana said. "I've parked up the hill."

"If you don't mind, I'll ring William." *Best to be safe.* "William Trevellyn. I'll let him know you're taking me so he doesn't worry." All she'd wanted was to climb into Oliver's father's familiar car and let him drive her home.

"Tell him it's Alana Mautone from Zennor."

Liliha made the call, and to her surprise, William knew Alana. She'd moved to the area when Oliver was a youngster. "William said hello." She walked beside her shorter companion up the quiet street. "This is very good of you." With Alana rushing her along, Liliha had no time to dwell on sorrow.

"Not at all. I haven't seen you before. How long have you lived in the area?"

"Nearly two years. I first came over to stay with William and Yvonne after my first husband left me." And now, she'd lost another husband—their son, more precious than life itself.

Alana flashed a glance across. "My husband and I moved from the Bronx some time ago to support his mother and dependent brother. Unfortunately, she's not well at the moment."

"I'm sorry." Choking on fresh grief, Liliha concentrated on the climb.

"I hope," Alana drew another breath, "you're happy here."

No need to mention Oliver's recent death. "I love it, but I miss my daughters. They live in Australia."

"That must be hard. How old are they?"

"Sixteen and seventeen. They visit during their

holidays."

"At least you have something to look forward to." Alana's words strained from lack of breath. "We'll have to get together sometime. I pass by the Peters' farm once a week to shop in St. Ives. Zennor's a small place." They hiked beside business premises until Alana stopped beside a parked car.

Before easing into the passenger seat, Liliha glanced along the street and caught the flash of a man's eye. He stopped and bent over his shoe, revealing dark hair. Prickles at the nape of her neck continued along her spine. The man from the train?

Chapter Three

Muted bird-trills outside The Barn's upstairs window roused Liliha despite a wish to shut out the dawn of another day without Oliver. After a trip to the bathroom, she settled in the bed's comfort again.

Her ring caught the first rays. Maybe she could fill the aching void with a satisfying vision. She composed herself—held still, sniffed. Nothing. She'd never been able to produce the effect at will.

A memory returned from many years ago. A vision had propelled her to Paris in one of the many random episodes. Afterward, a news report detailed events of a thwarted assassination attempt she'd experienced. The visions were real all right. Also, when she'd lost the ring, they'd stopped. The strange effect came from the ring rather than from a natural ability, no argument.

While she shifted position against the pillows, the desire to meditate dragged at her inner being. Perhaps some part of Oliver's spirit remained. She remembered snatches of their discussions on an after-life and the power of the mind.

With closed eyes, she concentrated on attaining a higher plane, letting go of the constant rattle of thoughts. Bit by bit, all sense of the tangible world eased.

A powerful force lifted, soothed, and healed her. Along with the knowledge of connection, her perception translated into words.

'Move on.' The meaning burned into her soul.

In ecstasy or relief, she reached for his essence with longing. 'Stay with me.'

'Later.'

God or Oliver? Inseparable. She strained to comprehend. Had yearning supplied what she wanted to hear?

With the force of sunlight piercing clouds, a new message emerged. *'Eternity waits. For now, you must carry on.'*

Her heart floated on a cloud of elation.

The presence generated love and light, and then withdrew with the swiftness of a flick of silk.

Strengthened by the experience, Liliha swiveled to the side of the bed, swung her legs to the floor and donned a robe in the morning chill.

Downstairs at the rear of the expansive open area of the remodeled barn, she turned on the electric kettle and leaned against the bench to gaze outside. Familiar skeletal trees filled the garden—guardians watching the property, ready to burst into leaf at the first hint of spring.

She prepared tea, and then carried the mug to the sofa. The first sip stung her tongue with pleasant bitterness.

With Oliver gone, isolation dragged her lower. Her cottage in St. Ives offered alternative accommodation. The place was free from holiday-makers at the moment.

Alerted by a knock, Liliha opened the door watched over by Buddha's smiling statue beside the step. The traitor hadn't bestowed luck on their home. Rather, the reverse. "How good to see you, Sarah." She stepped away from Sarah's reassuring hug. "Come in." Blocking a flood of emotion prompted by her friend's penetrating gaze, Liliha led the way into the huge main room.

Sarah shrugged off her coat to drop onto the brown leather sofa. "I hope I haven't called in too soon, but I'm on a mission." She softened her voice. "First things first. How are you holding up?"

"I won't lie. It's lonely on my own now Kaelyn and Alissa have left."

"So good your daughters were with you. Do you want to talk?"

Unsure, Liliha nodded.

"Did you ever find out why Beatrice contacted Oliver that day?"

"I saw her in a vision when she drove away. She was mentally disturbed. She wanted to take him back." Rather than remember the horrific stabbing, Liliha gazed outside. Branches swayed in the breeze with an enviable lack of emotion.

"She must have been unbalanced to leave Witness Protection." Sarah sighed. "Thanks for clearing it up. I won't mention the subject again." Head tilted, Sarah gazed at her finger. "You're wearing the ring."

"I promised Kaelyn. She thought the visions would give me purpose now ..."

Sarah's nod signified understanding. "Don't take offense at what I'm about to say. It's in your own interest. Why not consider moving into your cottage—just 'till you settle? The Barn is so big."

"William and Yvonne might be offended if I leave The Barn, seeing as Oliver," she swallowed, "borrowed money from them for the rebuilding."

"Why not see how things go? You can always come back."

Liliha nodded. "I guess there's no need to organize a sale just yet. A few days at the cottage might help."

"I could take you if you like."

A burst of annoyance bulked against Sarah's interference. "I'll stay here one more night and pack a few clothes. I could get a lift into town tomorrow."

"Really? You'll move?"

"Yes." No need for Sarah to go on pushing. "I'll talk to Oliver's parents then. I'd rather not face them yet."

Sarah nodded. "Good."

Liliha's sigh released her angst. "Sorry I snapped. I'm not controlling myself well."

"Perfectly understandable." Sarah rambled on about a conversation she'd had with her husband, while Liliha reviewed her own outburst.

***

At five in the afternoon, Ellen dove inside a doorway and onto an escalator inside Paddington Station. The loud pounding in her head dulled other sounds. London was packed at the moment and she meant to take full advantage of the crowds. The murmur of conversation and occasional shouts came from nearby people. Happy people. Not running, like her.

On the slow rise beneath the glass of the great arch, she gazed up at blue sky. If she believed in heaven ... *don't be daft*.

She lunged off the moving steps. Ahead, three trains sat between platforms. She slid between the crowds of people in the central area and followed their upward gazes to the signboard. Numbers flashed and changed.

Two dolled-up women stood alongside, deep in conversation.

"If you ever need to relax, come and stay with me at St. Ives," the younger woman said. "It's a great place. Look. The train's about to leave. Better run." She took a few steps toward a stationary train, and then faced her friend and waved.

Ellen searched the large open area but couldn't see Matt. For now, she was safe.

She made a snap decision and followed the woman to the closest train. No ticket collector stopped her. She might get away with it. After a probing search for the well-known blond head amongst the crowd, she leaped into an open doorway, spotted a gap between passengers and collapsed on the seat in the warm air.

Head lowered, she gasped until her breath settled, and then removed her parka with the fake-fur collar, shifting position so the elbow of the man beside her didn't connect. She rubbed one grubby shoe against the other.

The door slid shut. The train lurched before they rolled away.

What had she gotten herself into? With no belongings apart from what was in her roomy handbag, she'd have to cope.

The train picked up speed. Outside, drab suburban buildings sped by in a blur. She'd rather not think about the future. At least she was safe. One last quivering breath eased from her chest. Her muscles sagged inside the tracksuit. Other passengers wore better clothes than her. Too bad. She hadn't planned this trip.

A hiss pointed to the carriage door being opened behind her. She twisted to the rear. A guard was clicking people's tickets. Now what?

Avoid or pay? How much did the fare to St. Ives cost? She struggled to her feet and headed for the far door.

Another guard appeared, stepped in front of her and raised his brows. "Ticket?"

"Sorry. I didn't have time to buy one. I hope ..."

"Don't worry. You can pay me now. All the way to Penzance?"

She nodded. Didn't know anywhere else.

"Fifty eight pounds, fifty pence, please."

Ellen scrabbled in her bag although she couldn't afford the ticket, expecting to be thrown off at the first stop. She produced forty pounds and waited with droopy shoulders.

On her left, a smartly dressed young man with a seventies-type Afro hairstyle nudged her. He reached into his pocket, and then held out a twenty pound note.

She glanced from his eyes to those of the collector. Drawing a breath, she faced the man again, nodded and accepted the money. The guy who flashed the cash would demand a repayment. She understood what kind and beamed a fake smile. "Thanks."

After she'd bought her ticket and dropped the small change into her purse, Ellen faced the stranger. Maybe he'd be satisfied with flirting.

She'd do whatever was needed. No going back now. If Matt ever found her, she'd be nothing more than a zombie.

***

Alone on the private beach attached to the Peter's farm, Liliha took a morning walk, wrapped in coat and scarf to keep out the stiff, salty breeze. The memory of Oliver's gentle face, beaded with moisture under his wooly hat, drifted in the spume.

On the horizon, gray sky hovered over the water. Rough waves pounded and crashed on the sand ahead, and then retreated to the colorless depths. She veered away from a trail of clattering stones and broken shells to the drier sand, and then turned to face the ocean.

The beauty did nothing to rouse her from dejection. Oliver's death hung over her along with the pressure of the heavens. She longed for the reassurance of his arms while they gazed out to sea.

Why did she bother with anything? Why continue wearing the ring—go on day after day for what? Life held nothing. A desire to hurl the ring into the shallows made her breath come fast.

But no. She couldn't waste such a precious jewel. Better to donate her ring to the museum.

Her head dropped. Despite her best intentions, she'd failed to give them the bracelet after the jewel vanished from storage.

Why did she always have to be so levelheaded? She longed to let go of all her reasonable thoughts. A high lament slid out of her mouth.

Her legs buckled and she dropped to her knees while wracking sobs released all the pent-up sorrow.

Too much! Pain. Loss. Oliver!

The next day, following up on her plan to move from the isolated Barn to town, Liliha emerged in the late afternoon and closed the door of her snug little house. Cheese on toast would do for her evening meal. The coming discussion mattered far more than food. She passed other cottages huddled together on the cobbled street during the five minute uphill walk.

After rehearsing what to say, she paused outside Yvonne and William's home. Should she knock on the front or rear door? No sign of activity came from the pottery. *Better use the front.*

In a matter of moments, Yvonne's perfume and caring surrounded her. Inside, the familiar, low-beamed interior offered welcome while Liliha removed her coat.

Once greetings were over, she followed Oliver's parents to the dining room table. The area looked bigger without the extra seats at the table. Perhaps they'd cut out entertaining. Would life ever be the same again?

Yvonne hurried away. William patted her hand. "We can get through this."

Time passed in awkward chatter until Yvonne returned with a tray of steaming mugs and a snack. Cheeks daubed a shade too bright contrasted against her silver bob. She passed their drinks, offered biscuits, and joined William opposite Liliha.

"Have you lost your appetite, too?" Liliha asked.

William tapped his waist. "Never mind. Do us good." Deep rings beneath his eyes reflected sorrow.

"I've moved into the cottage," she blurted. "Just for the moment. The Barn is so big—so empty."

"How did you bring your things across?" Yvonne asked.

"Mr. Peters drove me. I didn't need much. Just a few clothes and stuff."

William nodded. "I understand."

"I'm glad," Yvonne said. "You look ..."

"...Well," William finished. "The olive green complements your complexion."

Their caring tenderness, full of patient understanding, showed what love could be. Liliha smoothed the folds of the mid-calf skirt. The silky fabric rippling over tan boots released a memory of when she'd shopped with Oliver. He'd wanted her to have it.

While they sipped in silence, Liliha tried to work out a way to approach the next subject. She cleared her throat. "I've been doing a lot of thinking lately. I miss Oliver terribly, but it's too painful to keep living in The Barn, knowing he'd remodeled it for me." After a gulp, she plunged on. "I thought ... I'm considering ... moving to town permanently."

"The Barn was your home with Oliver." William's

26

cheeks sank further toward his collar. "He never did anything wrong."

"Of course not." Liliha shifted in her seat.

Yvonne opened her mouth, and then gazed at William with a small frown. "I never liked Beatrice, but I had no idea she was mad."

"She wanted him back. She didn't know or care what a wonderful husband he was to me." Liliha tightened her shoulders, neck, and sentiment, willing herself to stay strong. "Our time together was short, but I loved Oliver so much."

"Nothing's the same any more." William's shoulders shook as though repressing sobs.

Liliha blurted, "It's just an idea. I'll only consider a permanent move if you approve." Breath eased out of her chest without a sound.

"Why not stay with us, dear?" Yvonne asked, voice husky. "Then, you'll still have money coming in from the cottage rent."

Liliha drew in a shaky breath. "Although I'd like that—"

"She wouldn't want to live with two old fogies," William mumbled to Yvonne. He turned to Liliha. "We don't need looking after."

Yvonne touched his arm, and then looked up, eyes glimmering.

Liliha blinked. "That's not what I meant at all." The last thing she wanted was to upset them. "I'll go back to The Barn."

"You do what is best for you, dear." Yvonne glanced at William who nodded before dropping his head. "Now, stay and eat with us. It's getting late and you probably haven't bought supplies."

27

"Thank you. I'll give you a hand." Best to stay busy. The see-saw of conflicting plans dragged at her emotions. Oliver was no longer with them to take charge. While they chatted, Liliha longed for a real purpose to fill the void. Up to her to smarten up, make a decision, and take responsibility for her life. She'd done so before. Could she do it again?

Chapter Four

Outside in the cool afternoon breeze on the second day since changing her location, Liliha tucked loosened strands of hair behind her ears and walked downhill toward town. She anticipated relaxing at the tearoom with Sarah. Feeling silly about criticizing her friend before, Liliha made a mental note to take extra care.

Historical cottages pressed together—sentinels on guard along the narrow street, beyond, a faint glimmer of the sea. Despite the ugliness in the world, beauty remained if one could appreciate the sight with an unclouded mind.

A man with dark hair and a set expression passed her on his way uphill.

Distracted from her uplifting contemplation, she recalled the passenger who might have followed her from the train. Nothing had happened. *Overactive imagination.* A gull circling overhead caused her to consider a way to channel excess energy into something positive.

An idea came. What had happened to the people she'd visited in her visions? Why assume her task finished at the end of each mental episode? She should follow up— ensure they walked along the right path.

A sign swung in the breeze ahead. 'The Double S Tearooms' triggered a memory of when she'd worked inside. Before she met—. *Stop. Time to move on. Think of something else.*

Nasheen.

Liliha brought to mind the last vision. If only she'd been able to help the mother and her children more. How were they getting on? Would Nasheen be home from the hospital now? Caring for her darling children with the deep, soulful eyes?

But the family lived in Northern England, too far away to visit. She needed to locate someone close to her in a vision.

Outside the tearoom, which nestled amongst a group of businesses away from the main shopping area, Liliha stopped to read a hand-written notice requesting temporary help. She pushed the door open, spotted Sarah and made her way across the room.

After she'd settled at the table, Liliha asked, "What have you been up to?"

"I've done a couple of sketches for a new painting to contrast the rich and the poor." Sarah leaned closer. "I want to show a man sitting in the gutter while a luxurious automobile drives by. Perhaps an old Daimler. Something to give an impression of wealth. It's giving me a heck of a challenge." She chuckled. "And, before you say it, I can't work from a picture on the screen."

"You're so lucky to have your motivation to paint."

"Right. Let's work out something to occupy you. What about your song writing?"

"I'll bring some manuscript sheets in case inspiration strikes me." No chance of a creative urge in her present frame of mind. Liliha leaned forward. "I'm thinking of speaking to Silvia about the job I saw advertised in the window."

***

Later, Liliha strolled home in a cold wind after chatting with her friend. Prior to their parting, she had taken the two-week job. The present waitress needed to stay with her sick baby in a London hospital. The hours were the same as before—eleven in the morning until four in the afternoon. With an occupation to fill her lonely days, she might buck up. Having no day off was the one disadvantage.

A few birds twittered from leafless trees away from town. No sign of occupation came from any of the homes surrounding hers. The longing for contact slammed into her chest hard enough to take her breath away.

She'd speak to plenty of people at the tearoom. Mental reprimand over, Liliha slid the key into the lock.

The Abyssinian cat Walnut, who lived close by, emerged from under a shrub, chocolate-colored fur rippling over shoulder muscles. The cat yowled, a cross between a howl and a growl. His almond-shaped, blue eyes and demanding attitude raised the hair on Liliha's head. "What's wrong?" She bent to stroke the gentle cat. Walnut lowered his ears, avoided her touch, and dived under the bushes.

With a dejected sigh, she entered the warmth of her cottage. The cuckoo clock ticked from the other end of the hallway. On the papyrus picture, the priestess's serene expression calmed her. Liliha clicked the door shut, placed her bag on the table beneath the picture, and strolled past the main room's doorway to the kitchen.

She pulled up short and frowned. The chopping board didn't line up with the bench top. A canister label sat skew-whiff, and the lid of the glazed pot rested off-center. She dragged in a breath. Someone had invaded her privacy.

With a tinge of nervousness, she turned left in the hall, climbed the stairs, and peered into her bedroom. The pillows sat a fraction out of place. The full meaning of living alone pounded into her heart with the regularity of waves over rocks.

The crash in her ears strengthened while she checked the second bedroom on the right. She braced herself, and then peeked in. Nobody. One step after the other, she eased along the landing past the staircase to reach the small study at the end.

She froze. The sound of a light scuffle came from behind. She glanced behind. Imagination. No use worrying about every creak and groan from the old building.

Finding the study empty, she braved the opening to the bathroom opposite. Nothing amiss in any of the rooms and no sign of an intruder.

Downstairs again, her chest heaved. A rustle came from the kitchen. Advancing with care, she peered past the door-frame.

A flash. She ducked. Walnut landed beside her foot with a howl.

A relieved laugh erupted. "How did you get in?"

The cat pressed against her leg, tail stiff and voice expressing a hint of complaint.

Liliha followed him along the hall and edged the door open. After he shot outside, she returned to the kitchen, blaming herself for not investigating the noise. Walnut could have come in when an intruder departed. The cat might have jumped on her bed but he could never shift a pottery lid.

A groan escaped her throat. If she reported her suspicion to the police, all she could say was, *'My pillows weren't in the right place.'*

What had the burglar been searching for? She owned very little of value. Perhaps the prowler had taken pity.

She dropped onto a chair and placed trembling hands onto the solid wooden table. Her attention returned to the familiar man she'd passed on the street.

***

The next afternoon, Liliha stood under the shower.

Warmth eased the ache in her spine. Her first busy day at the tearooms had brought the remembered stress of balancing work with tact. Now, the tide of activity retreated to leave her doubts exposed like crabs scuttling on the sand.

A blast of the sweet, heavenly scent of attar alerted her to an oncoming vision. She'd be safe under the warm water for the short mental journey. Her sight dimmed. Footsteps alternated with scrapes and faint thuds. Pondering on the sounds, she spun into the swirling aperture.

***

The familiar sensation of enclosure and random thoughts tell me I'm within another body already—a man, judging by the shape of the hand stretched out in front of me to touch a picture. I rely on what he sees to determine our location. The interior of a home comes into focus while we walk along a hall and pause at the doorway.

Our gaze sweeps an area set out in the manner of a typical suburban house in England, with a staircase opposite the entrance.

"Hopkins and Co is a thing of the past. From now on, it's just plain George Hopkins." Our chuckle resembles the recorded sound of a malicious fairground clown.

A bunch of keys hang from the wall papered with stylistic flowers on a brown background. The tag reveals a golden jaguar engraved with the XJ logo. We pocket the jangling cluster.

To probe deeper, I sift his inner dialogue until I reach his underlying reason for this visit.

Prompted, George goes over the memory again to strengthen his purpose. A client had canceled Hopkins & Co's services and switched to Bertie's protection. 'A deal gone wrong as the suits would say. All due to Bertie trying to muscle in. George had worked ... he couldn't say hard. His effort and particular skills paid off. But the crow, Bertie, had flown in to swipe the crust. Well, tit for tat. The boot's full already. The remaining goods will fit in the back seat.'

We walk while he rambles on. Partnerships never succeed. St. Ives is his town. Small businesses and holdings didn't need proper security with him patrolling the streets.

We enter the living room and lift a mobile phone from an occasional table—rough justice for the greedy sod who owned two phones. Tucking the device into our pocket, we swagger toward a pile of electrical equipment and cartons at the rear exit. Our mouth stretches in a sneer at perfect opportunity to get even, now Bertie's away for a two-day holiday.

I whisper, 'Don't do this. A man of your cunning can handle this another way. Think.'

He shrugs off my suggestion as if it's a cobweb.

We push the double doors open. The woodwork shows signs of George's forced entry. A gold ring flashes, engraved with an insignia of some sort. A horseshoe? We lift a weighty box with the ease of an athlete and carry the carton along the tiled drive. After a stumble, we admire our fancy, pointed-toed boots pacing beside the house.

'Leave everything there,' I whisper. 'He'll notice what you've done. Returning goods to their right places will be enough of a bother. You don't need to steal them.' I attempt to deter him by concentrating hard. Sometimes mind force works better than whispered words. We stagger on uneven pavement and shift the burden while facing the street.

I use the opportunity to observe the surroundings.

When we reach the pale blue vehicle, we open the rear door, and dump the load on the floor before returning for more items. Soon, we've loaded the luxury saloon with a stereo, television and several more cartons.

'You've proved you can take everything. Settle your grievance with a note. Leave the goods in the car and walk away.'

We slam the door and pause, which makes me assume I've succeeded.

But no. We pace to the front of the vehicle.

Here's my chance to withdraw from him so I can read the number-plate. I concentrate, jerk, and envisage the physical shift.

Despite my effort, he slides in and turns on the ignition.

The engine purrs and we reverse out of the drive with a screech. Our hand reaches for the gear stick. With a twist of the steering wheel, the vehicle roars off to merge with traffic at the junction. We chuckle.

How can I break his obstinate resistance? I remain silent and observant for several blocks, wondering why I'm still trapped within him yet unable to stop his flight.

His thoughts are filled with his role in town. Shopkeepers and businessmen think he's acting the role of protector, yet he simply takes bribes to leave them alone. Nothing big enough to alert the police.

Poised for a final act, he stretches in luxury and admires the way the Jaguar nestles rock-solid on the road.

'Do something with your intelligence to give you pride. Consider making yourself a real security guard for everyone to admire.' I share an illusion of him wearing a blue uniform on his stroll in the town. People smile and wave. I replace the delightful daydream with an image of him in an official role of apprehending a thief.

George chuckles about fooling everyone. Our foot

presses harder. The car accelerates to pass another with a surge of power.

I yell, 'Listen to your inner prompt.'

His own thought cuts in. 'Time to give Bertie a call. Rub his nose in how clever I am.' We retrieve the stolen mobile from our pocket, locate the number, and leave a gloating message to the person who answers.

After a surprised, "What?" from Bertie, we disconnect.

A sign flashes by the windscreen with the words, 'Hayle: 1 km.' So close to home? I scrutinize the landscape. On the left, the last rays of sunlight glint over an estuary. Boats float under a familiar bridge.

This is Cornwall.

After the revelation, I'm released to hover over the waterway. I didn't achieve anything. Frustration rides with me inside the churning tunnel.

***

Regaining awareness in the shower, Liliha groaned at her failure. George had discarded suggestions for his redemption.

This had never happened before during a vision. She should have converted his desire to punish his former associate into a joke rather than actual theft. Doubt about not having the fortitude to do the job lowered her mood.

She turned off the flow of water and stepped out to grab a towel, thinking over the last two years while she dried her back. Since inheriting the ring, she'd worked out, with trial and error, what to do for each contact. Just as a shell held to the ear seemed to whisper, her psychic probing acted in the manner of a conscience or inner voice. She never knew her destination or established a further link with her temporary host, instead, accepted each visit as a glimpse into another life. Before the bracelet came on the scene, every experience had rewarded her with satisfaction.

She bent to dry her legs. The coincidence struck again. Hayle was close to St. Ives—close to her. She couldn't ignore such a good opportunity.

Determination gave a new purpose. If—no, when— she found George, she'd need to convince him to change his ways.

Chapter Five

Liliha lifted her feet onto the footstool in the cozy living room and rested her spine against a comfortable armchair. Bliss after the second hectic day in the tearooms. No need to prepare a meal yet.

Before relaxing too much, she removed the ring from the chain around her neck and slid the satisfying weight onto her finger. So far, no vision had taken her unawares with this method.

Beneath the dull sky, bare branches swayed in the garden outside the glass door. A fur-ball revealed Walnut's presence under a rosemary bush, which relaxed her further.

Her hand rubbed across a slight wear-mark on the chair's chintz cover while she considered a furniture swap with items from The Barn. A few ornaments would personalize the cottage for now.

The way to make contact with George eluded her. But, if she wanted to find the thief, she must be positive.

Apart from locating the car, what did she have to go on? George had worn a signet ring and pointy-toed boots when he drove away from his crime. His actual appearance remained unknown.

Liliha fiddled with the plait trailing over her shoulder. An idea sprang up—explore sales outlets for the pale blue Jaguar XJ with Sarah, ostensibly to hunt for car types to paint.

She reached for the phone.

***

At five o'clock, the taxi pulled out of the idling traffic into a forecourt. Hesitant in a strange country, Georg van den Burg studied the paved driveway outside a mansion north of London. The narrow roadway they'd left seemed way too busy. Why didn't they build wide roads here?

He paid the driver and climbed out. Patted his pocket to ensure the security of his passport. His future in England depended on the forthcoming visit with a vague contact from South Africa. When the cab left, Georg approached the entrance.

His knock left a dull thud which merged with traffic noise. Took ages before anyone answered. He ran his hands over his curly hair and considered tying the length off his face. A tubby woman wearing an apron swung open the elegant door.

"I've got an appointment with Mr. Straten," Georg said.

"Come this way, sir."

He followed her to the rear exit of the luxurious home. Under open sky beyond the deck rails, a magnificent view of green plains stretched into the distance. They walked to the entrance of a newer complex built against the far side of the house. The woman opened the door and beckoned him into an area containing an indoor swimming pool. She nodded and left.

In the heated air, a fit, aging man wrapped in a fluffy towel, his blond hair dripping onto his torso, padded toward him. "And you are?" he asked.

"Van den Burg. You know my father."

"Ah, yes. From the old days. I'm Straten. Pleased to meet you."

After shaking hands, Georg wondered whether to sit or wait for an invitation.

"Just before we get comfortable, I'd like to see your passport. Can't be too sure. So many fraudsters about nowadays."

Georg handed the book to the over-finicky man, and then shifted from foot to foot.

Once his host had checked the photo and details, he returned the passport. "So. You've just arrived from Johannesburg. What can I do for you?"

The pool shimmered with an invitation. His muscles could do with a workout from the stress he'd endured after train trip from Cornwall. Georg didn't rate his chances. He slid the document into an inner pocket. "I wondered if you'd heard about any jobs going."

"Going? Where would they go?" Straten flung himself into a cast iron chair.

Picky with the language too. "Sorry," Georg said. "I need to find employment."

"Where are you staying?"

"A guest house down in Cornwall," Georg said. "Nice place, but I can live anywhere."

"What made you choose that area?"

"I want to see the whole country eventually. My father often spoke about the way you'd moved to London in your prime." Not recently though. He'd left without contacting the old man.

Straten gestured to a chair. "We need to have a good talk. I want to know all about you. Then, we'll see if something presents itself."

"I'd rather you didn't mention my being here." Georg held his breath.

The man arched one eyebrow and his mouth softened as though considering a private joke.

While the big cat played with him, Georg's expectations dropped with his body onto the hard chair.

***

George strode about 'his' town, as he called St. Ives.

Never wanted to visit faraway places. Lived here all his life—his father before him. He chuckled to himself about the stolen Jag. Old buggerlugs at the junk yard had let him use a slot between two cars meant for demolition.

He'd love to drive the car again. Pity he had to sell it.

"Hello, Hopkins."

George snapped to in time to catch the eye of Albert, the town guzzler, probably on his way to the pub for the evening. Didn't bother to return the greeting. Mind on other things. A thought moldered—soured his stomach. Funny how failings returned to haunt you.

Like a couple of days ago.

He brooded over the chain of events leading him to the cottage—the conversation between two women on the train, their mumbled talk about a priceless ring and furtive glances. He'd followed their car in his trusty Volkswagen from the station at Penzance to an isolated place beside the sea. Could have once been a barn. The tall one, who wore the ring, went inside and the other woman drove off.

George had handed the watching job to old Cedric the Sharp-eyed while he got even with Bertie.

Shouldn't have mentioned the ring. The old fart had been known to become Cedric the Loose-tongued. To be safe, he'd slipped Cedric a red note. Fifty pounds worked wonders.

The day after, the tall woman left the isolated spot with baggage and arrived at St. Ives. Cedric had trailed her to the cottage and returned the job to George.

While searching the upstairs rooms, he'd smelled fresh paint. Could be a holiday rental place. 'Course, it was easy for him to slide out the front door when she'd returned.

No need to worry. Next visit, he'd find the ring. Or, if she wore it constantly like his signet ring, he'd rip it off her finger one dark night.

Chapter Six

In the evening alone at the cottage, Liliha stared at an open page of her book. *Face up to life.* She reached for the phone. Although hesitant about how to broach the subject of her decision to remain in St. Ives, she punched the link and waited until Yvonne picked up.

Greetings over, Liliha said, "I'm still at the cottage. I start a temporary job at the tearooms tomorrow. Silvia needed someone urgently. Seeing as I'm here, I arranged to fill-in."

"You must do what you think is right, dear. We're just watching television."

"Me too. It keeps me from thinking. But this is why I rang. Could William spare some time tomorrow? I want to grab a couple of more things from The Barn." She couldn't face the empty shell alone.

"Let me check."

Liliha contemplated what to collect apart from a few more clothes. The roughly carved Egyptian cat with a broken ear should sit in the hall under the papyrus.

Yvonne spoke again. "We'll be flat out finishing an order tomorrow. Can you wait?"

"Of course. I've got enough to tide me over." Pierced by more rejection, Liliha slumped.

"What about late tomorrow afternoon? I'll prepare the meal while William's away. Come and eat with us afterward."

"Great."

When the call ended, Liliha sighed, longing for the sound of a loved-one's voice. Kaelyn's email mentioned she'd landed a job at the gym. *Don't bring up the subject of the bracelet. Let Kaelyn get over her horrible episode in her own time.*

After the conversation with Kaelyn about her new job ended, Liliha punched in Alissa's number at the boarding school.

The girl who answered the dorm phone yelled Alissa's name. The call rang hollow, bringing to mind a ghost at the other end of a dark corridor. At a rasp on the other end, Liliha perked up.

"Mum?"

"Hello, darling. I hope I didn't disturb you."

"You're my mother. It's just the best thing to hear your voice. Emails aren't the same at all." Alissa's deep sigh unsettled Liliha.

Better not question the root of the discontent. She'd rather soak in the warmth of Alissa's bubbly nature.

They chatted about classes while Liliha acted her familiar role as an absent parent. Maybe she overcompensated with love and understanding, but that couldn't be bad. Emotion surfaced as the conversation lost momentum. "I wish I'd been stronger. I should have stood up to your father. Not abandoned you and Kaelyn at a boarding school."

"You didn't. Dad arranged the whole thing. Anyway, what's done is done, as they say. Kaelyn's free now and soon I'll escape too. One more year to go."

"Stick with it, darling. Education is so important."

"I know." Alissa's sigh expressed aggravation. "There's another girl waiting to call her mother. Drats about not being able to use mobiles here. Anyway, I've got to go. Love you."

"I love you too. With all my heart. Won't be long 'till I see you." Liliha lowered the phone. Neither of her daughters really needed her. With Oliver gone from her life, she would float like a phantom, interfering in other lives, but never again be really necessary to the people who meant the most.

With a heave, she stood and paced to the kitchen. Restless hands lifted the plates from the rack and positioned them in a line along the timber-topped bench. She rubbed them with a tea towel and re-stacked them. *Such useless activity.*

Hold on tight. Make an effort.

She'd start with a new name for her home. Cottage Central or Headquarters. And her title? Easy. Psychic Detective. The assumed role should give her focus while making inquiries about the stolen Jag.

***

The next day, Liliha walked close to William along the drive in the approaching dusk. Once inside The Barn, she lit the main room. An air of abandonment lingered, as if her previous home sensed she never intended to return.

"Okay." William's expression didn't give away his emotions. "What do you want me to do?"

"Check the studio while I collect some clothes." They climbed the stairs together, each carrying an empty suitcase. "See if anything needs to be tossed." Her words sounded callous. "Like jars of cleaner or used tubes of paint."

On the landing, he frowned and glanced her way. "Glad to."

"You'll find bin-bags under the sink." Liliha's voice caught.

"I'll leave this suitcase here." He strode off.

"Thanks, William." He must be upset about her tactless command. No use running after him. Probably too late to fix the damage. Whatever she said came out wrong.

Grief shouldn't affect her this way. Must be this house.

Suitcases in hand, Liliha approached the bedroom. Neat, tidy ... empty. No sign of a shared life. She flung open a suitcase and jammed in blouses and trousers from the wardrobe. *Don't think. Just do.* Underwear next.

The granite cat peeked at her from the chest. She shoved the solid weight underneath the clothes. Bodies passed away, but material things, statues, remained.

She wouldn't crumple. With the suction of a limpet on a rock, she clung to the idea of finding George.

Next, she'd undergo the meal with Yvonne and William. Tiredness would make a perfect excuse for leaving early.

***

A sharp morning wind whipped about Liliha's face. Should have plaited her hair to be ready for work later. Dragging strands from her lips, she anticipated the task ahead—her first line of inquiry via used-car dealerships with Sarah.

Under her gloves in the cool air, the ring generated warmth and comfort.

Grandmother Luciana hadn't left any indication of whether she'd worn the ring. Liliha wished she'd known. She pictured her grandmother at Redruth and her mother before her. Ancestors occupying this ancient strip of land. The myths and legends of ghosts, giants and kings.

A memory of a former trip with Sarah along the coast to the far side of Redruth rose in her mind. Below the cliffs, her friend had sketched the ruins of Tintagel Castle.

Liliha turned the corner near the tearooms and headed for the town center. Her thoughts reverted to legends. Who knew if the ancient stories of King Arthur and his Knights of the Round Table were true? Tales passed along by word of mouth contained at least a grain of truth. Perhaps Tintagel was part of the same legacy.

On the walk along the main street, she caught sight of Sarah beyond a few pedestrians, and hurried to reach her.

"This worked out well," Sarah called. "Audley's glad to grab some extra time at the office."

"Bit chilly this morning, but the walk warmed me up." Liliha peered inside the glass window of SoundEmissions.com and waved to Audley sitting at his desk.

"Let's check out the closest car yard before a salesman arrives for the day." Sarah led the way to a side street.

"How are you getting on with your picture?"

"So—so. I'll be glad when I decide on the make of car—and the color." Passing houses and small businesses, Sarah's high heels clicked over the pavement. "Have you seen Harry lately?" She glanced away fast.

"What makes you ask?" Harry used to work with Audley as an accountant. What was Harry up to now?

"You two should get together. Catch up on old times."

"I saw him at the funeral." Liliha's emotions took a dive remembering the cemetery surrounded by pine trees.

"I'll have to invite you to our farmhouse one day."

"I'm not sure I'm ready yet."

"You can't put your life on hold." Sarah cast a sideways glance.

"I know."

"Don't be too hard on yourself." Sarah nudged her. "I didn't mean to judge you. God knows how I'd cope."

Change the subject. Where did the woman she'd met

on the train live again? Liliha grasped at the name. "What's Zennor like?"

"There's the old Mill House, a church, a few sheds, and houses."

"What about beyond, toward the west?"

"About the same—farms, sheds, barns, a few pubs and houses all the way to Land's End," Sarah said. "It's nice and peaceful where we live at St. Just." She scanned six cars on show inside the premises. "Nothing here."

"We could search other yards." Liliha frowned. How would she find George? Or the home he'd burgled on a residential street?

But the location wouldn't lead her to the man. By inquiring, she might draw undue suspicion to herself. A hopeless task.

So far, she'd messed with an improbable idea. Confronting a criminal presented a serious challenge.

Chapter Seven

After work, Liliha paced uphill to Yvonne and William's cottage. *Best to find out if they held resentment about her move.* Taking deep breaths after the stiff climb, she made her way along the garden path to large stone structure at the rear, swung the door open, and entered the warm atmosphere filled with an earthy aroma.

William flashed a welcome smile before focusing on the damp clay shape before him. He slid a moist paintbrush over the surface. "I'm just finishing this glazing."

"Good to see you, Liliha," Yvonne called.

Thankful about their normal attitude, Liliha ambled over to Yvonne, who sat at the wheel with her hands pressed over a spinning lump of clay.

"You look more cheerful," William called from the other side of the room.

Liliha raised her voice. "Sarah took me to Hayle this morning to look at cars."

William asked, "What about your other car?"

Rather than explain about her impossible mission, Liliha said, "Just searching for something Sarah can paint. I've parked my little Fiat in Mr. Peters' shed for the moment." A sharp pain pierced her heart. Oliver bought her the car as a surprise.

"Did you check the car ads in the local paper?" William cleaned and dried his brush.

"Not yet."

He stepped away from the table. "Come on, Yvonne. Let's finish for the day."

Yvonne's wheel slowed and she lifted the wet clay shape off the turntable. "Stay and eat with us. I've made plenty."

"Thank you."

After removing their aprons and cleaning their hands, they strolled with Liliha to the rear of the house. In the main kitchen, Yvonne prepared drinks. A savory aroma wafted in the air.

"I'll get the local rag." When William returned, he spread the paper on the table and flipped to the used car section. "What are you looking for?"

Yvonne joined them, hands wrapped over her mug. Loose trousers and top revealed her distinctive loose style of trousers and top, although she didn't wear the usual jangling bracelets while she worked.

"A Jaguar." Liliha reached for the paper and flicked page after page of cars offered for sale. "Nothing here." The probability of finding the stolen car dissipated.

"We'll drive you wherever you want to go," William said.

"I know. But you're too busy lately." Liliha shifted position. "You should hire someone to help with the work."

"We're all right." Yvonne's mug clattered on the wooden table.

At the same time William said, "We can handle whatever comes in." His rigid posture spoke of a need for self-protection.

Liliha flashed sympathy in her glance. "You're both looking tired." She shouldn't have called attention to their state of mind. "We've all been under a strain. Why not take things easy?"

"Work keeps me motivated." William clamped his jaw.

"Me too," Liliha said, relieved at the opportunity to make up for her gaff. "Working at the tearooms helps."

Torn between her need for advice and causing them

worry, Liliha asked, "Has there been much crime in the area lately?"

"Smashed windows in one of the local businesses," Yvonne said.

William studied Liliha. "Why do you ask?"

"I think someone was in my house the other day."

"What?" Yvonne opened her mouth and swiveled to William.

"Did they take anything?" he asked.

Liliha gave a little laugh. "No. I could be imagining things."

"You should have let us know," William said. "I'd have come to check your safety."

"Call whenever something worries you." Yvonne strode toward the kitchen and returned with a crock-pot full of steaming food.

After a delicious meal, Liliha stood to help with washing the dishes.

"No need," Yvonne said. "I'll stack them in the dishwasher. Get some rest."

"You don't mind?"

"Not at all." Yvonne walked her to the door and waved her away.

Outside, the light faded with every breath. No lingering daylight at this time of year. Once again, Liliha faced the fear of walking unprotected in the gloom. A longing to surrender to grief tugged at her while she strode in the twilight.

The briny smell on the breeze changed to perfume, which hinted at the scent of lilies. She paused beside a hedge, squatted and bent over her shoe for the short sojourn to follow, safe from prying eyes. With the ease of accustomed travel, she spun inside the flickering tunnel scattered with random colors into another reality.

***

I'm inside a room containing a sink and table. A strange, sour aroma drifts in the air.

I aim attention at a strong, well-endowed woman. Before I've had a chance to think, I lunge forward and merge with her—an easy transformation, and one to which I am accustomed. While we chop strong onions for a late meal, our eyes flood with protective tears. We glance at the Russian flag upright in a glass, which gives me the clue to her location.

Working at her chore, she's thinking about her wonderful husband. After a year of marriage, her love remains strong. His words echo in her head, "Luiza, my love." All her friends appreciate Mickhale's jokes, although her mother thinks he's a silly prankster. Luiza hopes to make out signs of a baby coming soon, which should stop the hurtful remarks.

I wonder what I'm here to do.

We run the fingers of our left hand along the six inch knife shaft to remove onion flecks.

A floorboard creaks. Our breath quickens and heat diffuses our body.

Horror at dealing with this unseen terror grips me. I dismiss my fear and concentrate on Luiza's reaction.

Her adrenalin rises. The house is locked. How could anyone get in?

At a further scrape, hairs prickle along our neck.

Strong arms grab us from behind. Our heart beats with the flutters of a trapped bird. We gasp for air.

Numb with the same fear, I need to free myself from overpowering emotion to make an assessment. I mustn't let something bad happen to Luiza. However, I'm trapped in her body, unable to see behind.

We grip the knife tighter, ready to protect ourselves.

I whisper, 'Turn to face your attacker.' I make an effort to mentally disengage, hoping to meld with the person behind her.

"Let go of me, you great bear," she shouts.

Determination fills us. The speed of the change stuns me and renders me immobile.

We jerk our arms upward and throw off the vice-like grip. Pivoting, we plunge the knife into the attacker under the ribs. Blood spurts over his shirt, releasing the distinctive sweet aroma.

Our combined horror flushes away all other emotions. My reflex stems from the violence, but hers is something else — she knows him.

"Mikhael," she screams. "What ...?"

"A joke," he whispers and sags.

Stunned, we drop to our knees beside him on the floor. The thud jars us. Our sight hazes over.

"I didn't know it was you." *Turning our head one way and another, we panic.* "I didn't mean to hurt you, my love. I thought it was a ..." *We reach out to withdraw the weapon.*

My whisper contains urgency. 'Leave the knife. Phone for help. Every moment is important.'

"I'll get the ambulance," Luiza whispers. "Hold on Mikhael." *We stumble to the work surface and grab the phone with shaking, bloody hands.* "Help. My husband. I've stabbed him."

We disregard the questioning voice on the speaker and drop the phone. They'll be able to identify the location.

I ooze with pain and regret, yet I must rouse myself from this sense of déjà vous.

We run to her husband and sink onto our knees once more. Leaning close, we try to stop the flow of blood by cupping our hands over the knife. Luiza whispers, "Don't die. Please, don't die."

Her anguish registers while I wait with her. I offer soothing words of comfort. 'Rest now. You've done all you can. Help is on the way.' Pathos and empathy swell within me.

His eyes crack open. His lips part. "Did I surprise you?" he whispers.

Stifling tears, we nod, willing him to continue breathing. "Why did you have to do it? Why? Why?"

But his eyes have closed again. If he dies, she will accept whatever punishment the courts hand out.

I'm stunned. What should I have done? Could I have stopped this tragedy? Her husband—killed by a knife. Just like mine. But she was the one to stab him, not some crazed former lover. What a cruel stroke. I hope she can live with her action.

A siren wails in the distance.

A familiar tug suggests my departure will follow. With one last burst to empower Luiza with strength, I float away.

Along with my regret, an apparition of our three bodies dancing with death accompanies me inside the aperture's spin.

***

In the grip of shock which brought fresh pain about Oliver's death, Liliha's eyes cracked open in the dim street. How could anyone recover from such a horrific event? Standing, she stretched the muscles on her legs, and then dragged her feet onward.

The hardest lessons hurt more. She and Louisa must carry on after their loved-one's death. Healing took time.

Liliha faced her dilemma. She couldn't have prevented the murder, so why was she called? Just to offer comfort? To avert the tragedy, Luiza needed to identify Mikhael. But neither Luiza or Liliha could see the attacker. In this instance, she'd been unable to use the trick learned long ago about how to leave her host's body and scan the surroundings.

Maybe her own recent tragedy had linked her with the Russian woman. Both alone in their houses. Frustration screamed inside. She should have done more. At least, she hadn't contacted Doom again. However, fear about an intruder had influenced her.

No use going over and over the situation—let it go.

The dilemma of her continued role persisted during five minutes of the downhill stride. Below, her detached cottage came into view, separated from the other terrace houses.

A man emerged on the path and glanced either way.

Had he come from the gap beside her Headquarters? She considered running back to William and Yvonne.

The streetlight glinted on the shiny surface of his jacket.

'Psychic Detective' indeed. How would she ever find George if she couldn't face her own fear?

***

Irritation boiled inside George Hopkins. He'd come away from the cottage empty-handed again. However, this time, the owner hadn't caught him inside. She must be wearing the darn ring. He'd get his hands on the jewel yet. Just had to work out how.

Intent on flushing away disappointment, George headed toward the Golden Lion in the waning light. He eased his pace. Didn't want to appear as if he was running away from a crime scene. Although he preferred Cuban heels, his rubber-soled trainers made no sound over the cobbles between old houses.

Another frustration bugged him. He lit a cigarette and inhaled. Someone had stolen his, or rather Bertie's, Jag.

No need to stress. He'd achieved his object in taking everything from old buggerlugs. Bertie would think twice before he tried another takeover. Apart from the crush of a setback, why worry about losing the Jag? The car wouldn't draw attention to him now.

Nobody got the better of him. Straightening to his full height on his downhill stride, he dragged in a lungful of smoke. The owners of the newsagent and the pub amongst other local businesses *'supported'* him while he gathered information for his benefit.

Mary at the launderette, with her stringy hair and wiry body, seemed keen on him, which stood to reason. Women were drawn to powerful men. All birds lost their appearance in the dark. He'd keep Mary dangling. Plenty of skirts hung on his every word in the town. He could always pop over to Truro if he got sick of them. But he needed a bit of ready cash to keep him going. Nothing in the cottage behind him had been worth taking.

He tossed his stub into a garden and continued on.

Once he reached the town center, he carried out his regular patrol. Nothing to it. He passed the bright window displays of local shops and strolled past the locked launderette. All quiet. Now for a drink.

Inside the familiar pub, filled with the smell of beer and smoke, several old codgers greeted him. He nodded on the way to the bar. An arrangement with the owner gave him the first pint without charge. All he needed to do was patrol the premises—the way he kept a check on all the other losers.

He pitied every business owner in the area with their naive, small-town attitudes. He'd continue to squeeze them for a percentage of their money. This was his livelihood. Robin Hood had the right idea. However, rather than passing his booty to the poor, he'd be joining them if he didn't keep the proceeds.

George perched on a stool and gestured to the bar girl. She nodded and ran the bubbling liquid into his glass, and then flipped the handle before passing the brimming container over. He gulped some of the bitter brew.

"How's things?" he asked.

"Pretty quiet," the bar girl said. "The boss wants to see you later."

He couldn't remember her name. Didn't care. "Right you are." George searched the faces to his left and caught sight of Collin dressed in the usual stained shirt. He gestured him over.

The guy carried over his drink, slobbering for George's favor. "All right, Hopkins?"

"Sure." A smart guy with a striped jacket bumped against his side. George spun. "Watch it."

"Leave out the attitude. Just an accident, old man."

Taller than the average of his race, the fellow looked Italian with his dark complexion. A hard man too, despite his polite manner. Better take care. He dropped his grimace at the chance of making another contact. "No offense. George is the name."

"Harry, as you're offering a name exchange." The suit ordered his drink.

"I've seen you before, haven't I?"

"On and off." Harry placed coins on the bar while the barmaid carried his brimming glass over. "Cheers." He paced away.

George seethed at the guy's dismissive attitude. He could take the suit on whenever he wanted.

"This is my town, you bastard. We play by my rules." The surrounding chatter swallowed George's words. Collin nodded and leaned closer.

Chapter Eight

Liliha dressed with care for her evening out. Sarah had insisted she come to dinner with a few friends and had arranged for someone to pick her up at seven. *Best to push aside a reluctance to socialize. Grief should be private and infrequent.* Part of a quote rose to mind. '*When you are sorrowful look again in your heart, and you shall see that in truth you are weeping for that which has been your delight.*' Ah, yes. Very accurate of Khalil Gibran.

She stepped into beige loose trousers and slid a coordinated tunic over her head. The blue stone in her ring shone against the plain material. She fastened a gold belt at the front and imagined Oliver beside her, taking delight in what she wore. In her reflection, the color went well with her dark complexion and hair. She slid her feet into flat ballet-style shoes, and then descended to the living area, loose hair swaying over her shoulders.

Besides her disinclination to venture out when she was tired, a terrible memory lurked in the dark. With any luck, she wouldn't pick out the ivy-covered shed—the shed where Oliver had bled to death after his murder. *Don't think about it.*

Just time to check on her daughter's state of mind overseas. She punched the automatic redial on her phone.

Kaelyn picked up on the second ring. She must have been close. "Hi, Mum."

"I won't keep you long. I know you must be getting ready for work."

"No probs. I can spare a minute while I wait for my ride. Eddie's left already. He caught the bus."

Lifted by Kaelyn's bright voice, Liliha asked

questions about her role at the gym and Kaelyn filled her in.

"Here's my friend's car, Mum." Kaelyn's voice contained urgency. "I'll speak to you soon."

"Love you." Their chat was too short, but Kaelyn's enthusiasm washed away any disappointment. She seemed to have put her bad experience with the bracelet behind her.

Rather than allow an explosion of sorrow before her ordeal, Liliha checked the security of the ground floor windows once more. At the sound of a knock, she slid her arms into her long padded coat and opened the door.

"Harry. You're the mystery driver."

"Fraid so. Can you handle it?" He flashed one of his confident smiles—a hunter bearing a gift. Errol Flynn came to mind in his role as Robin Hood, shrugging a stag carcass off his shoulders onto King John's table.

"I think I'll manage." Liliha accepted the peace offering in Harry's smile. Returning the grin, although she doubted her own expressed the same degree of happiness, she locked the door.

He ushered her along the tiny garden to the gate. "The car's up at the parking station. Sarah gave me strict instructions to take good care of you."

Liliha reached for his arm and they continued in silence. His lemon-scented aftershave wafted in the air.

"My lady." At the car, he opened her door and ushered her in.

Oh, how she loved this treatment. In her imagination Oliver replaced Harry striding to the other side. She leaned into the seat, which moved and settled with Harry's presence.

The car clunked as they drove away. Harry shrugged. "Not exactly luxury, is it? One day I'd like a good car. One that doesn't break down."

"A Jag would be nice." She recalled the smell and luxury of the car George had driven from his robbery.

"In my dreams," Harry said. "Never mind. Maybe one day."

"At least you've got a car." She caught the flash of his eye illuminated by the dashboard lights before he concentrated on the dark road again. They turned right, away from Hailing and far-off London. After a ten minute drive, they whizzed past the Peters' farm with The Barn behind it. Heart pounding, Liliha dropped her head rather than pick out the shed further along the dark road.

Must have passed the place by now. A deep breath strengthened her to peek out the windows while they passed Zennor—small as Sarah had said.

"Audley's renting an old farmhouse up ahead," Harry said. "I haven't visited before." His soft voice rasped in the dark interior. "You might remember we went to uni together. That's how I got the old job as accountant at the music office. I always did well at numbers. Of course, now I'm working on my own." He cleared his throat. "I'm talking too much. Don't mean to ... sorry about Oliver."

"It's over now." She closed her eyes. "I miss him so much." She swallowed and forced words past her blocked throat in the hope of repressing sorrow. "I wish I'd been to uni. I married too young the first time." Of course, without those circumstances, Kaelyn and Alissa wouldn't exist. And she might not have escaped to England and met Oliver. Everything happened for a reason.

A nasty inner voice scoffed and questioned the reason for Oliver's murder—an innocent man lured to meet his former girlfriend.

Harry didn't speak for several minutes. Liliha flashed a glance in his direction. He didn't acknowledge her. His next words jerked her to attention.

"I know it must be hard for you, coming out this way."

"Has to be done."

"You wouldn't want to take to black robes like the women in Sicily and become a bitter old widow."

"I guess not, although it sounds comforting," she said.

"They've given up on life. They content themselves with gossiping about their neighbors."

"I haven't got any."

"That's a pity." Harry swung the wheel to take a corner. "Of course the isolation was worse at The Barn."

"Which is why I moved."

"Just remember, your friends care about you. I know you must feel lonely. I'm always at the end of the phone. Call me if ever you need advice or help."

"Okay, here's your first task," she said. "Have you seen a pale blue Jag for sale?"

"Nope. Want me to look?"

The light banter amused her. "Yes, please."

"That was too easy." His voice took on a sharp tone. "And not relevant. I mean it, Liliha. Don't be flippant with my care."

His word *'care'* caused a frown. "How do you mean?"

"Surely, you know ... Give me a real task one day and I'll show you."

"I'll bear that in mind. You're one of the good guys, Harry."

"If only you knew."

After quarter of an hour of dreaming silence, the car's motion slowed. Harry leaned forward, concentrated ahead, and turned the wheel into a long drive across a field. They bumped over ruts and came to a stop in front of the house alongside several others obscured in the dark.

"Here we are." Harry helped her out.

Although tall in flats, she had to gaze up. "Thank you."

"Glad I could help." He hesitated, leaned close and took a breath. "Ready?" His deep voice came out as a murmur. "Or would you rather take a stroll in the field?" His teeth flashed. "Joke."

Something inside her clenched tight. She didn't want personal contact. *Bluff it out. He'd made a simple effort to lighten the mood. Way too touchy.* "I think we'd better show up, otherwise they might send out a search party."

The front door opened and a glow spilled out into the gloom.

"Hi, you two," Sarah called from the entrance. "Everything okay?"

The friendly voice revived Liliha. "We're fine."

"Come and meet the rest of the gang." Sarah led them inside.

Five well-dressed people stood in the living room. Liliha greeted Alana, the American woman she'd met on the train, Audley with the short silver hair, Chris, the musician with long locks, and his petite dark-haired wife Jessica.

Sarah gestured to a new man. "Liliha. This is George. George, Liliha."

A powerful presence emanated from the stranger. Under weathered facial skin, his body hinted at honed muscles beneath a smart suit.

"Spelled without an 'e' on the end." Georg raised his chin, flicking curly collar-length hair behind. "No need to bother pronouncing it South African-style."

Shaking his firm hand, Liliha didn't risk staring.

Her reluctance to socialize changed.

He could be the George from her vision—the one she'd been trying to find. The melding of minds didn't reveal the presence of an accent.

Chapter Nine

Sarah's living room put Liliha at ease with its polished wooden floor and shabby-chic leather sofas. She relaxed and stepped backward. Harry balanced her with a grip under the elbows.

She drew herself away from personal contact and, trying to appear casual, grinned. "Thanks."

"Any time, *cara*." Harry grasped two glasses of wine from Audley and handed one to her.

His use of the word *'cara'* brushed the air with a lingering caress. Rejecting his attention, Liliha approached Alana on the far side of the circle. She didn't glance Georg's way.

"I see you're wearing your wonderful ring," Alana said.

Liliha raised her wine glass. Flashes of light pierced the air from the facet within the star moonstone.

Sarah said, "Tell Alana what they told you at the museum, Liliha."

"This is fascinating," Jessica told Alana.

"The ring ... Well I should start at the beginning. About two years ago, I lost my ring at a former friend's house." Liliha sucked in her lower lip. No need to mention the woman who had stabbed Oliver. One fingernail rubbed a piece of fluff on her sleeve. *Better snap out of this daze.* "Then, it was discovered on a body, washed up on the beach." Everyone faced her now.

"A body? How awful! How did it get there?" Alana asked.

"Something to do with drugs." Liliha shot a glance at Sarah. Encouraged, she drew another breath. "I didn't know about any of this right then."

Sarah took up the story. "Apparently, the police gave the ring to a jeweler to be valued. He rang a contact at the British Museum. They showed interest so he sent it off to The Department of Ancient Egypt and Sudan."

"I took the train to London for an appointment at the museum." Liliha drew a breath.

Sarah frowned and tightened her lips.

Better not launch into the part about outmaneuvering the two men and refusing to be compensated from the Historical Resources Fund.

When Georg's gaze fixed on her finger, Liliha covered the precious jewel with the other hand. "They told me all about the ring's history. That's it really. No big deal." Liliha swept her glance over the standing group of people.

No guile showed in Georg's brown eyes and open expression. Shaggy hair resembled a mane framing his square face. Was he the one she was looking for? *Best to be wary.*

William had warned her not to be so trusting when she'd first met Harry. She flashed him a smile. Harry might not be perfect, but he'd been a good friend over the years.

"I haven't seen you around here," Harry said to Georg. "Are you visiting?"

"Just moved in up the road. These people," Georg nodded at Sarah and Audley, "have been kind enough to invite a newcomer out for a meal."

"I stopped to speak to him while I was walking my dog along the cliffs," Jessica said. "I mean to find out all about you, now." She grinned at Georg's embarrassment.

Liliha studied the mystery man while he chatted. She judged his age to be in the mid-thirties. No distinguishing features, straight nose, neither handsome nor ugly. Rather than crocodile shoes, he wore black polished going-out-for-a-meal lace-ups.

Too much of a coincidence to find the thief from her vision without any effort on her part. Liliha gave an inner chuckle about sending her wish out into the cosmos to bounce off the moon and beam the result to her. "Which part of South Africa are you from?"

"Johannesburg." Georg's eyes flashed with awareness, and then he hooded them. "What about you?"

"South Australia." Maybe he wanted to hide something. "I've lived here several years."

"Where?"

Playing the same game, Liliha said, "In town. Lovely here in Cornwall, isn't it?"

Alana opened her mouth and drew in a breath, kindly eyes becoming more alert.

Liliha gave a slight shake to her head to stop her revealing The Barn.

"And I'm from the Bronx," Alana said. "Been here almost ten years. Love it. So different from the other side of the pond."

"You have to wonder what brought such a diverse group to St. Ives," Chris said. "African, Australian, and American."

"And there's me," Harry said. "I'm from Sicily originally."

"If everyone's ready," Sarah said, "follow me into the dining room."

Liliha leaned close to Alana. "I got lonely in the country so I've moved back to St. Ives."

"Oh, is that why you didn't mention The Barn?"

Liliha nodded and took the seat Sarah indicated beside Alana.

During the meal, Liliha glanced across the table at Georg and caught him staring. She shot another quick look in his direction at his right hand gripping the glass. Sure enough, he wore a signet ring, although she couldn't determine the design.

Talking in fits and bursts, everyone concentrated on their meal.

Sarah cleared the dishes from the main course. Liliha chatted to Alana on her left. Murmured conversation came from the other end, where Audley and Chris discussed music, and Harry spoke to Jessica and Sarah beside the observant Georg.

Alana's cutlery clattered on her empty plate. "That was real nice," she said. "It's good to get out. I haven't done anything much with my husband away."

"You must be lonely without him." Liliha dabbed her mouth with a napkin while she changed the subject. "There must be lovely walks in your area."

"Bryan and I used to go over to the edge of Trewey cliffs. Pendour cove, it's called. The locals told us pirate ships sailed nearby in the old days before the decree was passed to get rid of the buccaneers roaming the high seas."

Alana's words about the locality brushed over Liliha. "If you don't mind me asking, how long will he be away?"

"Only a couple of weeks. The cottage seems so quiet without him. You know what that's like, I guess. What do you do with your time?"

Liliha leaned close. "I've found a temporary job at the Double S tearooms where I used to work."

"You must have plenty of energy."

"Not really. But I've just had a thought. A woman sells patchwork quilts at the shop," Liliha said. "People exhibit their work there. I know she needs help. Are you interested?"

Alana straightened. "Could be. But how would I ...?" Her eyes flicked under lowered brows.

"I'll contact her and find out."

"How kind of you." Alana touched Liliha's arm. "I used to love sewing."

After coffee, they wandered into the living room and listened to Chris play the guitar. Relaxed by the slow, haunting tune, Liliha closed her eyes several times, but jerked awake just in time.

"Come on," Harry said. "Let's get you home." With a grin flashing bright, even teeth, he grasped her hand and pulled her erect.

She glanced at Georg, wishing they could talk.

After goodbyes, Sarah accompanied them to the door.

Outside, the crisp fresh odor of dew hung in the air.

Harry lit a cigarette, and then ushered her past darkened shapes of vehicles to his own. When he settled on the seat beside her, his hands were free. He started the engine and reversed the car along the drive. After a few bumps, they traveled over a smooth road.

Liliha peered at Harry's silhouette. "Does Georg live close?"

"No idea." Harry glanced at her. "You're not interested, are you?"

Not in the manner he meant. "Harry! As if I could, with Oliver just ..." She shouldn't criticize. Harry accepted her just the way she was, didn't humiliate, or make her feel small. She relaxed and concentrated on the little she'd learned about Georg.

***

Liliha jerked her eyes open when her car door opened.

"Here we are," Harry said. "I've driven you right to the gate."

Fresh air raised goose bumps. "Sorry, Harry. I didn't mean to fall asleep." Her neck sunk into her scarf.

"Says a lot for my company. You did it on the way over too."

She climbed out and stretched in the breeze. "I'm not used to late nights."

At the edge of the garden, Harry raised her hand to his lips. "Good night, donna."

She smiled at his formal gesture, murmured a farewell, and then unlocked her front door. Harry waved and drove off.

Inside the quiet hallway, the papyrus of Lilihaffertiti faced her, standing calm and proud. Liliha slung her scarf and coat on a hook to the right under the stairs, wishing she'd found out more about Georg.

A natural inclination told her to retreat. He might take her interest as an invitation or worse, he could present a real danger away from other people's company.

Chapter Ten

Trapped in midafternoon traffic close to London, van den Burg chuckled and stretched out in the comfort of the roomy Jag. Orchestral music from the radio soothed him with memories of his childhood home. The theft of this fine example of British luxury motor coaches didn't worry him. Rather than borrow an old banger from a guileless bumpkin, he'd swiped the car from under the nose of a small-time thief in St. Ives. Just happened to be passing. Easy to tell the man was up to no good when the loser had left the vehicle in a wreckers' yard. He wouldn't have the log-book, that's for sure.

Georg changed gears with a nudge of the stick and passed a slower vehicle. Despite the risk of being seen, he'd driven the Jag to the diner-party last night. The country area had no street lights to give him away. What a buzz.

He glanced at his watch. Shouldn't be long before he reached his mentor's home. He relied on Straten for advice.

Forced to halt in congested traffic beside endless miles of housing, he changed the radio channel to a sport discussion. After listening for a few minutes, his attention wandered. Cornwall's fresh air and wonderful scenery was so much better than living close to other people.

At his first interview, he'd agreed to remain in Cornwall. Straten had made a few calls and arranged for a permanent place for Georg to live, right on the western tip of the land. Nobody occupied the three other flats in the converted farmhouse. The isolated spot lay miles from any neighbors, which suited him as well as Straten.

Georg clicked off the raised voices on the radio, sobering at the direction his solitary existence had taken.

However, he shuddered about the woman his father had suggested as a bride. Hence, he'd left. The longing for female company screamed into his mind with the call of a circling eagle. At the age of thirty-three, he lived the life of a gypsy, yet craved stability.

Breaking out of the line of idling traffic, he pulled the Jag into the paved drive of Straten's impressive house and parked under a bare central tree.

He slid off the leather seat and stepped out. Palms flattened, he smoothed the shirt into his chinos and centered his belt buckle. *Alright, van den Burg. Time to make your own way in this world.* He strode to the door set in the middle of six tall, narrow-cased windows on the ground floor.

Prepped with the silent encouragement, he knocked.

On the far side of a laurel hedge border, fume-belching vehicles roared along the opposite lane of the busy road. How did his employer stand the noise? The door opened.

Straten stared at him with expressionless eyes. "What's the problem?"

"Just calling in," Georg said. "I'm on my way up north. Did you check out the car?"

Straten allowed him entry and dismissed the woman who appeared by brushing the air with his hand. Silence engulfed the spacious hall. "All right." Straten folded his arms. "I'll go along with you. Where did the Jag come from?"

Dressed in a suit, the man must have just arrived home from the office. Probably explained his snappy mood. "Personal," Georg said. "But I need to get rid of it fast. Any contacts in Scotland?"

"You're a bit above yourself. You work for me,

remember?"

Chastened, Georg glanced inside a doorway on the right. A bottle and glasses sat on the sideboard. He moistened the corner of his mouth. "Thirsty work driving."

"Plenty of pubs in the area." The man slid his hand over his hair. "This is my home, and I don't want you here again without an invitation. Understood?" Anger glinted from his pale eyes.

"Just needed advice. I didn't know you'd—"

"Well, now you do. As you're here, I'll tell you this. Word's out about an ancient Egyptian ring down in Cornwall. Star moonstone set in old gold. Get back fast and see if you can locate the thing. Make contacts in the area. It's got my stamp on it, and nobody else had better wipe it off, understood?"

Georg frowned. "You mean...?"

Straten added, "I'll make an offer when you locate the item."

Georg drew a breath. "How ...?" Couldn't ask. Somebody had sung into the Cornish wind and the news blew all the way to London.

Could be pure coincidence, but he'd seen a moonstone ring on a woman's finger at the party the other night. Had an old look about it. Georg masked his expression while trying to work out how to revert the conversation to the car.

"My daughters will arrive home in half an hour." Straten grasped him by the shoulder, digging his fingers into the muscle on the way toward the door. "I don't want you in the way."

Georg shrugged. Bloody arrogant pig. "No worries, man. I respect your home. It won't happen again." Now what? "I'll do as you ask as soon as I can. Do you mind if I get rid of the motor first? Don't want to draw attention to myself. Unless you want me to leave it with you."

"You could drive the car out into the country to abandon for all I care."

"A car park or a country lane? Some nosy parker would find me traipsing along the road and link me to ..."

"Just a minute." With a sigh, Straten sidestepped to a hall table, pulled out a card from a drawer, scribbled on the reverse, and handed it over. "Contact Leith. He'll help you out ... this time." He frowned and strolled to the door. "We're not in the car business. I've got other plans for you. You're lucky I know your father from the old days."

Heartbeat hammered in his ears. "You won't—"

"Not unless I need to." The man's raised top lip revealed his over-white teeth.

"I'll be in St. Ives by tomorrow." Georg pocketed the information.

"Make sure you are." Straten closed the door behind him.

Flexing his neck as though in the man's stranglehold, Georg strode to the car and settled inside. The motor's initial clatter settled to a purr. He edged out between stationary traffic and roared downhill toward Watford, north of London. He didn't like the sound of Straten's suggestion. Make an offer? That didn't ring true. Georg clenched his jaw. Despite going for joyrides, he hadn't been raised to live a life of crime. Anyway, shuffling the Jag from one place to another didn't count.

***

Twenty minutes before closing time at the tearooms, Liliha polished the glass on the cold drinks cabinet. Activity reduced her sorrow somewhat. She dreaded the suspicion of a flare-up when she returned to Cottage

Central. Best to keep up the pretense of normality along with the make-believe role of psychic detective.

Two groups of customers remained. At one table, four people chatted together, amongst occasional bouts of laughter. At the other, two elderly people sipped their tea.

Working in the business of hospitality, she communicated positive ideas to people nearby, rather than during visions. She imagined ants exploring their surroundings, carrying food for the colony on their return, and sharing information each time they met. In her simple job of worker ant, she could influence the whole. Words from the bible echoed within her head. *'And the greatest among you is the servant of all.'* Rather than a lowly job, her work as a waitress mattered. The concept almost raised a smile.

A tinkle came from the door. Entering with a swirl of breeze, a scruffy young woman glanced about the room, lowered her head and traipsed over to a small table at one side.

Liliha retreated behind the counter, deposited her cleaning cloth and spray bottle, and then hurried toward the pale customer. "What can I get you?"

"I'm dying for a cup of tea," she said in a hesitant voice. "I've been walking most of the afternoon."

"Would you like something to eat?"

The young woman's mouth dropped open and her eyebrows lifted.

"I can offer a delicious banana muffin, or a wedge of rich chocolate cake, served with your choice of cream or ice cream." Liliha smiled. "Or scones, jam and cream."

The woman hesitated. Her head drooped and she huddled inside her padded, synthetic jacket. "Just tea, please."

While Liliha made the drink, she wondered about the customer's circumstances. She slipped a muffin onto a plate. Silvia would throw the food out at the end of the day. Better mention what she'd done to her employer. Liliha sighed at the approach of another lecture. Before she could change her mind, Liliha carried the tray over to the customer. "Here you are. Just leave the muffin if you don't want it. No charge."

The woman gazed up and blinked. "Thank you."

By the time Liliha returned to the serving area, the woman had already eaten half. The people from the table of four rose and ambled to the counter. Liliha took their payment and chatted, happy with her role. After they left, the elderly couple settled up, and then wandered outside hand in hand.

Liliha glanced at the last customer, slumped on the table. She hurried across with a glass of water. "Are you all right?"

The young woman's head rose and she blinked. "I just came over all dizzy."

"You've probably overdone the walking," Liliha said. "Rest awhile."

The woman gulped the water.

"You look a bit pale. Do you want me to call an ambulance?"

"I'll be okay in a minute. Please, don't make a fuss."

"Of course not. Take all the time you need." Liliha turned away. "Let me know if you want anything else." She placed the closed sign on the door before hurrying into the kitchen to alert Silvia.

"Better stay with her until she leaves," Silvia said. "We don't want trouble."

Liliha untied her apron. Was trouble the only thing

her employer cared about? She unlatched the gold neck chain from her neck, removed her ring, and slid the comforting weight onto her finger before reaching for her bag and coat.

On the approach toward the fire door, the first signs of dizziness came over her. A waft of lily perfume drifted by.

A vision already? Too quick. *Reach a safe place.* Liliha staggered to the area between the shop and kitchen and eased the door open. Inside, she pressed her spine against the rear wall behind the shop counter. Weak hands dropped her coat and bag. A quick glance revealed the customer gazing outside before Liliha tilted within the deviation toward another place.

***

I peer below with my telescopic vision and ignore the fuzzy edges and the surreal floating sensation. Below, occasional cars roar along a wide road on the right-hand side. Concentrating on this area, I hover under bright, late morning sun and get my bearings. To one side, stores line the roadside and people stroll along the pavement.

Ahead of a line of traffic, a car slows. The horn sounds.

A child stumbles along the edge of the road—a toddler on unsteady legs, dressed in pink trousers and top. More cars reduce speed.

I zoom toward the closest pedestrian and meld with a middle-aged woman. "Pay attention to the road."

With me inside her, she turns her head and notices the toddler. Her first instinct is to help, but she hesitates. I read a deep-seated problem inside her consciousness.

'Quick. Get the child before a car runs her over.'

Overcoming uncertainty, we dart forward and swoop

the little one up in our arms. "Well done," she whispers to herself. "When I tell my husband, he'll say, 'Good for you, Daphne.'"

We speak louder to the child to penetrate the traffic noise. "What are you doing on the road? Where's Mommy?"

The girl points.

Our gaze swings to a woman lying prone close to the gutter between cars, face tilted sideways. We tuck the child on our hip, hurry over, and lean close, adjusting our burden to compensate. "What's wrong?"

The disheveled woman mumbles. A strong smell of alcohol rises from her slack lips.

"Mommy, Mommy." The child squeals and wriggles. We lower her to the ground.

Worry seeps into Daphne's mind. Unless she reports the incident to the police, the child will be in very real danger and she can't remain with her. She's on her way to pick up her young grandchildren from school.

She doesn't want to call the authorities. Flashes of her unhappy childhood with foster parents rise to the surface. Welfare services took her from her own lackadaisical mother. She wouldn't wish a similar future on any child.

The slumped woman stirs, but then sags.

'Call the police,' I whisper inside Daphne's mind. 'Things might not turn out the same way for this child.'

The toddler tries to wander off again. When we grasp her, our gaze falls on the watch. We have to go. We scan the area for someone else to take over.

I issue a strong certainty to her. 'You must call.'

We flick open the phone and ask for help.

An American female voice says, "An officer will be

78

with you very soon. There is one just around the corner. Please remain with the child."

The little girl struggles, but we keep a firm hold on her dress strap. With a squeal of tires, a motorbike stops. A uniformed officer dismounts, removes his helmet and strides over.

I'm released. I float up and keep watching.

After explaining, Daphne alerts him about her need to leave while he bends to examine the woman. She blurts, "What will happen to the child?"

"Don't worry, Ma'am. We'll keep them both safe for the night, and if all is well, they'll be released in the morning."

Daphne hurries away to meet her grandchildren.

The scene fades.

***

Soft sounds in the tearooms eased Liliha's passage—the hum of the refrigerator, an occasional muffled clink. She'd love to find out what happened to the mother and little pink toddler—so innocent alone on the street. The child had no control over the circumstance of her birth. However, the mother's intoxication was a worry. She might pull herself together after the humiliating experience of being locked up for the night.

Acknowledging how Daphne had overcome her past pain to help the child, Liliha blinked away the lingering incident. The clock hand had advanced five minutes.

The last customer sat with her elbows resting either side of her cup. Lank hair hung close to a small face with an upturned nose and eyes which slanted downward at the edges.

With hesitancy, Liliha approached and murmured,

"Where are you staying? I could see you safely home."

"No need. Let me pay for the tea now." She reached into her purse and scrabbled for the change, making the amount up with small coins.

Liliha accepted the money and returned to the register. When she looked up, the slim form, unsteady on her feet, was leaving. Liliha hurried to the rear workroom. "Silvia, I'm going to make sure the customer's alright. She might wander onto the road in the state she's in."

Silvia dusted her hands and reached for the key.

Chapter Eleven

Outside the shop, Liliha located the young woman wearing a brown parka with a fur hood over navy trousers, trainers scuffed. Liliha hurried close. "Wait."

The young woman turned, eyes narrowed.

"I'm Liliha. Let me help you home."

"Ellen's the name. I might as well tell ya. I'm not staying anywhere yet." She lowered her gaze to the cobblestones and shuffled her feet.

"Right." A man approached on the footpath. Liliha considered a way to help while they shifted to allow him room. "Would you rather stay in a guest house or a hotel? I'd recommend a guest house."

"You're nosy, aren't ya? Why should you care?"

Liliha smiled, hoping to reassure her. "I thought you might need assistance in a strange town."

"If ya must know, I haven't found anyone who'll take me without a deposit."

"I see your a problem."

"Is there a homeless shelter close?"

"I don't know." Liliha gazed into the distance. "We could inquire at the police station."

"Not the police." Ellen glanced away. "No bother, please."

Another woman who didn't want to get involved with the authorities, like Daphne from her earlier vision. What was Ellen's reason? "Are you in trouble? Maybe I could help."

More people passed.

"There's nothing you could do." Ellen drew in a breath and straightened. "I just need to work things out."

"Where have you left your luggage?"

With blinking eyes like an owl caught in sudden light, Ellen shrugged. "Don't worry about it."

"Would you like to come home with me?"

"I said no. Leave me alone."

"I won't ask you any personal questions." Liliha gazed at a cast-off sweet wrapper on the pavement. Something inside suggested turning away. But she couldn't. *Best to let actions speak for themselves.* "Come on. You need somewhere to sleep. It will be dark in a couple of hours."

"I guess I've got nothing to lose if I go with ya."

A mental niggle alerted Liliha. But, the slender girl wasn't likely to do her any harm. "This way."

***

Ellen gazed at Liliha's hallway as if in a dream. So neat. And so beautiful. A fresh scent reminded her of standing under pine trees close to where she'd lived when Mum and Dad were still together.

What did this older woman expect? People didn't give anything away without wanting payment of some sort. Lily might want to set her up in the game. At least this job would be high-class. *Best to wait and see.*

Ellen licked her dry lips. She could handle herself. She'd escaped worse.

***

Unsure of her hasty decision, Liliha gestured to a hanging space under the stairs. "You can leave your things here with mine."

The ragamuffin guest unzipped her parka.

"Come into the kitchen where we can chat." Liliha strode ahead and turned right at the far end. She glanced behind to see Ellen tiptoe along and peer into the room.

"Another cuppa?"

Ellen nodded. "Coffee, please. I'm thirsty."

"Take a seat at the table." Liliha set about making the drinks. "First things first. You need a place for the night. Do you want to stay with me? I have a spare bedroom."

"Sure. Why not?" Ellen draped the strap of her bag over the chair support behind her.

A strange reply. Liliha shrugged. "Right. That's settled." She poured boiling water into the mugs and turned.

Ellen slouched in Liliha's normal spot with her hands behind her head.

Liliha carried the drinks to the table. "What brings you to St. Ives?" She settled in a chair opposite Ellen, viewing the room from another angle. Funny how one became used to a certain seat.

"Had to take a break." Ellen blew on her coffee.

"A holiday, I guess. Looks like things aren't working out the way you'd hoped. Tell me about the life you left behind."

"You said no personal questions." Ellen's lips resembled a slash drawn on a cartoon face.

"Are you running from someone?" Liliha took a sip of hot tea.

"From everything. And don't bother thinking you can catch me either. A bed for the night, but that's it. If you don't like it ..." Ellen edged forward, placed her hands on the table and pressed, ready to stand. "I'll leave right now."

Liliha frowned. Rather than give the girl a reprimand about her rude attitude, she should respond with gentleness. For one brief moment, Liliha closed her eyes and gathered her patience. "I'd like to help if I can. Relax while I fix something to eat."

"Oh, good." Ellen sipped her coffee, eyes flashing

about the room. She set her mug on the table and knocked her drink over. "Sorry," she gasped.

Liliha jumped up for a cloth and mopped up the spreading liquid. "Don't worry. It happens to everyone. Would you like some more?"

"No thanks." With a sigh, Ellen slumped over her arms.

"What you need is food." A motherly instinct replaced Liliha's frustration as she headed for the bench and prepared a meal.

When the bacon sizzled, she added sliced mushrooms to the pan. Before long, filled plates clattered onto the wooden table.

Ellen sat up, blinked, and stretched. "Something smells good."

"You must be starving." Liliha picked up her knife and fork.

Ellen clutched her knife and fork upright between mouthfuls, and then shoveled in more food before she swallowed.

Rather than dwell on her bad manners, Liliha chewed a slice of crunchy toast, savoring the way it cleaned her mouth from the sticky egg yolk. "What sort of work are you interested in?"

"Dunno." Ellen pushed her empty plate toward the center of the table. "I can't do much." Ellen dropped her gaze, hiding any hint of her feelings.

"I suppose you've checked the Job Center."

Ellen's head nodded without lifting.

"I found work hard to get too, without qualifications," Liliha said, placing her knife and fork together. "I just recently got the job at the tearooms."

"Do they need anyone else? I can wash dishes."

"There's an automatic dishwasher," Liliha said.

"Nobody wants to take me on. That's the trouble."

"Let's sleep on it. I'll think of something."

Ellen yawned. "Want me to help clean up?"

"What about having an early night? You look exhausted."

"What, no telly?" Ellen glanced out into the hall.

"Watch television if you like. It's through here." In the hallway, Liliha pointed out the layout to the bedrooms and bathroom upstairs. "If you want to clean your teeth, there's a spare brush in the bathroom cabinet."

"I'm okay." When they entered the living room, Ellen plonked into Liliha's favorite chair with the good back support. "Where's the remote?"

Swallowing annoyance, Liliha did no more than point at the item before she returned to the kitchen. Ellen's attitude riled her. Committed to taking the girl in and giving her a bed for the night, Liliha wondered at her hasty decision. But then, in the morning, Ellen would be on her way.

Chapter Twelve

Noise from the television drifted into the kitchen. Liliha wiped over the stainless steel sink one last time. With the wrung-out cloth, she dried the remaining drops. All shiny, she flung the cloths into the washing machine, removed her rubber gloves, and sighed in satisfaction at a completed job.

Now, to ring Alissa at boarding school before joining Ellen.

Someone must have answered although they didn't speak. After she asked for Alissa, a scrape came from the speaker before a cough. "Mum?" A husky voice.

"Darling, what's wrong?"

"I've caught a cold."

"You should start to feel better soon. Are you eating enough fruit and vegetables?"

"Yeah. Yeah. Always trying to teach me something." A pause. "I don't mean to be snappy." Alissa's voice took on an anxious tone.

"Understandable, when you're not feeling well. You poor darling. I won't keep you. Are you going to lessons today?"

"Matron doesn't believe in coddling a cold. She says you get over the symptoms quicker if you carry on."

"She might be right. But I wish I could wrap you up in a blanket and feed you lemon and honey drinks."

"Haha. You'd probably make me swallow whole cloves of garlic. I know you." The clearing of a throat grated from within the receiver. "The others are leaving now. Gotta go."

"I love you so much."

"Me too."

Alissa's words reminded Liliha of her deep-rooted desire to control other people's lives. In a pensive mood, she strode into the living room. Ellen had moved to the sofa where she slept, grubby shoes on the woven material. Liliha sighed. She needed to sort things out with her guest. Easing into her chair, she kicked off her shoes and rested. The actors on a television serial screamed at each other.

Liliha needed to suggest employment for Ellen or some course of action. Otherwise she might end up with a permanent non-contributing guest.

Unable to take the screeching voices any longer, she padded over the carpet and reached to grasp the remote lying beside Ellen.

The girl's eyes sprang open. "What?"

"I'm just going to turn this off. Do you want to go to bed?"

Frowning, Ellen licked her lips. "Anyone here?"

"Of course not. Just us."

Ellen sighed.

"Come on," Liliha said. "I'm tired, and I can see you are."

Ellen swung her legs off the sofa. "Why not? You don't get nuttin' for nuttin.'"

Liliha frowned and led her upstairs. Ellen hinted at certain modes of behavior. *Best to clear things up right at the start.* "We'll have a talk in the morning. But for now, you need rest, and I know I do." She gestured to the spare bedroom at the rear of the house behind hers.

"Want me to wash first?"

"Good idea." Liliha pointed at the bathroom at the far end. "Get a towel from the top shelf. I'll bring you a nightie."

"I sleep in the raw. Saves time," Ellen said.

"Right." Perhaps Ellen meant getting dressed in the morning. "I'll use the bathroom first, and then it's all yours."

Ellen leaned on the study door-frame opposite. She was still outside when Liliha emerged. Liliha said, "Okay?"

"Yeah." Ellen raised her shoulders, yawned, and let out her breath in a sigh. "I'll see you in a minute."

"No need. We'll speak tomorrow. The spare bed's all ready. Just get comfy and sleep well." Liliha raised the corners of her mouth in a way she hoped gave assurance and left Ellen entering the bathroom.

***

Ellen seethed with uncertainty. She'd slid out of her trainers on the landing. This Lily was hard to read. She didn't come right out in the open and say what she wanted, but she gave off enough hints. She might be satisfied with a sleeping partner, but Ellen didn't think so. Oh well, any effort on her part was worth a cushy night in a nice house.

She found a flannel and towel—both fluffy and white—and ran the water for a wash. Just face and private parts would do. Lily seemed eager for their coupling. Sex probably helped her sleep well. For Ellen, sometimes it did and sometimes it didn't. Depended on the toys. Some women liked to inflict pain, or the reverse: to receive it.

She rubbed the towel over her body. Lily looked gentle. Maybe she'd be nice. Bunching her castoff garments up under her arm, she emerged.

No sound except for a faint tick echoing up the stairwell. Liliha must be waiting. She approached the indicated room. Starlight penetrated lace curtain from outside. The bed was empty, flat. No Lily.

After dumping her soiled clothes in one corner, Ellen

climbed between fluffy sheets—flannelette and giving the hint of flowers on a summer day. Lily might come creeping in to surprise her.

For quite some time, Ellen lay stiff. When Lily didn't turn up, she climbed out of the bed and crept out to the passage. You had to cater for all sorts of tastes and personalities. The woman might be shy.

***

Edgy because a stranger occupied the house, Liliha shifted in her bed. A hint of perfume strengthened. Loud roaring which resembled the wind in a snow storm hinted at a coming vision. Too late to remove the ring. She clenched her teeth before tumbling within the spinning vortex toward another place.

***

I'm hovering over a yard filled with children. Judging by the fancy architecture of the buildings and the children's language, this must be France. I have no difficulty interpreting, which is one of the amazing things about my visions. Against the perimeter of the play area, twenty children sit in a covered shed with food wrappings in front of them.

I observe a young teacher standing in the yard. I read her name badge while I plummet toward her. Now, I'm with Marie, on duty during the break. She sweeps her gaze over the running children in an alert manner. Under a map showing many islands set in the ocean, a sign in big letters states French Polynesia.

I generate determination as if I'm a car engine revving up. I must succeed this time.

Children's high yells come from the shed. Expecting a fight, Marie, with me inside her, veers to one side to check. The noise increases and we jog toward the fuss. Children are leaning over a gasping boy on the ground. Sudden alarm snakes inside our awareness. The boy's mouth is open and he's flushed with bulging eyes. We push others aside, panicked by the prone child's protruding tongue.

Overwhelmed, Marie can't think what to do.

I experience the same anxiety as any parent. I'd expect a teacher to take charge. 'Ask his friends,' I urge. Will she listen to the advice?

"What's wrong with him?" Our voice rings loud amongst the assembled pupils while Marie recalls a recent first aid class.

Was the teacher's question coincidence or did she hear me? A jumble of high voices pipe up in reply.

"He just ate one of my biscuits."

"Then, he started choking."

"But he's allergic to nuts, Mademoiselle," a girl says.

"He only had a chocolate biscuit."

Time might run out. He could die. 'Concentrate. You know what to do,' I say, trying to calm her mind, slow her heart rate and control her breathing.

"Where's his kit?" Marie asks, swallowing her fear. He must have one.

"I'll get it, Miss." The girl, Amelie, runs off toward the rear of the school about ten feet away.

The memory of a sickly sweet odor increases Marie's panic and revulsion. Her older brother injected himself for his diabetes. She never wanted to touch a needle and wonders if she can deal with the procedure. She's never handled a needle before.

'Get over this,' I advise. 'The child's life depends on your next action. Don't be afraid. You'll know exactly what to do. While you're waiting, organize the children.'

"Hold the door open for her," Marie calls. "This is

an emergency."

I whisper. 'Reassure the others.'

"Everyone clear a path for Amelie."

'Ambulance?' I remind her.

"Luc. Run to the office and get the secretary to ring for an ambulance."

The children step away and allow Luc passage. Yes. She did listen. I pray she can save him.

With an overriding hope, we kneel beside the stricken child, whose tongue has swelled more. "The biscuit must have contained nuts. Once I've injected him, he'll recover." We glance up at the approaching Amelie and reach for the syringe.

I fight her revulsion, fill her with confidence, and project an image of the boy's recovery.

With a slight tremble, we flick open the cap.

I guide her hands and reassure her as we inject adrenalin into the lad's arm and massage it. "He'll be all right in a minute." We cradle him.

Discharged, I ascend while Marie carries the child inside.

✳✳✳

Liliha's eyes sprung open in her bedroom at the sound of a shuffle and blinked in the faint light entering the room from outside. Someone stood in her doorway. The robber must have returned. Should she wake Ellen?

Too late because the presence advanced. Liliha's heart hammered loud in her ears. What did he want? Murder? Or just to check if she lay sleeping? She closed her eyes and tried to make her breathing regular. Maybe he'd go away. The ring. He'd have to wake her. Her hand curled. The improbable idea formed of the ring being cut off a finger for the second time in its history.

The intruder crept closer. What could she do? Faced with too many choices, Liliha remained motionless. Breath brushed over her face, moved hairs on her head. She opened her eyes a fraction to check if he held a pillow ready to smother her. Perhaps she could talk him out of murder. She could hand the ring over, rather than lose her finger—or her life.

A light trail of spider's web or something similar brushed over her face. She inhaled a hint of dust or grime. She couldn't help the indrawn breath which came from her fear.

"Lily." A female voice. "Are you awake? Tell me what ya want."

"Ellen. Is that you?" Liliha sat up and clutched her heart. "What are you doing in here?"

Ellen brushed her hair away and stroked Liliha's shoulder. "Shhhh. It's all right. I'm here."

Liliha removed Ellen's hand. "What do you mean? I thought you were a burglar."

"Just me. Were you frightened? Move over and I'll hold you."

Liliha controlled herself. "I'm quite all right, thank you. You did startle me, I must admit. I'm usually the one who acts the motherly part."

"Ah. You want me to be the child." Ellen's voice took on a higher note. "Mummy, I'm scared. Can I get into bed with you?"

Liliha could hardly believe her ears. She blinked, at the strange notion of what Ellen alluded to. Understanding crept into her mind. A laugh started in her stomach. Arms gripping opposite shoulders, she shook while giggles erupted. "Go to sleep in the other room, Ellen," she said between chuckles. "You're safe here."

Head high, Ellen swayed her nude hips on her way out of the room.

What a life the poor girl must have led. Releasing a silent breath, Liliha held motionless. The explosive release of laughter had eased her nerves and healed her embarrassment. Her back didn't even hurt. Must be the adrenalin.

The discharge resembled the injection which had saved the little French boy's life. Thank goodness, the teacher had snapped out of her fear, alone with responsibility.

Tomorrow, Liliha had to work out what to do about Ellen.

Chapter Thirteen

Liliha cut fruit to begin the day, glancing toward the kitchen doorway from time to time while waiting for her guest to emerge from upstairs. She bit into a section of orange, savoring the sweet, acid flavor.

What form of employment could she suggest for Ellen? Despite a suspicion of what the girl was trying to escape from, stupid ideas came up one after the other. A dresser for catwalk models—Ellen lacked experience, a magician's assistant—lacked training, a food server in a prison—too attractive. Ellen might draw the men's eyes and their mind toward—. Don't even consider the implications.

Liliha flexed her shoulders. Use logic. What would her visionary persona suggest while occupying another body?

The difference lay in one simple fact. Liliha couldn't enter Ellen's mind and learn what she really cared about. The girl had already resisted some careful face-to-face probing.

The cuckoo clock sang nine times. Two more hours before she needed to arrive at the tearooms. She headed to the base of the stairs. The toilet flushed. Good. The bear would emerge from hibernation soon.

After waiting long enough to allow her guest to cover her presumably naked body, Liliha shouted upstairs. "Tea or coffee?"

Silence. Then a hesitant, "Coffee please."

"Come and join me."

In the kitchen again, Liliha glanced up at a presence in the doorway. "Sit down, please." She deposited a steaming mug on the table and gestured to the sleepy-eyed Ellen, who wore the same crumpled tracksuit. "You'll feel better after you take a sip."

"Thanks." Face blotchy and hair tangled, Ellen kept her gaze averted.

"How did you sleep?"

"Good. Really. I haven't slept in such a comfortable bed for ages." Ellen glanced up, and then away.

Liliha spoke in a soft voice. "Where did you spend the night before?"

"Close to the station. It's handy because of the toilet. There's a wash basin and everything." Ellen gulped her coffee and wrapped her hands over the mug. "'Course, you have to get in and out quickly, before the station master catches you."

Liliha chuckled and glanced at the cupboards. "What would you like for breakfast? Fruit? Cereal? Toast?"

"A bowl of Coco Pops. Don't go to any bother."

"Sorry. I don't have any of those. I use porridge or Shredded Wheat, both pure grain with no additives." Liliha raised her brows.

"Uggg. Not porridge. The other one."

"You haven't tasted my porridge yet. It's wonderful."

After a rejection, Liliha passed the cereal packet, bowl, semi-skimmed milk and raw sugar to the table, and then settled opposite while Ellen ate.

"What's all those funny squiggles on sheets of paper in the other room upstairs?" Ellen asked, spoon part-way to her mouth.

"I write songs in my spare time. Of course, I don't have much at the moment."

Ellen nodded and swallowed. "Thought so. Aren't you clever?"

Seeing as Ellen was used to snooping, she'd better relocate her guest as soon as possible. "Now," Liliha said. "A job for you is the next problem. Tell me what you'd like to do."

Ellen's laugh exploded without a touch of humor. "Laze around all day. At night I usually dress up for a party." She ate fast, shoving in spoonful after spoonful.

"Not exactly what I had in mind. Are you interested in children? Sewing? Talking to people? Reading."

Ellen swallowed. "I like books."

"They're recruiting people to listen to children read at the local school. The work is voluntary, but something could come along afterward."

"How would doing that help me to earn money?" Ellen crammed in another mouthful of cereal. "Anyway, I don't know any kids and I don't like spoiled brats."

Judging by the closed expression on Ellen's face, Liliha needn't pursue the subject. While carrying her empty mug away, she despaired at the pointless tussle of wills. The girl didn't want help. Why bother? Bent over the sink, Liliha considered defeat.

Tears welled up. Self pity raged inside her. *Let the girl go.*

The memory of Oliver's steady expression calmed her. She sniffed and straightened. Determination fired. All her experience led to this point. "What about calling in at the local pubs? They might be looking for a barmaid."

"Tried already." Ellen pushed her empty bowl away. "It's hopeless."

"How far did you get with your schooling?"

"Not far. I didn't want to learn." Ellen mumbled. "I wish I'd paid attention now."

"I know what you mean. I should have stayed longer.

But we can't change the past. Let's work with what we've got. You need a place to live. Someone would welcome your company."

"Yeah. Men do."

"What I had in mind is a companion for an old person, or you could help somebody disabled with basic jobs."

Ellen raised her eyebrows. "I've got no references."

"Do you have a record?"

Ellen slumped and let her breath out in a steady stream. "Nope."

With patience close to breaking, Liliha swallowed. Why didn't Ellen appreciate her? "Are you willing to try to find a job?"

Ellen gave a slight nod, although her raised eyebrows showed a sense of doubt.

"Go up and have a nice shower. We've got over an hour before I set off for work. I'll leave some of my daughter's clean clothes on your bed. I hope they fit."

Liliha grabbed the phone and rang everyone she could think of. At last, she turned to Sarah for advice.

***

As soon as the shower cut off and the bathroom door banged, Liliha shouted upstairs, "Grab your things and bundle your dirty clothes into the bag I left on the bed."

When Ellen appeared with a perky smile, they donned their coats. Alissa's trousers trailed over Ellen's shoes, but fitted well otherwise. "Have you got everything?"

"I think so. What's the hurry?"

Liliha beckoned her to the door. "A friend told me about a position that might be available."

"Where are we going?" Ellen zipped up her jacket,

jerked her head and scratched her neck. "My hair's not quite dry."

"It won't take long in the breeze." Liliha led the way toward the town. "The woman who runs the local launderette might be able to use you. Apparently, she's very busy at the moment. I think it will depend on whether the woman ... whether you like each other." *Perhaps too much to ask.*

"What? More begging?"

"You need a job. To get one, you have to approach people. Once you arrive, wash the clothes you wore yesterday." Liliha peeped at Ellen's expression, which remained neutral. "While you're waiting, you could approach her. Offer to help her fold the washing, or sweep the floor, or wipe over the machines."

"Where will I live?"

"That's the next problem. I'll walk with you to the launderette and leave you there. Meet me after work at the tearooms and tell me how you got on."

"I'm not sure I want to do this."

Liliha's patience snapped. "No more arguments. You have to take charge of your own life if you want to change. You're running from something, so here's your chance." With the pressure released, she couldn't prevent the flow of words. "I don't know what brought you to St. Ives, but I assume you enjoy the relaxed atmosphere. The locals are friendly, and maybe, just maybe, you could make a place for yourself here if you're willing to try."

"You bitch. Who said I wanted to change? You're not my mother." Ellen jerked to a halt, cheeks flaming.

"That's the way I encourage my own daughters," Liliha said. "Listen or not. Up to you." Chin high, she turned and strode away relieved of the responsibility.

Ellen's voice shouted, "Stop."

Turning to face her, Liliha waited, eyebrows raised.

"Okay. Just don't lecture me."

They continued toward the launderette in silence, and then stopped outside the glass exterior. Liliha handed over a few coins and flicked her head toward the door.

Left to her own device, Ellen might come to some arrangement.

***

On his return trip to London, van den Burg studied the passengers inside the train. He longed to hear familiar South African tones amongst the English chattering voices. The suited men opposite concentrated their attention between newspapers and mobile phones without bothering to acknowledge him. On the other side of the aisle, a few women wearing fur-lined coats and smart make-up chatted. Georg brushed a hair off his leather jacket. At least the action gave him something to do. He didn't need to dress in a swanky suit with his life-style. All the same, the women's lack of interest in him caused a prickly reaction.

However, the wad of notes inside his jacket cheered him up. The journey in the Jag to Edinburgh had been so much more pleasant than this return to London on public transport. He wished he'd kept the stolen car although owning it wasn't an option.

If he'd been home in Jo'burg, he'd enjoy a life of luxury with a similar car. The woman his parents picked for him to marry had cast a shadow over such a scenario. Horsy face, teeth and all. Georg shuddered, knowing he'd pay any price for escape.

Now, he'd work on healing the rift with Straten.

His mind jumped to the party the other night. Harry had brought a gentle woman wearing a ring which drew his gaze time and again. Strange name. Lily or something. No, Liliha. Full of grace and beauty. Once he'd established the ring was the one Straten had mentioned, he'd send word.

Didn't know if he believed his employer's assurance about a legitimate deal though. This left a quandary about the way to proceed.

Chapter Fourteen

After work, Liliha emerged onto the breezy street and glanced each way. No sign of Ellen. Hopefully, the girl had found a place to stay as well as a job. Liliha breathed a big sigh, somewhat relieved about helping a person close-by, rather than separated by the channel of a vision.

However, a small niggle of uncertainty remained. She turned toward the town to check on Ellen.

Feet driven by momentum on the downhill walk along the quiet street, she considered another undone task. Imagination brought forth a lineup of Georges living in the area. *'Please step forward, number two.'* She chuckled. Next breath she sobered to consider a local search of the popular name on the internet.

One thing at a time. Reaching the main shopping area, she surged ahead amongst the crowds to peer inside the launderette.

Ellen, bent over a pile of clothes, chatted to another woman of about the same age.

With a sigh of satisfaction, Liliha turned and headed uphill.

***

Inside the steamy atmosphere of the launderette, Ellen glanced at her watch. A few hours to go before tackling the problem of where to sleep. Her dad had given her the wristwatch out of guilt for sexual favors. Took a lot of scrubbing with toothpaste to keep the silver shiny. She'd managed to hold onto the object during all her trials. Each time something she couldn't handle came up, the watch served as a reminder of what to fight against.

Mary, a woman of about the same age, worked at a nearby drying machine. She had taken Ellen on faith, no

101

questions asked.

Ellen folded the last sheet in the customer's pile and smoothed the surface the way Mary had demonstrated. "What next?"

"Thanks for your help. Do you live around here?" Mary slid over another washing basket of dried clothes.

"Just moved in. Thanks for taking me on." There. That sounded polite.

"You sort out this lot and I'll put on another load to wash."

"Okay." Ellen folded a pair of jeans, flattening the creases.

"The ironing is up to the customer. I can't do everything." Mary stood upright from loading a machine. "Come to think of it, with you on board, we could offer the service. Are you interested?" She leaned on the tall vibrating machine, eyes scrunched.

"In ironing?" Ellen shrugged. Right at the moment, she couldn't think of anything worse. *Better make an effort.* She could always back out later. "Whatever ya' think." How could she turn this to her advantage? She folded a sweater. "But I need to find a ... another place to stay."

"You can crash with me if you like," Mary said. "It's nothing much. Just a little flat. If you like, we can share the rent, and I'll take the money out of your salary."

Ellen rubbed her chin to gain extra time. Just like everyone else, including Matt, Mary was trying to take advantage—make a slave of her. The rent would slice any earnings. She wanted fun. Rather than storming to the doorway in anger, she rocked on her toes. *Time to decide between security and freedom.*

What had Lily said? *'You could make a place for yourself if you're willing to work at it.'*

Did slaves have a place in the world? Maybe they did if you counted a place to sleep and enough food to stay alive. *Better try.* She faced Mary and nodded.

On to the next challenge. Nothing was ever the way it seemed.

***

Georg exited the train at the station in Penzance, worn out. A fresh breeze from the harbor blew hair about his face. The whole day of travel started in Scotland. He'd changed trains in London and boarded the final one to Cornwall. From here, he could arrive at St. Ives in ten minutes by car—if he had one. *Smarten up van den Burg. Find a way to shorten the last section.*

For a small island, the United Kingdom sure took a long time to traverse. South Africa was bigger, but routes went straight to each destination.

Come to think of it, the minds of the English inhabitants weren't limited by constrictions. Whatever you wanted could be achieved with ingenuity. And Georg wanted it all—just needed to negotiate the bends en route.

First, he had to work out how to slide the ring off Liliha's slender finger. Pretty sure the ring was the one Straten had mentioned. Too much of a coincidence. Foolish not to take advantage of what life offered.

He'd never been one for words—negotiations as Straten had suggested. Rather use seduction than burglar's tools.

Georg licked his lips. A quick pint of bitter first.

He strode toward the businesses facing the sea. Oh, sod it. He'd look for a sucker in the bar. An inebriated driver might offer the opportunity he needed.

Two cold pints later, Georg chatted with an old man

who couldn't pronounce his own name, much less grasp Georg's. All the same, Georg didn't bother to give his surname. The revelation might return to bite him.

"Well, that's me done." The man slid off his stool sideways, staggered a few steps to regain his balance, and waved to the bartender.

Only five customers. Probably get busy later. Georg frowned and leaned forward. "Hold on. Have you got far to go?"

The man gave a lopsided smile. "About a mile." He produced a bunch of jangling keys.

"The little lady might want you home in one piece. Perhaps you should walk."

The fellow behind the bar nodded.

After a scratch on his head, the drunk dropped his hand. "Right. Police on the prowl lately."

Georg faced his biggest obstacle. The barman or one of the locals might prevent him from driving the guy home. He lowered his voice. "Would you like me to give you a hand?"

The barman stopped polishing a glass and narrowed his eyes.

Silence stretched.

"You drive me. Problem sorted." The guy tapped his pocket. "I'll pay you ..."

Relief flooded into Georg. "What about taking a cab?" What did the fellow usually do when he drank too much? The customers nodded.

"Na. Na. Tha'sss all right. They take too long to arrive. You drive me." The fellow held out the keys.

"You sure?"

"We're all frien's."

"Hold on," the barman shouted. "How will you get

home? Denis lives out on a farm."

"Ah. I hadn't thought of that."

"The'ss a bus'ss going by every half hour." Denis held the keys high.

"Problem sorted," Georg said. "I'll catch the bus. First, let's get you and the car home safe."

The wizened customers studied Georg all the way out. They'd be sure to remember his distinctive hair style and accent. Up to him to return the car before the poor fellow recovered from his hang-over. Tomorrow, he'd feel bright enough to catch the bus.

Chapter Fifteen

Assured of safety, Ellen sat in the main room of the unfamiliar flat, dressed in her own track-suit once more. The mess lying on every available surface didn't bother her. God knows, she owned nothing much to scatter. She swallowed the last greasy wedge of fried potato before wiping her fingers on a tissue.

Lily's bundle of clothes sat on Mary's spare bed in the only bedroom. The small flat was nothing like Lily's orderly house. However, the place would do for the moment. Better than sleeping on the street.

Wearing fluffy slippers, Mary shuffled into the living room with two steaming mugs. "Just make yourself at home. That chair's none too comfy, is it? I got it from the tip." She settled on another tapestry one, worn in places. "This one was here when I took over. I think the flat was a holiday rent beforehand. The guy seemed pleased to have regular money coming in."

"Whatever." Ellen sipped her coffee and changed the subject. "I'll sleep well tonight."

"It's hard work at the launderette, isn't it? Looks easy, but you're on the go all day."

"How long have ya' been there?"

"About two years," Mary said. "I used to help out. When the lease came up, I took it over. That's why I don't have much cash to spare. Things will improve. What about you?"

"The guy I worked for in London got too pushy. I didn't accept his terms." Drugs. Not for her. Didn't want to end up the same way as those other girls, half out of their heads. "So I left. I thought Cornwall would be far enough away. I meant to head for Land's End, but a woman on the train told me there isn't much work."

"Yeah, it's a small place."

"This job's a change for me." Ellen fiddled with her hair. "What do ya' do for a laugh?"

"Money's too tight at the moment." Mary frowned. "Are you bored already? I didn't think you'd last."

"Nah," Ellen added before the other woman had time to think. "Just wondering what I can look forward to."

Mary raised her voice. "And here I was thinking you wanted work." Her mouth pinched.

"I do, but there's more to life than endless labor. Don't be so touchy." Ellen let out her breath in a steady stream. No sense in falling out of the push-chair just after she'd scrambled in.

"We'd better sort this out now." Mary met her gaze. "If you stay, you work hard. Or do you want to walk away right now?"

Ellen swallowed. She'd have no earnings left at the rate the woman siphoned money off. She glanced at the doorway. If she left now, she'd need to find another place to crash. "I said I'd stay, although I'm not so sure now." Ellen raised her chin. "We've only just started working together. Anyway, if ya' take rent money from my wage, we should be partners."

A glint sparked in Mary's eyes. "Bit soon for that, but I'll think it over."

"Only fair, as I see it." Ellen studied her companion for a reaction.

Slumped, shoulders drooping—probably regretted her words.

"I'm just thinking about what you said before. I wouldn't mind having a bit of fun." Scratching her scalp, Mary leaned forward. "Tell you what. Let's make sure we go out at least one night a week. We could afford a treat between us."

"Will your clothes fit me? I don't have anything suitable."

A smile slid over Mary's face. "We can check out the charity shop for party clothes. We could find a bargain or two."

"Not a bad idea. I could use some extra work clothes as well." Then, she'd have an excuse to return Lily's cast-offs.

"How come you didn't bring anything else with you?"

"I've left my stuff in London. No sense in lugging it about 'till I settle."

A sharp tap sounded. Mary hurried to answer the door. Ellen couldn't see who stood outside in the hall. Mumbled conversation penetrated with a draft of air. The name George. A laugh. The click of the door.

"That was my ... friend. Sometimes you have to stay pally with the likes of him." Mary nodded. "He won't bother you."

"Gawd." Ellen didn't know whether to be reassured or worried.

***

After leaving the old codger's car in the St. Ives parking area, van den Burg headed below to Market Place in the stiff evening breeze. A pint in the Golden Lion would go down well. Best place to gather information amongst the friendly bunch of locals.

Tapping his pocket against his signet ring to hear the jingle of change, he considered himself lucky to have a position of sorts. Although he didn't know Straten well, their connection to South Africa had worked in his favor.

Straten might be a self-important prat, but he'd bought Georg's loyalty. Best to go along with the boss's plans, using his own judgment of how to handle the job. His resolution included finding the ring.

Under pale moonlight, he glimpsed the pub's illuminated sign. Beyond it, a faint glimmer of the sea surrounded the pier strung with baubles.

His pace increased until he reached the popular hang-out. On the far side of the road, dark shapes of fishing boats dotted the sand.

Outside the establishment, he bent under the low entrance, and entered the room's cozy atmosphere with its dim lights and a fire to one side. The door banged behind him while he headed toward the chattering people at the bar.

The dark haired Harry called over the yells and bursts of laughter, "Hi, Georg."

Georg headed over. Oh yes, this was where he belonged.

A wide grin slashed Harry's dark complexion.

A few women sat at a table on the far side of the room. Brash and boisterous. He couldn't picture Liliha here. What did she do for fun?

Men shouted about the latest football fiasco. He pushed between the crowd and approached the bar. Harry sat at the far end, nattering to another ... man? Hard to tell under the lank hair obscuring his face. Not that he had anything against the length of a person's hair. At least his own was clean and shiny with a bit of a curl to give style. The closest bartender tilted his head. Georg raised his voice to order, and then placed his coins on the counter. When his drink arrived, he took a gulp and carried the glass toward Harry, who glanced over with raised eyebrows.

"Come and join us, Georg. You remember Chris?"

Georg nodded. The arty guy from the dinner party. Georg asked, "What's happening?"

"I'm just about to leave," Chris said. "Jessica will kill me if I don't get home soon." He gulped the remainder of his drink and slammed the glass on the bar.

"See you tomorrow," Harry said.

Georg strode past Harry and eased onto the vacated seat. The well-built smart-ass was nice enough, sitting with his beige jacket open over a white shirt, floral tie askew. Georg sipped his bitter and licked froth off his top lip. "I've just got back from Edinburgh. Boy, it was cold up north."

"That's why I like the mild climate here in Cornwall. Have you lived in the area long?" Harry eyed him.

"A month or so." He didn't bat an eye. "Nice of Audley to give me the invite the other night. I need to meet people." One in particular.

"They're a good bunch." Harry took a long glug. "What do you do for a living?"

Georg shifted position while he worked out a story.

Harry flicked his gaze toward a man entering the room.

Ah, the guy was edgy, same as him. "I'm working for a man in London," Georg said. "He's interested in one or two things in the area."

"Property?"

Georg nodded. How convenient.

The corners of Harry's mouth twitched, as if he anticipated the punch-line. "I'm in security." He leaned close. "We can help each other out from time to time."

Georg chuckled. Now they were getting somewhere.

"What are you after?" Harry asked.

Georg picked a speck of dust off his jacket sleeve.

"Something of great value."

"Ah. Not land. Have you tried the antique shops?"

Georg bellowed with laughter. "We speak the same language. Let me buy you a drink."

"Sure. I can handle one more. Gotta drive home yet."

Georg didn't bother asking how far away. "I like a man who knows his limits." He gestured for two more pints and pulled out his wallet. A young woman behind the bar flicked a lever and filled a glass with a frothy brew. Georg faced Harry. "Changing the subject, is that woman, Liliha, local?"

With hooded eyes, Harry reached for his fresh pint. "She reminds me of the donnas back home."

"A boyfriend hanging close?"

"Hold on. Don't get pushy. She's getting over the death of her husband. Oliver was a nice guy. Give her the time and space to heal. Anyway, I ... never mind."

Georg tried to read the other man's expression. He could be interested. "Sure thing. I won't cause problems."

"You'd better not," Harry growled.

"No worries, man. I've gotta drive over to Penzance tomorrow. Return a car I borrowed. How regular is the bus service? Do you know?"

"Never had to travel by public transport. You should hire a car."

"I might just do that." Georg gulped more cold liquid. "On another subject. I noticed her ring the other night. The moonstone. They're symbolic in Africa." He didn't worry about making the detail up. "Has she ever told you about where it came from?" He recalled some story about the British Museum's interest. Must be the one he was looking for.

"Her ring is very precious to her. Her grandmother

left it to her." Harry adjusted the sunglasses perched on his head, and then dropped his hand to expose a calloused knuckle. "Leave her be."

With his muscled body and keen mind, the guy knew how to defend those he cared about. Georg lowered his brows and nodded. "We should invite her for a drink one night. Get her out a bit and take her mind off her troubles." Up to Harry now. When the fellow clenched his jaw, Georg straightened, ready to use more persuasion.

Chapter Sixteen

Liliha flicked the fresh sheets over the spare bed. How she wished they smelled of sunshine. At least they had dried in the airing cupboard. In Australia, she'd left washing outside almost all year round. Bring on summer.

A bird twittered outside. By the sound of the musical notes, it could be a rare Cirl Bunting which had been released in Cornwall to breed.

She hoped the birds had drifted to St. Ives to seek shelter. She'd done the same years ago. Nobody stayed put nowadays. The movement of people brought to mind two other newcomers—Georg and Ellen.

The girl had thrown kindness back in Liliha's face. The word, *'Bitch,'* rung in her ears. By giving refuge, had she been too trusting? A deep hurt burned inside her chest at Ellen's lack of appreciation.

At a sudden burst of loneliness, Liliha perched on the side of the bed. She missed Oliver. So much. Head in hands, she surrendered to sobs. Hot moisture flowed over her cheeks until the pain subsided.

After drawing a deep, recovering breath, a dizzy feeling tugged at her. Accompanied by a whiff of perfume, soft thuds projected her into the spinning tunnel toward another place.

***

The fog clears after the transition. Emotionally drained, I peer down at a sagging body. I've melded already, judging by the splayed legs beneath a floral skirt, and the wrinkled hands grasping a bucket. While we totter along a garden path, I try to grasp her name, but her concentration doesn't allow my penetration.

Our bent position makes lifting our head difficult.

With my scoliosis, I know the discomfort she feels although age makes her condition worse.

We approach the border of her front garden. Determination drives her to maintain her own grounds. No use relying on others. She once stood tall and straight before the ache in her back set in. Youth long gone.

What can I do for her? I watch and wait without interference.

We grasp cutters and gloves, lower the bucket onto the lawn and set to work. Progress is slow and careful. Soon, a pile of cuttings lies on the ground alongside.

A child's whistle comes from behind. When we attempt to straighten, we gasp in pain and clutch our rear. Brakes screech. With shuffled steps, we rotate to face the street. The young boy living next door leans his pushbike against the fence. Our mouth stretches to express a greeting.

Life passed her by after her family left home. Loneliness chips away at her will to carry on.

He glances toward us, returns the greeting, and then strides toward his house. We nod and smile, thinking he's anticipating a cool drink.

Bending to collect the cuttings, pain pierces our spine. We thump onto the ground, body light and fragile.

Helpless and disoriented lying on our side, we roll a shoulder and ease over until we face the sky. We lift our torso in an attempt to rise. After a jerk forward, we fall to the former position.

Embarrassed and uncertain, she hesitates.

I suggest a moment of rest. Then, with a shift of consciousness, I propel my attention toward the boy with a prompt to return. No need to enter his mind. I hover overhead to watch.

He spots the prone form on the ground and approaches. "Here, Mrs. Potts. Are you all right? I'll run inside and get my mother."

She groans and assumes a brave smile before he leaves.

After a few moments the boy's mother hurries across. "Can I help you up?"

"Thank you."

"You shouldn't be alone. From now on, I'll keep an eye on you." The neighbor assists Mrs. Potts into her house, gesturing to the boy to collect the greenery.

With my job over, I drift away.

***

With tears still weighing her lashes, Liliha whispered to whoever answered her prayers, "Thank you." Her own problems dissipated after assuming the clearly defined role.

A sigh released former angst about Ellen. Liliha stood and faced the bed. She flicked the folded quilt. Giant pink tulips on a white ground settled over the surface.

Satisfied with the smooth appearance, the tension drained away from her shoulders. Any assistance she had given Ellen might tip the scales in the girl's favor.

***

From his bed, Georg reached for his ringing phone while he struggled to un-glue his eyes. He mumbled, "Yes."

"Are you ready for work, van den Burg, or are you about to go off on another personal side-trip?"

Georg jerked up onto one elbow, dragging his mind into gear. "Ready boss. What do you have in mind?" He covered the mouthpiece to block out his yawn.

"Get yourself over to Truro." Straten's voice went quiet. "Do you have a car?"

115

"I picked one up yesterday." Could he delay the return?

"Right," the voice went on. "There's an exhibition about to open in a little Truro art gallery up the coast in Cornwall. The consignment should arrive this afternoon."

"You want me to look after it? Don't they have guards arranged?"

"Of sorts. Nothing official. The batch consists of ancient Egyptian stuff from a private owner. This would be an excellent opportunity to relieve him of a few items."

Whoa. "What do you mean? Steal it?"

"I'm in business here. I've already spoken to the owner. He'll be just as happy to collect on the insurance if the load goes missing. Do you want the work or not?"

Georg's mind snapped into gear. He'd better accept rather than face unemployment and the loss of the accommodation related to the position. "Is there much?"

"I'll leave it to you. Some of the items are quite heavy. Just take whatever seems appropriate."

"Right. I'm on it."

Straten gave him the location details. "Don't let me down." The line cut off.

Legit in a manner of speaking. An insurance scam. Georg swung his legs over the side of the bed. *Fate. Kismet. All arranged.*

Perhaps getting his hands on the ring would work the same way.

On the way to the bathroom, conscience pricked him. He'd vowed to return the car to the old codger he'd met in the bar. If he hurried, he could do so, catch a bus to Penzance, and then hire a car.

Chapter Seventeen

Ellen set off early with Mary for the ten-minute walk to work. Tired and out of sorts, Ellen waited in the quiet main street while the other woman unlocked the door. They entered the musty interior and pulled the shutters away from the windows.

"Prop the door open, Ellen. The breeze will flush out the stale air. Let's get cracking and wipe over the machines. The first customer will be here soon."

"Right." Ellen ambled into the small rear room with a bathroom built into one corner. The table, the hand basin, and a broom propped beside hooks on one wall presented a dismal picture. What had she run to? Did she really want this life of drudgery rather than parties—hard work instead of a life of lying on her back?

Better rethink. The old days weren't all rosy. She recalled bad times, beatings from rough men, and threats from her pimp, Matt. The name made her shiver.

Ellen moistened a cloth. At least she should make an effort like Lily had suggested.

***

Two hours before the exhibition opened, Georg veered the new hire-car away from the Saturday traffic into an out-of-town parking station. *Prepare yourself to meet the challenge, van den Burg.* On stepping out, afternoon air hit his face with bracing freshness. He headed for the center area of Truro.

Treasure-seeking had excited him as a child. In his imagination, splendid armor replaced his leather jacket, jeans and boots—a conquistador marching over Mexico. He became Francisco de Coronado, from a noble Spanish family, consorting with the Zuni Indians while searching for El Dorado.

But anxiety tugged his stomach at what he might face. Although Straten had assured him the deal had been prearranged, probably an insurance scam, Georg would take the blow if something went wrong.

He strolled past shops leading to the front of the art gallery, noting the exhibition sign. Someone moved about inside, so he didn't stop, but continued along the street to the next side turning. Picking up pace, he headed toward a rear lane, just wide enough for a single vehicle. In the distance, a white van with open rear doors blocked the way. A man inside passed a carton to someone on the ground.

Georg slipped into a gap behind another property.

After hearing a few shouted words, Georg peered into the driveway. A lone man shifted a few cartons. The bulge under his jacket could be a weapon, which implied their goods were of extreme value.

The other guy might return at any moment. He'd have to charge right in to remove the treasures. *Better use reason first.* On his approach, he called, "How's things?"

"Step aside, man." The man straightened and faced him, hand on hip. "We're not here with food orders. Official business with the gallery."

Good. The right consignment. "Did your boss tell you he'd arranged for me to come?"

"The two of us can take care of this little lot. I said shove off."

Now what? No agreement? Leave or—?

The fellow fumbled with his holster. Probably never fired at a live target. "Brody. Give me a hand," the fellow shouted, loud enough for his partner to hear if he was near.

Urgency and panic drove Georg to vault into the rear

of the van. He used the trick of throwing his jacket over his left side. With the man's attention elsewhere, he landed a swift jab, palm down, on his opponent's carotid artery at the side of the neck. Shock waves spread from the side of his palm along his arm. Although his elbow throbbed, Georg grabbed the collapsing man's lapels before he hit the van's floor, stepped to one side and dragged him into cover behind the remaining cartons, marked with the gallery's name. He made sure the boxes hid the unconscious body.

Before he straightened, Georg checked the man's pulse. Thank the good Lord, he was alive. The name tag on his uniform read Jeff Hughes. He'd got away with aggression—this time. He'd rather not indulge again. Had the other guard reported the outcry?

Footsteps rang on the pavement while Georg rubbed his throbbing hand. What story could he use to throw the returning guy off?

Georg pulled his fogged thoughts together. "Jeff's gone for a coffee at my shop next door."

The man tucked his chin in and drew his brows together.

"I'll watch the rest of this stuff, while you take a break with him." Georg gave a smile to resemble the one Harry used—he hoped. "The governor at the gallery and I are good friends. You'll be okay." He winked.

"I'm not sure—"

"Ten minutes. You've got time."

The man hesitated, and then turned.

Georg's hands shook from his earlier action. "Go along the lane to the street. You'll see the coffee bar. They'll take care of you." He sat on the edge of the open hatch, swinging his legs in an unconcerned manner.

The man veered to face him. "Nah. Can't leave the van unattended. Wait till I see Jeff. I'll give him a piece of my mind."

Georg lunged forward to land on his feet. "No worries."

The man flexed his shoulders and stomped his feet. "Better get the next lot."

"Can I give you a hand?" Georg asked checking his name badge, "Brody."

"Nah. We're supposed to keep an eye on the goods." Brody glanced at the cartons. "On the other hand, it wouldn't take long. You say you're a friend of the owner?"

"I told him I'd check everything's going well." Georg flashed another smile. He might swing his maneuver yet.

"Okay then."

Heart hammering, Georg waited until Brody clambered onto the bed of the van. A quick glance assured him nothing gave away a sign of Jeff's unconscious body behind the cartons. But the man shouldn't approach. Georg grasped his ankles and tugged to unbalance him.

Brody dropped forward, on the way hitting his head on the opening.

Bad business. Could have killed him.

Georg reached into the truck bed, tugged Brody to the edge, and then supported him all the way to the gutter. He breathed a sigh of relief when Brody's pulse registered. Someone would be along soon from the gallery to check on him.

With no time to lose, Georg slammed the rear van doors and jogged toward the front. He checked the vehicle's side for insignias. Plain. Luck remained with him.

He climbed up into the driver's seat. No key in the ignition.

Jeff might have it. Georg angled his arm into the gap behind the driver's seat to search the unconscious man's pocket. His fingers shook while he extracted a bunch of keys. Once in the ignition, the motor fired. He familiarized himself with the vehicle's workings, and then eased it forward.

Should have dragged Jeff outside too. No time now.

After driving a few blocks, Georg pulled up beside a park. No sounds came from behind. He jumped out, sprinted to the rear and flung open the doors. Placing one hand on the van floor, he vaulted up, approached, and leaned over the fellow.

The guy lifted his head, eyes clouded with confusion. "What the—?"

Ha. Not familiar with the gun. Georg jerked his elbow into the side of the other man's neck again, hard and fast. Jeff went slack. "Sorry, old man."

Outside, two women joggers glanced over. He raised his voice to reach them. "Sleep it off in the park."

Georg dragged him to the edge of the van door, jumped to the ground, and then pulled him feet first. The man balanced his weight on his feet. Georg spoke loud enough for the watchers to hear. "I told you not to drink so much. Can't take you home in this state." He supported the tottering Jeff all the way to the closest tree and placed him in a sitting position against the stout trunk. Recovery wouldn't take long, judging by the twitches under his eyelids. Although the joggers were out of earshot, Georg kept up his pretense. "You should've eaten first, you silly sod."

Georg jogged to the van, slammed the rear doors and returned to the open driver's door. Springing into the seat behind the wheel, he drove on.

Although the action was implied, Straten's orders didn't include roughing up the guards. But then, nothing went to plan. Now both men could identify him and he didn't have the bulk of the consignment. It remained to be seen if they could trace him to his digs. The isolated spot could have been part of Straten's strategy.

Relieving someone of their goods had seemed harmless enough. But now he'd stooped to brutality. A memory surfaced. Straten had questioned him about his training. The boss had known something like this would occur.

Best to push the idea to one side and concentrate on the present. He couldn't offload the goods from the stolen van into his hired car at the parking station.

After a ten minute drive in traffic, he navigated the roundabout, and then pulled up in a lay-by close to Truro's industrial area. He couldn't wait to find out what sat inside the cartons. Must be five in all. Had the delivery men already removed the most valuable items?

Leaving the motor running, he jumped out, strolled to the rear, and opened the van doors.

Inside, he undid the restraint and opened the closest carton sitting on top of another. Layer after layer of plastic wadding filled most of the space. At the sight of a solid package, he slowed his mad scramble and lifted a six inch wide pine box. Nothing special. He assumed the rough container had been made to fit whatever lay inside. They'd secured the lid well with wax and a metal chain and lock. Sod it! He didn't have time for this right now. He tossed the box into the gap leading to the front seat, and unsealed the next carton.

This one contained paintings. Straten might like them. He lifted the empty carton off and reached for the edge of tape sealing the larger pack underneath.

Georg turned at the sound of a motor cutting off behind him. Not a police car. The driver lifted a clip-board.

Better move, quick smart! He jumped to the ground and closed the rear doors.

Settled once more in the front seat, Georg drove away. He'd leave the van in a safe spot, collect his hire-car and return for the goods.

Chapter Eighteen

Ellen gazed at the street outside the launderette. People hurried past clutching umbrellas. No use denying the job bored her. She folded a tee-shirt in the way Mary had demonstrated. For the moment, this work gave the assurance of pay at the end of the week, and somewhere safe to sleep.

A dark-haired man hauling a black bag entered and headed for the rear. He winked at Ellen, and then leaned close to speak to Mary. Old friends chatting in the steamy atmosphere, surrounded by humming washing machines and dryers.

While doubling tea towels, Ellen balked at doing other people's laundry.

Only one way to balance her state of mind—go out at night. Other girls her age worked in boring office jobs with one thought on their minds: a weekly bender. Get plastered. Get laid. They didn't have to class their sleeping around as a job. Probably didn't know how bad a problem could get—wouldn't be likely to notice in their drunken state.

While she folded a fluffy blue towel, the customer left his bulging bag beside Mary.

"I hope you both have a great day," he called and ambled outside.

He didn't use the sloppy form of 'ya.' People here spoke well.

A sudden fear of Matt sent a shiver along her spine. Better stop thinking about living free. Way too soon.

"All right, Ellen?" Mary asked. "What about a cup of coffee?"

"I'll make it." Ellen hurried to the little staff room.

She should speak better—revert to the way she'd been taught. Why had she slipped? How weak to fit in with other people's way of life.

***

Cuban heels clicking over the cobble-stones in *'his'* town after depositing his week's washing, George Hopkins nodded to a passing resident. Further along the main street, he slipped into the barber for a shave and trim. Old buggerlugs caught his glance before facing his customer to finish with a flurry of activity. George handed a junior his padded black jacket and stood with his arms folded, refusing a seat.

When the customer took his time leaving, George moved closer. The fellow got the message. The barber brushed the customer off, and he scooted out.

"Come, sir." Buggerlugs gestured him over with a sweeping motion, and George sauntered across to be pampered. Free of charge, of course.

Halfway into his shave, his phone played the Queen's anthem. The barber stepped away while George answered.

"Terry here." His crony spoke with enthusiasm. "I've seen her in town, mate. The tall woman with straight dark hair."

"Yeah?" Terry went up in George's estimation. A bit dumb, but eager.

"She's at the bank right now."

"Well, keep your eyes on her." He edged forward on the chair. "Don't let her leave. Make up some reason to keep her in the building. I'm on my way." He flicked his phone shut. "Wipe this muck off. I've gotta leave."

"Yes, sir." The barber swiped a damp cloth over the rest of the shaving cream while George made shooing gestures.

He grabbed his jacket and left.

Before he'd got halfway along the street, a panda van roared by, siren blazing. He slowed his pace and followed several curious rubbernecks. The police car sat outside the bank.

Standing behind the other people gawking at the emerging twosome, George's stomach dropped with the swiftness of a coin tossed in a fountain. A uniformed officer pushed Terry ahead of him to the copper car and secured him inside. So much for wishes coming true. Another officer glanced about the area before climbing in behind the wheel and driving away.

What had Terry done? The stupid blind mole! Ah well, the dead-beat should feel right at home when he returned to the nick.

Fine rain licked George's face. People drifted away, but he remained, hoping his quarry was still inside the building.

He eased his weight onto the other foot, than then straightened. The tall woman who held his interest emerged from the bank entrance and opened a colorful umbrella. He checked her hands. No ring. All wasted.

Nothing to do but follow her along the slick footpath.

At last, she entered a tearoom. When she didn't appear again, he scratched his head. She might have left the ring at home this time. Turning up the collar of his waterproof jacket, George spun on the balls of his feet and strode toward her cottage. Couldn't get much wetter.

***

Parked in the idling white vehicle beside a public square on the outskirts of Hayle, van den Burg pondered his predicament.

Straten had arranged the use of a storage shed on a

derelict farm in Cornwall for any bulky merchandise. Far enough away from the heist. The alarm must have gone out by now about the missing art exhibits. The theft might have been reported to the authorities along with the vehicle's reg.

He drove to a suburban street. Houses nestled together, resembling pigeons sunning themselves on a wire. Cars lined the road either side. When he came to a vacant area between two cars and reversed into the gap. Now to find a replacement car for his get-away.

The hand-sized box on the van's seat beside him must contain something unique. They'd used the entire carton for one item. Rather than get distracted and peek inside right now, he tried to slide the container into the pocket of his jacket. When the bulk wouldn't fit, he shoved the box inside his waistband and buttoned his jacket. Tight, but it would do. Right. Off to find a replacement car.

Keeping a lookout for twitching curtains, he ambled along the street. An aging car sat in the exact spot he needed, out of view from surrounding houses. The door of the Peugeot came open in his hand. He slid behind the wheel and reached for the fine screwdrivers he had brought in case of emergency. Once inserted into the ignition, he fiddled until the motor caught.

And they're off. His reluctant steed eased onto the road under Georg's coaxing. He back-tracked to the van, parked alongside, and left the motor running while he jumped out and opened the rear doors. A few hasty moves stashed the four cartons into the rear section of the Peugeot.

He perused the street in a casual manner, slammed the car's boot, trotted to the driver's door, and slid inside to drive to his hire-car.

Chapter Nineteen

Outside the tearooms, Ellen squinted in the sudden bright sunshine glinting from behind black clouds. When the older woman emerged from the doorway, Ellen waved and held up the plastic carrier bag. "I've brought ..." she brushed aside the first word springing to mind, 'ya,' and changed it to, "... your ... clothes back."

Lily smiled a greeting and pulled her long waxed coat tighter. A pale, smooth stone in her ring caught the light. "Thanks." She approached with a serious expression and took the bag.

Ellen's heart sank. What had she done now? "Everything all right?" Maybe Lily took offense at her earlier outburst.

"We had a problem while I was at the bank. The police arrived and took a man away. I'm still uptight."

After a quick breath of relief, Ellen asked, "What happened?"

"Apparently, the teller got suspicious when he saw a man with a bulging pocket pacing at the rear of the queue and pushed a button under the counter. The police arrived pretty quickly. They must have been around the corner."

"I'll bet you'll be nervous next time."

"Silvia's going to arrange for a security firm to pick up the money from now on. Thank goodness." Lily took a deep breath and drew herself up. "How are you coping?"

Her caring attitude took Ellen to a time in childhood beside a favorite aunt. "Mary and I are getting along well. She's going to take me on. We might set up business together later." Ellen drew a breath. Her involvement as a partner hadn't been agreed.

"Great," Lily said. "I'm glad."

"Thanks." Ellen hesitated, unsure of how to approach the subject. "But we're sharing one room. Not one bed ... I've got my own." She giggled to remove embarrassment. "But the flat's too small to invite anyone to visit."

"No need."

"I didn't mean ..." Ellen drew a breath and plunged in. "I might want to get to know someone better, and I'd never be able to with the three of us, and Mary listening to every word."

"Couldn't you talk at the pub? Or the movies? Or somewhere else?"

"Mary said there's no money for going out just yet." Steer the conversation away. "I'm going to start ironing clothes to earn a bit more."

"I hope everything works out for you." Lily glanced along the street.

"Do you want to go? Sorry. I shouldn't keep ... you." Phew! Remembered the right word just in time. But they hadn't arranged anything yet. She needed somewhere to go for a bit of hanky-panky.

Lily straightened up a fraction. "I'm longing to sit down." She stroked her smooth hair. The rest was clamped behind in a plait. "Come home with me and we can have a proper talk."

"Thanks, Lily, but I need to get to work. I slipped out in a quiet period but Mary will expect me back. Could I call in and ... see you after work some time?"

"My name is Liliha. Nobody calls me Lily. You say it much like Lilian, but it's Lilia. As to your question, of course you can visit me another time."

"Gee, thanks. Well, I'd better run." Ellen turned away.

***

129

Liliha frowned as Ellen hurried toward the town below. Nodding, she turned toward what she liked to call Cottage Central. Plenty of people ambled in the sunshine now the shower had cleared.

Relief fired at achieving her aim in helping Ellen and parting on friendly terms.

Further along the street, her steps halted beside a dusty bookshop front and she gazed inside, unseeing. Maybe she'd been too hasty in expecting an immediate result with Ellen.

The atmosphere charged the air with power. Zaps and buzzes foretold a coming vision. Somehow, the sound didn't bode well. Liliha clenched her stomach as consciousness faded. Sweet ambrosia accompanied her while she penetrated the churning disparity.

***

I'm standing in the dark—inky blackness ahead, but lights and muffled sounds come from behind. Legs beneath me adjust to a lurch beneath our feet. I've already merged with an intoxicated mind. Not sure if the dizzy effect comes from within or without. Where are we? The wind roars. Hair whips into my face. Her face.

Another lurch makes the surface slant beneath our feet. I tighten our muscles and whisper, 'Careful.'

"Jamie," a female voice calls. "Come inside. The sea's rough out there."

Ah. We're on the deck of a ship.

Dizzy, we lean over a railing. Goose bumps rise on the bare arms emerging from her light evening dress. She's just left two friends to get a breath of fresh air on the Princess Seaways ferry. We're in the North Sea.

The surface underfoot tilts.

We lose balance.

Topple head first over the barrier. Flail the air. Plummet below.

Hit. Swishing noises.

Our vision blurs. Can't breathe.

She's going into shock and dragging me with her.

'Wake up. Your life depends on it.' Thrash. Kick. Skirt catches on our legs. Try to reach a faint glint against the drag of downward momentum. Flaying arms take us up and up.

Head breaks into the air. Breathe one lungful after another. Glimpse hundreds of lights while waves lash our head.

Submerge again.

Gasp. Break surface again and breathe. Movements jerky. Cold numbs our limbs.

Yell. Someone might hear over the raging storm, otherwise this holiday will end in death.

Too weak. So cold.

Keep moving. Look at the lights.

No. They're growing smaller with each lunge.

Concentrate. I must keep Jamie alive until help reaches her. Chances are against rescue. Yet, why am I here if the task is hopeless? First, give comfort, and then search for someone to help.

I breathe assurances into her mind. 'Keep afloat. They'll search for you. Never stop moving. Your chances are good. The propeller didn't suck you under. You only need to survive for a short time. Focus on the comfort of the coming rescue. Think of your loved ones.' Don't let her worry about the unimaginable.

Although regret sears me, the desperation of her plight impels me to leave her. Abandon her.

While she fights the paralysis in her chilled limbs, I

disengage and soar up and over toward the lights. On the lower deck, uniformed men toss an inflatable overboard and others hold the rope firm. Commands swirl in the wind while people scramble aboard. The outboard motor roars.

In the black night, they battle the waves. The throb of the ship's powerful engines fades. Shouts from hopeless voices penetrate the raging storm.

I hover over the inflatable. Inside, the men strain forward.

I concentrate on Jamie's whereabouts because they have to decide which way to search. With my guidance and calm assurances broadcast into their collective minds, the searchers set out in the right direction despite the lashing waves. I'm relieved they picked up my message.

In a flash, I've returned to Jamie.

Numbing cold. Hard to move. Tired.

'Fight,' I whisper. 'Never give up. Help is close. Kick for all you're worth.'

Why bother? Too cold.

She needs a memory to give incentive. I emerge deep into her mind and find Darren—laughing, full of life and love. She grasps the image. 'You need to prove worthy. Show how you can fight any adversity. Think of the stories you can tell your children.'

Warmth washes over her to mix with the alcohol and adrenalin in her blood. I've cheered her—for now.

One more task. Direct the men to find her in the howling sea. I zap over to the inflatable to check their position.

"She must have drowned, Tom," one man says to another.

"She's been in the cold too long."

132

In a flash, I've merged with Tom and read his concern. Nobody has ever been recovered alive in these conditions, if found at all. I whisper, 'On the left, between the waves. See the flash of movement?'

We train the torch in the vicinity. The swell heaves and rolls.

'Look,' I whisper.

"Try the starboard, Tom."

"Wait," he says. "I think I saw something." Tom, with me inside him, focuses on an object bobbing behind the spray. "There," we shout. "Steer that way."

With a sigh of relief, I lift away.

The men head for Jamie while she bobs, sinks, and breaks surface again.

After shouts and activity, they assist her dripping body into the inflatable. My consciousness fades.

***

A quick glance either way along the street assured Liliha no one had spotted her during the out of body experience. Heartbeat pounded in her ears without the raging storm to drown out other sounds. Impossible to remain unaffected after the rescue, but somehow she managed to calm her shaking limbs and continue walking. Although the odds were against a rescue, Jamie hadn't succumbed to defeat. Liliha appreciated the firm path under her feet. She should follow Jamie's lead. Find George and complete her mission.

What blessed relief to have no further episodes of fighting with Doom. Why had she been apprehensive? No good came from worrying about an event which might never happen.

Liliha drew a breath at a blinding realization. The young woman had been alone on the deck. All the recent visions had the theme of lonesomeness.

Further along the street, bird-call took on a magical tone which tickled the base of her head and rose up to the crown. Could be a skylark judging by the wonderful musical notes. Nature itself was magical. Why didn't she appreciate birds and animals with every breath? And plants. The leaves on trees caught dust and pollution all summer, and then shed them before growing new, fresh ones in the spring.

The memory of her beloved trees at The Barn waved her on. But her former life was over. She turned the corner and approached Headquarters' gate.

Walnut emerged from the side of the cottage and ran toward her. Liliha stopped to pat his soft fur. He twitched, stepping one way, and then the other.

"What's the matter? Has someone been inside again?" Everything pointed to an intruder. Walnut bounded away.

Chin up, Liliha turned and unlocked the door.

Inside, everything looked the same. In the kitchen, the chopping board sat straight in alignment with the edge of the work surface, the tea pot lid was jammed into the top in the right place. No, nothing to worry about. Nothing at all.

Little bubbles of doubt rose one after the other.

***

Georg carried the four cartons into his flat to dump on the floor beside the brown settee. So much for the returning conquistador. But then, Francisco de Coronado never found the Seven Cities of Gold either.

The owner would find his stolen car soon enough at the Hayle parking station. No need to feel too guilty.

Come on van den Burg. Time for a peek before

storing the haul in the lock-up. He shrugged off his jacket and tossed the leather garment onto the sofa. After hauling the small box out from under his belt, he flicked on the wall-mounted television. The announcer on the evening news spoke about a young man killed on an underground station.

The recollection of his own violence slammed into him with the charge of an elephant. What had he done in Truro? He should have lifted the things Straten wanted without resorting to violence. The events rose one after another while he searched for other ways he could have acted. *Too late now.*

Before he rang the boss, he opened the cardboard sections on the lid of one carton and studied the paintings with more care. Nice, but not for his wall. Two more contained sculptures, uninteresting jewelry set with plain stones, painted material which looked to have been been chiseled from old walls, papyri and dull clay funerary objects. Dejected, he stripped the tape away on the last unopened box. Shredded paper hid the contents. Could be something interesting.

He tossed a handful of filling onto the carpet and removed a cold, flat surface to reveal a smooth highly decorated wooden casket, as long as his foot and more than half as wide. Colorful pictures made up of brilliant, miniature sections of stone, mother of pearl, different metals, and ivory embellished the surface. Some as tiny as a pinhead formed the hieroglyphics.

Different intricate scenes covered each side, made up of similar materials. The box must be meant to stand in the center of a room so every angled could be appreciated.

He grabbed his mobile and punched buttons. "Can you talk?"

Straten answered, "Go ahead."

"I only got four cartons." He crossed his fingers in the way of the tribe people. "But I think you'll appreciate the contents. Paintings and various articles in three of them and a highly decorated marquetry casket, I think it would be called, in the other. I can't tell their worth."

"Right. Store them in the lock-up. Make sure damp doesn't get to them. Pack them up well."

"Sure thing, boss."

"You're not holding out on me, are you?" Straten asked. "I'd like to think I can trust you. On that matter, I'll speak to you soon." The phone cut off.

The call left an unsettled feeling, but Georg brushed it aside. Before replacing the box, he slid his hand to the bottom and touched a cold, heavy piece. He raised a smooth, brown statue of a cat—probably granite.

He replaced, covered, and surrounded the items with protection, and then sealed all boxes with tape. Too tired to drive to the lockup now. He'd store them tomorrow. But wait. He'd forgotten to check the contents of the small rough wooden box sitting on the settee. The one he hadn't mentioned to Straten. His shake didn't produce a rattle.

On the bench, he made fast work of the lock with a pair of cutters, slid the metal chain off and broke a wax seal underneath. Both box and seal were new, perhaps constructed for transportation.

Once seated, he pried the lid open. Set in more orange wax, a decorated golden bracelet glinted at him with a deep blue lapis lazuli scarab decoration. The jewel raised his spirits. Someone went to a lot of trouble to keep it rigid.

He slid two fingers under the edge. A sharp prick resembling an electrical charge zapped him.

Two loud knocks came from the door.

Chapter Twenty

Georg flicked his fingers and shook his wrist, but opposing sections on the gold bracelet's joints clung on. *How could an object do this? Come on, van den Burg. You must be mistaken.*

The enamel scarab might contain a battery— something to cause this shock surging along his fingers. A dizzy sickness overcame him. He swallowed bile, unable to sum up strength to answer repeated knocks coming from outside his door.

Energy zapped about his mind. Not sure what caused it—or if he liked the sensation. Drunk ... or drugged. The prickling in his fingers didn't hurt so much now. *Could have got used to the pain.*

Right. Overcome any obstacle. Never give in. Never had, and never would. Clenching his teeth, he flicked the tips of his fingers. Hard. *Drop, damn you.* While mesmerized by the bracelet, he considered the time he'd faced a charging elephant and stared with determination into those small eyes—jumped out of the way at the last moment and squatted behind a boulder.

Section by section, the heavy bracelet clinked into the box. The band coiled like a snake with the bright blue scarab facing up.

Stunned, Georg snorted to clear away the traces of ... Not sure what. Drawing another breath, he reached for the lustrous gold, but dropped his hand. Something niggled, although the cause eluded him.

Unsettled by pounding on the door, he dragged his gaze away. He shoved the closed box to the rear of the sofa behind a cushion, deciding to return the first chance he got.

Head reeling, he stood, staggered to the doorway and opened a crack. "Yes?"

"Van den Burg? Straten sent me."

Cheeks burning, Georg opened the door.

"You look a bit dopey. You been asleep, or what?" The man pushed past leaving behind the smell of jojoba oil. Burly and blond, with his muscles bulging and his attitude suspicious, he glanced at the contents of the room.

A few scraps of shredded paper remained on the floor. No time to hide them. "Bit late for a social visit." Georg shook his head to clear lingering fragments of his obsession. He needed to concentrate. Lucky he'd closed the cartons again.

"Nothing social about it. Business." The hard-man shoved out his hand. "Matt Albright."

Of a similar age to Georg, the man gripped his palm, leaving no doubt about his strength. Under short trendy hair, a bright scarf showed at the neck of a high-buttoned belted jacket over plain taupe trousers.

"As I thought," Matt said. "The cartons are here."

Fully alert, Georg followed him. "Are you taking over now I've done all the hard work?"

"Just checking them out." With his mouth twitching, Matt nudged a shred of paper with the toe of his polished boot. "He's had me waiting in the area for you to arrive. Knew you wouldn't head straight for the lock-up." He snickered. "I'd do the same, I guess."

"Take a look if you like." Penknife in hand, Georg slit the masking tape of one carton again and flipped open the top sections.

Matt lifted the edges of several paintings and dropped them again. "What's in the others?"

"Hasn't he told you already?" Georg asked.

"Didn't know what you had." Matt's expressionless blue eyes stared Georg out.

"A few bits and pieces. A highly decorated box, a granite cat statue, and a pottery fox-man in a skirt. Want me to open them up?"

"Don't bother. I think I arrived before you had time to squirrel anything much away. Seal this one again." Matt marked crosses over the top and overlapped a scribbled signature between the tape and the cardboard on each carton. "Where will I sleep?"

Georg jolted. "You're staying?" He sighed to give himself time to think. "Want to kip in the double bed with me?" He forced himself to remain away from box's the hiding place. "I promise I'll behave."

"The sofa will do."

"Sorry. No spare duvet." Georg held his breath.

"Brought a sleeping bag." Matt turned toward the door. "Make me a hot drink while I bring my stuff in. We'll be ready for an early start in the morning."

Georg's head pounded. He needed to move fast. The sound of Matt's steps faded.

Lifting the shaggy brown cushion, he grasped the box under his arm and headed for the kitchen. Hide it in a saucepan? *Too small.* He dropped the rough container amongst the trash and veered away as the front door opened.

***

Latish the next morning, Georg, escorted by Matt in his late-model gray Fiat, stopped outside a group of sheds close to a derelict farmhouse. The blond man hadn't left him alone during his stay at the flat. The sooner he attended to business, the faster he'd see the back of the burly minder. Georg climbed out of his hire-car and opened the boot.

Matt strolled close. "What else you got inside, van den Burg?" He indicated the shed with a flick of his head.

"Electrical equipment. Odds and ends that were stored in a car." The information would reach Straten. He'd better explain. "A private job. The boss knows. I'll get rid of the stuff today, hopefully." Georg lifted one of the cartons and headed for the door. "Give me a hand."

Matt grabbed the container with the paintings.

Propping the carton on his hip, Georg unlocked the heavy padlock and pushed the door open.

"Do you know many locals?" Matt hauled his box inside.

"A few. I haven't been here long." Georg set his carton on the floor.

"What about a new girl?" Matt eased his box beside the other. "Thin face, twenty five. She's a slut on the run."

"I don't mix in those circles," Georg said. "What's she running from?"

Matt didn't respond on the way outside to grab the remaining goods. "I know she's here somewhere."

"Why here?" George twisted his ring to cover impatience. Better act nice so the minder would leave with a good impression. Hopefully, soon.

"She blabbed to one of her customers who told her about Land's End. Said she wanted to go to the end of the earth. He let the information slip to another girl."

"Is that why you're in the area?" Cunning buzzard. Pick one carcass clean while watching another.

"Yep. The boss knew I was here. I'll keep looking. Wanna grab a bite of lunch once we stash these?"

What the ...? *No avoiding the next entanglement.* "St. Ives is the nearest. Plenty of tourists and newcomers about. Nice pub lunches." Closer to London, the minder might take the hint and leave him alone.

***

Van den Burg entered his flat close to four o'clock in the afternoon. Matt's lingering scent of jojoba hung in the air. At least the aroma was the only reminder of the thug, who'd headed off on foot to search for his girl in town. Georg made for the rubbish bag. When he swung the door open, a smell of stale food hit him.

Plunging his hand in amongst crumpled paper, empty food packages and soggy tea bags, he grabbed the wooden box and brushed crumbs off one side. The smeared stain on the rough unsealed timber wouldn't matter.

Time to snap out of whatever was holding him to the spot. He rocked and drew in a deep breath. A compulsion to look inside the box drew him with such force he shuddered. Rather than allow his shaky legs to collapse, he dragged one foot after another to the sofa where he flopped, box on his lap.

He shook his head to try to clear his foggy mind. What had gotten into him? *Reach out and open the lid.* Couldn't raise his heavy arm. As if it didn't belong to him. *Stop this right now. Take charge.*

Breath came short. Excitement surged. His stomach tightened. His hand reached out.

He opened the box and sudden brain-waves promised all—a juicy hen to a fox, a half-eaten carcass to a hyena, or a treasure beyond his wildest dreams. The latter expanded. As if watching a television program, concepts played over in his brain of big cars and beautiful women toying with him.

Nestled inside the box, the bracelet glinted. The blue scarab drew his gaze. Did it move? Trick of the light. Just to be sure, he flicked the deep blue lapis lazuli enamel with

141

one fingernail. The beetle didn't recoil. Just a decoration. He pulled his hand away a little too fast for his liking.

Better hide the thing for a while. He'd gain police and media attention if he tried to sell the bracelet right after the heist at Truro. Where to stow it? Not the lock-up where Matt or anyone else in Stratens' employ could find it.

He glanced at the beautiful object again. Stunning. Dragging him with a lure he found hard to resist. *Remember the charging elephant. Time to scramble out of danger's path. Get rid of the thing.*

Decision made, he raised his chin and used a handkerchief to prevent his fingers touching the jewel again. With his continued pressure, the band locked in place over the yielding mold.

Lid shut, he grabbed his lighter and spurted the flame. The wax melted and sealed the box. Last of all, Georg pressed his signet ring into the congealing blob, chuckling at the notion of imbedding a royal seal. *Better rough the surface.* He swiped the soft wax on the side of his jeans.

Pleased with the smudged result, he dropped the box beside him. His accommodation offered plenty of choices for the box's temporary home. Best not get rid of the thing until he'd considered the implications. Couldn't be sure whether he cared about the bracelet itself, or the weaker individual who might lift the scarab from its lipid nest.

Another jewel slid into his mind. Liliha's ring.

Chapter Twenty-One

After work, Liliha's desire to relax beside the ocean turned her steps downhill. For too long, she'd avoided a particular spot on the walkway overlooking the beach. Painful memories had to be faced and overcome.

She'd promised to meet Harry at the pub in an hour. The diversion would save a needless trip home.

Securing her scarf tighter against the breeze, Liliha strolled along the main thoroughfare of the town. A For Sale sign hung on one of the shops, a boarded-up window defaced another. All over the area, things were changing in small ways. Clothing displays in windows announced the coming summer, although the hot season was months away. Everyone appeared to be in a hurry to get on with the future. She'd rather slip into the past.

At the beach, she halted on the path and drew a deep breath. Salty freshness replaced the tearooms' stale coffee aroma. Beyond the expanse of sand, the choppy, gray sea stretched to the horizon. Lengths of cloud strung across the sky. An unseen host had pinned streamers from one side to the other in celebration for her visit.

Each step carried her along the familiar route. Oliver had been with her in this spot a few weeks ago.

Once perched on a wooden bench seat, she removed the ring from her necklace and slid the solid weight onto her finger. She didn't intend to repeat the mistake of wearing it too soon after work. Time passed in daydreams of the past.

The smell of brine changed to perfume while an angel drifted by, leaving a trail of spiritual essence. A dizzy sensation alerted her to an impending vision. Her eyelids closed. How pleasant to spin away to another realm while sitting beside the sea.

***

I arrive in the confines of a dark enclosed space. Pain pounds inside my contact's head. I block it out so I can think. Dim light enters from a tiny window on a bare wall opposite. What I observe doesn't make sense. Cartons cover the ceiling.

Take hold. The reason I'm here is for the person whose body I'm occupying. We turn to gaze the other way. I'm with a man, judging by the shoe size and sturdy shape. To concentrate, I override the throbbing in our left leg too.

We're suspended by one leg. Gnarled hands grip a ladder. Pressure pounds inside the veins near our eyes. The door overhead, which opposes the window, remains open. How long has he been dangling here before I joined him?

"Well, Sid. What's to be done?" He draws a breath to answer as if he's asked himself this many times. "Gotta think. Seems like I've been here forever. Slipped late yesterday. Checking the cellar for rats." We grunt. The pain in our ankle alternates between being unbearable and numbness. "Came through the war unscathed, just to perish like a fox caught by its leg in a trap."

Reading his nervousness about rats, I search for a way to assist. Can't loosen our ankle because I'm not physically present. The injury to the leg is severe. He needs help.

Our dry voice mutters, "Maybe I'll get a medal to go with my father's." After a manic chuckle, we shout as if we're trying to reach someone on the other side of the world. Our throat is raw from hollering and, although tired, we won't give in to sleep.

I concentrate on his musings to find out what I can.

The postman will visit this afternoon to deliver some

of those pesky advertisements. Judging by the shift in light, the man should arrive soon. My host, Sid, usually sets his clock by the time of delivery. However, the postman arrives upstairs, and won't know we're trapped below.

One gnarled, arthritic hand grips the ladder tighter to take the strain from our ankle. "It's killing me. Well, throbbing. I know it's swollen. Can't twist up enough to take a peek. Damn body. Letting me down. Who'd get old?" Our head lolls. Memories return about playing on climbing equipment.

I place reassurances into his mind. 'Remain calm. Someone will arrive to help soon.' My positive idea will sustain him a little longer. He's focused so I make a mental jump to hurry things along.

It worked. Great how I can slip between the molecules of cement, bricks and earth. I guess my form is similar to a ghost, or a spirit.

I emerge onto the street. Buildings press together, each similar to its neighbor. I take note of his house position, before soaring over slate roofs. I see a red postal van between parked cars. In this episode, I'm free to move. Perhaps I'll be able to mind-shift into another body as well.

A uniformed man hurries to a red post vehicle, climbs in, and then it takes off. After the van pulls up at one end of Sid's street, the postman emerges, holding mail bound with an elastic band. Making his way along the leafy street, he deposits junk mail and letters into each letterbox while birds twitter and swoop on passing insects.

Good. I know he'll visit Sid's house. But, I must work out how to alert him to Sid's cries. The plucky old man won't last much longer. If the postman doesn't hear the yells, Sid will die.

Rather than leave circumstances to chance, I ease

into the postman's mind as he approaches Sid's door. He wants to shove the advertising brochures into the slot quickly, before the old boy collars him with another complaint.

Now what? How can I prevent him from leaving? Send in a dog to bite his ankle? Although desperate, I can't search elsewhere because the postman's gaze is focused on the letterbox.

Rather than disengaging, I call with my mind to catch a passing bird. 'Come. Come. Peck this hand for food. Nuts. You love nuts. Come. Now.'

A blackbird dives with a flurry of dark feathers and a flashing yellow beak, but flies away with nothing. The postman jerks his hand away in pain and drops the bundle.

Guilt troubles me, although my command will be justified if I achieve my aim. I urge the postman, 'Listen.'

He shakes his hand, where blood wells from the peck. "Bloody bird. What did you do that for?"

'Listen,' I whisper again. 'Hear a faint voice? Someone needs you.'

He breathes in. A weak yell reaches him from inside. Must be the old man. Better get on with the postal round. Time's slipping by. He grabs a handkerchief, wraps his hand, and steps away.

'He's calling for help. You couldn't leave someone in distress, could you?'

The postman sighs and leans forward to shout inside the slot. "You all right in there?"

"Help. I'm hurt."

He hears the faint voice this time. Concern replaces annoyance. He shouts, "What's wrong?" *When he gets no reply, he takes out his phone and calls the emergency number.* "There's an elderly man in difficulty at this *address." After giving the particulars, he lifts the post flap on the door and bends to shout again. "The ambulance will be here soon."*

As I disengage, blackbirds squabble and peck at each other in a tree close by, enforcing my distress. I resist the prompt to return to my own life. I want to know if Sid will recover.

I hover until I hear siren's wailing. A police car arrives. An ambulance pulls up at the curb. After smashing a small pane of glass in the door, policemen enter, and then medics run into the house. They emerge and collect a trolley. When they return, Sid is strapped onto the stretcher. Although attached to a drip, he glances at the activity with bright eyes.

I strain to see the dimming scene below.

"Try to relax," one medic says. "You're a tough old bird, aren't you?"

Sid's chuckle fades. I barely catch his next words. "I've been through worse than this."

I lose consciousness in this reality and drift away.

***

Liliha opened her eyes on a bench seat, glad she wasn't trapped in a cellar—alone. She should follow Sid's lead and keep her spirit high.

Over the two years since inheriting the ring, visions had presented snapshots of life. Each person she contacted faced a problem, some of their own making.

A longing to share the experience with Oliver drifted on the briny air. She should never have come. Her shuddering sigh emerged to mingle with the breeze. Would every experience remain untold for the rest of her life? A heavy weight dragged her mood toward despair. She could help others but not herself.

She didn't want the responsibility associated with the ring any more. Once, she'd have been tempted to hurl the thing away. But Oliver hadn't betrayed her and the ring couldn't be blamed for his death.

Frustration boiled inside. Apart from showing resentment, she'd suppressed her feelings with her first husband Gareth, and anger hadn't been necessary with Oliver. But here, alone, she could allow emotion full control. Life flashed before her. Why didn't Ellen appreciate her? Why didn't Sarah leave her to grieve in peace? Harry was just as bad—always hovering close by and making her do things she wasn't ready to face.

Her mood sunk lower. Realization hit deep. People she really loved didn't need her. Even contacts in visions ignored her advice—well, George hadn't listened. Breath caught in her throat when the crux of the problem rose. Why couldn't she be happy? She deserved it.

A seagull screamed and circled overhead in the breeze, echoing her frustration. Yet, she'd chosen to fill her empty days with the task of finding George.

A laughing family strolled along, obscuring her view of the sea. In the blink of an eye, her loved-ones replaced the group. Raging thoughts dispelled. How silly to get angry about a twist of Fate. Nobody could prevent life's ups and downs.

Distant surfers spotted the sea. By remaining active, they stayed completely in the moment. She must do the same.

A blond man approached. She dropped her head and gazed into her ring. Trouser-clad legs came to a halt in front of her.

She glanced up into a plain face, devoid of any

emotion.

"I wonder if you can help me?" he said in a gravelly voice. "I'm searching for my girlfriend. I can't find her anywhere."

Liliha tilted her head. A chance to help someone in real life. Would the friend be super-fit too? "What does she look like?"

"Mid-twenties. Thin face, brown eyes, attractive. She might have got lost without me to guide her. She's not one for paying attention to her surroundings."

A shiver of worry at his lack of information about what she was wearing at the time produced immediate denial. "There are always tourists coming and going. Your friend could be with those surfers." Liliha nodded in the direction of the beach.

"Thanks for your help." He strode off toward the steps leading to the sand.

Trying to recall whether Ellen had mentioned a boyfriend, Liliha stood, cast a worried glance after the retreating figure, and then left in the opposite direction.

Chapter Twenty-Two

Ellen peered at her watch. Close to six o'clock and nearly dark. The days were so short in winter. She unhooked the keepsake from Dad to jam into her pocket. Didn't want to look rich. She teased her tangled tresses and knocked on Liliha's door. The old trousers picked up at the second-hand clothing store completed her costume.

Hard to believe how a stroke of luck had led her to the tearooms the other day. She'd just about given up hope. Times were difficult, but she meant to do so much better.

Liliha could help with her air of—what would you call it? Decency, maybe. Ellen sneered at the older woman's trust.

After a light flicked on, the lock clicked and the door swung open. Liliha peered out, eyes narrowed, deepening fine lines spreading from the corners like cat's whiskers.

"It's me. Ellen."

Liliha straightened. "How nice to see you. Come in."

Sure of her mark, Ellen traipsed after her. The spotless hall led to the sitting room, where a lovely perfumed aroma hung in the air. A chunky candle set with shells burned on the mantelpiece.

"Sit on the sofa and get comfy. I'm just watching a program about hiking in the mountains up north." Liliha gestured to the television.

"Yeah? I fall asleep if I watch one of those." Ellen ran her fingers over the floral woven texture beside her. Ah. The luxury of sitting on a soft chair.

"Just what I was doing when you knocked." Liliha switched off the television. "Would you like a drink?"

Ella shook her head. "Not unless you're offering

150

alcohol."

"Sorry." Liliha's gaze could have pierced a sheet of metal. "Ellen, are you in trouble of any sort?"

"Of course not. I've got a job, thanks to you."

"It's just ... Well don't worry about it."

"What?" Ellen held her breath.

"A fit-looking man spoke to me at the beach. He was searching for his girlfriend."

It couldn't be Matt. He'd never locate her so far away from London. All the same, Ellen's heart hammered while she waited until Liliha relaxed her stern expression. Rather than ask for his description, Ellen changed the subject. "Tonight Mary's washing her hair. I had to get out of the flat."

Liliha nodded. "Have you ever worn your hair a different way?"

"You mean like this?" Ella grabbed a handful and lifted the weight to the top of her head.

"That looks good," Liliha said. "You should wear your hair up."

"Would you do it for me?" Hand quivering, Ellen took a breath. This meeting couldn't have gone better.

"Have you brought your own brush?"

Ellen frowned. "Why?"

"We can't use the same one," Liliha said. "It's not hygienic."

"I don't mind using yours. You sure are fussy."

Liliha rubbed her head, and then glanced up. "You're acting in a very demanding way." Her face went red and she blurted, "I've already had a frustrating afternoon, waiting alone in a pub when my ... friend ... didn't turn up."

"Sorry." So Liliha was seeing someone. "I didn't think. I never do before I speak. My mother used to thrash me when I acted cheeky." Now what had she revealed? "I guess punishment didn't teach me anything."

"Tell you what," Liliha said. "How about I—"

"Don't bother. I didn't realize you'd be tired."

Liliha tilted her head. "I shouldn't have taken my mood out on you. I'll bet I can find a spare brush. Come upstairs while I fix your hair."

Ellen followed her out of the room and glanced up the stylish staircase. Yes. She was in.

She didn't falter on the way to Liliha's bedroom where she sat, meek as a child on Miss Muffet's tuffet. Play-acting the nursery rhyme, her eyes opened wide when Liliha grabbed her brush. Instead of a thrashing, the bristles scratched Ellen's scalp and tugged when they snagged on tangles. Rather than jerking away, she swayed with each stroke in an attempt to lessen the pain.

"How long have ... When did you last do this?" Liliha asked.

"What, properly? A week or so ago. I usually tease it. Easier to handle that way." She admired her image in the mirror. After several minutes, the brushstrokes soothed her.

"Now. To tie it," Liliha said.

"I've got a rubber band off the mail in my pocket." Ellen reached into the gritty lining and produced her trophy.

With expert movements, Liliha secured Ellen's hair on top of her head and splayed out the ends.

"That looks real pretty," Ellen said. "Thanks."

"I've done this for my daughters." Liliha's eyes went all misty.

Ellen relaxed in the warmth of acceptance, happy to take advantage of whatever came along. Perhaps she could set up a career on her own here in St. Ives. "Well. I'll leave ... you ... to get your rest. I'll let myself out."

"I appreciate the way you are making an effort to speak better, Ellen. It shows you're willing to change." Liliha nodded. "I'll see you out, and then lock the door properly."

Drat. Should have known. Ellen flicked her head. Loose hair bounced on top. *Too soon to ask for a spare key.* Her glance fell on the brush. "That's nice. Can I have it?"

"It belongs to Alissa."

Ellen used her wheedling voice. "She can get a new one."

"She likes that brush. Besides, it's something I can remember her by."

"Why are you being mean?"

"You can't barge in and take what you want." Liliha's cheeks tinged red. "I know you're making an effort to fit in, but you've gone too far."

"Didn't mean to be rude," Ellen said. "I learned to grab what I wanted." She shook the thought of her dad away.

"If you want to be friends, you need to respect my foibles. After all, I'm older. And, I hope, wiser." She nodded to herself and went misty-eyed again. "Come on." Liliha led the way downstairs.

Ellen screamed at the retreating stiff back. "Don't be so tight. You've got plenty and I've got nothing."

When she turned, the light had left Liliha eyes. "I've earned what I have with labor and tears." Raising her chin, Liliha walked to the door and ushered her outside.

Fuming, Ellen stalked off. She'd worked hard in a different way, with nothing to show for it.

***

Liliha wrapped her arms against her body on her way to the living room, pushing aside the nagging gloom after her failed attempt at telling Ellen how to behave. Her role with visionary help must be giving her a false sense of importance. *Better squash her old personality flaw of being too pushy—too controlling.* Her daughters had made no bones about pointing out her bossiness in the past. *Should have remembered.*

On the other side of the glass door, the last of the sun's rays softened a cloud to a dreamy pink. Straining to alter her perspective, Liliha focused on the brilliance. Other people, like Ellen, would jump at the chance to swap positions with her, free from danger and owning two houses.

The ringing phone jolted her into the present.

"Liliha. Harry here." The lowered voice hinted at a shared secret. "Just a quick call. I've rung to 'fess up and face the music. No, don't stop me."

"I wasn't going to." Remembering how the apology from Ellen had ended, Liliha said, "Go on."

"Sorry I didn't turn up. Things came on top. You know what that's like."

Liliha allowed silence to linger. Although his words sparked her sympathy, she determined to make him suffer a bit more. "Tell me."

"Aw." A low growl hit her ear. "One thing and another. I won't bore you."

Liliha held her breath and counted. Releasing the air, she said, "Don't bother to ask me out again, Harry."

"Don't hang up." His whispered voice held a desperate note. "I'm really sorry."

"Well. You should be. I don't go into pubs alone. You know I'm feeling vulnerable with Oliver gone. Not a pleasant experience."

"I can imagine how you must have felt. God, Liliha. I

am sorry. Believe me, I am." After a short grunt, Harry said, "How can I make it up to you?"

"No need, Harry. Let's leave it."

"Jees, Liliha." A sigh. "Can we get together and talk?"

"Ha. Ha. No, thanks."

The silence went on and on while she shrugged off her cocoon. "Apology accepted." A sudden thought hit her. "Have you seen Georg lately?"

"Once or twice. Why?"

Her piqued tone covered rising trepidation. "I'd like to talk to him about his life in South Africa." Hesitancy choked the breath in her throat. He'd guess her lame motive.

"I'd stay clear, if I were you."

"You're probably right. Even though you didn't turn up for the last meeting, you're still my friend. We've been through so much together." Closing the conversation, Liliha slumped against the chair support. Outside, dark confined her to loneliness, mirroring her thoughts.

Take charge—ignore Harry's advice and find the George from her vision.

Chapter Twenty-Three

After their third day of working together, Ellen made a big show of clearing away the Chinese food containers and bags in Mary's flat. While Ellen appreciated a place to stay, extra work was the last thing on her mind.

Mary sat facing the television while Ellen, in slave mode, stacked the boxes together as best she could without getting sticky remains on her fingers. She pranced across the room and shoved the food packages inside the flip-top lid of the refuse container by the door. "Want me to take the bin bag outside?" Mary should be impressed. Maybe she wouldn't notice the manipulation.

"Just leave it in the far corner of the lane," Mary said. "The collection is tomorrow."

Leaving the dull room with its faded floral wallpaper and a tiny window's view of the streetlight, Ellen stepped out of the rear door. In the cool, fresh air, she hauled the bulging bag to the other side of a littered yard not much bigger than a child's playhouse.

A memory struck like a shard of lightening, illuminating the memory about squatting inside her tiny hideaway, Dad's approach filling her with fear.

A shake of her head removed the past. Depositing the bag beside others, she turned and barged inside the flat, determined to replace the squalor with bright lights and laughter.

"Mary, what about washing our food down with a cheap drink?"

The other woman dragged her gaze away from the screen. "What?"

"If we go to the pub, we could ask for a glass of tap water with ice and a slice of lemon. You look out for me

156

while I pour the drinks into cocktail glasses. Once we finish, one of the fellows will shout us a refill. We can say it's a cocktail. They're not to know what we're drinking."

"Where did you learn that?"

"I've done it before." Ellen shook the hair out of her eyes. "Come on. Let's go out for a bit of fun."

Mary glanced at the screen, and then straightened to brush her sloppy tracksuit.

"Let's get glammed up." Ellen strode toward the bedroom.

"Hold on," Mary said. "I'm settled here."

"You stay if you like. I'm going."

"Why should you have all the fun?"

"Come on, then." Ellen winked.

With a sigh, Mary stretched, and then nodded.

Inside the small bedroom, Ellen reached into the black bag containing the clothes picked up at the pre-loved clothing store. The sparkly top would dress up jeans. No need to worry about the creases. They'd drop out with body heat. She reached in again and grabbed high heels.

Mary hovered in the doorway and eyed the garments strewn across the bed. "That looks sassy. Let's see what I can come up with."

Yes!

***

Alive again after a fun evening at the pub, Ellen stood beside a *customer* in the cool air. She'd left Mary nattering to girlfriends. Must be after eleven o'clock, but the light was still on inside Liliha's cottage. When the front door opened a fraction, Ellen said, "Hi, Liliha. I've brought a friend." She hugged herself in the bitter cold.

The door opened wider. Liliha peered into the gloom. "Come inside out of the wind."

Ellen gazed at ... what's-'is-name? ... ah yes. "This is Jack." She waved in his direction. "An old friend." She cleared her throat.

"You must be freezing in that skimpy top, Ellen." Liliha frowned ever so slightly, perhaps catching on. "Come and get warm." She led the way into the living room.

The whites of Jack's eyes flashed from behind the hair covering his eyes. "This is nice." His grubby trousers and the rip on the shoulder of his lumber jacket stood out in the tidy room.

Ellen frowned and glanced outside where light spilled onto a shed in the rear garden.

Liliha gestured to the sofa and sat in her chair by the glass door. She shifted about as though her seat was hot. "How long since you've seen each other?" she asked.

The fool's mouth dropped open. Ellen jumped in before Jack could spoil everything. "Ages. I hardly recognized him." She nudged him. "We went to school together."

"Where?" Liliha asked.

"Manchester," Jack said.

At the same time, Ellen said, "London." She recovered. "Of course. You transferred home before we finished." Phew. She'd got out of the hole she'd dug.

The dodo frowned.

"And what are you doing in St. Ives, Jack?" Liliha asked.

"Came with a group of friends. We're staying in a guest house on the far side of town. She said you might—"

"... be a friendly local," Ellen finished. "I haven't known Liliha long." She faced Jack. "But she's been so kind to me, taking me in and looking after me."

Liliha pursed her lips and sighed. "Ellen. You're treating me like a fool. At least you could offer me the respect of being open about what you're doing."

"Sorry." Ellen dropped her head, hoping to talk Liliha 'round. "It's so cold and I needed a place where I could catch up with Jack. Away from everyone else. Ya know?"

"Surely the pub was warm. But talk is all you'll do." Liliha's eyes lost their welcome. "Seeing as you're here, how about I make us a cup of coffee?"

Ellen adopted her cheeky face. "Thought you'd never ask."

When Liliha left the room, Ellen reached out. "Come here and let me give you a proper welcome." He tasted of smoke and beer.

"Let's go to bed," Jack said.

"Not yet," she whispered and brushed her lips over his ear. "Maybe next time." Depended on how he behaved. "Don't worry. I won't leave you frustrated." She rubbed one of his sinewy arms.

A dazed expression softened his face while he slid his hand under her sweater.

During Jack's fumble, Ellen's gaze drifted about the beautiful room. Her life hadn't been roses. She wanted perfume, not the thorns which had nearly hooked her.

Footsteps in the hall alerted her to pull away. Just in time. After small talk with Liliha about Mary's flat and how her job was going, Ellen finished her coffee and smiled at Jack. After dragging him upright, she mumbled thanks on the way to the front door.

Outside, she drew Jack along the side path, high heels stumbling over uneven ground. Jack stopped and pulled her into his arms. His kiss burned her up. His breath came fast.

She leaned away. "Come this way. There's a good

spot out of the cold."

Leading him to the shed, she murmured, "This'll be exciting. Much more fun than the room upstairs."

She flicked the catch. Not locked, thank goodness. Stepping into the small area she turned to face him. "Close the door."

"Come here," he whispered. "I'll warm you."

Her ministrations came easy while Jack glided to closure.

Ellen blinked at a sudden light and froze. Just a house light.

"What the ..." Jack gasped, and then shriveled.

Hopefully, he'd still pay.

***

On evening patrol, George narrowed his eyes at two figures ahead. *Time for a little fun, Hopkins, my boy.* Smoke rose under the street light. Raucous laughs erupted.

Whistling, he approached a couple of lads concealed in the dark lane behind the school. The town was becoming too quiet. *Better make a show to keep his clients willing.* Business owners needed an extra incentive to pay his security fees.

The two runts hid their cigarettes and leaned over their pushbikes, speaking low.

"Want to earn a little something and enjoy yourselves at the same time?" George asked.

"What?" a half-broken voice asked.

"What I had in mind was a rouse." George grinned, knowing they'd be snookered by his word.

The boys straightened. In the gloom, he made out longish hair on one of them leaning close to the shorter lad.

"What's that mean?" a deeper voice asked.

"A stir-up," George said. "How do you fancy

breaking a window, and then running away?"

"I can't get in any more trouble," the short lad said. "Mum'll go mad."

"You won't get caught." George moved closer.

"How much you paying?"

"A packet of cigarettes each."

They looked at each other and frowned.

They'd be off in a flash if he didn't stop them. Then, he'd have to retaliate. Violent scenarios came to him while the boys murmured together, casting quick looks at him every now and again. He grunted, "Want the job or not. This is a one-time offer. I'll find someone else who'll jump at the chance."

After murmured conversation, the half-broken voice said, "We'll take it."

"Right," George said. "Get yourselves over to the launderette. When I give the signal, hurl a stone at the back window." He cleared his throat, relieved he didn't need to break their knee-caps one dark night. "You can bugger off. I'll say I couldn't catch you."

"Is that all?" the larger of the two lads asked.

"That's it. Job done."

"What about the ciggies?"

George pulled a couple of packets out of his jacket. "I'll leave them right here." He lifted up a rock and placed them on the pavement underneath. "Now, hightail it."

They straightened their bikes and glanced at the hiding place. "How do we know you won't take them when we leave?"

"Smart kid. I'll be right behind you. Off you go." George followed his trainee henchmen toward town.

Chapter Twenty-Four

Liliha studied different packets of beans inside the busy supermarket, mung beans, borlotti, cannelloni—so much to choose from. And cheap. A person didn't need to spend a fortune to eat well and stay healthy. She selected a can of butter beans to go in a salad for her evening meal. She'd mention including beans, legumes and vegetables in meals to Ellen next time she visited. The girl was too pale. Rather than ban Ellen, she might as well try to be a good influence.

At the sound of her name, she glanced up. "Yvonne, William. How good to see you."

William flashed a smile although his eyes didn't light up.

The grief they all shared slammed into her with such ferocity it took her breath away. Oliver's image replaced her earlier happy thoughts. She touched William's shoulder, gaining comfort from the rough fibers of his gray mohair jacket. "Everything okay?"

At his nod, she breathed a shuddering sigh. Oliver's parents were coping, and so should she.

"You'll have to visit us soon." Yvonne leaned close as another customer pushed by in the isle, sending a hint of spicy perfume into the stuffy air. "Get away from," she mouthed, "tourists."

"You're right." Liliha rambled on to fill a pause. "I met a new woman at the tearooms the other day. Ellen. She's in her mid-twenties and doesn't have any friends in the area. She needed to find a place to stay."

Yvonne frowned. "You didn't invite her home?"

"Just for the night. She's found a flat with a friend

now. I'm afraid we don't have much in common." *Only a feeling of exclusion from the life*. Liliha nodded at the irony of two such different personalities united in loneliness.

No need to mention Ellen had brought her boyfriend when she visited last time. Something going on, but Liliha hadn't quite figured out what. Maybe she was hiding from the fair-haired burly man who'd asked about his lost girlfriend. If so, she acted way too cheeky.

William murmured, "Be careful. You don't know what you're getting into with a newcomer."

Here came a lecture. Liliha clamped her teeth, knowing she shouldn't involve herself with strangers, especially now.

"William," Yvonne said. "Leave her alone. She always brings out the best in people."

"All right, all right. I'm just saying."

Liliha inspected her cuff while a wry thought crept over her. In a game like pass the parcel, everyone influenced each other. "On another subject," Liliha said, "do you know anyone who makes picture frames?"

"Plenty about in the area, to cater to all the artists. I'll make inquiries."

"Thank you. I'd like to re-frame the papyrus in the hall." Relieved at steering the conversation away from a touchy subject, Liliha chatted for a while before they parted.

***

Ellen stood in the dark with Derrick outside Liliha's cottage. Tall and rugged, he dressed much better than Jack, who had left the area. Being a fussy woman, Liliha might prefer Derrick in his trendy cardigan and jeans to the other fellow she picked up.

Sure enough, when the door opened, Liliha gave a

163

hesitant smile before inviting them into the warmth of the cottage. After introductions in the bright hallway, they removed their coats and trouped into the living room.

The older woman edged close and spoke in a low voice. "Ellen, I don't want to appear mean, but you can't treat my house like a ..." she blushed and swallowed, "boarding house."

"I just wanted you to meet Derrick." Ellen spoke loud enough to include him. "When he mentioned sheet music, I knew you two would get on."

Liliha blinked a few times. "Take a seat, Derrick. Are you interested in songwriting?"

"Sure." He dropped onto the sofa. "My friends and I have a little band. I wrote a song last week before we came on vacation. Called it, 'Don't Ya Know."

"Sounds catchy." Liliha said.

Ellen smiled at Derrick, but frowned when Liliha spoke again.

"I want to have a private word with you."

She wriggled her wrist out of Liliha's grip. "Of course. Can it wait for a moment? Let Derrick settle in first."

"You two go ahead." He glanced at the screen flicking with scenes from an old movie.

Liliha beckoned. "Come into the kitchen."

Ellen bounced backward onto the sofa beside Derrick. "I love Casablanca. Wait 'till I see this bit."

Derrick glanced from one to the other. "I see you're old friends."

Ellen grinned at the fool, and then turned to Liliha. "I meant to tell you. You'll never guess what happened last night. Someone smashed a window at the launderette. Mary's man chased them away or they might have broken in. He arranged for someone to come and fix the damage."

"The crime's getting bad here lately," Liliha said.

"Nothing like London, though," Derrick said. "I read about someone being knifed in the street just about every day."

"I don't go to London often," Liliha said. "It's so crowded."

Ellen clamped her mouth shut. The less she said about her old life the better.

"It's trendy in the Camden area," Derrick said. "There's a great little theater tucked away on a back street. My group's played there a few times ..."

"Won't be a minute." Ellen left them talking, strolled along the hall, and made her way upstairs to the bathroom. Just a little more time, and she'd convince Liliha to let her use the spare room.

Her mind jumped to the action in the shed with Jack and the money in her hand afterward, despite the interruption. Who needed a so-called protector? She could operate on her own as long as she kept her activities private.

***

Once he'd socialized and shifted the goods found inside the stolen Jag, Georg van den Burg jumped in and roared away from Penzance, headed north over the dark, narrow roads to St. Ives. He grinned. Why did he ever think fitting into Johannesburg society was for him?

A few underhanded moves had set him up here in England. *Couldn't be helped.* All the great storybook heroes acted the same way. After all, Sinbad stole the lamp and turned out a hero at the end. Businessmen finalized deals on the sly to get ahead. Called themselves entrepreneurs. The title suited Georg fine. Once he'd stashed away a bit of money, he'd settle down with a good woman by his side. Too edgy at the moment, what with one thing and another.

With the car parked on outskirts of town, he strode toward the pub in the chilly night air.

Very few people occupied the street at this time of night.

He passed several rowdy teenage boys. The kids expressed his enthusiasm. They'd probably never had a setback in their lives. When they did, they might not recapture the same joy. You had to be tough to rise after a fall—take advantage of every opportunity—even if it went against the grain.

Sea air cleared out his lungs as he neared the Golden Lion. Reaching the entrance, he bent under the doorway and entered the bright, cheerful atmosphere. Customers laughed and shouted at tables. Harry glanced over from the bar—always shifty.

Georg headed over to his new friend.

Harry grinned. "How's things?"

"Not too bad," Georg said. "You?"

"Fine." Harry nodded in the direction of a scruffy man, whose black hair curled over his ears. "Same name as you."

The hard expression on the man's face filtered out any emotion, yet, at the same time, oozed with threat.

"Yeah? It's a common name." Georg raised his hand to the bar girl with her bright expression under the blonde hair most of the local girls favored these days. He pointed to his drink of choice. "A pint, please."

An unusual woman with dark hair, blue eyes, and a face like the Mona Lisa eased into his mind again. Tall and attractive, Liliha represented the ideal beauty to him. But she was too soft, too gentle. He didn't mind the age difference between them, but she needed roughing up a little—bring those sad eyes to life. And of course, he had to get his hands on the moonstone ring Straten mentioned.

After paying for his drink, Georg asked, "Seen Liliha lately?"

Harry sucked in his lips, and then blew them out. "Nope."

"Trouble in paradise?"

Harry took a long gulp of his drink. "We had a few words on the phone."

"These things happen." Georg took a quick sip while he regrouped. "Now we have to work out how to get you into her good books. Stunning women don't hang about."

"Leave her alone. She's grieving." Harry lowered his brows and fiddled with a cigarette carton.

"I wouldn't mind helping her get over it." The guy avoided eye contact and he held his shoulders way too low. Perhaps Harry was interested. Georg leaned forward. "You don't mind, do you?"

Harry shrugged. "None of my business. But I won't stand by and see her hurt." He headed for the door where other smokers huddled together in the cold.

Georg released his breath. In the future, Harry might make his grand plans difficult.

Chapter Twenty-Five

Liliha searched for a way to broach the subject of Ellen during an unexpected afternoon stroll along the sand with Sarah. Her friend's opinion might help her decide how to speak to the girl rather than rejecting her altogether.

Amazed at finding strength after a day on her feet at work, she allowed the seaside to work its magic. *Must be getting used to the extra exercise.* Chuckling at the illusion of herself as an athlete, she glanced at Sarah. "This breeze is bracing."

"Clears the lungs." Sarah's coat flapped against her legs. "I found the type of car for my painting, by the way."

"What sort did you choose?

"A maroon Rolls Royce."

"Show me when you finish, won't you?" Liliha gazed out at the flat, gray-green expanse of sea stretching to the horizon. "I love the beach when the weather's wild. Look at the foam on top of the waves."

A crash from a nearby breaker sent an incredible burst of ozone into the air. Fingers of spume extended along the sand, depositing more seaweed on the heaped debris. The water retreated with a swish.

"The tide kissed the shore," Liliha said. "The line's from an old sixties song."

"They were more romantic with lyrics then."

"I know." Liliha trudged along the squeaking sand. Gone were the days of kissing for her.

"You should get a dog, Liliha. Take him for walks along the beach after work."

"More advice for a lonely widow?"

Sarah grinned. "I'm just saying."

"Cats are more my style. I wonder if Walnut would

come with me." She chuckled at the improbable idea.

"Cats won't get their feet wet," Sarah said.

"Anyway, I'm not lonely." The perfect spot to mention Ellen. "I've made a new acquaintance. Ellen's new to the area."

"What's she like?"

"She's a bit younger than we are." Liliha hesitated, and then blurted, "I think she's running away from something in her past."

Sarah's stare stirred deep worries.

"If people can't look after each other," Liliha said, "what sort of a world would we live in?"

"Just help without becoming involved." Sarah kicked a broken shell.

"That's a bit harsh." Liliha gazed out to sea. *Better mention the rest.* "Lately she's been bringing men friends to visit."

Sarah stopped. "Whoa. Where's this going?"

Liliha faced her. "Maybe she thinks of me as an aunt."

"Aunts tell you what you can, and can't, get away with." Sarah frowned. "Are you laying down the rules?"

"I gave her a piece of my mind, but I didn't make it quite as formal as establishing guidelines. I feel sorry for her, the poor kid."

"Better sort things out before she takes over," Sarah said.

Strolling further, Liliha considered how to set parameters without being too controlling.

The briny air charged with intensity. Must be overdoing the exercise. Hard to breathe.

A whiff of fragrance drifted by.

Chiding herself for a sudden reluctance to leave

normal life behind, Liliha halted and gazed out to sea. Dizzy and disoriented, her essence tumbled amongst a kaleidoscope of swirling colors toward the unknown.

***

I arrive in a large room. I've already merged. Judging by the size of the fingers playing with bright plastic toys and the trousers on small bent knees before me, the youngster is roughly three years old. Our hands lift and dive a truck onto joined sections of a runway.

"Timmy, do dat." Seeking Mummy's attention, we glance across the expanse of white carpet.

Two adults sit on the other side of the room. Mummy and another man. They're looking at each other.

I feel the tug of Timmy's smile as if I'm expressing my own need for reassurance.

The big people are cross. Mummy's speaking with the voice she uses when Timmy's left his wet bed to crawl in with her. He pushes his truck along the track all the while roaring louder and louder.

I murmur to Timmy, 'Play quietly. Mummy will speak to you soon.' Without knowing why I'm here, I hum to the boy. 'Hush little baby, don't say a word. Mummy's gonna buy you a mocking bird' ... and continue to the end of the tune. I hold myself ready to help.

A man bursts into the room. Daddy. Timmy lunges to his feet and runs across, shouting with delight.

Managing our little legs is difficult, especially when we're unsettled at the way Mummy's ignoring us.

We hug Daddy's leg, but Daddy pushes our hands away. We burst into tears, grief and frustration released in our howls. Daddy's looking at Mummy.

I can't penetrate Timmy's pain right now, so I wait. Unsure of what's going on, I speculate. The man's not an

170

uncle or Timmy would know.

Daddy strides toward Mummy and bends low to her face. "Did you think I didn't know?"

Mummy's face scrunches up. "What are you doing home at this time of day?"

We run and bury our head in her lap, desperate for comfort, and unable to work out why everyone's so cross.

Mummy pats our head as though we're a doggy. We hold still while the men's voices rage.

Timmy doesn't understand what's happening, but I do.

"Get out of here."

"I was invited."

"Don't cause a fuss," Mummy says.

"Outside. You and me." Daddy's red face frightens us.

"Any time. She doesn't want you. You'll see why I'm the better man."

"Calm down," Mummy says. "It's not what you think."

"That's not what the bastard beside you says."

"No." Mommy's voice goes quiet and she stops stroking. "Stop it. You'll upset Timmy."

"Did you think of that before you invited him here?"

"Let's have a proper talk."

"Nothing to say. I'm taking Timmy." Bending, Daddy lifts us. We reach our feet out to grip him. Daddy holds us against his big body.

"I go with Daddy?" We glance from Mummy's face to Daddy's.

Mummy reaches out, blinks away tears and stands. "Leave him here. Don't take him away—"

"You've lost any right to him now."

"What did I do?"

"What Mummy do?" we ask, wiggling in Daddy's arms. We want to run to Mummy.

"Look, old man—" The other man stands up.

Mummy stretches her arms to us, and we yell with relief. Mummy's gonna take us. It'll be all right.

Daddy holds on too tight and steps away. We reach out toward Mummy's arms, squealing in frustration. A sudden terror pounds inside our body.

What can I do in this tense moment? Should I wait until they're calmer? I whisper, 'Hold still until Daddy and Mummy talk.'

"I'm taking Timmy," Daddy yells. "That's final."

We release one last whimper. "The zoo. Daddy take me."

I grasp this idea. Can I make it work? 'Talk about your favorite animals,' I whisper. 'Lions and tigers.'

"Garamaraffs," we shout. "Big and long like my toy." We search the other side of the room for the stuffed giraffe.

"He'll never give you a moment's peace," Mummy says. "Once he gets an idea, he won't let go."

We squirm, trying to get down. Should I engage with the mother or the father? Who will benefit Timmy the most.

Daddy whacks the side of our head. "I'm the adult here. I say what goes."

At the blow, I strengthen his neck with a clench of muscles, while Timmy howls with shock and pain.

By suggesting talk about animals, I'm partly to blame for this abuse. I've got to call a halt before Timmy suffers more. I try to leave, but I'm blocked—locked inside this little body. I'll have to sort things out from here.

Mummy shouts, "Don't hurt him."

"I'm calling the police," the man says.

"There's nothing to report. Mind your own business. You're the one who caused this mess."

"Then I should leave." The man stands up.

"Don't bother. We're going," Daddy says.

In panic, we scream, "I stay wiv' Mummy."

"Let's settle this between us," the man says. "Leave the boy out of it."

I whisper to Timmy, 'You must be very quiet now. The big people need to figure something out.'

"Ice cream?" he whimpers.

With a surge of strength, I assure him he'll get his reward if he lets his body relax and stops yelling. He complies so suddenly I'm taken aback.

In the silence, Daddy says to the man, "Right. Outside." He lowers us to the floor.

We run to Mummy. When she lifts us, we snuggle into her arms while the men walk outside.

Mummy murmurs, "It's all right, darling. It's all right now."

Her arms hold us too tight, but with my whispered advice, Timmy remains still and listens to her rapid heartbeat.

"What dat noise, Mummy?"

"The men are sorting things out. We'll go up to your room." She rubs his head. "I'm sorry, baby. I'll make sure you're safe from now on. Mummy promises."

"Ice cream."

"We'll take some with us. How about that?"

While Mummy walks to the freezer, Timmy leans into the comfort of her body.

Assured of the toddler's safety, I lift away.

***

Liliha opened her eyes facing the sea. The regular pounding and hissing of retreating waves sent calming emanations into her head. Did she do enough? At least the youngster would remain with his mother. A child couldn't survive alone.

"Want to turn back now?" Sarah's faint voice drifted on the wind.

Liliha faced her approaching friend.

"Where were you? Another vision? Or thinking of Oliver?"

"You noticed." Liliha gazed at the sand. Despite Sarah's knowledge of previous visions, Liliha discounted using Sarah as a sounding board. She longed to share her experiences, but the task should be reserved for a constant companion and nothing could replace Oliver's support.

While they headed toward the distant steps, the remnants of the recent vision receded, leaving Liliha to consider her future. Okay, Ellen made things difficult, but she could sort out the problem with a few timely words of warning.

The pungent smell of decay filled her nostrils. Amongst the flotsam ahead, she picked out the body of a floppy, lifeless seal. "Don't come close," she called to Sarah.

At the knowledge of life's brevity, Liliha's optimistic mood slid out with a receding wave. Safety could never be taken for granted—for Timmy or the little French boy from a previous vision, for Ellen, and, in a more permanent way, for Oliver. *Best to take advantage of each moment.*

Chapter Twenty-Six

Georg van den Burg stepped outside the busy St. Ives pub after a Plowman's lunch of cold meat, cheddar cheese, pickles, and bread. These English knew how to satisfy a man. Fortified by a pint to wash the food down, his step quickened in the direction of the parking station, reliving the conversation about how he'd cajoled Harry into inviting Liliha out. A swan grieving for her mate. *Easy pickings.* He swung his body into the car, started the engine and headed west.

With an occasional glimpse of the sea on the right of the quiet road, he passed an empty lorry. Hardly anyone about. At this time of day, the farmers labored while their wives prepared their meal. Georg didn't envy their simple life.

But he wasn't so clever. He still had to work out how to reach Liliha and gain her treasure.

In the Rapunzel tale, the roving king's son had climbed her long hair to the tower. Georg needed to surmount every obstruction in a similar way to achieve his objective. He gave a wry chuckle. *Better cut out the daydreams and smarten up.*

Closer to the isolated area where he lived, the low afternoon sun disappeared behind clouds. Although daylight skies were gray here instead of the wonderful blue of South Africa, the expanse of ocean reminded him of home.

On his drive along the side road past the lock-up arranged by Straten, the sun hit the protruding top of the shed door.

Alerted, Georg jammed his foot on the brakes.

Dust filtered the rays while he skidded to a halt, reversed, and pulled into the dirt driveway between tall weeds. Jumping out of his car, he crunched over the rubble to the door.

The hinge on the forced lock hung loose.

Georg slammed his palm into the timber. "Shit!" Everything had been going so well. He eased the door open. Inside, light pierced the single window to slant onto the empty floor. The cartons containing the Egyptian loot were gone.

Heart pounding with a sense of violation, Georg brushed dust out of the hair trailing over his collar. Nobody but Matt knew the whereabouts.

Two options presented themselves. Let the boss know, thus risking accusation, or skip away like a springbok before a lion's charge. Georg stilled his natural inclination to run. After all, he was the lion here in Cornwall. Better act like an entrepreneur and work things out to his advantage.

Before he reported the burglary to Straten, he needed a plan.

On his way to the car, he slapped his forehead. Matt might have broken into his flat too. What if he'd found the small box containing the bracelet?

***

In the fresh breeze outside the tearooms, Liliha drew a breath, anticipating home and rest.

A tall form lurched from the wall.

"Harry. What are you doing here?"

"I popped into St. Ives on business and decided to stroll along to meet you after work." He took her elbow and steered her toward town.

She struggled. "I go that way."

"Thought you might want to come to the pub for a quick drink."

Ignoring her gripe about him not turning up before, she countered, "Should you be drinking if you're going to drive?"

"Who said I'm leaving? Anyway, I could have an orange juice."

Liliha raised her brows. "By your sly expression, I'd say that's the last thing on your mind. Anyway, I don't think this is the right time. I've had a tough day and I'm longing to rest."

"What about tomorrow night?"

"Sorry. Not yet. Give me time to plan."

"I thought you wanted to talk to Georg. He'll probably turn up. The fellow doesn't seem to work regular hours."

"But, I find it difficult ... I'm not ready to get about more." Surely he understood her reluctance.

"It's hard." Harry touched her shoulder. "Force yourself. Socializing gets easier."

"Have you had personal experience?"

"Sure. Who hasn't?"

"Who ...?" Liliha touched his arm in sympathy, and then pulled away with embarrassment.

"No need to go into it." His eyes glowed. "Let's just say I miss someone." Harry leaned close.

"Now you're being evasive." She inhaled aftershave, the gel on his hair. Despite her intentions to rebuke him, she smiled. "Okay. Tomorrow."

"All settled." He leaned away. "Golden Lion. We'll have a fish meal at the bar."

"Fried food isn't very health—" She smiled, this time with politeness and acceptance.

"I'll pick you up at six o'clock," Harry said. "Want me to walk you home now?"

"No, thanks, Harry. You get on with what you were about to do."

He tilted his head. "You sure?"

She nodded.

"See you then." With a sigh, his shoulders slumped.

Liliha veered away and tramped up the hill. What had gotten into him? Had she been mean for denying him what he wanted? *Don't be silly.* Her needs were just as important as his.

If she planned to get on with normal life, she'd better make a start. Tomorrow night offered a perfect opportunity.

***

After securing his car on the deserted road behind bare trees, Georg approached the building he lived in with stealth. Set in isolation surrounded by scrub rustling in the breeze, his was the only occupied flat of the four. Acting the part of a lion seeking prey, he blended with the trees while his senses probed to detect movement. Satisfied, he headed for the front entrance, glanced along the road both ways, and then checked the lock. Secure.

When he entered the small space, one swift step took him to the far side of the door in case of attack from behind its cover.

The buzzing in his head stopped. Instinct told him the room was empty. He closed the door and lowered the blinds in the living room, kitchen, bedroom and bathroom. Finding no sign of disturbance, he relaxed.

First things first. He strode to the laundry basket, flung aside soiled shirts, and grasped the rough wooden box hidden amongst them.

The object seemed to greet him—to send a buzz of

recognition and a warm glow inside him. *Enough of fairy stories*.

He assured himself his motive was security while he searched each room for the perfect spot to store the box. If someone broke in, they'd find every place he considered.

In the small kitchen, he opened the pantry door. Too apparent to any burglar if placed amongst a few grocery items on the shelves. His boot caught on the raised edge of a floorboard at one side of the small space. Resting the container on a shelf, he bent. An inner voice suggested breaking the seal to lift the lid and gaze at the beauty again.

George ignored the temptation. Demands in his ears plagued him while pacing away to retrieve a tool to pry up the wooden floorboard.

Chapter Twenty-Seven

They'd arrived early this time, straight from the fishing boats. Once inside Liliha's cottage, Ellen gazed at the neat hallway and nudged Derrick. So much depended on this visit.

Derrick bowed and handed the paper parcel to Liliha.

"What's this?" Liliha's smile brought her eyes to life.

Ellen melted at the other woman's enjoyment. *Don't get soft.* "I'll give you a hint. Food."

"Come into the kitchen."

They ambled along behind her to the end room where she unwrapped the crackling parcel on the bench. The large fish flopped over the paper, glistening body and bright eye.

"How lovely. Thank you so much."

"John Dory, fresh from the harbor," Derrick said.

"We arranged to meet after I finished work." Ellen smiled at him. "So glad we did."

"This is far too much for me," Liliha said. "How about I cook it for our supper? It's just the right time."

Ellen stopped herself from punching the air. "Great. Sure ya don't mind?"

Derrick muttered something about fried fish.

"I'd love the company. I'll even cook it the way you want. You two go and make yourselves comfortable while I whip up some batter. Don't forget where you are, Ellen."

"Okay. Come on, Derrick." Ellen led him away. In the living room, she veered to face him. "Come here." She kissed him, softening her lips in invitation. His body pressed against hers. What should she charge him for time spent in a proper, clean room?

***

Liliha washed the mixing bowl and wiped the work

surfaces. She'd set the table for three, and placed the fish in the oil. Voices and music drifted from the television. A sense of living in the moment, of entertaining happy guests and cooking their meal, added to her contentment.

How could she present rules to Ellen, a girl who substituted her own family for now? Liliha chuckled and hung the towel on its hook. She didn't have any trouble setting the limits for her own daughters.

Shoulders braced, she marched into the living room.

Nobody in sight. Heart pounding, her imagination focused upstairs. No. Surely Ellen wouldn't take him into her private space? *Maybe ... No use speculating.*

She darted out of the room. Halfway up the stairs, a groan followed by a high cry drew her on to the landing. Mumbles came from the direction of the spare room. She stomped over the carpet. Swung the closed door open.

Inside, Ellen pulled the sheet over the masculine body pressed over her. "We're just trying out the comfortable bed. Derrick's not too sure so he lay on top of me." She jabbed him.

Derrick flopped onto his side and faced Liliha. Flushed and disheveled, he raised himself on his elbow and swallowed. "All right?"

Liliha clenched her jaw. They all needed time to think and work out how to recover. "I suggest you get dressed and join me. The meal's nearly ready. We'll talk when we've eaten."

"No worries," he said.

Liliha jerked away and descended to the kitchen just in time to remove the fish from the hot oil. She'd get through this. Working to assemble the meal soothed her disquiet. Derrick should have behaved better in a strange house rather than taking his cue from Ellen.

181

What sort of a home did Ellen come from? Could any child shoulder the blame for their upbringing, or change once the mold had set? Liliha made the decision to be firm, understanding and kind—treat others the way she'd want to be treated. Steps on the staircase penetrated the thump of her heartbeat. "In the kitchen," she called.

Blinking faces peered in, followed by her ill-at-ease guests.

"Come and sit down," Liliha said. "I can't wait to taste this fish."

"Looks good, Liliha." Derrick ran his fingers between the spiky strands of his short hair. After an outward breath, his arms lowered under a plain knitted cardigan worn inside out.

Liliha pointed to a chair at the other side of the table. He eased onto the seat, a wary expression settling over his features.

"I don't have salad very often." Ellen plonked on the middle chair. "Any tomato ketchup?"

Liliha rose and grabbed a plastic bottle. Kaelyn liked the stuff. "Try squeezing a section of lemon over your fish instead. You'll find the juice works just as well and it's better for you." She settled beside them to eat. Both her visitors used the ketchup.

Concentrating on her own food, Liliha savored the succulent John Dory while she geared herself for her coming lecture.

Derrick finished, pushed his plate away, and gulped the apple juice in his glass. "Nice." He rubbed his neck. "Um, thanks." He glanced at the doorway.

"If you've got something else to do," Liliha said, "take off. Ellen and I can finish up here."

"Do you mind, Ellen?" he asked.

Ellen frowned at Liliha, and then faced Derrick. "I'll catch you later."

His chair scraped on the wooden floor. "Well, thanks for cooking the fish." Derrick flashed a glance at Ellen and rubbed his jaw. "See you soon."

"Right." Ellen lifted her chin.

Liliha accompanied the silent man to the door. Once again in the kitchen, she drew a breath. "I expected better from you. But I'm not your mother."

Ellen clamped her lips.

"Didn't I tell you to stay downstairs?" Heat rose into Liliha's face. "You can't use my home as the place you bring men to ... to make love ... for sex."

"But where else will I go?"

Despite rising frustration, Liliha made her voice as firm as possible. "You'll have to work something out."

"I like it here. Why are you being so mean? You've got a spare room."

"I've had enough of your cheek." Liliha gave in to building pressure. "You're a selfish little slut. Why I ever invited you to stay, I don't know. You've done nothing but demand and whine since I first met you. If you were my daughter, I'd send you to your room and withhold privileges. But we're way beyond that."

Ellen shot a glance at the exit.

"Yes! Get out! And don't bother coming back!"

Ellen's flashing eyes and flushed cheeks spoke volumes. "You're just like everyone else."

"I'm human all right. I'm trying to get over a traumatic event. My husband was murdered by a former girlfriend and he bled to death in my ..." Vision. *Don't share that.* Liliha closed her mouth to block the torrent of words, emotions and pain. Her hands quivered while she led Ellen to the exit.

After Ellen ducked outside, Liliha slammed the door and wiped hot tears from her face. She missed Oliver so much, imagined his comforting arms, wished he would save her. From herself. Had she really called the girl a slut? Where had her prized compassion gone?

***

Georg van den Burg lifted the phone and punched in a number. Better get the bad news over with. Although he'd waited a day since the theft, no plan had formed.

Straten answered with a grunted name.

"The cartons have been stolen from the lock-up," Georg blurted.

"What the f—. Is that you Georg?"

"I'm sorry to say, it is."

"I'm in the study." Straten spoke with a growl. "You can speak freely. You'd better explain."

"Can't tell you much. Lock busted, goods gone—and after Matt examined the contents and signed the seal."

"How convenient. I've only got your word to rely on."

"How could I prove my case? Nobody else knew about the haul." Georg dabbed his forehead.

"I'll have a word with him first. I'll ring you back."

"What will that prove? Matt will deny any knowledge of the theft."

"Just like you." Straten's pause contained nothing but heavy breathing.

In the silence, all Georg's plans stampeded away like a herd of wildebeest. Should he promise the ring?

A voice grated in his ear. "Why do you suspect him?"

Georg drew breath into his empty lungs. "I wouldn't

be able to get rid of antiques. I don't know anyone in the business and I don't have residency yet. They'd be sure to check once they hear my accent. If you think about it, you'll see I'm right. Only Matt could have done it."

"The bastard. I'd hoped to leave the goods resting until the hoo-ha died down. I shouldn't have trusted him. Way too convenient for him to be in Cornwall already. Right, you'd better find him. I'll give you his address in London. Can I leave it to you?"

"I'll drive up first thing tomorrow."

"Why not now? You can get here in seven hours."

"That'd put me in London at roughly three in the morning," Georg said. "If you don't mind, I'll set off early tomorrow."

"You'd better be able to prove what you say."

Chapter Twenty-Eight

At the expected knock, Liliha slid her arms inside the waxed coat, shrugged the comforting protection over her shoulders and grabbed her bag. She greeted Harry and left Cottage Central, ensuring she locked the door. Now, to find the George from her vision.

On the walk past town toward the harbor, time passed in pleasant reminiscence while night drew in. A distinctive smell of brine drifted in the breeze.

"This isn't so bad," she said. "You've made venturing out simple for me."

"See? Told you it gets easier."

They turned the corner at the end of the road. To the right, moonlight picked out odd angles of fishing boats and glinted on the tips of waves in the distance. They headed for the pub.

Liliha entered the low doorway. A fire burned in the nook on one side, sending flickers of shifting light over twenty or so people inside the room. In a brighter area, customers ate at tables, talking. One group of diners broke out in raucous laughter. Not so different from the tearooms, except for louder voices and the smell of spilled drinks and smoke. Clatters came from a room behind the bar.

Harry waved to someone seated on a stool, and then ushered her to a circular booth in front of the window. While she removed her outer clothing, he scrambled in front of the seat, perched in the center, and patted the closer spot beside him. The lift of his mouth and twinkling eyes welcomed her.

She moved his jacket a fraction, threw her coat over the backrest, and slid along, stopping before she touched his elbow. "Whose glass is that?" She pointed to an empty on the other side of the table in front of a brown leather jacket.

"Georg's."

Her breathing quickened.

"Georg van den Burg. We met him at Sarah's party." Harry nodded in the direction of a scruffy man by the bar. "Not that one."

Anticipation mounted. "It's a common name."

"George Hopkins. I won't introduce you. He's not your type."

She needed to think about this new development without staring at the stranger. She hadn't considered what to do when she confronted two Georges.

She ran her gaze along the customers at the bar, trying not to single him out. Curly dark hair surrounded a face creased with hard living.

"What'll you have to drink? Shandy?"

She nodded, pleased with the suggestion of lemonade mixed with beer, and followed Harry's upward gaze.

"Hello, Liliha." Georg, dressed in smart jeans and navy windcheater, bent to place two glasses full of brown liquid on the table.

She shrunk under his gaze and prepared a line of questioning. Couldn't see his shoes, the only way she could identify her quarry from the vision. She should ask if he knew Bertie.

"She wants a shandy."

While Georg retreated to the bar to get her drink, Liliha pondered. Of the two Georges, the one at the bar looked a more probable thief. Nothing like the smart appearance of Harry beside her. Maybe she should approach this rough George. Not a pleasant thought. Aged about thirty years, the scrawny, dark-haired man carried his shoulders high. His narrowed eyes shifted to fix on sudden movements. Her gaze slid along his jeans to his feet. Pointy-toed boots with Cuban heels.

The stranger's eyes rose to catch hers.

Liliha flushed and glanced away fast. So much for avoiding his gaze. The man from the train? Couldn't tell from the few times she'd glimpsed him.

"The waitress will be here to take our meal order soon." Harry reached inside his jacket pocket and pulled out a notebook. "Take a look at this. I'm trying to figure out what to say on my business card." He handed his jotted words over. "Hope you don't mind if I leave you for a minute. I'll be back before you know it." He slid out the other side of the table and headed toward the rear of the room.

She peeked at dark-haired George at the bar before glancing at Harry's writing. 'Seeking an accountant to maximize your company's financial goals? Harry Mendoza, accountant at large.'

Light and dark flickered. Perfume wafted into her senses. Glad about being alone, Liliha tightened her muscles ready for the impending vision. With a sudden tilt, her perception spun out of control.

***

Below, a streetlight illuminates houses. Slender legs carry me along. High-heeled shoes click and echo in a dark street. I'm within a woman already. She recollects a recent conversation with giggling friends, during which someone calls her name. I experience the movement as Trudy glances over her shoulder at the man following her, wishing she could return to safety.

Unlit houses stand side-by-side along the street fronted by small gardens. Trudy increases her pace toward the corner ahead. She abandons an impulse to hammer on one of the doors. Another friend lives close. If she can just reach the end, she'll run to safety.

With me inside, her breath comes fast. We stumble.

'You can do it,' I whisper in her mind in an effort to calm her. 'Concentrate.'

Gasping, we straighten and hurry on.

Her jumbled thoughts override mine. 'Get to the gate. Someone better be inside. What if they're not? Can I reach home? Shoes are awkward ... throw them off. No. I'd have to stop.' We sob.

I generate a surge of strength to her, and then make a mental leap to deal with the follower. Thank the Lord I'm not locked into Trudy on this occasion.

In a flash, I hover over the man lurching behind, and then meld. He's young and drunk, out for a thrill. His inebriated thoughts don't divulge his name. I snatch random information. His plans for the woman ahead are lustful, possibly violent. Needing some street-cred, he'll tell his mates about his exploit.

What can I do to slow him? He's bilious. I send the idea of doubling over and suggest a comforting image of relief.

We stop, grunt and spill the contents of our stomach into a garden. Not pleasant. A house light flicks on. A growled curse comes from a high window. We gaze up at the twitching curtains. Humiliation withers our erection.

A sour taste produces another retch. We swerve and retreat.

All he wants is to crawl into bed—feel his mother's soft hands on his head.

'You should be ashamed,' I whisper. 'What will she think of this behavior when she hears reports?'

He listens to the voice of reason. Rising alarm causes a stumble over a jutting pavement slab.

He'll remember this lesson. I leave his revolting body.

I surge forward and rejoin Trudy, too panicked to notice his absence. I whisper, 'It's all right now. Slow down.' I hope she's listening. I empathize with the girl the same age as my own daughter Kaelyn. Before I leave, Trudy needs to conquer her fear.

Someone ahead. We pull up, heart fluttering.

"Alright, love?" An old man stops and his dog sniffs her.

"Help me," we gasp. "There's someone following me."

"Wait here," he says. "We'll take a look, won't we, Tiger?" They reach the corner and halt. "No one here. Come and see."

Trudy doesn't want to advance. What if the old man's tricking her? We flex, ready to run.

I whisper, 'You're safe. The man came from the opposite direction.'

After a huge breath, we step toward the man, checking his body language. He remains impassive. His dog jumps beside him, giving the occasional impatient yip. Taking a deep breath, we approach. The stalker is nowhere in sight.

"Thank you."

With relief replacing terror, Trudy's open to a nudge in the right direction. I whisper, 'When alone at night, carry a Mace spray. Always let someone know where you are. Take a mobile phone to contact the police.'

With a determined nod, she accepts my suggestions as part of the normal inner voice guiding her.

I lift away.

***

Inside the pub surrounded by chatter, Liliha rubbed her eyes. Appealing to someone's better nature usually worked. In a roundabout way, the method influenced the stalker. Most people possessed the inner prompt, just as they sometimes acted on outrageous ideas.

Harry and Georg approached the table together.

Georg presented her drink with a flourish and a slight bow before sitting opposite.

She returned Harry's notebook and accepted the cold glass, slippery with condensation.

Georg sighed. "I've had a rotten day."

"You're not alone." Harry slid his pad away. "Alright?" he asked her.

"I like the words you've written for the card, Harry."

"Thanks." The smile he gave lacked his usual optimism. "Bottoms up. Drink makes every problem go away." Harry focused on his lifted glass. "Reason being: you can't remember."

"I doubt I could forget this one. Everything's gone wrong." Georg gulped half of his pint.

After taking a sip of the refreshing drink, Liliha's gaze fell on Georg's signet ring. Her heart picked up its beat while she recalled the one the George from her vision had worn. Pulling her thoughts together, she said, "The best thing to do is to concentrate on a good outcome."

The men glanced at each other with raised brows.

"Keep your outlook positive," Liliha said. "I believe thoughts can influence everything around you—even the rest of the world."

"Rather strong statement," Georg said. "How on earth would that work?" His laugh rang with derision.

She sipped the bubbly, sweet drink, which left an

aftertaste of bitterness. Caught up in her conviction, nothing deterred her from speaking. "I think you connect to the universal consciousness, and everyone works together." Her awareness rose. The air sparkled with possibility.

Georg said, "Do you really believe that? Or are you just spouting off?"

Fired with enthusiasm, Liliha drew in a breath to explain.

"As we're expounding theories," Harry said, "I think we were seeded by aliens long ago."

Liliha leaned forward. "Go on."

"Like the little gray men they found at Roswell." Harry lifted his chin. "What if aliens implanted early man and sat back to watch how we progressed over time? And those guys are keeping a watch on us."

"I'm not keen on your idea." Liliha sipped her drink. "It wipes out the bible story of creation."

"What about," Harry asked, "when the sons of God mated with the daughters of man?"

Georg cut in. "That was a fragment taken from a myth. All nonsense. We're in charge of our own life. Here's what I think." His rugged face pinched up. "The creator is a computer programmer. He's set mankind up as avatars and let us loose to see who works out the best. There are no rules."

"I agree," Liliha said. "Each person is free to choose good or bad."

"What if the programmer," Harry said, "is the leader of the little gray men?"

"I like to think of the programmer as God," Liliha said, although neither man took notice.

"Let me make my point," Georg said. "We avatars run around grabbing as much as we can get away with. The one who acquires the most is the winner."

Liliha asked, "Well, how come the programmer didn't create all his avatars the same? Why are some weak and some strong—mentally and physically? That's just not fair. How could the weak win?"

"It's up to them to rise," Georg said, "any way they can."

Harry leaned forward with a frown. "The little gray men could have just left us to breed and interbreed, obeying all the laws of nature." He glared at Georg. "In nature, the strongest survive."

"My point exactly." Georg's voice rose. "The strongest make off with the goods."

Liliha glanced from one to the other. "I don't think life's about personal wealth."

They both turned on her.

"What is life about, then?" Georg asked, maintaining a stern expression.

"Making the right decisions," she said. "Putting the needs and desires of others on the same level as your own."

"We're not ants," Harry said, "working for the colony."

"Or bees," Georg said, "gathering honey."

"We're people," Liliha said, lips a little looser than usual. Probably the alcohol. "We should help each other."

"Are you okay with this discussion, Liliha?" Harry asked.

She nodded. *Not exactly.* But at least the debate made her think.

"Do you share everything you have?" A strange light shone from Georg's eyes.

Liliha gulped the rest of her drink. "Not everything. I need to keep enough to survive."

"What about your ring?" Georg stared at her star moonstone.

Liliha sighed. "We can't share everything. Somebody has to own each thing."

"That's my point," Georg said, loud and strident. "It's up to each individual to accumulate."

"I speculate to accumulate," Harry said with a laugh. "On the horses."

"Say I wanted your ring." Georg drew a breath and concentrated on Liliha. "Would you give it to me?"

Liliha tightened up inside and said, "No."

"If I begged? If I told you I needed it?"

Liliha placed her other palm over the smooth stone. "The ring belongs to me."

Harry shifted in his seat beside her.

"By what right?" Georg asked. "The programmer wants me to have it. I got a direct message." He gazed up at the smoke-stained ceiling.

Liliha fiddled with her empty glass. "Your great programmer sent the ring to my grandmother and she passed the inheritance on to me."

"But we should share," Georg said. "Help me out here, Harry."

Harry leaned closer to Liliha. "Leave her alone, Georg. She needs another drink."

"Let me try the ring on," Georg held out his hand. "At least you can share. Go on."

She shook her head.

A slight frown creased Harry's brow. "You're acting like a bully."

"Give me one good reason why you won't share," Georg said.

An edgy laugh escaped her. "Because I don't want

to."

Georg gestured with his outstretched hand, curling his fingers toward him. "Let me hold it."

"I could just say no."

"You wouldn't want to be selfish," Georg said.

Anger rose inside her. "I could leave, right now."

"Don't go away mad." Georg's voice took on a teasing tone. He reached for her hand.

She shrank inside, wishing she could pull away, but unable to be rude. The gentleness of his touch surprised her. Turning her hand over so the palm faced up, he stroked the sensitive center with his thumb.

Harry leaned away with a laugh. "You had me going there."

Georg sighed. "I'd hoped you could practice what you preached, Liliha." At his release, her hand landed on the table between them with a soft thud. "I didn't intend to keep the ring."

Now she'd offended him. She glanced at Harry. "What do you think?" She blinked and tilted her head. "Should I?"

"Up to you." Harry gulped the rest of his drink. "He's promised to give it back. Who's getting the next round?"

At Georg's assurance, she cradled her ring hand and gazed into the stone. With a soft sigh, she eased the ring off her finger and clutched the weight in the palm of her other hand. Inch by inch, she stretched toward Georg, and then relaxed her fingers to expose the ring. Why did her heart flutter so much?

In a light gesture, Georg lifted the ring. He leaned away from her and sighed. "Hello, little ring." He slid the band over his smallest finger.

A young woman approached to take their food order.

Harry asked for more drinks. Making a quick selection, Liliha chose tacos, something she'd never prepare at home. Uneasy and unsure, she gazed at Georg's finger.

Chapter Twenty-Nine

Georg glanced up from the ring, noting Liliha's slight frown and flickering smile. He'd spouted a lot of nonsense to extract this insignificant item of jewelry. Still, if Straten showed an interest, he should make an effort. Georg froze at Harry's watchful gaze. The guy seemed to know his plans. "The pair of you are looking at me as if I've just made off with the crown jewels."

"The ring's important to Liliha," Harry said.

"Nice ring," Georg said, "but probably of little value." He needed to take the item to Straten when he left for London tomorrow. "This old thing is hardly worth all the fuss. Nothing against your grandmother, Liliha."

She opened her mouth as if to speak, but instead sighed and relaxed, never taking her gaze away from the ring.

George gave an internal chuckle. *A doe all right.*

A barmaid brought their food to the table and Georg devoured his fish and fries.

Now she'd parted with the ring, he'd have to blind her with nonsense. "Back to our conversation about the computer programmer and the avatars." He gulped a mouthful of bitter to wash away the greasy taste, and then slid the ring on and off his finger.

Harry groaned. "Go on." He pushed a piece of lettuce aside.

Liliha extended her hand as if she wanted to snatch the ring, but instead, picked up another taco.

"Let's say the programmer wanted me to have this ... ring."

"How would you know?" Harry asked.

197

"I'm aware of everything. I left South Africa—another twist of the dial from the programmer—and arrived in Cornwall." He probed Liliha's down-turned eyes until she gazed up. "We were destined to meet."

She frowned.

"The natural progression is for me to acquire the ring. Fate. Kismet. The stars." He gave a hearty laugh and reached for his glass.

"I've already avoided giving it to the museum," Liliha said.

"There you are." Georg swigged a few bitter mouthfuls. "Just shows you had to save it for me." He settled his glass on the coaster and ran his thumb over the smooth stone. "Nice. Thank you programmer."

"Liliha gave it to you, not the pro—"

"Thank you, Liliha."

"I didn't ..." Liliha leaned forward, "give it. I let you hold the ring." She reached for his hand, hers unsteady. "Hand it over, now."

Georg avoided her reach, twisting the ring on his finger. "I'm not finished."

"Look," Harry said. "This is getting out of hand. Enough is enough. Give the ring to her." He drew himself up. The light of camaraderie in his eyes changed to opposition. "Let Liliha relax and enjoy herself."

"Take no notice. I'm having a bit of fun." Georg waved his hand in the air. He'd try to keep them talking, although he might have to take drastic measures if things didn't go his way. Pity about Harry—he liked the guy.

Liliha's soft voice cut the air. "Have you had enough of a laugh, now?" Despite her gentle outward manner, Liliha's inner strength shone in her piercing blue eyes, raised chin and prominent cheek bones.

"Let's have another drink and pursue the subject. It's thirsty work."

"I should be getting home." Liliha checked her watch and recoiled. "I didn't realize the time."

"See what happens when you're enjoying yourself?" Georg asked.

"I wouldn't say—"

"Or when your mind is stimulated." Georg rose and slid his hand into his pocket. "I'll get another round."

He left Harry murmuring with Liliha. Flexing his little finger to order the drinks, the weight of the ring registered. A nearby customer glanced over with raised eyebrows.

When Georg returned with brimming glasses, Liliha leaned closer to Harry. "Hey, you two. Don't leave me out." Georg passed the drinks across the table and eased onto the seat opposite her again.

Liliha extended an open palm. "My ring, please, Georg."

"So polite."

"She's getting anxious now, squire. Hand it over."

"I'm not programmed to return the ring." Georg made a show of slurping the froth off the top of his drink. "Cheers."

"I, for one, am not programmed." A flush rose over Liliha's cheeks. "I have free will to act the way I please. I take pleasure in helping people in need." She drew herself up. "But you're not needy, Georg. And that's my ring, which I allowed you to hold out of the goodness of my heart."

"And what a big heart you have, my dear."

"It's not funny, and it's not a game," Liliha said.

"Return the ring now." Her outstretched hand didn't waver, and neither did the strength of her gaze.

"Do I get a reward?" Georg's chest expanded.

"What?" Harry said.

The fellow didn't bother him. "A kiss would release the ring," Georg said, making love to her eyes.

Liliha said to Harry, "It's okay." Half standing, she leaned toward his cheek.

At the last second, Georg turned so his lips met hers. She tasted nice and he wished the table didn't separate them. As she withdrew, he rose and savored her warmth until they separated.

Harry frowned. "You've gone too far. Give her the ring and we'll leave."

Liliha held her shoulders rigid. "Give me your ring to look at in exchange."

A sudden notion jolted Georg. He liked her. A pain erupted in his stomach. *Don't get soft.* "Another challenge," he shouted to deflect his shock. "Which ring should I choose?"

"The game's over now," Harry said. A threat hung between them.

Rather than spoil this wonderful sense of belonging and hold his purpose inside, Georg allowed his determination to collapse. "'Course I will. Here you are." He pulled at the ring with little enthusiasm. He could say the band was stuck. Why did he enjoy the feeling of the ring on his finger so much? When he slid the weight off, a sense of oppression overcame him. He handed the item over. "Thank you, my dear. Very charming of you to play with me. Please excuse my manner. I never meant to offend you."

Liliha accepted her ring with trembling fingers, and

then replaced it on her finger. Breathing out with a soft sigh, her worried expression cleared.

"It's only a ring," Georg said. What now? His plan wasn't about to eventuate any time soon, and certainly not before he left for London.

***

After waving to Harry, Liliha switched on her hall light and closed the front door behind her. She leaned against the solid frame. In the space of a day, two people had demanded her possessions. Why didn't she give in? Everyone should share. Something nagged at her—an opportunity to change and grow. But she balked at Ellen taking Alissa's brush and took exception to Georg claiming the moonstone ring. She'd stand her ground, protect her rights.

The effects of the alcohol went to her head. The trip home had hardly registered with her mind stimulated by their discussions. Nobody had ever asked if they could wear her ring before. She'd twitched the whole time about the possibility of Georg being swept into a vision.

Once again, she pondered on the significance of her visions. Apart from learning more about the world and the people who lived there, she wondered if she'd ever figure out why the mind-shift occurred. A search on the internet looking for the connection between inanimate objects and memories hadn't produced any results.

She strolled along the passage and into the kitchen. All straight. Nothing disturbed. Pausing, she propped herself against the work surface to stop the alarming vertigo. Although drinking too much might be the answer to reducing pain, the practice didn't appeal.

Georg van den Burg couldn't be the man from her vision. Anyway, he didn't give the impression of a house thief. He'd taken her ring, but surely he'd done so in fun. If he'd really intended to steal it, he wouldn't have acted in such an open way. And Harry had been with her to oversee the whole thing. Okay, Georg wore a signet ring. He hadn't fallen for her ploy to inspect his ring either. But she'd need concrete evidence before she could condemn him, especially now she'd seen the other George—a far more likely prospect with his seedy expression, Cuban heeled boots, and lank, curly hair.

The bench supported her while she adjusted to the unsettling way the room lurched. She wasn't the best judge of appearances now or in the past. Some men, including her first husband, could show any side of their character they chose. Best to remain wary of any man—particularly one called George.

Chapter Thirty

Before dawn, van den Burg headed east for London. So much rested on finding Matt.

Surrounded by idling cars on the outskirts of the city, his mind drifted to the intriguing conversation with Harry and Liliha in the pub the night before. He'd taunted her with his guile, but she remained so firm in her opinion. The closer Georg got to his destination, the more Liliha's ethereal beauty lured him. However, she wasn't for him. A fairy and a garden gnome made strange companions.

He needed a woman of his own. One he picked for himself—one who shared similar ideas—not someone his father foisted on him.

But his lifestyle might need adjusting to appeal to this unknown person.

The glint of the scarab bracelet entered his mind. He rubbed his forehead, shocked at his reaction to a possession. A car pulled onto the road from the curb. Slamming on the brakes, he drew in a breath to avoid yelling. *Hold on, van den Burg. You decided to get rid of the jewel. Before the enticement got into your head any further.*

Now he understood why men accumulated treasures. Paintings, antiquities, diamonds. Was the bracelet any different? Or the ring?

He'd convinced Liliha to hand it over once. Having won her confidence, he could do so again, in a gentle fashion. Wouldn't want to crush her fairy wings.

When he reached the London suburb on the address Straten had supplied, he parked at the station. With no inspectors in sight, he didn't bother to purchase a ticket from the machine. Leaving his vehicle, he hiked along the busy street, checking the slip of paper.

A flight of stairs behind a row of small shops led to the flat number. He followed the rail to the front balcony, and knocked on Matt's door. No sound came from inside. At almost midday, the thieving jackal should be awake.

The roar of traffic below combined with a bus's squeaking brakes. Stifled by the fumes, Georg knocked again.

An old man emerged from the stairs he'd just mounted, approached on bowed legs and glanced over.

"I'm looking for the man who lives here," Georg said.

"He's been away a couple of days now." The old man shuffled on.

"Thanks." George's footsteps echoed on his gallop downstairs to the shaded ground behind the building. Litter spread from one corner and scattered paper lifted in the wind. What a place to live. Not for him.

Heading for his car, he passed young women chatting together while pushing babies in buggies.

He caught sight of two policemen and ducked into a newsagent in panic. He'd left fingerprints on the white van he'd driven away from the heist. The guards had seen his face too. Pretty sloppy.

Take a breath. Nothing linked him to the heist in Truro.

Heaviness dragged at his chest while he stood rigid. Why had he fallen in with Straten's plans? He'd acted the part of a scavenger—taking advantage of an opportunity.

When he'd completed this job of finding Matt and getting the bastard to admit culpability, he'd search for another position.

The shop attendant looked over with narrowed eyes. Georg purchased a newspaper, and then turned to the entrance. The officers passed by. He perused a car magazine before slipping outside.

This trip had been a bloody waste of time. Cursing Matt, Georg strode toward the car park.

A man in uniform strode past the taxi-rank, clip-board held ready. Georg hurried to his car, climbed in and started the engine.

The inspector knocked on his window. Georg shouted, "I'm just going." He forced a smile, waved and sped away.

***

Ellen reached deep inside the warm dryer to remove a last sock. Straightening in her comfy tracksuit, she grabbed its twin. Mary worked beside her as if they'd known each other forever. Ellen envisaged an easy life.

A man with short blond hair passed by outside the launderette window. Ellen drew a breath in alarm and froze, unable break her gaze from his strutting walk. Matt!

He stopped and turned.

He'd found her. *Quick. Hide.* Ellen blurted, "I'm just going out back."

"Are you all right?" Mary asked. "You look a bit pale."

Ellen nodded and ducked out of the steamy atmosphere. No time to explain.

Ellen stood panting in the small storeroom. She glanced from the high window over the shop door, and then to the exit. Run or hide? At least he couldn't see into the room. She checked the lock to the rear lane. She'd be all right here, as long as he didn't force his way past Mary. Had she ever mentioned Matt? Couldn't remember.

Without meaning to, the woman might give her away.

After using the toilet, Ellen wondered what was going on in the main room. Machines bumped and whirred. Occasional chatter. A man's voice rose. She recognized the tone. Mary could come in to check on her at any moment. She had to get out of here. Matt couldn't catch her again.

Ready to leave, she struggled into her coat and grabbed her bag. She should change her appearance. But how?

Pile her hair on top the way Liliha had shown her. The change might mask her for a precious fraction of a second. All done, she turned the key and eased the door open.

Sighing with relief at the sight of an empty lane, she closed the door, and sped away. Perhaps she could get lost in the crowd closer to town. Nobody followed, but she couldn't relax, knowing Matt's ways. Dominant, leader of the pack, he always reached his goal. And he'd owned her—sent her out to earn him money. Matt wasn't a man to give up.

How did he track her here? Panting, she tried to remember if she'd revealed where she was going. Then she recalled a conversation with a customer about the western tip of England. Did she give him the impression she'd go there? Surely, he wouldn't pass idle talk on. She tripped on uneven pavement and slowed her pace.

Tears stung her eyes when she reached the street. Although other people filled the footpath, she didn't feel safe. The man who passed her might never know what went on in the lower side of life—first in line to her door, but last to think of her fate.

Her choices lay between a life of punishment filled

with a haze of drugs, or death. She couldn't face taking her own life. Didn't have the courage. She rejected police protection. After awkward questions, they wouldn't help someone like her.

A woman pushing a baby stroller hurried past. Ellen couldn't ask her for a place to hide, or the two older ladies strolling together with bulging carrier bags.

She'd already used Liliha's cottage for her own ends and couldn't expect help from her now.

Ellen scurried inside a shopping mall. Light penetrated from the glass roof. *Find somewhere dark.* She rushed on, dodging between hurrying and dawdling people, push-chairs, and occasional motorized wheel-chairs. Everyone must be out today.

She couldn't return to the flat. Matt might have found out she was staying with Mary. He told a good yarn to charm the ladies. He'd hooked her the same way.

Don't think about the past. Her former existence was over.

She caught sight of a blond head bobbing amongst the crowd. Panic held her rigid.

Relief surged. Not Matt. Her body bumped against a portly man. "Sorry." She wrenched herself away and stumbled on, upset about the memory of Liliha's kindness, which she'd abused. Why did she forget the best, most important thing in life? Trust and friendship.

Hide, hide, hide.

Chapter Thirty-One

After returning to his digs in Cornwall, Georg flicked on the light. The bracelet, hidden inside the dark confines of the boiler cupboard, had been on his mind during the long drive from London. But what if the box went missing too?

Head pounding, he grabbed a screwdriver and headed for the kitchen to check. *Better lower the blinds from prying eyes.* Once completed, he grasped the tool again, levered up the loose floorboard and opened the lid.

His stash was safe. "Thank God!" At least he might make some money out of his ... deception.

The shift of events worried him—a botched heist, and then the cartons stolen from his shed. To top things off, he hadn't found Matt. *Come on van den Burg. Don't give up.*

Fingers sliding between strands of his hair, he returned to the kitchen. Food or a hot drink didn't appeal. Too agitated to sleep, he retraced his steps outside, hopped into the car, and headed for St. Ives.

***

With slippers on her aching feet, Liliha prepared food in the kitchen. At a slight rap, she strode to the front door and peered out. Nobody. She glanced either way along the dark empty street, frowned and closed the door. The knock came again, but from the direction of the living room, which opened onto the rear. She approached the glass door and peered outside into the gloom. Someone outside.

She leaned closer to the door. An outline of swept-up hair. Ellen. Liliha released her breath and clicked the lock.

The girl stumbled inside, hunched over as though rain lashed her. "Liliha. I'm sorry. Do you mind if I ...? Can I

...?" Tears slid along her cheeks.

"What's wrong?" Liliha eased her arm over Ellen's shaking shoulders. "Hold on." Liliha flicked the lock, and then faced Ellen. "Start at the beginning."

"I've been hiding in your shed."

"Why? Sit down and tell me." Liliha jumped at the chance to make amends for her earlier outburst. Grief didn't excuse the rude things she'd said.

Ellen brushed the trousers of her tracksuit and glanced at the sofa. "I'm grubby."

"You're cold too. Let me get you a blanket." Liliha lifted a rug from her chair and spread the soft folds on the sofa. "Sit on top and we'll wrap the ends around you. You can take your coat off. You'll warm up soon."

Once she'd dropped her outer garment on the floor, Ellen snuggled inside the blanket. "Thanks." Her high voice vibrated in the top of her nose. "I don't deserve your kindness." More tears spilled before she caught her breath. "I need somewhere to hide."

"You're safe here for the moment. I'll make you a chocolate drink. Could be shock. Sugar will help. Just relax and get warm. I'll be right back and you can tell me everything."

The girl closed her eyes.

Halfway along the hall, Liliha's steps halted beside the papyrus of Lilihaffertiti, considering how to deal with Ellen.

Inhaling a blast of perfume, she pressed against the wall. A familiar motion sucked her into the breach between her existence and the mind of another.

***

I'm occupying a toned body—male by the appearance of the broad, smooth hands gripping both ends

209

of a stretched towel. Sunlight penetrates from overhead windows and the hint of sweat rises in the steam. Shouts fill the air—young male voices with American accents, loud and demanding.

I attempt to disregard the overpowering personality I find myself within. Everything about him screams alpha male. We enter a changing room and shove a stray football helmet onto a shelf.

"Shaun." The voice echoes.

We stretch the fabric again and turn to face Shaun, all elbows and knees, his jaw covered with fluff. Our hands flip an end at his protruding hip bones.

"Cut it out." Shaun cowers against the wall, his dropped towel covering one foot.

I pick up Ralph's thoughts. 'Why didn't the weenie flick the thing in my face? Maybe I'd stop giving him shit.'

One of the coaches frowns at the boys before collecting a pile of towels. He walks from the room. The assistant coach finishes patching up a kid's wound and follows him.

Urged on by his companions' glances, Ralph strokes his chin. "You're a wuss. Why don't you stand up to me?"

"You and all the others," Shaun says in a squeaky voice. "Ten against one. How's that fair?"

"You scared? You have to go with the flow, roll with the punches. My old man taught me that."

"I want to play ..." Shaun stutters. "Give me a chance."

While the adolescents jeer, I whisper into Ralph's forceful mind. 'Leave him alone. It's not his fault he's small.'

We rub our forehead. Shaun's a late developer like Ralph's own brother, one year behind him in age. Cried when a fox ate his pet chicken. Ralph sighs. "Never mind, you pansy. I don't have time for you." We grin at the closest boys. "Hey. Did you see the legs on that red-haired cheerleader? Hot."

A big adolescent with cropped hair pounds on a locker. "I'll finish him."

"No skin off my nose." Conscience battles with Ralph's desire to lead. We stroll to the seat. Uniforms drape over the bench beside us.

Taunts fill the air.

A coach pokes his head into the room. "Settle down, boys. We're about to have a meeting. Behave your damn selves." The door closes.

After a subdued hush, the adolescent voices grow in strength. "Shove him in the locker."

The youths laugh. Shaun jerks to avoid a grip on his elbow, but someone else grasps his arm.

'Are you going to sit there and let them torment him?' My question doesn't raise a response. I urge, 'Whatever comes of this, you'll all be lumped together. You're their leader.'

Muscles relaxing after a hard game, Ralph frowns when a couple of kids grab a rope from the wall beside the fire hydrant. "Shut up, you guys," he calls. "Why are you so bothered by a sub?"

The room stills. Two boys who are tying the rope on Shaun glance over.

'They're yours to lead right here, right now,' I whisper. 'You might never get another chance to do something strong and worthwhile. You're at the crossroads. On one side you're a good example, on the other you're a bully. Choose.'

Ralph stands. "Chill out, guys. We just played one of

211

the best games ever—hard, too. We killed them, twenty-one to nothing."

A few cheers erupt.

"I don't know about you, but I want to get better and better." Our glance sweeps over the youths' slack mouths. "Anyone who gets their fun with a jerk off, needs to think again. I'm out."

Their expressions tighten.

'Give them more,' I whisper. 'Talk about Shaun.'

We drop onto the bench. "Can't you see it? He ain't nothin'. Leave him alone." Ralph fidgets when nobody changes their stance. Like his brother, Shaun needs to learn how to fight. "Bring him here."

Two youths lead their prisoner forward. Shaun struggles against them. Some fold their arms and nod.

Ralph sighs. He wouldn't want his kid brother to be in the same position.

'This is it,' I whisper. 'Make or break.'

"How'd you like to learn to fight?" Ralph asks.

"Against how many?" Shaun whines.

"Yeah, yeah," voices shout.

"Cut the crap," Ralph snaps. "I'm trying to work something out." We pull a jersey over our head.

"What?" the big youth jeers.

"Set him up in the middle," a half-broken voice yells. "Whoever he faces gets to punch him."

"That'll teach him."

"Are we a team or what?" Ralph growls into the enthusiastic yells. "Or just a bunch of chickenshits?"

Voices hush. A few youths bite their lips and shuffle their feet.

"Listen." We stand tall, and then shove our dirty jersey into a bag. Number sixteen. They'll remember him

for a long time. "This is our final year before college. We need to stick together. Who's with me?"

One by one, they relax and nod to each other.

"Just kidding, Shaun," one murmurs.

The boys remove the ropes and slap him on the back.

I give Ralph a prod. 'Have the talk you were planning.'

We pat the bench beside us and bend to tie our laces. "What about it? Want to learn self-defense?"

Shaun nods.

"Come over to my house every Tuesday after school. I'll arrange something with my brother and his friends." We mock-punch his arm.

Pleased at Ralph's acceptance of my prompt, I drift away.

***

Liliha opened her eyes and faced the kitchen. Shaun's isolation because of his size had caused the problem. Why did everyone have to conform? At least Ralph had been decent underneath. Most people contained a spark of morality. Thank the Lord, she hadn't needed to deal with the influence from the bracelet during the vision. The task of changing Ralph's outlook had been difficult enough without Doom's presence. Perhaps the person who'd taken the bracelet, with its wicked suggestions, had worked out the problem and locked away the evil influence.

Somehow, Shaun's experience tied into Ellen's problem. Did the runaway need to defend herself? Maybe so.

First things first. Make the drink. Then find out what troubled Ellen.

***

Noisy chatter interspersed with occasional shouts

filled the pub where Georg sat drinking. Several empty glasses and two full ones dotted the table.

Harry returned from the cigarette huddle outside, seated himself, and fixed his attention on the overseas soccer match which was being played in sunlight on the big screen.

The barmaid obviously couldn't keep up with the demanding crowd. Georg didn't mind. More people made the place a hub of activity. He could think uninterrupted.

A whistle blew, marking half time. Harry faced him and sighed. "Can you follow the rules?"

"I'm getting there," Georg said. "We like rugby in South Africa. Not this soccer you English call football."

"Who cares what you call the game? I've had a hard day, trying to drum up business. I don't know how I'd relax without this." Harry raised his drink.

"I know what you mean. My day didn't go too well either."

"Exactly what line of work are you in?" Harry asked.

Georg scratched his cheek. "Product development." He gave a cocky grin.

"Interesting. What sort of goods?"

Georg searched for an answer to keep the guy sweet. "Cars, if you must know."

"Ah." Harry's eyes assessed him. The guy suspected. "New or used?"

"Logistics." Relocating items belonging to someone else without their consent. Georg frowned in concentration.

"What?"

"Too complicated to go into when we're drinking."

"Right." Harry faced the screen where experts discussed the first half of the match. "None of my business."

"One thing you could help me with."

Harry turned with his brows raised.

"Have you seen any strangers hanging about?"

"What sort of question is that? This is a holiday town." Harry's smile could belong to a movie star, but warmth didn't reach his eyes.

Georg leaned close. "A blond bloke, with fair skin and huge attitude, if you know what I mean."

"You're searching for someone. Friend or foe?"

"Someone who's pissed me off."

"I'll ask and let you know."

"How many contacts do you have here?"

"Enough for your purposes," Harry said. "You can go somewhere else with your questions for all I care."

After a whistle blew, the television commentary began.

"Don't take offense at my ways. South Africans are known for their direct approach."

"Better adapt if you want to stay." Harry's features tightened. "And stay away from Liliha."

Or what? Georg sipped his drink.

***

After a long talk with Ellen, Liliha led her guest upstairs to the spare room. "The clothes you returned are in the wardrobe. You might as well use them tomorrow. A shower will relax you. Pop into bed when you're finished." Liliha grinned. "Unless you feel like painting the town."

Ellen shook her head.

Liliha gave a mock frown. "No sleepwalking."

"Sorry, Liliha. I thought that's what ya' ... you ... expected. Payment, like."

"I tried to tell you." Liliha touched Ellen's shoulder. "I'll call the launderette in the morning and give your

215

excuses. Don't worry. Just stay here and relax. I'll think of a way to help you by tomorrow."

Ellen's sigh sent her hair tendrils quivering. "Thanks."

With a blank mind, Liliha padded downstairs. Harry might suggest something. She reached for the phone and selected his number. Faint commotion accompanied his answer.

"It's Liliha. I've got a problem and I wondered if you could advise me."

"Hold on. Too noisy here. I'll pop outside."

The sounds dulled. He must be walking.

"Right." He exhaled. Probably smoke. "Let me have it."

She explained. "The poor kid's terrified. God knows what sort of hold he has over her."

"I can guess. Leave it to me. I'll see if there's anyone new in the area, acting suspicious. Funny. Georg just asked me the same thing."

"Did he? Sounds fishy." Liliha drew a breath. "Something else too. I think someone broke in here last week. I found signs of disturbance. I need a new lock fitted. Do you know anyone who could do a good job?"

"Now we've got two problems. Is she safe with you?"

Chapter Thirty-Two

Liliha opened the door to admit Harry. His wonderful smile relieved her. She didn't have to shoulder Ellen's appearance alone.

He glanced about the hallway. "Where is she?"

"Asleep upstairs. Come into the living room." Liliha led the way and gestured to the sofa. Harry perched on the edge, hunched forward over his knees. Liliha settled into her chair. "Sorry about the slippers."

Harry batted the air, and then swallowed a yawn. "Sorry. I can't hack early mornings, and I've got another one looming tomorrow."

"I know what you mean." Not true, but her sympathy might reassure him. "All things considered ..." Liliha drew a breath. "Do you think it's advisable for Ellen to stay here with me?"

"Depends on who's after her and whether they can get in."

"She didn't tell me much, but I gathered she worked as a prostitute for a man named Matt."

"Could get nasty." They stared at each other for the space of several heartbeats.

Harry broke the silence. "I think she should find another place to hide for a few days. Somewhere secluded. You don't want a thug trashing your home because of her." He jerked to attention. "Oh, yeah. You mentioned someone breaking in before. Did they take anything?"

"Just shifted things about. Guess they didn't think I'd notice."

His glance swept the room. "You would." A smile lifted the corners of his mouth.

"Where could she go?" Liliha asked.

"That's the problem." He yawned again. "Meantime, I'll see if I can get the lock changed for you. Sorry I can't offer more help."

"Thank you, anyway." Liliha rose.

He tilted his head. "What if I stay here and guard the place? By tomorrow, you might have worked out somewhere else she could go."

"Would you?" Relief surged into her.

Harry nodded. "Set me up on the sofa. I can sleep here just as well as in my flat. Don't worry. I won't smoke inside. I'll pop out into the garden for a quick puff and look-around soon."

"Good." Liliha relaxed her shoulders and hurried to gather bedding.

The consideration of a strange man sleeping in her home overnight brought up the image of his tousled hair in the morning. She replaced the thought with Oliver's beloved image while she headed upstairs.

Tomorrow, she'd have to work out what to do with Ellen.

***

Pale light suffused the sky. Liliha crept downstairs wrapped in her fluffy bathrobe. With no way to see into the living room, she eased by the doorway.

Ideas swirled inside her mind in the chilly air. She set them aside. After gulping a full glass of water, she placed the tumbler beside the sink with care so she wouldn't disturb Harry, and then retreated to her bedroom instead of the living room to start her exercise and meditation routine.

Half an hour later, a plan had formed. The world presented a much more ordered spectacle on the way downstairs.

She peeped into the living room. Empty! Harry had

left without alerting her with a creak or a shuffle. Nothing. A note told her to re-lock the door.

The cuckoo chirped eight times. Her visitor in the bedroom overhead remained silent. Liliha wandered into the kitchen and selected some fruit. An orange delighted her palate with explosions of sweet, acidic juice. While she ate a slice of pineapple, she thanked the creator for the gift of taste and the wonder of nature. Everything balanced in a perfect way.

A faint swish alerted her to the toilet flushing.

She strode to the base of the staircase and yelled, "Don't go back to sleep, Ellen. Take a shower while I work on something." The water spray might wake her up.

Liliha hovered in the hall, perusing contacts, and then rang a few familiar people out of the area. No luck.

Running out of options, she remembered Alana from Zenor. The woman's matter-of-fact presence on the train had given her such comfort during a vulnerable time. She seemed like a strong lady.

"Good morning, Alana. I hope I'm not ringing too early."

"Liliha. I'm just finishing breakfast. I've got a busy day ahead with my sewing."

"Great." Pleasure about the successful link she'd arranged flooded Liliha during her stroll to the living room. "Are you enjoying the work?"

"Loving it."

"It's good to have a purpose, isn't it?" Liliha settled in comfort on her chair. "The reason I'm calling is to ask how you'd feel about giving a young woman a place to stay for a few days."

Alana's voice deepened. "What's up?"

"Don't worry. I'll understand if you'd rather not have

a stranger in your home. Or if you don't have room for someone else."

"I'm just thinking," Alana said. "Bryan's caring for his mother and his brother's condition can make things difficult. I should do the same for someone else."

"Wait until you hear about her history before you commit yourself. You see, she's on the run from a man who used to send her out to work at night in London. A hooker." Liliha stroked the armrest twice to let information sink in, and then continued. "I think he's found her here in St. Ives. She's staying with me at the moment." Liliha cleared her throat. "I must warn you. Doing this could place you in danger too if he traces her."

"The poor kid. What's her name?"

"Ellen. She wants to change, honestly she does. I think she's a decent girl. She's just wandered down the wrong path."

"Say no more," Alana said. "I'll take her. If you vouch for her, she must be all right."

Better warn Ellen not to prowl into Alana's bedroom. "I'm not sure if ... No. I think she's okay. She wouldn't harm you." A twinge of doubt caused Liliha to swallow. "She's never hurt me. She's just awkward, without social skills. You have to be firm."

"I can handle her. She can tell me her story in her own time."

"How will we get her out to you? I could ask—"

"I'll come and pick her up." Alana cleared her throat. "She should be in disguise when she leaves the house in case anyone's watching."

"You're right. I'll help her." Liliha drew a hesitant breath. "Are you sure? It's not too late to back out."

"Nonsense. Let's just take one step at a time. It'll

probably be a couple of hours before I finish up. Then, I'll deliver my work, and take ... Ella?"

"Ellen." Liliha said. "That'd be great. If you get here before eleven, I'll still be here."

"I think I could manage. How exciting."

Liliha said, "Don't forget to take care. It's a huge risk to you. Hopefully, if she's left St. Ives, he won't find her. Don't tell anyone she's with you or do anything different from your normal routine. Okay?"

"Sure thing." Alana disconnected.

Liliha's heart pounded loud in her ears. What if she'd done the wrong thing placing Alana at risk?

She filled the sink and plunged her breakfast bowl into soapy water. A knock alerted her. She flung the rubber gloves onto the drainer and hurried along the hall. A stranger stood outside.

"Hello, missus. I've come to fit a new lock for you." The lank-haired workman lowered his toolbox, hands ingrained with dirt.

"Ah, good." Liliha slid her hand over her hair. Perhaps Harry had asked him to come. "Who sent you?"

"Dunno who. I just got the work order and here I am." His eyes narrowed. "You want the work done, don't you?"

Liliha blocked the opening with her body. "I'd like to know who I'm dealing with. What's the name of your company? I'll give them a quick ring."

"Peter McLaughlin. I work for myself. You can ask anyone in the town. I'm well known." His mouth formed a straight line.

"No card?"

"Not big enough."

"Just a minute. Wait there while I call my friend."

Leaving the door open a crack, she grabbed the mobile phone from the hall table, but then glanced at the entrance.

In a few strides, she closed the door while she selected the number. "Harry? Liliha here. Did you arrange for someone to come and fix my lock?"

"Sorry, Liliha. I'll organize something as soon as possible. Things came on top."

"That's all right. It's just ... A workman has turned up and I don't know who sent him."

"Get rid of him, now." Harry's abrupt words overrode occasional clatters and voices.

Liliha checked outside. "Ah, he's gone. What a strange thing. He didn't even wait until I made the call."

"Suspicious. Did you open the door to him?"

"I shouldn't have, should I?"

"Be wary in future. You never know who's outside."

"No harm done. I'll let you get on. Don't worry about organizing the lock. I'll wait a while." Once her job finished in just over a week, she'd have time to oversee the workman. Hopefully, the process wouldn't be too late.

***

Hopkins sauntered into the newsagent on his daily round. The man behind the counter was taking money from the queued customers as fast as his hands could move.

Old Pepper met his glance and nodded. George picked up his newspaper, a part-payment for his security services, and flicked the page to the nude woman. Not bad, although her breasts sagged a bit too much for his liking. He turned away and bumped into a big blond bloke. George shouldered him aside.

"Watch it," the hulk said.

"Or what, buggerlugs?" This was his town and he'd make bloody sure any newcomer got the message.

The guy drew himself up. "You'd better mind who you're talking to."

"A smart-arse from the big city by the look of your fancy clothes. You couldn't brush a mosquito off your nose."

"You piece of shit. You need to be knocked off your perch. Outside."

"Hopkins," Old Pepper called. "No need for trouble."

George ignored the shopkeeper. "Don't mind if I do." He stepped into the fresh breeze to face his well-dressed opponent. The man couldn't do much in his belted jacket with a fancy scarf at his neck. "The owner doesn't want trouble, but I've got other ideas. If you want a good hiding, I'm your man."

"You're full of shit," Blondie said. "What could a weedy little guy do to me?" He stood with legs apart and arms hanging loose.

Several people hurried by with their eyes averted.

George flexed his shoulders. They were stronger than they looked, as the blowhard would find out. His voice rose, matching his anger. "Plenty." He took a swing at the arrogant jaw before him, but the fellow avoided his reach with a sneer.

A passerby glared at them. "Cut it out, the pair of you."

A woman's voice yelled, "Go somewhere else if you must behave like that. We've got children here."

Without a word, Blondie veered toward the beach.

George strode after him, appreciating the padding on his own jacket.

"Leave it. I'll call it quits," the fellow called.

Darned if he would. Who was this fellow with the huge attitude? George determined to look for a chance to topple the brute. On the ground, he'd be easier to overpower.

They reached the deserted pathway at the edge of the sand. George dived at the sturdy legs, but Blondie avoided his grasp. A laugh swirled in the breeze and George landed on his knees. Up in a flash despite the throbbing, he flipped to avoid another charge and growled. He'd never let the guy get the better of him.

They faced each other, circling, while George probed for weakness. He lunged and landed a punch on his opponent's hard jaw. His lucky signet ring raised a welt but didn't break Blondie's skin, worse luck. George clenched his jaw and shrugged off the pain in his hand.

The hulk raised his fist and pounded George before he could dodge aside.

His jaw smarted. He ducked another blow and missed one of his own, breath released in explosive gasps like those of his opponent.

George circled. No pain registered. He'd teach this muscle-bound newcomer who was the better man.

Several people walked by while George avoided a punch.

"Why are those men fighting?" The rest of a child's words blew away.

George charged. They fell and rolled apart.

Blondie didn't spring to his feet this time on his polished boots, but flexed his shoulders and eased onto one knee.

Panting, George stood, hands clenched by his side. His numb jaw throbbed. He couldn't take much more but refused to give in. The bastard would have to kill him.

With his red eyes narrowing, the brute stood and raised fists in front of his face.

Chapter Thirty-Three

Liliha leaned against the kitchen doorjamb and yelled, "Ellen." She jerked her work shirt straight and called again. "Ellen. Breakfast." Why did young women find starting the day at a decent hour so hard?

"Coming." The voice drifted downstairs.

After a pause, Ellen's legs appeared on the stairway, followed by her torso. She yawned when she reached ground level and dawdled behind Liliha into the kitchen.

"Bare floor's cold on my feet."

"Sit down and eat while I explain what I've arranged."

Ellen picked up the steaming mug Liliha set before her and took a sip. "Not sweet enough." She pulled the sugar closer and turned to accept a spoon.

"I want to tell you my plan to get you away from town."

"Where will I go? I can't—"

"I've arranged for a friend to take you in. It's a little place called Zennor."

Ellen grabbed a slice of toast reached for a knife. "What? I'll be trapped in a hick town."

"Alana's a kind lady." Liliha settled at the table with her tea. "She'll make sure you're safe for a while. Friends of mine, Yvonne and William, did the same for me when I first arrived."

Ellen slathered butter over the toast. "I like it here with you." The knife clattered on the table.

Liliha's fingers gripped her mug tighter. Why didn't Ellen appreciate her efforts? She lowered her drink to the table. "I thought you wanted a place to hide. St. Ives isn't safe."

The sulky look disappeared when Ellen took a bite. "But what if Matt sees me when I leave here?"

"Let's disguise you. Got any ideas?"

Ellen munched. "Change my hair color?"

"Not a bad idea, but we don't have time. You've got one hour before Alana arrives."

"I'll cut my hair off. Really short." A particle of food shot out of Ellen's mouth. "Punk. I can make my eyes black. Lips too. Who'd recognize me then?" A frown settled over Ellen's face. "I can't get ready so fast. I'll have no time to think."

"You'll manage. You're strong and adaptable." Liliha assessed her. "Don't be too extreme with your hair cut. Just make it shorter. You'd better adjust the way you walk though. Think mid-forties, instead of sassy fox." She reached out to touch Ellen's arm. "I know you're worried. It must be hard, but you need to change everything about you—even your former life. In the future, don't let anyone push you into doing something you're not happy with. You should make your own choices." Liliha considered how that sounded. Better offer a choice about this too. "Do you want to follow my advice?"

"I ... guess I do." Ellen headed for the stairs. Her trailing voice lacked conviction. "I'll think about what I do from now on."

When the sound of the dryer ceased, Liliha hauled out Ellen's tracksuit. She folded the soft garments, ready to pass on to her guest like more useless advice.

***

George's sight blurred after the newcomer's last punch. The old Hopkins desperation called for another plan. "Sod this. Are we gonna slog each other all day or what?" The distant roar of the sea did nothing to mask his ragged breathing.

"You're a wiry little bastard. More muscle and guts than I gave you credit for." The guy climbed to his feet.

"Quits?"

"You got it."

George shrugged, keeping a watch for any further challenge. "A lot of fuss about nothing."

Blondie held out his hand. "Matt Albright."

After a quizzing stare, George gripped the hand and introduced himself. His knuckles throbbed. "What are you doing on my patch?"

"I'm taking care of business."

George snapped. "This is my area."

"Seems to me, we could help each other."

"I'll help you leave all right."

"Soon as I find what I'm looking for. I'm searching for a woman."

George gave a single explosive laugh. "I know a few."

"A particular woman. Goes by the name of Ellen. Thin face, brown hair. She'd be new in town."

"Yeah. Plenty of tourists. What's it to me?" *If the smart-arse thought he could push old Hopkins around, he had another think coming.*

"As I said, we could watch each other's backs."

George sniffed. "What did you have in mind to help me?"

"Let me know what you need. While I'm in town, I might as well keep busy. You expanding?"

"Could be." George wouldn't mind taking over the clothing stores security. Matt dressed well. So could he. But, this guy could be about to pull a swiftie, like Bertie had. "Come and have a coffee in my pub. We can talk business." George rubbed his painful jaw. "Need a shave," he added, rather than show Matt his weakness. He led Matt away.

"You own a pub?"

"I'm the minder. How long are you planning to stay?"

Matt's expression hardened. "'Till I find her."

"Won't be easy, but I've got a few contacts who could keep an eye open." George licked his swollen lip. He'd keep the guy close. Matt could be useful.

***

On the drive along the coast road, Ellen lifted a stiff leg and flicked the strange trousers.

"You can take off your coat," Alana said. "Nobody will see you here."

Ellen sunk lower. "What if he's right behind us?"

After a quick glance at her face, Alana said, "What's wrong? What are you so afraid of?"

"He owns me." Ellen twiddled her fingers. "He'll never let me go. I thought I'd be safe here, but he's followed me."

Alana nodded. "We'll figure something out."

They drove in silence. Ellen pulled the beret low and snuggled into Liliha's woolen scarf. She inhaled perfume and thought of the kindness so freely given. What made these women help her and expect nothing in return?

A sign flashed by and the car slowed.

"Here we are," Alana swung the car past an old church on the corner onto a side turn. They bumped over rough ground alongside sheds and a large house, and then approached a line of houses facing the fields.

"These were old Victorian miners' cottages," Alana said. "You've probably seen similar ones in London."

"Yeah."

"The ocean's over there." Alana pointed into the distance on the right. The car stopped in the middle of the row. Scrawny bushes grew in a little strip of garden outside the door.

Ellen stepped into the strong sea breeze and pulled the hat over her ears. Rocks in the distance silhouetted against the gray sky. She shivered and turned to retrieve her old tracksuit, the one change of clothes she'd brought until she could collect her things from Mary.

"See the large smooth stone sticking up above the others? Giant's rock. There's a story about giants flinging the rock here in a battle long ago."

"I don't believe in fairy stories." Ellen dragged her feet. Dangling trousers swept the path to the door. If Matt found her in this isolated spot, he'd kill her and toss her body into the sea.

***

At four o'clock, Georg waited outside the tearooms to surprise Liliha. He leaned one elbow against the brick wall facing the door. It shouldn't take long to charm her out of the ring, but he needed to outwit Harry. Great Hunter van den Burg aimed his imaginary rifle at the door. Within the space of a breath, the opening disgorged the aroma of coffee along with the long-legged doe. When her eyes widened, he lurched off the wall.

"Georg." Her long lashes batted over the blue depths.

He bent toward her. "How good to meet you again."

She wavered before his old-world charm, glanced along the street, and then faced him. "How did you know where I work?"

"I have ways of finding out." No need to let on she'd mentioned the tearooms to Alana at the dinner party where they'd first met. *Treat her like a lady.* "What about a stroll along the sea front. Or are you too tired?"

"I could do with a rest after the busy day we've had. Sorry. Perhaps some other time."

She might be in a higher place with spiritual leanings, but she failed to deter him with such a flimsy excuse. "It's perfectly all right. I'll come home with you and we can talk while you relax."

Liliha frowned, eyes swiveling from side to side as if searching for escape. "Look, if you don't mind ..."

He grasped her left elbow and ushered her along. "Not at all. I respect a woman who knows what she needs."

Once away from onlookers, he could ensure things went his way. He shook his head, mane swaying in the breeze. Could he pierce her genteel veneer?

"Don't mean to be rude, but I'm dying to rest." She eased her arm out of his grip.

A flash from the moonstone ring taunted him. "I just wanted to chat." He fingered his lips. "I enjoyed our banter the other day. And ... I've got to admit, I'm lonely." To sweeten her up, he added, "Don't tell anyone. I shouldn't have spoken. No need to feel sorry for me. Honestly, I'm quite all right."

"Okay. We'll catch up some other time." She veered away to stride uphill.

Georg cursed. So much for his strength, stealth and agile mind.

***

Liliha squeezed between several people and headed home. All she wanted was to grieve alone. However, footsteps sounded close behind. Intuition told her he was following. Georg offered no threat. Nothing like a man with too much alcohol under his belt on a dark street.

Her original quest taunted her. She went over the circumstances again. During a vision, she had failed to prevent a theft. This presented the ideal occasion to settle any confusion about which George she should contact. With a sigh, she turned. "Maybe I was too hasty. Want to join me?"

He nodded, glanced at the pavement, and then strolled uphill beside her.

Once inside what she referred to as Headquarters since her hunt began, Liliha chatted while she made drinks. The forthcoming challenge wiped away her former tiredness. She couldn't expect to choose a convenient time.

She handed him a mug of coffee and led the way into the living room rather than suffer discomfort on a kitchen chair.

Sprawled on the settee, Georg lifted his square chin and shook a stray hair off his face. "It's hard making new friends when you move to another country, isn't it?"

"I was lucky to already know people in the area." Liliha pressed her aching spine against the support on her chair. "They took me in until I got settled. What about you?"

"I didn't know anybody, apart from those at Audley's dinner-party."

"What made you choose St. Ives, then?"

Georg's eyes flicked in the manner of moths hovering over a patch of cabbages. "The sea. I love living on the coast."

"I feel the same way." Liliha sipped her bitter tea. "Harry will look after you. Why not go out together?"

"Dunno where we'd go."

"What about visiting one of the local sights? There's the Eden Project which grows every plant in the world under giant domes. They're built in the hollows left by an old mine."

"Good idea." His teeth flashed. "Not sure if Harry's interested in sight-seeing though. Why don't you show me?"

Undeterred, she carried on in her role of problem-solver. "Perhaps you and Harry have common interests. What do you do for a living?" At least Georg should recognize the value of her help.

"I'm a dealer. All kinds—electrical, furniture, art. You know the sort of thing."

She understood if what sprang to mind was correct— the items George had stolen in her vision. Time to clear things up. Irritation made her voice snap. "Televisions?"

"Maybe."

The non-committal answer didn't prove anything. "What about luxury cars?"

He frowned. "Why do you mention cars?" His eyes pierced her.

What did he expect to find? "Do you like them enough to steal one from an acquaintance?"

"Who are you? The police?"

What had got into her? She never used enough tact. "Sorry. That was rude. I'm alone too much. I hope you'll forgive me."

His jaw tightened and the friendliness left his expression. "Are you trying to upset me? If so, I'll leave." He shuffled forward on the seat.

"Please. Don't take offense. I'm tired and grumpy. I don't know why I'm entertaining a strange man in my home when my husband has just died." Despite trying to prevent the surge of emotion, tears filled her eyes and trickled along her cheeks.

"My fault," he said in a gruff voice. "I forced you to invite me." He took a sip of his drink.

Relief flooded her. She should try to patch up her gaff. "I took my problems out on you," she murmured. "So sorry."

A tiny tap came from the direction of the glass door. She glanced outside. At ground level, Walnut's pink mouth stretched open in a silent meow and he swatted the glass again. She dragged in a shuddering breath and straightened. "I'll just let the cat in."

"Why disturb yourself?"

"I guess he's just saying hello." She slumped. "He used to live here. Visits every day."

"All the more reason to leave him outside," Georg said. "He reminds me of an old statue of a granite cat, with his long neck, big ears, and dainty feet. Like your rough one in the hall." He fiddled with his ring.

"Where did you see the other one?" Her interest picked up. Another Egyptian statue similar to the one she owned?

Rather than meeting her gaze, his eyes did the moth-type flit again. "At an exhibition." He clasped his hands behind his neck.

"I'll bet it was the London Museum. They've got a fantastic array of Egyptian artifacts, haven't they?" After his nod, Liliha took a gulp of her cooling tea. Her straight skirt pulled against her thighs, making her shift about in discomfort. No use flicking her shoes off either. He'd take her action as a sign to stay. Suspicion crept into her mind about how he'd eased into her surroundings. Someone had entered her cottage last week. "Have you been here before?"

"You've never invited me." He winked. "Or shared any of this with me." The twinkle in his eyes signified his recollection of their earlier conversation.

To cover herself, Liliha blurted, "You see, I used to rent the place to holiday makers. Just thought you might be one of them." She couldn't tell by his reply if he was hiding something. "Anyway, this is my home now, Georg. Everyone has to live somewhere."

"Now, we've returned to the old subject of ownership and sharing."

She swallowed, longing for the conversation to end. "As long as we use what we need and share any excess with others, we're not spoiling the earth we live in."

Georg sat straighter. "Who is to say how much each person needs? One might need more than another. The way a lion needs meat and a lamb needs grass."

"You're right." She'd make one last try to reach an understanding with him. "What do you need?"

"A good job. A place in the world. A spot to sleep and keep my things."

At a sharp pain in her spine, Liliha eased to one side. Would she ever get rid of him? "Look. I've had a hard day. I need to relax properly, change clothes and rest." She stared at him until he nodded.

"Okay. We'll continue this conversation later."

Way too tired to think of a retort, Liliha nodded before leading him along the hall. He swung his coat behind and slipped his arms into the sleeves. At the door, she released him into the breeze.

What drove her to take in every piece of flotsam the tide tossed onto the beach? Like Georg—or Ellen.

Her inner voice cautioned, *'Be careful what you wish for.'*

Chapter Thirty-Four

The breeze whistled with threat on Ellen's solitary walk along the cliffs. Why did she give in to the impulse to leave Alana's stuffy cottage? Surrounded by magical twilight, anything could happen. Her body could fall from the cliff into the sea.

Any one of the strange clicks and roars on the wind could be Matt following her. She glanced either way, but couldn't see anybody. Better return. She picked a safe route over loose rocks to Alana's house.

Skin tingling, she knocked on her guardian angel's door. The overhead glass section lit up. The door swung open, enveloping her in the aroma of the lamb chops she'd eaten earlier with Alana.

"Come in."

Ellen scuttled inside and hung her coat on the hook to one side of the hallway. "I made it back in one piece."

In the main room, a crochet rug hung over a chair. Flames licked over glowing coals in the fireplace. Photos of family sat on the mantle.

"Is this your husband?"

"That's Bryan. He's away at the moment." Alana settled in her chair and pointed to another by the fireside before lifting some cloth onto her lap. "I never walk outside in the dark on my own. It's dangerous over by the cliff and I'd hate to lose my footing." She poked a threaded needle into the material and pulled them to the other side.

The fire popped. Ellen jumped, and then relaxed on the indicated seat. Only the logs settling in the fireplace. "I don't rely on anyone to keep me safe. Couldn't."

"Sounds to me like someone wants to harm you." Alana's needle hovered.

"Looks that way." The cocky mood left Ellen. She had taken a needless risk.

"Do you want to talk? I won't pass on anything you tell me." Alana faced her.

The kindness in Alana's expression melted Ellen's defenses. "I don't know what you'll think of me."

"Don't worry about me. Just tell me how you got to this point."

"You'd never understand the sort of life I've led. I left home young." Ellen hesitated.

"It's hard to make your way without the protection of home."

"Mine wasn't ... I had to leave. Anyway, I met a man ... somebody who would protect me and he set me up with work. Know what I mean?"

"Uh, huh."

Ellen gripped her hands together and checked Alana's face for signs of disapproval.

"Go on. I'm still listening."

With her former occupation disclosed, Ellen flexed her shoulders. "Everything worked out fine for months. Sure, I had to share my takings with him, but the arrangement was fair, seeing as he was looking after my best interests."

Alana's sharp gaze pierced right to the bottom of Ellen's thoughts.

"Well, maybe not, now I think about it. But I had other girls to talk to and a fairly good life, considering." Not true. She'd been fooling herself all this time.

Alana took up her stitching again. "What changed?"

Ellen hesitated. "He wanted me to take drugs. He told me some of the ... clients ... enjoyed their time more if girls were ... more abandoned, he called it." She blurted, "That's one thing I swore I'd never do. I remember what drugs did to my mother." She choked on a sob.

Alana nodded.

"But I couldn't ... He insisted. One afternoon, he left the rooms where we were living to take a private call." Her voice got louder. "I ran. I didn't have time to take anything. Didn't know where to go either. I just ran and ran. I finally came to my senses outside Paddington station. A train was about to leave for Cornwall so I jumped on."

"Oh, boy. You really took a chance there."

Stifled in the hot air, Ellen undid the buttons at her neckline. "I wanted to escape to Land's End. Sounded about as far away as I could go. By the time the train reached Penzance, I'd worked out what to do. Get as far away from Matt as I could. I followed other passengers, changed trains and ended up at the end of the line in St. Ives. I thought he'd never find me."

"I can imagine how stressful that must have been."

"I saw him the other day. I don't know how he found me."

"But why does he care so much about you, Ellen?"

With the pounding in her head, she couldn't think straight. She drew a breath to explain, but closed her mouth and breathed out with sigh. Might as well carry on after blabbing so much. "We used to be lovers. He told me we'd never be apart. I promised him I'd stay with him forever." Now, Alana understood the worst—not only about the degrading work, but not sticking by her word. If the woman threw her out, she'd walk over to the cliffs.

Alana smoothed the material resting on her lap. "When you made the promise, the circumstances were different. If someone changes the rules, you are within your rights to disregard your promise."

Alana's words confused her. "Do you think so?"

"I'm sure of it." Alana's breath came out in a soft sigh. "Despite what you told me, I can tell you're a decent girl. Let's see if we can make a new life for you. One step at a time." She folded her work. "The first being to keep you safe."

Doubt crept into Ellen's mind. A soft woman like Alana couldn't protect her from Matt's control.

***

Liliha glanced at the dark window, and then paced into the kitchen to make a drink. After tipping milk into a pan to heat, she mixed cocoa powder with sugar and a dash of milk in the bottom of a mug, stirring until the mixture formed a smooth, frothy paste. The warm drink had helped Ellen stop shaking last night. Her mother always dealt with worries this way and the routine soothed her.

Was the girl safe in the isolated spot at Zennor? Or Alana? Liliha chewed her bottom lip. Her suggestion seemed mad in retrospect.

Tiny bubbles formed at the edge of the pan and Liliha flicked the gas off.

Perfume replaced the sweet steamy aroma. The saucepan in her hand clunked onto the stove top.

***

I hover in the night sky. Below me, traffic chokes a street flashing with electric signs. In the distance, the outline of a tower and a giant wheel reveal the UK's distinctive Blackpool illuminations. Three giggling girls dressed in short skirts congregate on the footpath outside an eatery. A young teenager hurries toward them. My psyche softens toward her. She's my target.

"Hi. Are they here yet?" She hitches up her tight tee-shirt.

"Not yet, Charlene," the girl alongside murmurs.

With accustomed speed, I meld with the new arrival and read her thoughts. At fourteen years old, she's excited about her outing.

'Time for an adventure. Only kids stay at home.' We peer into a window at the people eating inside. 'Snuck out to meet girls from school. Naughty girls Mum wouldn't like. I don't care. This is exciting.'

"When they get here, let them do the talking." An older girl, with bigger breasts glances along the street. "Here they come."

Two men in their twenties approach with a swagger, glancing either way.

Now I'm alerted.

"Right, girls." The shorter of the two speaks in a deep voice. "Hungry?"

Everyone nods, me included. I'm here to help Charlene.

"Okay," the tall olive-skinned man says. "Follow me."

While we troop inside, I anticipate trouble and whisper into Charlene's mind. 'This is dangerous.'

We giggle and nudge each other. The other girls flutter their eyelashes. Our head is pounding the way it does before opening an expensive present. At the counter, we reach inside our purse.

The stranger's hand halts us. "I'll buy chips for you all. My treat." While he orders, the girls shuffle their feet, pushing each other to get closer to the man. His wink sets them giggling again.

"Is it okay to let them pay?" we ask the girl beside us. "The teacher told us about this sort of thing."

"What?" The girl sneers.

I urge Charlene to speak.

"When men buy you something, they expect something in return."

"You softie," one girl says. "You should go home to Mummy."

Pain stabs us. We clench our hands.

Although she wants to belong, these men are too mature for Charlene. I whisper, 'Your mother wouldn't approve.' When she shrugs my suggestion off, I probe her mind for someone she admires. 'What about your sister? She'd tell you this isn't safe.'

Despite my words, Charlene clenches her jaw and pulls her denim mini-skirt down a fraction.

The tall man passes them small buckets of hot fries. Excited by his eyes, our stomach flutters.

Once outside on the pavement, the girls munch, keeping their mouths open to let heat escape.

We blow on a steaming wedge. So hungry.

"The car's parked in the lane," the shorter man says. "This way, girls. Soon, you can have a nice glug of vodka."

'You shouldn't go,' I whisper. 'Stay in the busy area where you're safe.'

Thoughts inside Charlene's brain battle for supremacy. 'Don't do anything stupid. Remember the news reports. But ... this is fun.'

"These guys like us," a girl whispers.

"Do you think they've noticed we're too young?"

"I've seen stories on the news," Charlene says. "You know, when girls get ab ... ducted."

"Na. These guys are all right."

"Stick your tits out," a girl says to a chorus of giggles. "Come on."

We traipse along, gobbling fries. The warm food

satisfies us but the salt makes our thirst worse. She longs for a drink to wash away the fatty taste.

'You should ask for juice.'

My suggestion makes our mouth water. We call, "Can I have orange juice with the vodka?"

One of the guys glances our way with a smile and a shake of the head. A couple of the girls titter.

When we reach an old car, the short man opens the passenger door. Indoor lights reveal a roomy seat. "Slide in girls."

I've got to take action. 'You know you shouldn't. You've heard about girls being kidnapped. Say you want to remain outside.'

"We can stand here and drink," we say between Charlene's lips.

One by one, the girls slide in.

'Don't go,' I whisper.

The tall man hovers beside the door holding a bottle and some plastic beakers. He gestures for us to join our friends. The other girls call to us.

Once we climb inside, we reach for a half-full beaker. "I didn't get any juice."

"Sorry, luv. Didn't have any."

The door closes. The men settle in the front and turn, bright eyes probing. "We'll get whatever you want soon."

Despite my warning, we giggle with the girls. Holding the strange-smelling liquid under our nose, we swallow. When we gag, the other girls sneer. Overcoming the urge, we swallow every last drop, clamp our mouth shut and screw our up our face at the burning in our throat.

"Let's go for a ride." The driver edges the car out of the lane to purr along the road. Traffic idles on both sides. Passing headlights illuminate the interior.

The other girls slump with sagging mouths and drooping eyelids. Deciding to join them in a rest, we lean against the girl beside us.

She's way too pliable. Each sound and shuffle distorts into slow motion. I give her a mental shake by planting pictures of her running away from grim chasers.

A deep voice from the front seat cuts into the silence. "They're reacting fast."

"Hope they stay awake. I don't fancy carrying them."

"We can get some of the guys to help us if necessary. They're expecting a good time."

"Yeah. Use them and toss them. That's the best part."

I whisper to Charlene, 'Keep your eyes open. Don't go to sleep. These men want to harm you. As soon as you get a chance, you've got to escape.'

Our heart beats with alarm. "All 'wight?" The girl beside us mumbles.

I send Charlene a surge of alarm to keep her alert. 'This isn't right. She can't talk. These men have drugged your drink.'

Although dopey, we clear our throat and sit straighter. The car slows. We bunch our legs, ready for flight. 'Pretend to be docile when you get out,' I whisper. 'Be ready to run as soon as they turn away from you.'

I hope they do. I issue strength to our slumping body while we step into the deserted area. People stroll past illuminated windows in the distance.

"This little 'un is all right," the tall man calls to his friend who is helping another girl to climb out. "Just stand there for a minute, luv," he says to Charlene. "I'll get your juice."

'Nod,' I advise her.

"Good to see you," a gruff voice calls from within the

building.

We force our eyes to remain open. 'This is bad. Gotta stay awake.'

"Smile,' I whisper. 'Act excited.'

"Good times are coming, baby doll." The tall man winks. "Just you wait."

"Here, give me a hand." The short man yanks a girl's arm from inside the car and shoves her toward the other guy. He reaches out and grasps her in the crook of his arm. His friend pokes his head into the interior again.

'Get ready,' I whisper to Charlene.

Another bleary-eyed girl emerges. "One more baby doll." The man dives inside again.

'Now,' I whisper. 'Run as fast as you can toward the lights. Scream for help from the first person you reach. Tell them about the other girls. They're in danger.'

Adrenalin combats the drug as we dash away.

'Take no notice of the shouts.' Using a force generated inside me, I give her legs strength until she reaches the lights and stops in front of a man and woman.

"Help me," she says, and sags onto the pavement, panting.

They bend over her with worried expressions. The woman reaches for her phone.

'Don't forget to tell them about the other girls,' I whisper.

When I leave, the group has disappeared from the street. I lift away, hoping someone reaches the girls in time.

***

A sweet aroma eased Liliha's tension during her period in the spinning tunnel. Those foolhardy girls hadn't been aware of the danger, out alone on the streets.

In the kitchen, her gaze focused on the saucepan. Her

243

hand guided the pan to the mug, and, stirring with the spoon, Liliha combined the milk with the paste. The aroma of chocolate calmed her.

Why did each person have separate trials? She'd often wondered. Maybe such situations occurred to test an individual's will and stamina. To change them for the better. At least Charlene would never repeat her mistake.

Something similar to the events in the vision could have induced Ellen into prostitution. Trapped women needed extra assistance to leave. *Let the other girls be safe.*

Problems chased each other inside Liliha's mind. What had she once told herself? She should temper her advice in the visions to ensure her distant contact had learned all they could from their experience. Charlene met the requirements.

But, had the runaway Ellen learned enough to alter her behavior?

***

George's footsteps pounded over the pavement in the dark. "Any luck with your inquiries?" His new shadow Matt strode beside him.

"Nope." Matt held himself rigid.

Must be frustrated at working alone all day. George grinned at the way Matt's body language revealed his need for help. "I don't mind a bit of company, but don't think you can muscle in. This is my patch."

"Yeah. As if I'd want this town. I told yer, Hopkins. I'm just here for the girl."

"Do you want me to call you Albright, seeing as we're getting all formal?" George slowed his pace. They'd reached the unlit area in the high street, marking the end of his patrol.

"Suit yourself."

George faced the way they'd come. Bright shop fronts guided him along his route.

"Did your contacts tell you about newcomers?"

"Plenty." George clamped his jaw. No sense in saying he didn't know anything. Anyway, what if the other guy swiped the ring from under his nose—or worse, grabbed all the minder business for himself? "Do I have your word you're only after the girl?"

"You've got it. Once I find her, I'll take her out of this little backwater."

The final insult irked, but old Hopkins wasn't stupid enough to release his temper in another round of punches. The guy belittled his status. Couldn't be trusted. Ways to retaliate came up one after the other.

Chapter Thirty-Five

Liliha pressed the phone to her ear after dial tone replaced the beloved voice of her daughter. She heaved a big sigh and appraised her empty home. Outside in the luminescent gray light of morning, birds twittered on the bare bough of the neighbor's tree.

In the manner of a water bird, she'd prepared a nest in St. Ives for her chicks. Perhaps, a cuckoo had deposited Ellen to replace her daughters. But now, Ellen had flown away too. A prayer rose from Liliha's heart. *Let Ellen find peace. Let her live a happy life.*

A knock sounded.

Liliha hurried along the hallway. When Yvonne called from outside, she opened the door.

"No time to chat," Yvonne said. "Just popping in to check on you. Haven't seen you for a few days."

"All I want to do is sit when I get home from work."

"What about that girl you took in?"

"She's gone now," Liliha said. "I'll ring you tonight and tell you all about it. How are you and William coping?"

"We're fine. Working, as usual." Yvonne glanced outside. "I've got to dash. Speak to you tonight."

Everyone else had a life of their own to occupy them.

Liliha waved Yvonne away in the same manner as she had about contacting George from a former vision. Rather than giving her a reason to carry on, the task forced her to admit her own inadequacy.

***

Hopkins strolled along his beat, nodding to acquaintances as he passed. All the while, the old brain ticked over, probing for an edge to raise him above the cooped chickens.

At a hail, George swiveled to face Old Locky and grunted. "Peter."

"Got some information for ya."

The guy had never given up anything interesting, but there was always a chance of the old mine turning up a glimmer of fresh metal.

"Thought I'd drum up some new business the other day and I tried my luck at the cottage where Helen's dad used to live." Peter tilted his head as though he expected a pat on the top.

George perked up. He'd visited the empty place several times searching for the moonstone ring. "I heard the cottage sold years ago. Anyone there?"

"A woman answered. She must have been the owner. About forty. A looker too, if you like them past forty. When she rang a friend for advice, I high-tailed it."

"Is there a point to this?"

"I'd already checked the back garden, as you do." The fellow waited for George to nod. "Easy access. On the way past the kitchen window, I heard someone organizing a place for a young woman to stay. It was all very hush-hush. She mentioned danger."

George couldn't help swallowing. "Go on."

Eyes glinting, Old Locky held out his hand. "Want to know her name?"

George handed him a twenty pound note. "Keep the information coming." When the hand remained extended, he added another.

Peter slid the money into his pocket. "Ellen. I made a note of the name when the woman yelled to her. The shower was going upstairs, so someone else was inside." He scratched his neck with stained fingernails. "Thought you might be interested."

"You never know. How long ago was this?"

"Few days ago."

"You should have told me sooner." George strolled away. What if the girl was on the run from Matt and had stayed in the same house as the woman with the ring? Seemed too convenient, but stranger things happened all the time. One instance was how he'd linked up with Matt the other day. Made him wonder if some things were meant to be.

Breath came fast and George's awareness of the shops faded. He could use Old Locky's information to his advantage. If he and Matt got together ... took turns in watching ...

***

After returning to the living room with a second steaming mug, Ellen sat beside Alana on the settee and listened to her instructions. "I'll have a try," Ellen said. "I haven't done any sewing before."

"Why don't you cut out some squares first? It's easy work as long as you have a sure eye and a steady hand."

Ellen knelt beside the low table, spread out a short length of material and cut along the weave as shown. "Alana. Do you think I could ring Mary and tell her why I didn't turn up for work?" She longed to chat with someone younger.

"Is that a good idea? You've already told me you saw the scumbag at the laundry. What if she lets something slip?"

"Yeah, you're right. But I don't have to tell her where I am."

"That would be a bad mistake." Alana glanced up.

"I could just say I've been called away."

"She'd ask you when you're coming back. What

would you answer?"

"Not sure. By now, Liliha might have spoken to her and explained. She said she would. But I still feel bad about ... you know ... letting Mary down."

Alana leaned across and patted her arm. "Your heart's in the right place. Think you can manage without pulling everything on top of you? Whatever you say, don't give away where you're staying."

"I'll be careful."

***

Hopkins strode into the launderette filled with clanks, engines grinding, and the high whine of spinning machines. The customers didn't deter him while he approached Mary. "How's things? Anything to report?" Darn woman kept moving. "Stand still while I'm talking, will ya?"

"Busy. The bloody girl took off."

"What?" George's interest rose. "The one who was helping you? How long did she plan to stay?"

"She never said, but we'd made arrangements. Now, she's done a runner." Mary shoved more laundry into the machine.

"Did she take her things?" George tilted his head.

"Why do you care?"

He grabbed her arm and jerked her to face him. "When I ask a question, I want an answer."

She did a double-take. "What happened to you?"

"Never you mind." Keeping a grip on her arm, George touched his tender jaw while he worked out how to use the bruises to his advantage. "If you must know, I defended you when a stranger mentioned your name. Said your business was run-down. You know I look after your best interests." His gaze never wavered. "Back to what we were talking about. Did she leave anything behind?"

"She left a bag at my flat." Mary struggled.

He kept hold of her. "When she calls, find out where she is. If she won't tell you, get her to collect her stuff." *Pretty smart.* He could run rings around Matt. "Let me know when she plans to come."

"What's she done to you?" Mary clenched her jaw and her mouth dropped.

The ugly cow narrowed her eyes and swung her foot.

Her kick landed on the base of the machine right beside him. "Watch it, you bitch." Out of the customers' sight, he jabbed his elbow into her stomach, hard. "I'm the one who says what's what."

She doubled over, drew in a breath and glanced at a nearby woman pulling wet laundry from a machine.

George muttered, "I'll wait to hear from you." He strode out the door.

Chapter Thirty-Six

Working alongside Alana, Ellen wiped the lunch dishes, her mind going over what to say to Mary. On her morning walk, she'd followed Alana's instructions to get to Giant's Rock without a worry, so why agonize over this? After more deliberation, she worked up the 'bottle' to make her excuses, picked up the phone, and clicked in the number on the note. A familiar voice answered.

"Mary. It's Ellen. I'm so sorry—"

"No worries. Liliha already explained." Hollow clanks sounded.

"That's good." Ellen's shoulders relaxed. "I hoped you'd know I couldn't help leaving."

"Where on earth are you? That's what I get for trusting you I suppose. You're more trouble than you're worth. You've got me into trouble with my man."

Ellen raised her voice. "I didn't leave on purpose. I'll be back to work for you, I promise."

"Not sure if I want someone unreliable."

Ellen's voice rose. "Just let me sort this out first."

"We'll have to see. You've left your clothes at the flat. I can't keep them while you dither. You'd better come and collect them."

"But what if he spots me?" Ellen shot a look at Alana, who shook her head. "I can't come."

"Do you want me to send them? Where are you?"

Ellen leaned forward and rocked. "I can't tell you in case he latches on somehow."

Alana raised her hand.

"Just a minute." Ellen covered the speaker while Alana spoke, and then nodded. "I can get the bag collected tomorrow."

"All right." Mary mumbled, "Just when I thought I'd have help, this has to happen."

"Sorry, Mary. Honest." After a click on the other end, Ellen disconnected.

***

Van den Burg kept up his search for the traitor Matt amongst St. Ives holiday crowds in all the likely areas. Stratten hadn't made contact for a couple of days. The boss's lack of communication could mean trouble.

Close to the Tate Gallery, Georg caught a flash of fair hair in the distance. He took off running, pushed aside sauntering tourists and skidded past a dustbin on the curb only to find the head had vanished. Bastard!

Thirsty work. He slipped in the side door of a small pub, occupied by a few men dressed in baggy trousers, sitting on stools. No Matt. A table surrounded by tourists wearing loud colors spewed chatter to match.

At the bar, he ordered his drink, pulled out change from his jeans pocket, and adjusted the belt buckle. Good belt. Elephant hide tanned by the local people south of the Sahara Desert. Made to last a lifetime. He fingered the rough patches on the clasp, cast by a blacksmith on an open fire.

"Here you go." The barmaid placed the full glass on the towel with a flourish, never spilling a drop.

With a laconic smile, Georg handed over his change, observing the cheeky miss. He took a long gulp. Nobody in the world made bitter as well as the English. "Crisps, please, my lovely." He shook a stray length of hair from his face.

She placed a crackling packet in front of him.

Popping the top open, he crunched the contents. More

drink washed away the salty taste but not the frustration at his lack of locating Matt. After glancing at his watch, Georg made his way into the fresh air outside.

Time for Liliha to finish work soon. He strode past businesses on his way uphill. He'd surprise her outside her cottage. This time, she wouldn't fob him off.

***

Hopkins stood in a side path between houses, pointing at the cottage opposite where the woman with the ring lived. "It's pretty quiet here. Never see signs of life in the other places. I've searched inside the cottage a couple of times, but didn't find anything valuable."

Albright's eyes narrowed. "After anything in particular?"

"The ring. You said you'd keep your hands off." Of course he couldn't trust Matt, but he should make the point.

"What are you planning?"

"Barge in and grab it," George said. "There are two of us and you'd frighten the fur off a cat." His wiry guile would beat the outsider any time. But, as far as appearance, Matt won with his smooth face and trendy haircut. Until you caught the cold glimmer in his stare.

"What's so special about this ring?"

"It's just a moonstone."

Interest flared in Matt's eyes before he glanced away. "A man's just rounded the corner."

"Duck back here." George crouched behind the fence and peered downhill. "He's coming this way. I've seen the guy at the pub talking to her."

"Looks as if you're out of luck then." Matt leaned on the side fence, eyes unfocussed.

"Wait a while. She's not home yet." George peered past a shrub. "He's hanging about outside."

"Might as well go." Matt glanced downhill and shuffled. "I thought you were going to help me locate my girl, Ellen."

"She's still in the area."

"How do you know?" Staying out of sight, Matt handed over a stick of chewing gum.

George tore off the paper and grunted with satisfaction. Sweet mint exploded in his mouth. "It pays to cozy up to people. One of my clients passed on some information about her."

Matt hunched his shoulders and made fists with his great hams. "Where is she? What are we doing hanging about here?"

"Hold on. I don't know yet. She was at the cottage a few days ago. Tomorrow, someone's going to pick up a bag of clothes from the place where she was staying. We can track them back to the girl."

Matt straightened. "Good." He yawned. "It's taking too long to find her. I guess I'll spend another night at the guest house."

"How are you planning to redeem your ... goods?"

"None of your business how I make my money," Matt said. "Let's just say they're on the hoof."

"What?" George frowned. "Never mind. I don't want to know."

"There's a woman coming."

George took a peek. "She's the one I'm after. She lives here."

"She's a looker." A slow grin crept over Matt's face. "Tall, dark hair. I've seen those penetrating eyes before. Reminds me of a movie star. What's her name? Sandra Bullock. They're both hot."

"Don't tell me you want her." George concentrated

on the rugged face before him. Hard as a pebble washed up on the beach.

"I've got no prejudice. Young or old, every woman has her uses. I haven't had one for a while."

As a possibility dawned on George, blood pounded in his temples and a bulge strained against his jeans.

Chapter Thirty-Seven

Georg straightened beside the cottage door before Liliha reached her gate. Right, van den Burg, time to charm the flighty doe. No shaking the hair, no gestures of dominance. "Hi, there. I hope you don't mind my waiting for you out of the breeze."

She raised her brows. "What a surprise." Her polite expression didn't embrace him.

"A nice one?" he asked, soft as a lion's yawn.

"I'm getting used to your ways."

"You don't want company. I can tell. I'll leave you to it." He'd flung the bait.

"You'd better come inside." She removed both gloves. No ring. Slender fingers gripped the key while she unlocked the door. Work as a waitress had left no impression on her smooth hand. He'd keep talking while he figured out where she kept the ring. "Your skin is darker than the locals."

"Probably my early life in Australia." She swung the door open and stepped in. "Same as yours in Africa." Long legs strode ahead. She didn't build them up with high heels either.

He passed the papyrus in the hall. The rough granite cat underneath jogged his memory of the missing Egyptian haul. Pacing after her, he wondered if he was acting the part of a predator or a buck.

"Come into the kitchen. I'll put the kettle on. My friend Yvonne will join us soon." She flicked the light on.

He hung his coat on the hook in the tidy hallway and followed her to the kitchen.

While she prepared the drinks, he scraped a chair over the floor and sat. *Get her talking.* "I'm having a hard time working up enthusiasm for football. Do you follow a team?"

"I'd rather read a book." She faced him and leaned against the counter.

"What interests you?"

"I guess I like Egyptology."

"Ah." Georg pinched the crease of his chinos to keep his focus sharp. "The picture in the hall is Egyptian, isn't it? Nice."

When two full mugs clicked onto the surface before him, she sat opposite with drooping shoulders and a bowed head.

"Is something wrong?"

"My back. Scoliosis. I'm not used to working on my feet for five hours a day any more." She stirred her coffee.

Probably to avoid looking at him. "Ah." Georg added sugar to his drink. In nature, the frail were taken as prey. Right or wrong, society, especially England, chose to support the weaklings. Yet, rather than being feeble, she showed mental strength. He admired the way she worked despite her pain.

"What about you?" she asked. "You must have weak points."

What could he safely reveal? Maybe he should play with her. "I love old jewelry—especially rings." He took a sip and sighed with satisfaction.

She laughed, deep from the belly. "You're right. That is soft. You want to shape up."

"Let me hold the ring, just once more." His shoulders slumped, pretending defeat.

She strengthened her voice. "I don't know what your intentions are, but you're annoying me. Do you want my friendship, or do you want to steal the ring?" A pink tinge suffused her face.

"The answer is I want everything." He cocked his head. No use bombarding her with more talk.

"Well, you won't get either the way you're acting." Silence stretched while she ran her finger over the grain on the table. "Drink your coffee. I've had enough chat for today." She took a gulp and faced away to stare out the window. A wistful expression raised the muscles on her cheeks as if she'd caught a glimpse of a good memory floating on a cloud.

No use being offended if he wanted the ring. George murmured, "Sorry. I'll behave. I'd like to stay."

***

Liliha frowned at the man she'd hoped to convert. The George confusion overwhelmed her. Why did she ever think she could trace the thief? Fancy inviting danger in, relying on the pretext of Yvonne's imminent arrival. He outsmarted her every time they were together. "Georg, I'm a simple woman—as in direct, not stupid. I see situations the way they are, and try to handle them as best I can."

"What are you referring to?" He sat upright, mouth lifting at one side with a smirk.

The gesture annoyed her. "You're trying to outwit me. I'm so sorry to throw you out, but it's getting late. Would you mind?"

"Of course not. Sorry if I've offended you."

"Not at all." The false reply covered her while she rose and headed into the hall. His mug clattered on the table and his faint words came closer.

"Let's part on a pleasant note."

"We'll catch up another time. Perhaps next week after my job ends. Harry can arrange it." She dragged tired legs along the hallway. She should postpone the challenge of following up on her vision until she felt stronger. When would that be? Ever?

At the entrance, she waved him away and leaned against the frame. How could she hope to penetrate Georg's defenses?

***

Hopkins nudged Albright. "Now's our chance."

"She's not in any hurry to get back inside either." Matt pulled his balaclava over his head in a swift yank.

Time to collect. George raised a handkerchief over his lower face. Smelled a bit dusty, but did the job. The city man had good ideas.

While the woman concentrated on her guest striding downhill, they darted across the street behind her line of sight.

George lightened his footsteps, hoping she didn't hear his Cuban heels clicking on the road.

"Make it quick," Matt mumbled from behind. "Too many other windows facing the street."

She stepped inside. George dashed to the closing door and grabbed the handle.

Beside him, Matt kicked until he got the tip of his boot inside, while George pushed, steady and sure. The door gave.

"What are you doing?" the woman shouted. "Help!"

"Grab her."

After her high scream, they shoved her inside, entered and closed the door.

Matt held her tight against his chest, one hand over her mouth and the other under her arms. "Where's the ring?" he muttered into her ear.

George grabbed her bag and searched the contents. Lipstick, tissues, little bits of paper. In the wallet, a few five pound notes and a photo of two smiling girls.

She jerked in Matt's grasp.

Frustrated, George yelled, "The ring!"

"Give it up now or I'll snap your arm." Matt said.

She tried to speak between Matt's fingers until he loosened his grip.

"Around my neck."

"Go on," Matt said. "Take it."

George reached under the collar of her blouse, snapped the fragile chain with one jerk and slid the ring into his waiting palm. He spat his gum onto the carpet. "Got it, you bitch."

She struggled in Matt's grip.

"Tie her up," George said. "We don't want her calling the cops."

"Just hold her."

George slid the ring into the coin pocket under his belt, reached out and swung her backwards into his waiting arms.

She kicked with her heel, gave a cry of pain, and struggled harder while he jammed his hand over her mouth again.

"Keep still." Matt removed hypodermic syringe complete with needle from his inner pocket, slid the cover off and inserted the point into a little bottle. "This'll knock her out."

"Why are you carrying that?"

"To use on Ellen when I catch her. Don't want any trouble." Matt gave the woman a shot. "She'll be all right tomorrow. Go to sleep, my love."

Her eyes widened and her nostrils flared. She threw her head from side to side and thrashed her legs. George held her against his chest until her movements slowed. One more breath and she sagged.

Matt chuckled. "Works fast."

"What's in it?" George stiffened.

"I've mixed a special Mickey Finn—Darkene, Rohypnol and a fast acting sedative."

George lowered her to the floor. She looked like one of the models in a magazine. Hard to tell her age. Smooth skin, legs spread slightly under a rumpled straight skirt. Her defenseless pose turned him on.

"Wanna have some fun before we go?" Matt asked.

Now he'd got what he came for, George said, "Why not?"

Matt pushed him aside. "Me first."

Chapter Thirty-Eight

A faint scream ripped the still evening air, high, a child in distress, or a threatened woman. Hard to tell where the sound came from. Van den Burg paused, knowing he had to check.

With his ears pricked to catch sounds beyond his ragged breaths, Georg pelted uphill to the cottage he'd left a moment before. Daylight faded along with his soft tread on the approach. Brightness showed from the little window over the entrance. Rather than pound on the door, he hurried to the rear of the house and peered into the living room's glass door. A shaft of illumination entered diagonally from the hall. Maybe she'd left the light on for security. A cat hissed from the bushes. He stepped away and gazed upstairs at the darkened windows. Far too soon for her to have turned out the bedroom light. On alert, he raised his hand to knock.

A shadow crossed the doorway in the hall. Then, another. Two? Something wrong. He hammered his fist on the glass. "Liliha. Are you all right?"

A pause. The scuffle of feet, followed by silence.

Georg strode to the front and found the door ajar. Nobody in sight. Wary, he stepped inside.

Liliha lay unconscious beneath the base of the stairs, skirt bunched over her hips but panties and tights intact. He checked her pulse. *Alive. No wounds. Regular breathing.* Relief surged. He'd call for help to get her seen to. Could have been a robbery judging by the broken gold chain on the floor.

Leaving the door open a crack so he could return, he stepped outside the gate and searched the street in both directions.

Two figures ran away in the distance. He took off full tilt, heart and legs pounding.

***

Hopkins gasped for breath on his flight downhill. No need to panic. Plenty of places to hide nearby. "He must have come back." No sense in confronting the man. "Don't worry. Nobody knew we were there." Superior in his leading role, George rounded a corner and headed for the lane ahead with Matt's breath hot in his ear. The fellow would be floundering on the sand without him to show the direction to safety.

"The sod." Albright's voice choked. "Let's get him. There's two of us."

"I've got a plan."

"What?"

"You'll see." George slowed his pace and came to a halt. Bent double to catch his breath enough to wheeze out a few words. "You in or out?"

"I'm in."

"This way." Straightening, George led his accomplice into the dark lane.

***

Van den Burg reached the crossroad where the men had disappeared. He caught a glimpse of movement to the left, pulled out his mobile and punched the emergency number. He might not return to help Liliha, and he needed to call for help. She had been kind to him and didn't deserve what had happened. He'd catch whoever destroyed her dignity. Someone would pay.

A remote voice asked, "What is the nature of your emergency?"

"Send an ambulance to number thirty-eight Talworth Street. There's an unconscious woman inside the door." He gave false details for himself, and then disconnected to hurry on.

Fair hair flashed under a streetlight ahead before the men disappeared. He ran to the spot, feet hardly touching the cobbles, and then peered into the dark recess of a lane.

Signals inside his head screamed a warning while Georg advanced one step at a time. Gateways and overhanging trees offered ideal hiding spots for someone to wait. The odds weren't in his favor. Why had they entered Liliha's cottage after he'd left? Coincidence? Or had they been watching him?

A blur on his right. He turned. A fierce explosion of pain. With no sense of motion, the ground met his fuzzy sight. Boots. A kick to his kidney. He grunted. Footsteps faded away. He tried to rise. Woozy ...

***

At a sense of her body in motion, Liliha groaned. A bad headache blurred her vision and she couldn't think straight. She forced her eyes open. A man in uniform? Cold. Discomfort in her spine. What? A rug covered her. Something soft supported her head. Flashes. Why was she here?

Fuzzy. Must be night. A dream. She didn't have to go to work for hours. Just lie still. A dull drumbeat pounded in her head ... Eyes closing.

***

Van den Burg woke with a vague memory of staggering back to his car. A bird announced daybreak with gusto, making him wince. Shivering, he snuggled inside his coat. Must have passed out. God, what a night. Liliha. Was she ...? Yes, he'd called the ambulance. First things first. He needed to pee and he longed for a hot drink.

Georg clambered out, locked up and took a few

tentative steps in the cold air. Plenty of cafés close by. He had to reach one. He'd freeze otherwise.

Locating the public toilets beside the parking station, he used the facilities, and then splashed water on his face. The condition of his head reflected in the cracked mirror. Looked as if congealed blood had covered the surface and sealed the wound. He fastened the stiff mass of curls behind his head with a rubber band from the floor. Leave nature to heal. He washed his hands, left the building, and shuffled downhill. His leather jacket pockets provided much-needed protection from the cool morning air.

Once he reached a café, he entered the comforting warmth of a room occupied by a bunch of men eating and talking, voices merging with clatters and clicks. Probably all working the same shift. Georg approached a vacant plastic chair beside a table with five other men. No need for embarrassment here. He fit right in with the workmen, who were occupied with eating.

A man wearing overalls nodded a greeting. "Order at the counter, mate."

Georg thanked him. Yawning, he wandered over and selected bacon, eggs and toast with coffee from the menu board.

After returning to his seat, Georg went over the events of last night. The scenario made no sense. Why didn't they break in at some other time? No, what had occurred must be something to do with him. The way he'd placed Liliha in danger pricked his conscience.

The waitress arrived with his breakfast and he tucked in, sudden hunger spurring quick bites and swallows. He buttered a crunchy slice of toast. What had the intruders wanted?

He recalled the gold chain on the floor beside Liliha.

Had the ring been hanging from it? His silent curse proceeded rising guilt. Fancy thinking of his own interests.

Mouth full of toast, he stopped chewing when the cafe door opened. Two men entered.

The fair-haired one was Matt.

Chapter Thirty-Nine

At the sound of wheels trundling along a hard floor, Liliha opened her eyes to daylight and warmth. Drowsy, she recalled her body in motion earlier and the high whine of a siren. Someone had lifted her. She recalled bright lights, murmured words and cold prodding in the depths of her privacy.

"Good morning. You slept right past breakfast."

Liliha gazed up.

"Open, please." A nurse poked a thermometer into Liliha's mouth and held her wrist with one hand and her watch with the other. She removed the probe and made notes.

Liliha ran her fingers over the smooth floral hospital gown. Steam rose into the air from a cup of dark amber liquid on the tray straddling her legs. Other occupied beds lined the room, each with a drink on their table.

"Where am I?" she asked the nurse.

"Edward Hains Community Hospital. Don't you remember last night?"

"Not much." A pair of fancy boots came to mind.

"Someone will be along to speak to you directly." The nurse pushed the medicines' trolley to the next patient.

With a sudden jolt, Liliha realized she should be at work. What was she doing lying in this ward? *Dream or vision?* She raised a finger. Real all right. *Wake up.* She made a terrific effort to sit, body so heavy she just wanted to relax again.

Yvonne would know what to do.

"Excuse me," Liliha called, forcing the words past her dry throat. "Can I have a phone, please?"

"I'll send one along as soon as I finish this ward."

The nurse studied the notepad on her trolley.

A figure in a white coat entered the room, spoke to the nurse, and then approached. The young man with a stethoscope hanging from his neck placed a banana on her tray. His earnest expression reassured Liliha.

"Eat this when you're ready." He checked his notes. "We've run a few tests. No rape occurred. Looks as if whoever slipped you the Rohypnol didn't finish what they started."

"How did you find me?" Liliha raised herself onto one elbow.

The doctor studied his notes again. "You arrived in an ambulance." He pulled a chair close to the bed and sat facing her. "How are you feeling?"

"Dopey. Drowsy. Will the effect wear off? The word you mentioned. Is it the date-rape drug?"

He nodded. "Were you at a party?"

Indignant, she frowned and dropped her head on the pillow. "Two men forced their way inside my home. I didn't know them."

"The police would have been called. Don't worry right now. I want to find out how you're handling your trauma. You need to talk."

"Bit too soon. I don't know what's happened yet. My thinking is fuzzy. Please, get me a phone. I've got to speak to my friend about work."

"Stay where you are for now. Later, we'll assess whether you can be released." The man stood and moved the chair away from the bed. "I'll send a porter in with the phone. Speak to you after lunch when you want to talk." He approached the older woman beside her and said, "Good. I see you're dressed, ready for your discharge."

Liliha struggled to sit upright and swayed. Did her

head belong to her body? This must be what people underwent when they had a hangover.

When the porter rolled the phone to a position beside her, she sighed. The operating instructions mentioned coins. "Wait".

The man turned to face her.

"I don't have any money."

"Sorry. No change." The man paced away on rubber soles.

Tears filled Liliha's eyes. Everything was too hard.

The woman approached from the bed beside hers, holding out coins. "Here, dear."

"Thank you. How kind."

"Not at all. I'm just sitting beside my bed waiting to go." The woman tottered away.

Liliha punched in the number needed. "Yvonne. Something bad has happened. I don't know what to do." She took a breath to prevent blurting further worries.

"What's wrong, dear? Start at the beginning." The sound muffled. Yvonne must be speaking to William.

"Two men grabbed me while I was shutting my front door and they ... I don't know."

"What?"

"I've just woken up in hospital."

Muffled conversation.

"We'll come right over."

"I'm not hurt, don't worry. They're just keeping me in for observation. I'm very dopey after the men injected me with a drug."

"What?"

"I'm okay. I just want to lie here. What time is it?"

"It's past ten o'clock."

"That's the problem. I don't think I can get to work."

"You stay right where you are," Yvonne said. "Wait until you're released. I can ring the tearooms and explain what happened. Someone else will have to fill in."

"Thank you. I don't think I could face Silvia." Liliha folded her arms and sighed.

"Let us know when you're due for release. We'll pick you up."

"Thank you for always being there for me." Liliha hung up the heavy receiver and shot an appreciative glance in the kind woman's direction. "Thanks."

While eating the banana, Liliha reached for her necklace. Panic hit her when she touched her bare neck.

No ring.

Think. Hospitals always removed jewelry. They'd probably stored her ring somewhere. A snake of worry made her stomach lurch. In fact, she wanted to throw up the banana she'd eaten.

***

Van den Burg turned away from Matt and the other man who approached the cafe counter. Heartbeat pounded in his temples. The best way to avoid being spotted was to blend in. Who'd notice one more wildebeest grazing with the herd?

The twenty or so chatting workmen in the room sat in front of empty plates, gripping their steaming mugs.

Elbows out and hunched forward, Georg took another bite of salty bacon. The simple meal had started to revive him. He lifted the collar of his jacket in case his tied-back hair gave him away. His scalp stung, but he avoided touching the spot.

"Looks like rain," he said to the man beside him.

"Better not. I'm working outdoors today." The man chuckled.

His acceptance gave Georg the cover he needed. "I know what you mean." He gestured with his fork at the window. "Dicey."

He mopped up the last of his egg yolk with toast. Although he wanted to confront Matt about the theft from his lock-up, he should consider the possibilities. Face the man right here, or follow him with a chance of recovering the stolen cartons. Straten would prefer the second option.

Georg shot a quick glance at Matt out of the corner of his eye. His blond hair contrasted with the other fellow's dark curls. He'd seen Matt's companion before but couldn't recall where.

The black-haired man murmured to the woman serving, waved at the cook working in the kitchen behind the counter, and then faced the customers. His gaze lingered on each one.

Georg ducked below the table to tie his shoelace. He called to the man beside him, "This could've caused an accident."

The workman winked. "That's one of your nine lives gone."

By the time he straightened, the two men were heading outside. "Better get on with the day." George sipped the remains of his coffee. Didn't want to find them waiting.

When he emerged, nobody occupied the street. He'd delayed too long. Now, he'd have to search for the thugs.

***

Another day in Paradise. *As if.* Ellen stopped cutting a strip of floral material, rubbed her thumb, and glanced at the door in Alana's living room. "The scissors are hurting me." She held up her hand. "I'm getting a blister."

Alana looked up. "I'm sorry. Poor little fingers. They

aren't used to the strain. What about helping me with this sewing?"

"I don't think I could."

"Do you want to learn? Maybe not, by the look on your face. What *are* your plans for the future?" Alana dropped the material onto her lap.

"I can't make plans ... not right now."

"Well, what do you want to happen?"

"I wish Matt would give up and leave me alone. I wish I lived an interesting life with someone I care about. I don't mean you. I mean a man—a partner. Someone who made me feel special." Ellen shook her head and slumped. "That'll never happen."

"Don't give up." Alana's eyes lit with a faint glow. "It's wonderful to find someone who loves you. My Bryan is a good man. We've been together so long." She drew a breath and bundled up her work. "Nearly eleven o'clock. I'll take this lot into St. Ives now." She stood and stretched her arms.

"And collect the bag of clothes for me."

"Of course."

"Try to make Mary realize I'll be back as soon as I can. I liked the job. I got to talk to all sorts of people. It made me feel part of the town."

"I'll have a chat with her." Alana headed for the door.

"Be careful."

"Do you think I should wear a disguise?" Alana chuckled.

"He doesn't know you. You should be fine."

***

George's mobile played '*God Save the Queen.*' Brought out the old Hopkins' snigger every time. Before the words reached the end of the first phase, he answered.

"Mary here. You asked me to let you know—"

"Yeah, yeah. Someone's called in for the bag?"

"An older woman's here right now."

"Keep her talking." He set off at a run. "Matt and I will be there soon."

"I'll try."

"You'll do it, if you know what's good for you."

Chapter Forty

In a maze of hospital corridors, Liliha lurched to her destination on rubbery legs. At least they'd let her wear her own clothes instead of the shapeless gown. People hurried by, some with stethoscopes or clipboards, others assisting elderly patients.

While she searched for the department indicated on her form, frustration bubbled. What had she done to deserve the assault and robbery? Hadn't she always helped other people? Surely her effort counted.

A well-endowed woman glanced up from behind the desk. "Can I help you?"

Liliha handed over her details and waited while the woman studied the computer screen. She assumed she'd speak to the doctor who visited the ward.

"Take a seat and wait until your name is called."

Frustrated, Liliha faced a room full of patients. At this rate, she'd never get home. Nausea quivered in her stomach while she approached a vacant plastic seat and eased down. Where had she seen Cuban heeled boots before? The full memory wouldn't surface.

Events piled on top of her: Oliver's death, the violation of her privacy and the loss of her ring.

The odds of seeing her moonstone ring again were slim. The scene in the train flashed into her mind. She'd been unwise to show the item off to Alana in front of everyone. People had overheard their conversation.

The artifact should have gone to someone stronger or the museum.

Did her loss of the jewel for the second time signify she shouldn't wield such amazing power over another person? With the ring gone, she'd have no visions. But ...

Truth blinded her—she'd never been worthy. The ring had passed on a false sense of her value.

An unfamiliar name rang over the loudspeaker. The man next to her made a move. Liliha shifted to allow him to stand, which renewed her queasiness.

After he left, she slumped forward and rested her chin on her hands to ease the throb in her head.

She longed to go home. But, what did the future hold?

***

Hopkins halted, drew in some much needed air, and entered the steamy launderette ahead of his city companion. Today he'd solve Matt's problem. Then he'd be rid of the guy who had plagued him for days. He spotted Mary behind a few customers at the rear.

Matt pushed ahead. "Where is she?"

"Hold on, I'll handle this," George muttered. He approached Mary. "Well?" Her doleful face told him all he needed to know.

"She's gone and taken the bag with her."

"What the—" Matt glanced outside.

"I couldn't keep her talking any longer." Mary glanced from one to the other. "A friend of yours?"

"None of your business. Where'd she go?"

"She said she had something else to do in town."

"How long ago?" Hands on hips, George flexed his shoulders.

"About five minutes."

Matt uttered an expletive and kicked the closest machine. His leather boot made a dull thud.

The bitch wouldn't dare kick now. "Where's she going?" George asked.

"She said something about sewing." Mary's voice screeched in his ear. "I couldn't take it all in."

"What did the woman look like?" Matt asked.

"Short, about fifty."

"Hair?"

"Brown." Mary straightened as if she had remembered something important. "Held in a clump at the back by a pin. She's not one of the locals who use this laundry." She bunched her lips and raised her penciled eyebrows.

"What was she wearing?"

"One of those dark green trench coats."

George eyed Mary. "I'll speak to you later." He led Matt away, pushed past the door, and glanced in either direction.

"Well?" Matt asked. "Any suggestions?"

"I say we go to the central parking station and keep a watch inside the entrance. She probably used that one, seeing as it's convenient. We might see her when she approaches. Hard to spot her inside a car." He turned toward the busy part of town.

"I've parked my Fiat there," Matt said. "If we have to follow her, we can use that."

"Good thinking." George grinned. Saved using petrol on his trusty Volkswagen. "No point in rushing. She's going somewhere else first." George straightened to gain height. "Nothing's lost yet."

"All very well for you to say. You've got your ring. I'm the one who's made a loss here." The fellow glanced sideways, eyes narrowed. "What are your plans?"

"I'll sell it, of course."

"If I don't find the girl, you can share the proceeds with me for my trouble."

276

George picked up his pace along with his expectations. How much did the big guy think the ring was worth?

***

The two men emerged from the launderette. Georg van den Burg raised his newspaper, inhaling fresh ink, to cover his identity. He followed them over the last day with the intention of delivering Matt to the boss. Now, they were out-and-about early. Not sure how he'd go about that particular procedure yet. He'd improvise. The boss needed to question Matt. Therefore, do whatever the situation required. Despite his faults, Straten represented a ticket to remain in the country. Although he didn't want to, George considered returning to Africa if circumstances became too hard to handle.

The sharp wind penetrated his tied hair and stung the wound on his scalp, bringing to mind the memory of Liliha on the floor, helpless. They were both victims, but only one was innocent.

The contents of the box under the floorboards in his kitchen cupboard presented another problem. Why hadn't he told Straten about it? No use speaking to him now. He'd be painted the same red as Matt, and branded a thief. Maybe the description fit, although he excused himself because he'd worked under guidance from his employer.

Georg lost the flash of fair hair behind a corner ahead, dodged a bulky tourist with two suitcases and sped up his approach until he caught sight of his quarry. What were they up to? And how did Matt, a stranger to St. Ives, know the other man?

Georg's shoulders slumped at the thought of his own actions. The ease with which he grabbed other people's possessions made him think he lived a charmed life. Yet he'd believed parting Liliha with her ring would turn a setback into a success. He shook his head. *Get some sense, van den Burg.*

Ahead, Matt and company ducked into the entrance of the mall. Georg followed.

Chapter Forty-One

George van den Burg came to a halt and caught his breath. Just after nine in the morning. Even this early, conversation buzzed inside the busy St. Ives shopping mall below the parking area.

He spotted Matt, whose companion nudged him and pointed to the far side of the crowd.

A short middle-aged woman dressed in a dark green trench coat approached the lifts. A probe the size of a pencil emerged from a knot on her hair.

The dark-haired man shook his head, scratched his neck, and smiled in a satisfied way.

They appeared to have a problem sorted. Whatever they were up to didn't concern Georg. He had to persuade Matt to hand over the goods he'd stolen. However, this wasn't the ideal spot.

The two men strolled to one of the fast food stalls in the center and stood chatting while they waited for their order.

Out of sight, Georg purchased a cheese sandwich and a cold drink at another booth. He sunk his teeth into the soft bread and devoured the whole thing while he observed his prey on the far side of the food hall. They tossed food wraps into the bin and made a move. Matt entered the lift to the car park area.

Georg tossed his rubbish, shoved the drink can into his pocket and pounded up the stairs.

From one level to the next, he searched until he located Matt. Just in time, Georg ducked behind a car while the burly fellow strode by toward the lift.

Georg ran to the exit. The door banged behind him as he galloped downstairs two at a time and emerged into the busy ground floor area before the lift door opened.

When Matt met his companion, they spoke a few words and headed for the lifts again. Judging by Matt's purposeful stride, the men had found what they came for. They'd leave soon.

Georg made his way to the car exit at the side of the building, and then stood on the first level with a view to the ramp. He'd managed to park along the street, so he could follow as soon as they appeared.

Several cars approached the exit, followed by a new gray Fiat similar to the one Matt had arrived in. Catching a flash of blond head beside a dark haired man, Georg vaulted the cement edge and landed six feet below. Behind another barrier, he crouched to take note of the number plate as the car headed away.

He pounded along the pavement to his parked vehicle.

***

Liliha blinked and sat up in her own bed. Peace surrounded her instead of the constant noise of chattering nurses, coughs and hospital equipment. A glance at the clock showed she wouldn't have time for meditation. She'd overslept.

With clumsy movements, she dressed for work, determining not to think too much about her ordeal yesterday. So many other women had experienced the same or worse. She'd handle the investigation soon enough. A phone call from a police officer had given her a crime reference number and arranged a convenient time for a visit.

She pared the fuzzy skin off a kiwi fruit, and then used her fingers to prize oily fragrant rind off a mandarin before devouring both. At least her appetite had returned.

However, worry about her loss drained her while she wiped the bench, tidied up, and emerged into the cold wind to pace downhill.

Wary about her reception, Liliha entered the tearooms a few minutes late. Never one to be talkative, Silvia nodded and flicked her head toward the rear. Liliha hurried to change into her apron.

While tying the bow behind, she glanced up when the fire-door opened.

Silvia said, "Everything okay?"

"I'm so sorry I'm late. I suppose Yvonne told you I was attacked."

Silvia opened her palms. "Tell me what happened."

"Two men pushed past my door and grabbed me. I woke up in hospital."

"God, Liliha. Are you all right?"

"Right after they entered, they injected me with a strong mixture of drugs so I collapsed." She drew in her breath. "And they stole my ring."

"Did you get a look at them?"

"It all happened so fast. They wore covers over their faces."

"Get yourself a cup of strong coffee," Silvia said. "Take your time to recover. Just concentrate on serving the customers. It should be a quiet day. You can leave early."

"Thanks." Assured, Liliha staggered into the main room and surveyed four tables occupied by customers. A man and woman gathered their things and approached the counter.

Make an effort. Chat nicely.

When the door shut behind them, self-pity slammed into her with the sensation of landing at the bottom of a slide. The intruders hadn't killed her, but used the rape drug. Why hadn't they gone the whole way? Someone must have scared them off—the same person who had called the ambulance.

Rather than slump in front of customers, Liliha made herself a drink as Silvia advised.

She wiped the counter, mulling over a long-time belief. Possessions would return to a person who had done no wrong. She should listen to her own advice. *Be strong. Believe things worked out according to a plan and good triumphed over evil.*

Rot! What about her? Always doing the right thing. A considerate attitude hadn't gotten her anywhere. She flung the cloth into the sink. Life wasn't fair. How could she live without both Oliver and the ring?

Give them back!

At another table, customers made a move. Liliha clenched her jaw. She'd act the role of waitress, while inside, she'd suspend the belief in everything she held dear.

***

Home early after work, Liliha hurried to answer an expected knock. "Who's there?"

"Police."

When she opened the door, a uniformed man and a woman stood outside.

"Mrs. Trevellyn?"

Oliver's surname stole her breath away.

"We're here to follow up on the break in." The tall man held out his warrant card and quoted the crime reference number.

"May we come in?" the female officer asked.

"Yes, Yes. Of course." Liliha led them into the sitting room where they perched on the edges of chairs opposite her and went over the details of what happened.

"We don't have much to go on," the male officer said, "but we'll look into the matter and update you at least once about progress." He answered the two-way radio strapped to his shoulder. A voice spoke and he replied before he faced Liliha again. "I've been called away, but my colleague will remain to have a word if that's all right with you."

Liliha nodded.

"I'll let myself out." He left the room.

Liliha faced the policewoman.

"This must be very traumatic for you. Please, let me explain what we can do. I'll go over the security you need before you open the door in future. We'll supply the name of a workman to fit a chain so you can see who's outside. Ask for identification and they can slip their card into the letter box."

"But I was just closing the door after my guest when they rushed at me. The visitor had gone already."

"Do you trust your guest?"

Liliha nodded. "It wasn't him." She frowned. "I just remembered. A man came last week. He said he was here to fit a new lock, but he disappeared when I rang my friend."

"Can you remember what he looked like?"

"A dirty man in overalls." Liliha gave as much detail as she could remember.

"We'll look into that. Best to be careful from now on."

"I think someone broke in before," Liliha said. "They moved things about, but didn't take anything."

"Perhaps they were searching for the ring. Unfortunately, they've got that now. We'll patrol the street from time to time." The officer leaned forward. "Was your ring very valuable?"

"Sentimental of course ... and there's a certain amount of the past associated with the keepsake. I lost it once before. The ring turned up on a body and was sent to the museum. They told me it was priceless because of the Egyptian history. You'll have a record of that." Liliha gave the date.

The officer made a note. "I'm sorry. We'll do everything we can to return your property. You're undergoing counseling at the hospital, I assume."

After Liliha's nod, the policewoman pulled a card from her file. "Dial nine, nine, nine if you see anything suspicious; otherwise ring this non-emergency number."

"Thank you for your help." Liliha examined the card, and then led her to the door.

With a wave, the woman strode away in sturdy rubber-soled shoes.

No use feeling sorry for herself. People from her visions were much worse off. Would she ever get another chance to change the way the world worked, one person at a time?

The street she'd once considered picturesque took on a depressing aspect. She sighed. First she'd lost her daughters, then Oliver and now her ring. What else could go wrong?

Oh, yes. She'd cope. But the joy had drained from her life.

Chapter Forty-Two

After revealing all the distressing details of her plight, Liliha gazed at her friend's sympathetic face.

"I'm so sorry about your ring." Sarah sighed. "Are you all right living here alone? I wish I hadn't suggested the change now."

"I'd already thought about moving. You're not to blame. The same thing could have happened at The Barn just as easily." The kettle clicked off. "The police are keeping an eye on the cottage." Liliha poured boiling water onto tea bags, at the same time erasing the title of Cottage Central. "I must admit, I'm a bit nervous though."

"You should be. I'll call in more ... every night before I pick up Audley." Sarah sighed and gazed outside. "It's a bad state of affairs when a woman can't feel safe inside her own home."

Liliha passed over a mug of steaming liquid. "What am I going to do?" Her eyes welled up with tears. "It wasn't enough for Oliver to die, but fate had to take my ring too."

"Not fate. Those thugs did the damage."

"But don't we always say everything happens for a reason? What if I wasn't meant to have the ring at all?"

"Nonsense. You're the most deserving person I know. Don't let grief affect your reasoning."

Wrapped in Sarah's arms, Liliha gave in to sobs.

***

Van den Burg followed Matt's gray Fiat into the turn-off leading to a dead-end in Zennor. He'd explored the whole area. The car would have to drive right by him when Matt left.

George glanced at the glove-box. The odds and ends

inside would give him the upper hand. Sturdy rope, sedative, bottled water, packaged food, and a soft cloth to use as a gag.

The vehicle didn't return. The men must intend to stay awhile.

The surrounding area consisted of a couple of old houses and a run of rooftops in the distance. Stepping into the fresh air, he closed the door, and then leaned against the car body to lift his face to the sun. The boom of distant waves crashed. The briny air smelled fresher away from habitation. A perfect spot to keep an eye on things, parked out of the way beside a derelict barn.

He fished the can of soft drink out of his pocket, opened the slit and gulped. Although the liquid had lost its chill, the beverage cleaned his mouth.

A sudden thud blended with gulls crying into the wind. Could be a closing car door. He lurched away.

***

After a late lunch of toasted sandwiches and what Alana called fries, Ellen strode into the breeze wrapped in her old brown parka. Who'd have thought she would walk for pleasure? She followed the flight of a big bird, and then shook her head to feel the strange effect of short hair caressing her face.

The Queen wore a scarf over her head, tied under her chin. Probably to keep her perm neat. Anyway, she took her stiff-legged little Corgis and Alana didn't have a dog for Ellen to walk. She sniggered. Anyone would think she was comparing herself to royalty.

The sea drew her with soft sloshes and the occasional bang. Probably waves hitting the rocks below the cliff. Nice. Sort of dramatic. She'd never had much to do with nature.

She climbed the first gate, and then followed the hedge to the right over the rocky surface, bypassing bushes and small trees.

How long would she need to stay at Zennor? She missed the excitement of her old life. Not the pain and dread, though. A sigh merged with the breeze. Long ago, she'd learned to take the good with the bad. *Life's way.*

Did she really need a string of men to mess up her life? Other women found just one man to live with. Sure, they split up sometimes, but at least they were happy while the attraction lasted. No such destiny for her. Who'd want a woman who'd been used by hundreds of men?

While she hoisted herself to the top of a second gate, she lost her footing and clung to the metal support. Out of the corner of her eye she caught a flash. Blue. She turned. Two men. Following her. One dark and . . . A glimpse of blond hair and a bulky body outlined against the sky. Matt. Her heart made a bid to leap out of her ribcage.

She ran over loose stones on the ground toward Giant's Rock in the hope of protection.

***

Pleased at locating the girl outside shelter and following her to a deserted spot, Hopkins nodded at Albright's signal. One rock protruded past other boulders in the area like a pimple on an unblemished face, out of place in the surrounding low shrubs. George circled the smooth rock to the right, leaving Matt to approach on the left. The chase excited him. Pushing between the undergrowth, he stumbled on loose rubble. The noise blended with the wind. From now on he'd take more care. Didn't want to alert the little skirt. He hadn't seen much of her—just a silhouette of a short-haired woman wrapped in a parka. She must be special if Matt was prepared to go to so much bother to find

287

her. Of course, some people couldn't let go.

No skin off George's nose. The ring nestled in his denim jacket pocket, buttoned and secure. How much money would he make? Wait till he told the dealer the story about the museum wanting it.

He crept on toward the faint sound of rubble clicking. At a gasp, he paused. Someone very near. George squashed against the flat rock towering over him. Must be twenty men high and just as round.

The sounds grew louder. He imagined the woman's cautious steps approaching. If he stopped her running off, Matt would have to show his gratitude. That'd make Hopkins a name to remember.

He tensed. Hold on one more moment.

Someone emerged from one side of the rock. George dived at the feet. The big body landed with a crash.

Matt lashed out and swore. "It's me you numbskull. Where is she?"

The insult built on all the previous derogatory comments. Just because he was from London, the guy considered himself so much better than anyone here. George stood and brushed his knees. Bloody bastard. The guy would never find her if he had any say in the matter. "I haven't seen her." He'd show the city slicker who was the numbskull. Nobody would take over his town.

Chapter Forty-Three

Ellen hunkered down behind the boulder leaning against Giant's Rock. Birds fluttered, took off, and cried noisy warnings into the breeze. *Quiet. Don't let Matt hear.*

The gap she'd discovered yesterday when she'd bent to tie her shoelace might be a way to escape. Could her body fit? While she squeezed into the space, damp earthy odors filled her nostrils. She pressed deeper, crawling on hands and knees to a lower level. Dark surrounded her, bringing to mind scenes of her childhood hiding place. She didn't like the whimper that escaped into the musty air. *Take charge.* Don't let the panic tightening in her chest freeze all action. Her mouth hang loose. She gritted her teeth.

The tight space barely allowed her to turn and face the light. She froze. Someone's ragged breathing penetrated over the thump of her heart, and then the click of stones followed by silence. He'd be back. Matt always got what he wanted.

She had to escape right now—couldn't stay here. They'd make a thorough search next time and trap her for sure.

She crawled to the entrance. Could she chance a peek outside? Breath came ragged as she crawled forward. *Mustn't whimper again. Strain forward just enough to see.*

Nobody in sight. They'd return soon. Bent double, she tiptoed out into the breeze, and then reverted to the left. Breath came in gasps while she crept toward the shrubs below the rock.

Wherever she went, they'd see her. Rather than hide under the growth, she skidded over the rubble to the gate.

No use heading for the cliff area by the sea. They'd trap her at the edge.

Just concentrate on not falling. Climb the gate again. Continue along the hedge to the left. Exposed and panicking, her breath came fast. She couldn't hear them. Maybe they'd fallen behind. The last gate faced her. *Over and away.*

She sprinted for Alana's house. With nothing tall enough to hide behind, she pounded over the rocky ground. Laced canvas shoes held her feet firm. How far could she run before being spotted from behind? She dodged low growth.

Someone loomed ahead. One man. No!

Defeat weighed her down. Matt must have brought help.

***

Van den Burg reached out and grasped the running woman. "Whoa, there." Someone chasing. She needed help. A flash of Matt's bright hair flashed between bushes behind her.

"Leave me alone," she screamed into the wind while making a dash sideways.

"It's all right." Georg caught her arm and swung her to face him. "I'm not going to hurt you."

She whimpered, sagging. "Let me go, please."

"Get behind me. I want that man."

She frowned. "You're not with them?"

"Not on your life." He forced her slender body behind his and faced the approaching thugs. Couldn't have planned the confrontation better. But now he had to fight two men. He murmured out of the side of his mouth, "I might need help."

He felt, rather than saw, her nod.

Matt advanced first, hands spread and legs bent. The other man stayed behind. Breathing fast, Matt yelled against the shriek of the wind, "Fancy seeing you here."

"Straten wants you."

When Matt made an aggressive move, Georg lunged. A large fist flew toward him. Georg ducked aside, leaving Matt swiping empty air.

Georg spun, jerked his elbow at his opponent's side, and then barreled into Matt's upper body before bouncing away.

Rather than fall, the big blond spread his legs and clenched his fists.

The black-haired man stood watching with a smirk.

Matt's arm thrashed forward again.

Georg stepped out of reach. Fast as a snake, he grabbed Matt's arm to twist behind. "You should learn martial art, my friend." He pressed a thumb into the point in his opponent's shoulder to cause the most pain.

Matt bellowed and glanced behind Georg.

The other man advanced on his toes.

"You want some too?" Georg asked.

The girl dived under the moving man's legs. He tumbled over her. She rolled away, and then sprang to her feet and landed on Matt's back.

"Hold him like so," Georg guided her to grip Matt's arm twisted behind him at the point of breaking the shoulder joint. While making sure she had a proper grip on him, he watched thug number two scramble upright and circle them.

Georg spun on the ball of his foot and kicked the man's chin with the other.

The fellow collapsed and rolled away. "I give up. I don't want the bitch anyway." Dragging himself to his knees, he spat blood. "I've got the ring anyway."

"Ahhh!"

The high scream alerted Georg to Matt's action. He'd managed to get the better of the girl and held her under the bend of his elbow.

"Right. I'm off now," Matt said. "Thank you everyone. You in particular, George."

"What?" Georg said.

"What?" the black-haired man said at the same time. "You can't. How will I get back to St Ives? We had a deal."

"Deal closed," Matt said. "Game over." He hurried away, pulling the girl by the arm while her feet scrabbled to gain purchase on the scree-covered rock underfoot.

Georg faced the other man. How could he overturn the situation? "Looks as if we have more in common than just a name. Want to team up?"

"I bit my tongue." The other George frowned, licked his lip, and then glanced up. "Guess I can't blame you." He stepped closer. "What's in it for me?"

"You don't want Matt calling the shots, do you?"

"The scumbag. I'm not letting him pull a swiftie on me."

Matt had dragged the girl about twenty feet toward the houses in the distance. She shot an imploring glance at Georg before Matt yanked her again.

A memory stirred. Looked like the girl without cash he'd helped when he'd first traveled to Cornwall on the train. "Any good at running?" Georg muttered. "They'll be too far ahead soon."

The man nodded. "Call me Hopkins. What you got in mind?"

"You know where the Fiat is. See if you can get there before him. The girl should slow him. Meanwhile I'll try to head him off."

"No worries. I'll reach his car first." Hopkins took off.

Determined not to lose Matt, Georg pounded over the ground to the right of the cottages toward the derelict barn where he'd left his car.

***

When Hopkins reached his destination, panting from an alternate route in the hope of secrecy, Matt and the girl already occupied Matt's gray Fiat. "Open up." George spread his feet on the loose sandy soil and grasped the door handle. Unsuccessful at opening the darn thing, he ran to the bonnet. Lucky this model gave access without the need for releasing the lock.

The engine fired.

Blind with fury at Matt's disloyalty, George flung the hood up, reached in, and tugged a coil of wire, hopefully an ignition cable.

After the motor spluttered and died, the door burst open and Matt stepped out.

George aimed a punch at Matt's head. The blow landed on his opponent's ear. "Ha. Too quick for you."

Matt roared. Another door slammed. They both turned to find the girl running toward the houses. Matt shouted and took off after the girl.

With haste, George reconnected the cable, climbed into the car, and roared away.

The other Georg would be somewhere ahead. He'd leave him to sort things out with Matt.

When he reached the road without being stopped, George tapped his pocket. He had the ring, and the other guy might take care of Matt alone. Why worry about the girl? He'd improved her chances already.

Chapter Forty-Four

Despite the fear of being trapped for good, Ellen wrestled inside the crook of Matt's arm. Pointless. He'd make sure she wouldn't escape again. After all, he'd come all the way to this God-forsaken place in Cornwall to find her.

Matt yelled, "Bloody bastard!"

She winced at the strength of his shout at a retreating car. He shoved her toward some outbuildings.

He forced her along. When she stumbled, he kept her upright with the grip on her arm. Her elbow jerked out of alignment enough times to dislocate. How long would it be before Alana wondered why she hadn't returned?

Matt slammed her against a doorway and reached beside her for the handle. "You're a poor sight in those sloppy clothes."

The light of affection didn't shine from his eyes any more. Only temper. Tears of outrage clouded her sight. He didn't care about her. From now on, he'd use her to make money. All her fears about drug use haunted her—the very thing she'd tried to avoid.

She ducked lower, but couldn't escape his arm. After a metallic grind, the door squeaked open. She bit the coat covering his bicep.

His pressure released, and then his fist slammed into her chin. Without waiting for her to recover, he pushed her inside a large space, big enough to take two cars. Disoriented and in pain, she swallowed the salty taste of blood. *Better not fight. Just sink into a dream-like state.*

He pulled a hypodermic needle from his pocket.

Here it came—her life as a druggie. *Don't sob.*

"No use. I can't carry you for miles."

How had she ever loved him? His big, muscled body repelled her now. His mouth was too wide and his eyes too close together. As he shoved the needle away in his pocket, she swallowed bile at the thought of their earlier tenderness.

When she lunged for the door, he caught her arm again, dragged her to one side and pushed his hip against her stomach while he gazed at the syringe in his hand. "Where's the other guy? Has he gone too?" he mumbled. "We'll wait here a while. He might leave." He eyed her.

"Matt, I don't want the job any more." She rubbed her elbow. "Wouldn't you rather keep girls who love the life?"

"Shut up, bitch. Let me concentrate."

Wrong approach. Maybe ... With a hesitant move, she touched his shoulder. Played the game he'd trained her for—pretense at affection. "It used to be just you and me. What happened?"

"Business." His top lip lifted in a sneer.

"I didn't want to change. Why couldn't we—?"

He pressed his body harder against her pelvis and raised the needle. "Do I need to use this?"

"No. I'll go along with whatever you want." Her heart hammered with fear.

"Give me your word."

She dredged up her special smile from somewhere deep inside. "I promise." *Had to lie for her own safety. Anything to escape the drug.*

A stone clattered outside.

Matt jammed his forearm into her throat and pocketed the needle.

Coughing, she dropped to her knees. Deep gasps racked her body.

"Shut the fuck up." He cuffed her over the head.

With a huge effort, she swallowed each explosive urge to choke and sagged onto the grimy floor beside the bare metal ridges of motorbike wheels.

A knife replaced the syringe and the blade flicked open. "Make a move, and I'll cut your face." He pushed her body onto the cold floor, and pressed a foot over her.

With her head wedged sideways, she strained to make out what he was doing.

The motorbike! The weight pressed over her.

"That'll hold you." With one final adjustment, he left her pinned under the bike and skittered behind the door. The old wood eased open, hiding Matt from the intruder.

Nothing to lose. She yelled, "He's behind the . . ." Her awkward position made the next word difficult.

***

Georg kicked the door open and spun away from the entrance in one practiced van den Burg move. The door thudded—hopefully onto Matt inside.

Scurrying along the left of the shed outside, he ducked under the window to listen. A faint scrape came from his right. He crept along the full circumference of the structure to reach the open door again.

No sign of Matt. Could have come outside. However, the girl sprawled face down with an old bike pressing on top of her. She lifted her head and her eyes flashed.

Georg advanced one step at a time and whispered, "Hold still. I'll get you as soon as I've—" He paused at a thump, and then swiveled to the doorway as the light darkened.

Matt blocked the exit.

In sham, Georg dropped his arms, offering himself as bait. He opened his eyes wide and allowed his jaw to drop.

The man ran at him.

Georg stepped out of the charge at the last moment, grasped Matt's arm, and spun him close.

After a jab to his throat from the other elbow, Georg lowered his chin and drew a chocking breath. A shift sideways and he slammed his shoulder into Matt's chest.

Arms grasping at Georg, Matt lost his balance and toppled onto the floor.

Georg sprawled on top of his opponent.

The big fellow reached toward his trouser leg. A blade glinted.

Chopping the side of his palm against Matt's wrist, Georg knocked the weapon to the floor.

They both lunged for the knife. Matt managed to straddle him. Georg bucked him off and pressed his weight over the bastard. When Matt's hand stretched toward the weapon, Georg squeezed the guy's throat and held on while Matt struggled. The fellow slumped.

Could be dead. Didn't care right now.

Georg dragged in a breath and called to the girl, "All right?"

Under the dull light from the window, her eyes flashed.

"Just a minute." On the other side of the shed, Georg spotted a roll of plastic bags. Breathing hard, he sprang to his feet and strode over. Shot a glance at Matt who hadn't recovered. Georg grasped a screwdriver and slit one of the bags, and then tied sections together. "This will work nicely. I don't know how long he'll be out." He flipped Matt onto his front. Worse luck, he was breathing. Georg secured his hands behind.

"I'm coming over for you, now," he said to the girl. "Let's get this machine off you." He strained, levered the bike away and dropped the weight to one side. "Can you move?" he shouted over the clang of metal.

She wriggled onto her side and sucked in a great breath. Hand over her chest, she gasped, "I think so." She was anxious to leave by the glance she shot at the door.

"Wait. I'll anchor Matt in case he comes to." After making more plastic strips, he strode over and secured the man's ankle to the motorcycle, and then tied the lot to the wooden bench leg set into the cement floor.

"He should be secure for a while." He'd phone Straten with the good news when he'd settled enough to think straight.

"He's got a needle in his jacket." Her eyes flicked. Probably nerves.

"Not for long." He patted Matt's pockets, found two offending articles and smashed them with a hammer from the cluttered bench. Swallowing rage, he grabbed her arm and they left the shed. "Do you live here?"

She shook her head and opened her mouth, but didn't speak.

Traumatized, by the look of her. Better be gentle. "I'm Georg." Perhaps she had something to hide. She might have been on the run when he'd helped her in the train. "I'll come back for Matt. With him wrapped up like a package, he'll be easy to return to a sender in London. Do you want me to take you to St. Ives on my way past?" He took her uplifted eyebrows and indrawn breath for a resounding yes.

***

On the jog past the houses with the stranger, Ellen pointed to the left. Desperation about what to do pulled her in different directions. "Wait." She drew a ragged breath. "I've been staying with a woman over there the last few days. I can't just leave without telling her where I am." Although he didn't dress as smartly, this stranger could be as bad as Matt. Better to stay in safety with Alana.

The man slowed. "You could ring her later. Or would you rather stay?" With a firm grip, he swung her to face him. "What's your name?"

His accent soothed her. "Ellen." She looked into a pair of kind eyes, which surprised her because of the violence he'd shown. "Don't bother trying to take over. You'll end up with a dead girl on your hands." She stuck out her chin in defiance.

"Hold on. I'm the guy who's just helped you. In fact, I've helped you twice."

"And I'll be forever grateful? Think again."

"Stay here then. I'll take Matt away. You don't have to worry about him anymore."

A scratch under Georg's eye ran to his hair line. Short breaths lifted his muscular chest under the tight tee shirt below his jacket. The tied-back hair could do with a wash, but all the same, not bad. How could she test him? "Come and meet Alana if you're so lily white."

"If you like."

You could never tell if men were decent. "Come on then."

He faced the houses. "Which one is it?" He ran his hand over his head and winced. "Hope I look presentable."

Breath escaped her in a sharp sigh. "You'll do." She leaned close and inhaled the clean odor mixed with sweat. Seeing he was willing, he didn't need to finish the test. Besides, Alana wouldn't appreciate a testosterone-filled male—a lesson learned after visiting Liliha with men. "It's okay. I've changed my mind. I'll go alone." Maybe Alana could advise her.

"Right." Georg glanced into the distance, and then touched his mouth. He didn't wince. "Here's the plan. I'll collect Matt and get him settled in the car. I've parked by the sheds at the turnoff." He pointed in the direction of the main road.

"That'll give me time to get my stuff." And also she could decide whether to leave with him.

"I'll pick you up shortly." Georg strode off.

She couldn't tear her gaze away. Something about him drew her. His strength, his openness. She'd read stories about women falling for their rescuer. And what did he mean about helping her twice?

Excitement over, her legs dragged on the way to Alana's house. The front door opened after her knock.

"What's happened?" Alana asked.

Ellen almost sobbed with relief. With the woman's perfume wafting in the air and her arm supporting her, Ellen entered. They ended up in the living room although she didn't remember walking there.

"Could I have a biscuit, please? I'm kinda shaky."

"Be back in a flash with something to tide you over."

Once seated and satisfied with food and a sweet drink, Ellen told her all about the fighting and how they'd left Matt tied up in the shed. "Don't worry. I'm not hurt. Only shaken. Anyway, Georg is coming to drive me to St. Ives in a minute."

"What will happen to the other man?" Alana frowned. "We should ring the police."

"Georg said he'd deliver the scumbag to someone in London. They'll probably deal with him there. He deserves what he gets."

"Do you want to press charges against Matt?"

Ellen's stomach tightened. "Don't involve the police."

"Sure?"

After a swift shake of her head, Ellen blurted, "I'm not sure about Georg, though."

"What do you want to do?"

"I don't know. How can I figure out whether to trust him?" Decisions were always difficult. First he looked as if he was saving her, and then he seemed like the worst pimp in the world.

"What does you intuition tell you?"

"Mixed signals. What if Georg is working with Matt and they're trying to trick me?"

"If you have any doubts, stay here with me."

"Then you'd be in danger." Ellen scrunched up her eyes. She couldn't do such a thing to Alana. "Georg seemed to hate the guy like I do. I should trust him until he gives me a reason not to."

"What you've experienced would frighten anybody."

"I'm alright now. I should go." She'd rather stay safe, but when he left, she'd wish she'd gone with him. "He'll be here any minute."

"Come upstairs. We'll collect your things while we talk."

"Luckily, I haven't taken everything out of the bag," Ellen said.

"You know, somebody could have followed me when I picked it up from the launderette." Alana led the way to the bedroom, and then folded her arms and leaned on the door jamb.

"Never mind. It's over now and I'm safe." Ellen hoped everything would work out while she collected her bits and pieces, stuffed them beside the clothes, and then flung her brush and lipstick into the top.

Alana sighed, and then gave a reassuring smile. "I've enjoyed our time together. It lifted me out of my rut."

Ellen hugged her. "Thanks."

"What goes around comes around. Each time you help a person in need, someone else helps you. Strange how everything works, but it makes sense."

A crunch of loose stones came from outside.

Ellen grabbed her bag, hurried downstairs, and left the ... what did they call it? *Sanctuary —like where nuns go.*

Outside, a sea fog shrouded the area. In the car, Georg sat behind the wheel and Matt rested against the rear headrest with his eyes closed.

Ellen gave a wave, and then climbed into the passenger seat.

"Are you sure you want to go?" Alana called.

"Don't worry about me. I can take care of myself." She wished her words were true.

Chapter Forty-Five

Van den Burg tingled all over. *Probably adrenalin.* As his assignment to deliver Matt to Straten neared completion, he drove the hire-car beside misty fields on the minor road toward St. Ives. Georg hoped the steady pace would give him, as well as his shocked female passenger, time to relax.

Every now and again, he took a peek at Ellen, her expression strained and her focus distant. He broke the silence. "Keep an eye on Matt for me. We don't want him to wake up and give us a surprise."

Ellen glanced across, sighed, and then strained to view the rear seat.

Reflected from the rear-vision mirror, Matt slumped on the seat with his mouth gagged and his hands tied and connected to his ankles. He should remain dozing after being forced to drink a dose of sedative last time he'd woken.

"Still out." She wriggled to face the front, and then rubbed her elbow. "Can he get away when he comes to?"

"I've tied one leg to the seat support."

"What if he dies?"

"We'll toss him over the cliff." Georg made an effort to laugh. His throat didn't co-operate and a grumble emerged instead. "You wouldn't care, would you?"

"Not on your life." Her vocalization echoed high in her nose.

He took another peek at her. *Stressed all right.* He didn't blame her. "Want to tell me about it?"

"He used me, the fucking bastard," she hissed like kitten surprised by a predator. "Wouldn't let me go. You'd think I'd be safe close to Land's End. But no, he had to chase me."

He wouldn't alert her to his involvement with Matt. "He could have been here for a different reason." His words might settle her.

"As if." Ellen folded her arms, strong, defiant. The trauma would have dragged weaker women down like an animal on the veldt hunted by a loin.

"Look, don't sweat it," Georg said. "He and I work for the same guy in London. He just came to check on something." He'd rather not explain. She was freaked enough already.

"What a coincidence," she muttered. "I thought Matt worked for himself. He never mentioned a boss."

"He wouldn't." Georg changed the car's gears and passed a tractor.

"So, I'm out of the frying pan into the fire."

"What do you mean?" He withheld a groan.

"You're both in the same line of work."

"In a manner of speaking. I don't mistreat women, though." Amongst bare branches, the St. Ives sign flashed by in the dimming light. "We'll be there in ten minutes. Where do you want me to drop you?"

"Anywhere close to town will do. I can walk."

"Guest house?"

"I'm staying in a cottage with a woman called Liliha." She shot him a frown, and then glanced away fast.

She probably regretted her words. "Small world," he murmured. "I know the place."

"Another coincidence. Were you following me?"

"What makes you think so? I was in the area at Zenor when you ran at me."

"Why were you there?"

Once again, his insides melted under the fervor of her

spunk. "Following Matt, if you must know." *Watch out, van den Burg. A woman like that can be addictive. Might not be a bad thing though.*

"Sounds like a set-up. You and Matt might have staged the whole thing." Despite her words, she remained approachable.

He faced the road, decreased speed and swung the wheel to round a bend. "Okay." He let his breath out in a steady stream. "I was tailing Matt, alright?"

"What do you really do?"

"I'm in the process of changing job descriptions." Georg couldn't block out conflicting thoughts of attraction to her and his desire for secrecy. Motor pressure built up sufficient revs for Georg to change gears, while his heartbeat made an effort to keep up.

"An action man like you could get work, no trouble."

"I'll find something to keep me occupied."

She stared outside.

A wispy haze floated by, which added to his sense of surrealism. A blink didn't clear his crazy sense of the world spinning. Had their meeting on the train been preordained?

Her feminine scent hovered in the air, mixed with oil and dirt. A reluctance to let go of this delicate, confused and abused woman tugged at Georg. Same as a lion, he wanted to cuff her and bite her neck in affection.

"I'll leave Matt tied up in the boot at the car-park and escort you to Liliha's door. I seem to remember there are driving restrictions in town today."

"I can go on my own."

When her elbow bumped him, he glanced across.

She drew a breath and hugged herself. "Don't leave him alone. He'll get away even if he's unconscious now."

"I'll make sure you arrive safely." Georg pulled off

the main road into a secluded lane. "First, give me a hand with Matt. We'll put him in the boot." He cut the motor.

"You're joking, right?" Her voice got louder. "I'm not touching that creep."

***

Ellen opened the car door and pelted away. Escape— nothing else mattered. Every man wanted to catch a woman and use her.

She hurtled along the verge of the small roadway toward a jumble of roofs in the gloom.

Crashing footfalls from behind made her heart jump.

She had to trick Georg so he couldn't find her. He'd worked with Matt for sure. He might have untied him by now. A sob mingled with her rugged breaths. Ducking beneath a jumble of entwined branches, she yelled with what she hoped resembled pain. She groaned and hoped he'd think she had fallen and couldn't get up. Instead, she crept beside thick undergrowth. No Giant's Rock would shelter her here.

Thuds approached. Scuffles told her he must be searching. She crept uphill between damp bushes. Distant roofs lured her to the safety of a farm and outbuildings. A branch dragged at her trousers.

She wrenched the stem off and straightened. Couldn't see him. In a burst of speed, she ran toward a roof which nestled beneath giant trees. No time to check behind her. Reaching a driveway, she bounded along crunching gravel. Rather than an old barn as she'd hoped, the building was a smart, glass-fronted home with a Buddha beside the door. Although no sound came from within, and no lights were on, she raised a hand to knock.

"Got you." A South African accent accompanied ragged breaths.

While she kicked, he pulled her against his strong chest. Her heels bounced off his legs, despite the arms binding her in a strange comfort.

"Don't act like a flighty springbok. I won't hurt you." Georg turned her to face him and clamped her biceps.

She yelled, "I'm not yours to use." Someone might hear her and send Georg away.

"Calm down. You've got the wrong idea."

The house was too quiet. She slumped—waiting for her chance. Nobody would trap her again.

"Despite what you believe, Matt's my enemy. He stole from me and now I'm taking him to London for punishment." His grip on her back softened. "Do you believe me?"

"Why should I?" She broke his hold and faced him, poised to escape.

"No reason, I guess." He gazed inside the picture window. "Nice house. Imagine living in a place like this. Maybe one day."

Freed, she tensed and shot a quick look past him.

"I'm going to check on Matt. I'll wait five minutes while you make up your mind whether to join me or not." He turned and paced along the driveway. He called, "Five minutes."

Ellen knocked in case someone missed her yell. Nothing but the twittering of birds. She dropped onto her haunches, face down. Did she, or didn't she, trust Georg? The fur collar of her parka hugged her neck. Out of sight, branches whispered promises of good things to come. *Don't be daft. Think!*

Liliha told her to defend herself if faced with danger. Georg didn't threaten her or rough her up. His face seemed decent with its square jaw and steady gaze. But, if she relied on him, she'd give up any chance of freedom.

A quick study of the area revealed plenty of places to hide. Should she run—or trust? She didn't like either option. The ground beneath her bent legs sent spiders of cold to wrap her into a statue pose. She must snap out of this mental fog.

Other people had helped her already—Liliha, Alana. Good people really lived in the world, not just in books. Her shoulders relaxed. Georg had never hurt her despite several opportunities. She pictured his stance when he'd raised her from under the bike—his gentle eyes. She lifted her head to the sky. Why not believe in Georg?

Breaking free from her cramped position, life flowed up her legs and into her heart.

***

Once Sarah left the cottage from her regular afternoon visit, Liliha collapsed onto her chair. A sigh slipped out and lingered in the quiet room. Soon, she'd be finished the two-week stint. Then she'd face a life with no purpose.

At least she had a friend her own age, although at the moment Sarah acted the role of a patrol officer and counselor.

Unable to prevent ideas popping into her mind, Liliha sagged in submission. Worries demanded attention—the ring, failure, and her own stupidity. Each affected its neighbor—a line of dominoes falling.

Restless fingers reached for the non-existent ring. An uncharacteristic grunt forced her to confront the reality of the ugly white dent on the finger of her right hand.

No use regretting the past. Giving every bit of strength to the push, she stood and wandered toward the kitchen. A knock startled her.

She faced the entrance and called, "Who's there?"

"Ellen."

After fumbling with the lock and checking the safety chain, Liliha opened the door a crack and peered into the fading light. "What are you doing here?" Something must be wrong.

"I've brought a man to visit." Ellen's voice conveyed a faint touch of humor.

Surely they'd passed that stage. Liliha opened the door wide, breath catching when she recognized Georg. "Do you know each other?"

"Yep." Both spoke in unison.

"Can we come in?" he asked.

"Of course." Liliha stepped aside, taking in the scratch under his eye and the sack he carried. "Have you two been in a fight?"

"We sure have," Ellen said. "And I've brought my clothes as the trophy."

The visitors removed their coats and left the bag beneath the stairs. Liliha ushered them to the kitchen. "Want a cuppa?"

"Yes, please."

Liliha paused. Alana had done a good job in teaching Ellen manners.

"I'm gasping for one," Georg said.

Ellen brushed the knees of her grubby track-suit, and narrowed her eyes at Georg.

While they settled at the table, Liliha filled the electric kettle and flicked the switch. Georg's hair looked mud-encrusted and she caught a glimpse of dried blood beneath. What had happened to friendly Cornwall? "I won't be a minute." She hurried upstairs and grabbed the first aid

309

kit.

When she rounded the kitchen doorway, her guests' mumbling broke off. She tried to dispel the grimness creeping up inside as she said, "Show me your battle scars." After preparing a bowl with antiseptic, she wrung out a cloth.

"Thanks." Georg held still under her ministrations.

She cleaned the edges of the cut beneath his eye with light dabs to avoid disturbing the skin. "That's deep. The wound could need attention." Disregarding his shrug, she removed the rubber band on his hair, cleansed the head wound, and then moistened the surrounding hair before mopping the blood. "The skin's closed. Might be alright, but you should get proper attention. The hospital is—"

"I'll be fine." A raised jaw showed his impatience. "I've got things to do."

Liliha hovered. "What about you, Ellen?"

"I'm okay. Just a few bruises." She gazed at George and scrunched up her eyes. "With your hair loose, I recognize you from somewhere."

Georg turned side on in a pose and grinned. "Remember the train trip to St. Ives?"

"You're the one ..."

"—who helped you out with the fare."

Ellen's mouth dropped open. "Small world. And you didn't pressure me for a refund."

"I offered to help you." His gaze lowered and his mouth twitched. "The money was a gift."

"I've always believed things happen for a reason," Liliha said, restored to the familiar role of guidance, albeit without reaching the achievement by way of a vision.

Georg's focus shifted to her. He rubbed the skin

under his eye. "You're not wearing your ring."

"Something awful happened to me, too." Liliha leaned against the bench. "After you left, someone broke in. I woke up in hospital without my ring. They must have taken it." Instead of allowing anguish to beat her, she took a mental shift. "A very kind person called an ambulance. You?"

His nod assured her while she prepared the drinks.

"I'm so sorry," Ellen said.

"It's over now." Liliha passed the mugs to her guests along with milk and sugar.

"I've brought a whole heap of trouble," Ellen said.

"No, don't be silly. How could you have caused the break-in? But tell me what happened to you."

The couple spilled their adventures in a jumble of words. Liliha strained to take the information in. A fight between three men and Ellen's escape.

Liliha frowned. "Was Matt the man ...?"

The girl nodded.

"Where is he?"

"He's safely tied up. I'll drink this and run before he comes to." Georg glanced at the window with a slight frown. "I plan to deliver him to London. The drive will be easy in the dark."

"You won't hurt him any more, will you?"

Georg frowned. "No need."

Worry cramped Liliha's stomach. "Who was the man with him?"

"George Hopkins—local scum."

Liliha raised her eyebrows. The other George.

Georg placed his mug on the table and rose to his feet. "Well, I'll leave you now and get on with my job."

"Your job?"

"In a manner of speaking." Georg rested his gaze on Ellen. "I hope I see you again."

The girl's cheeks colored. "Not sure I want to."

"Is there a problem?" Liliha asked.

"I accused him of working with Matt." Ellen's sigh sounded fed up. "Maybe I was wrong."

"I don't blame you," Georg said.

Ellen blinked, rocked, and dropped her shoulders. A faltering grin lifted a corner of her mouth. She shot a look of inquiry in Liliha's direction.

"You'll stay with me, of course, Ellen." Sight unfocused, Liliha gazed in the direction of the clock. George Hopkins. The man had stood at the bar while she and Harry sat together in the pub. Perhaps, he was the man from her vision. Without the ring, her responsibility to get him to change his ways dulled.

Chapter Forty-Six

With nobody inside the used car yard, George Hopkins used his spare key to open the gate, and then maneuvered Matt's gray Fiat between a couple of clapped-out motors. He'd speak to old buggerlugs when he returned to his so-called office tomorrow.

Owzat for a game of cricket? First, getting his hands on the ring, and then outsmarting Matt at Zenor. He chuckled at his cunning. At least he'd got something from the know-it-all Londoner for his trouble. With any luck, Matt would leave St. Ives now he'd found the girl.

Hands in the pockets of his black jacket, George strolled into town. The click of his Cuban heels added to his glow as the street lights flicked on. He'd spread the word to his contacts in the hope of discovering Matt's whereabouts. Anyone could spot the man with his blond hair and muscled body.

George hitched the prize out of his pocket and hefted it. Heavy. Solid. The ring's bright gold shone with purity. He recalled the furtive words from the two women on the train about the museum's interest in the ring which had started his search. On closer inspection, the stone didn't look special. Just a pale blue, cloudy hunk of rock, not even cut with facets to catch the light—smooth and plain with a tiny flaw which marred the clarity.

He'd make inquiries on the quiet about the value. A couple of local dealers owed him favors. Given a rough idea of what to expect, he'd be armed when he offered the item for sale to the London fence.

He shoved the ring inside his pocket, patted the bulk, and headed for the pub.

***

After changing into fresh trousers and sweater, Ellen clattered down Liliha's stairs. She'd need a suitcase soon with all the things she'd picked up along the way.

Metal clanks came from the end room. In the hallway, Ellen headed for the bright kitchen, passing the poster of the Egyptian woman. Despite the pots on the stove and bowls on the work bench, the room looked tidy.

Liliha stood with her head strained toward the radio sitting on the work bench. A voice ranted on about a stolen Egyptian consignment, whatever that was. She straightened, eyebrows lowered.

To draw attention, Ellen said, "I want to have a kitchen just like this one day."

"I'd like to get new cupboards installed later." Liliha glanced about the room. "But I love things from the past. See the old Clome oven?" She pointed to the blackened metal contraption built into the wall. "In the olden days, they baked bread inside."

"Nobody bakes any more. Ya ... You just buy bread at the shop." Pleased at her correction, Ellen plonked onto the chair Liliha had previously pointed out at the table.

"Everyone's too busy, I guess. The effort of working for a living takes so much out of you."

"I've got to think about what I'll do now." Ellen lifted her chin.

"Not working at the launderette?"

"Mary didn't seem too keen when I rang to apologize. I could go back to London, although I don't want the same life I had before. But then I'd have to find somewhere to stay. London's so expensive." Ellen gazed at the black oven while she blabbed on. "What would I do? Here, you've helped me find a job and a place to stay."

"Let's hope Mary will take you on again." Liliha faced the modern cooker and adjusted the heat under a saucepan. Steam rose into the air.

Smelled rank, like vegetables. "I'll talk to her tomorrow. Not sure I can face her at the moment. I need time to think."

"You've got some big decisions to make." Liliha placed two dinner plates on the bench beside the stove.

"Could I ever make a life where something I do matters?" Ellen asked. "Or have a home?"

"You have to work hard toward any goal. But first you need to decide what you want. Do you want to be independent or find a partner?"

"Depends on who comes along. I don't think you can plan for a partner."

Liliha studied her. "You're very wise, you know."

Ellen averted her eyes. Compared to the older woman, she'd never be good enough. But she lived a different life than Liliha.

The image of Georg's face wavered before her like the hero of a television program, with his candid brown eyes and square face. He'd probably keep a scar under his eye, which would give him rugged appeal. With him by her side, nobody would approach her unless she welcomed them. But would she need anyone else if she had Georg? Ellen's stomach clamped. The only thing she'd ever committed to was a life with Matt. Look where that got her.

She straightened as Liliha served the food. "Why should I decide what I want? Why not just go with the flow?"

"I believe thoughts affect every other thing around you. Not just the way people respond to you, but circumstances. Like fate." Liliha passed over a plate of steaming vegetables.

Ellen brushed aside the confusing words. "I smell cheese."

"I've made cheese sauce to add to the protein in the chick peas so we have a balanced meal."

"Why don't you just have meat?" Ellen took a mouthful of broccoli smothered in sauce. "Nice."

"I like vegetables." Liliha licked a white glob off her bottom lip.

Ellen savored a mouthful of thin green beans dipped in the sauce. The beans squeaked when she bit into them. Were they crying about their end or did they accept whatever came? How silly. As if vegetables had worries. She finished everything on her plate faster than Liliha, and then straightened her fork. The least she could show appreciation for the meal. "I've ... taken you for granted. How can I make up for that?"

Liliha's face lit and she chuckled. "I wish you could get the chewing gum out of the carpet in the hall."

"Of course. I know how, too. Mary told me." Ellen glanced in the direction of the door, pride filling her with enthusiasm.

"Tomorrow will be soon enough. I'm ready for bed." Liliha carried the plates to the sink.

"I'm so jumpy, I don't know if I'll sleep."

After they'd washed the dishes, Ellen smoothed on fragrant hand cream while climbing the stairs. Didn't feel like watching television.

Could she be sure Matt would stay away from her?

If she lived with Georg, she'd feel safe. But he seemed perfectly happy without her. She stopped beside the bed. What was wrong with her? Why did she grab the closest man and try to link up? Didn't she want to be independent?

Anyway, until she knew Georg better, she didn't know how to judge him.

***

North of London, Georg Van den Burg drew up in the forecourt outside Straten's mansion, thankful to have arrived without incident. They'd pulled over beside the road for pit-stops during the seven hour trip and avoided contact with others. Didn't want to arrive before the boss woke up.

Georg shrugged off his tiredness from the overnight drive, climbed out of the car and jogged to the passenger door. The laurel trees inside the old brick wall muted the traffic noise somewhat. "Don't try anything here." He jerked the sullen Matt out by the arm and retied his hands behind. The man's crumpled clothes didn't look so smart now. Linen. He wouldn't be caught dead in it. "Ever met our boss?"

"Never needed to."

Pleased at besting Matt by knowing the layout of the place, Georg centered his belt buckle and glanced at the door. Better use the rear entrance. "This way." He hauled Matt to the right, into a storage room built against the house, and emerged in the open rear area which overlooked the landscape. He reminded himself he needed this job if he wanted to remain in the country and keep the flat Straten had provided in St. Ives.

Escorting Matt, Georg climbed the steps to the long open veranda and stopped at the main rear door. "Let's find out what he wants done with you."

Matt remained impassive.

Georg knocked and waited. Footsteps approached from within. The door swung open. "Mr. Straten home?" he asked the housekeeper.

"Just a minute." She eyed the scruffy Matt before shutting off their entry.

After a long time, during which they both fidgeted, Straten appeared dressed in a smart suit.

"I've got a package for you." Georg shoved Matt forwards.

"Well, well, well," Straten said. "A thief."

"I'm not the only one," Matt blurted.

Georg's stomach tightened, ready for his exposure.

"A bastard in St. Ives stole my car and—"

"That doesn't concern me," Straten said.

"There's another matter, too," Georg said. "He held a woman unlawfully in a shed until I found her."

"We need to talk, Matt, man to man," Straten said. "Maybe I'll call the police, maybe not. Depends on what we agree to. In the meantime, Georg, take him to the shed and lock him in."

Matt squirmed against his grip on the walk over the wooden boards. When Georg closed the door, footsteps sounded behind.

"Just a minute. Step away."

Georg complied. What now?

"While he's tied, I want you to soften him up. Make it easy for me to question him."

"What?"

"Go on, man. What are you waiting for?"

"No way! I'm not beating a helpless man." With fury triggering his steps, Georg headed away.

"Wait!"

Georg turned to face Straten, his hand on the doorknob. The tips of his ears burned and he found breathing difficult.

Straten locked the door. "That was a test," Straten said, face stern and eyes narrow. "You passed." Straten led him to a table on the balcony, where the housekeeper placed a covered pot and two bone china cups and saucers before withdrawing.

With a sigh, Georg's tension eased. Now what?

"Take a seat." Straten, blond hair lifting in the breeze, gestured to the pot. "Coffee to wake us up. I've got an appointment at ten."

Weary, Georg pulled out a chair facing the view. Past a garden dotted with occasional horses, green fields bounded by trees swept to the skyline below. Better not relax in his employer's acceptance. The calm wouldn't last.

"I see you're a man of your word." Straten slid his gaze over Georg's body. "Not much good at the other work though."

Georg shifted position.

"How do you like St. Ives?" Straten asked.

"Nice place."

"Would you object to returning to London?"

Georg's heart beat picked up. "Not at all. What do you have in mind?"

"I have an opening for a chauffeur. The old boy's had a heart attack—fortunately, not behind the wheel. How would you fancy driving for me?"

"I think I could handle the job."

"Seeing as you made a mess of your former position, this easy job might suit you better."

Unsure if they'd sorted out the mix-up about what his earlier job entailed, Georg nodded. "I'll give that some thought." Couldn't very well face the man about the instructions he'd given for stealing the Egyptian display articles at Truro.

Calm and well-groomed in the morning air, Straten poured coffee for them both.

"I remember the trouble-free days back home." Georg pushed his ambivalent attitude away. "I prefer things that way." As long as he could make his own choice of a partner.

"I'll provide accommodation. My daughters need someone to take them from one place to another at short notice." The direct stare from Straten made Georg feel like a rodent caught in a snake's stare. "You understand, this is a position of trust. These are my daughters. Nothing bad will happen to them. I expect your complete assurance that you'll look after them."

"Understood." Georg held the man's gaze until Straten looked away while his mind raced. Maybe Ellen could share the living quarters with him.

"You look fitter than the old boy anyway. Have you kept up with your martial arts since you've been in Cornwall?"

Georg fiddled with his cup. "Sure have. I practice on the cliffs." He opened his mouth, and then decided not to speak.

"What is it, man?" Straten asked.

"What are you offering in the way of lodging?" Georg swallowed a mouthful of coffee and fought off the urge to choke.

Calculating eyes assessed him. "You haven't found a woman, have you?"

"Just wondering." Georg rubbed the rear of his head.

"There's plenty of room in the original groom's quarters. Either way," Straten said, "as long as your association doesn't cause hassle for me, report here in two days. Otherwise, I'll hire someone else."

"Understood." Although the weight of uncertainty lifted off Georg's chest, he now faced another challenge. Silly to think of Ellen. He hardly knew the girl.

Chapter Forty-Seven

After snoozing in his car beside a park on the outskirts of London, Georg made the return journey to Cornwall. Didn't bother with the radio—needed silence to think. He could rest properly tomorrow.

At least he'd won Straten's approval after Matt admitted to stealing the cartons from the lock-up. He had no idea what sort of threat Straten would impose on the pimp, but Matt would be unlikely to seek out Ellen in St. Ives again.

Released from the need to locate the moonstone for the boss, Georg pictured himself floating on a stream while the surge carried him to safety and left his recent way of life behind. His circumstances would change now with the prospect of a regular job so soon after arriving in the country.

At the turnoff to Truro, Georg pulled up before a roundabout, and then used the exit which led further west and escaped his nagging sense of guilt about the robbery.

The traffic thinned after a few miles and his thoughts went inward. B took goods from A. C stole them and passed them on to D. What senseless work.

Georg gritted his teeth, wondering why he hadn't admitted to the theft of the box from the Egyptian consignment. Now, with no idea what to do with the golden bracelet sealed inside the box, he considered his options. He should get rid of the item as soon as possible in light of the respectable life he intended to lead. Better sell in a different area, otherwise someone might alert the authorities. The news of the exhibition heist must have got about. Perhaps he could take the bracelet up to Scotland.

And what of the two women at the cottage in St. Ives? Although different, both pulled at him.

Ellen's young face, a kitten, cheeky and pert, offered excitement. What future lay ahead for them? Ellen didn't trust him. Not without reason. Her life had been bad. Horse-face in Jo'burg would never have survived if their circumstances had been reversed. He imagined Ellen born to wealth in South Africa—dressed in fashionable clothes, hair cut in a flattering style instead of the blunt ends framing her face now.

And the older woman. Tall and elegant, Liliha shone with the calm pale light of the moon. Rather than affecting the tides, she swayed his mind—made him think about the way his life was headed. Could have influenced him to become the prospect for a respectable job.

At a flash of movement, Georg gripped the wheel, and slowed the car to allow a small animal to run to the side. A sense of injustice pulled at him. Small creatures had no chance against man's mighty machines. In a similar way, the gentle Liliha had been defenseless against her attackers.

The annoying itch in his head pointed to healing. He'd make it his business to put the situation right—just as Liliha had helped with his wound. Armed with a clue, he'd find the violator and return her ring in the two days before he left.

Of course, he'd also have a reason to visit Ellen again. He glanced at the dashboard display. He should arrive at his flat by nineteen hundred hours. He'd have a good night's sleep and catch up with them tomorrow.

Life had a way of turning events upside down. Facing the right direction now, he might even contact his father and set his mind at rest.

***

"I love you too, Alissa." Liliha patted the phone as if the contact was her daughter in the flesh instead of her sleepy visitor upstairs, and then carried on preparing breakfast. Where had the woman who gave visionary advice to the needy gone? This empty casing couldn't be the person who whispered into a stranger's mind whenever they raised a figurative shell to their ear.

Numbness occupied the place where joy should have been, but she would do her best to act in a normal way.

Upstairs, the bathroom door creaked open.

Once ready, Liliha called Ellen, served the food onto two plates and placed them in the warm oven while she made mugs of tea.

Ellen wandered into the kitchen fully dressed, short hair still damp. "I slept better than I can remember."

"Good morning." Liliha bent to the oven and brought out the food, and then joined Ellen at the table.

"I'll go and see Mary while you're at work." Ellen reached for toast. "I hope she's not mad at me."

Liliha swallowed a slice of hot tomato before it burned too much. "So do I. Do you want to stay in St. Ives now?"

"I've made good friends in you and Alana. Friends are hard to come by. Let's see how Mary feels."

"Very sensible," Liliha said. A piece of grainy whole meal toast soothed her mouth.

"I'll call Alana and thank her. You go to work and leave the clearing up to me. It's the least I can do. When you get home, the chewing gum will be off the carpet and everything will be tidy."

Liliha nodded. "That would be great." From now on,

she'd curb her tendency to dictate her perfectionist ideas onto other people's lives. Ellen was improving without her help.

***

Ellen entered the launderette dressed in comfortable clothes, ready to start work if asked. No more skimpy skirts and short tops for her. Women stood chatting in the packed room while they folded dry laundry from the hot machines. At the rear, Mary accepted two full plastic bags from a man before he headed for the door.

Stomach quivering with worry and hope, Ellen approached. "Mary. I'm sorry I left you in the lurch the other day."

"No need to explain. You had to get away. I understand. Some men make life hard."

Ellen drew in a breath and smiled, looking forward to being accepted in this new life. And Georg? *Well that would come.*

Mary didn't meet her eyes. "But I have a business to run here. I'd already accepted extra work with the ironing." A frown creased her forehead. "I'm sorry. I didn't know when you'd be back so I arranged for someone else to take your place."

Ellen followed her gesture to a jolly woman speaking to a young man beside a machine. Every hope and plan slid down the drain with the gurgling wash water. Her stiff jaw felt awkward. She drew a breath but didn't shout. A reluctant nod accepted the replacement. Tears of rage and hurt blurred her vision on the way to the door.

"I hope you find something else soon," Mary called.

"Thanks." Ellen trudged outside.

***

Van den Burg arrived at the Golden Lion pub during

325

the busy lunch hour. Well rested from a good night's sleep, he ambled toward the bar. No sign of the local George Hopkins, but Harry's spiky hairstyle caught his eye.

Thinking of the friends he'd left behind in Jo'burg, Georg made for the stylish man dressed in a suit with a striped tie loosened at the neck. He mock-punched Harry's shoulder. "How's it going?"

"So-so." Harry's gaze wandered over Georg's tied-back hair. "That looks smart."

Georg accepted the comment without explaining his need to cover the wound and turned to order a pint.

Harry took a gulp of his drink. "Staying for a bite to eat?"

"I think I will." Georg accepted his brimming glass from the barmaid, took a sip and said to Harry, "I thought you had a job."

"This is my lunch break. I've ordered flounder. It's fresh today. The cook's frying a batch now."

"I'll have the same." Georg pointed to the chalked sign on the board and the barmaid nodded. He faced Harry. "I'm on the hunt for George Hopkins. Have you seen him anywhere?"

Harry's eyebrows gathered. "You wanna stay clear of him. The little mouse is crawling around eating so many crumbs he's gonna grow into a rat."

"That's what I'm worried about." Georg glanced up at the barmaid delivering their food. He dug into his pocket for cash.

They carried meals to a free table at the rear of the room.

"Did you get the cut under your eye from a rat's claw?" Harry asked.

Georg sat opposite Harry. "Kinda." He stuffed a

wedge of hot fried potato into his mouth. "I think Hopkins made off with Liliha's ring."

"No." Harry's jaw slackened, his eyes losing focus. "Poor Liliha. How much more loss can she take?"

The guy seemed overly concerned about her. While he filled Harry in, Georg finished his meal.

"Want some help?"

"I'll let you know. Meanwhile, keep a lookout for George."

"Don't turn now," Harry bent closer and touched his shoulder, "but the blighter's just arrived."

The hand steadied Georg's hunter instinct to turn.

Chapter Forty-Eight

George Hopkins stepped inside *'his'* pub door, strolled over to join a few welcoming locals at the bar, and ordered a large beer. The barmaid slammed his drink on the counter and then headed toward the other side of the room. He wiped the spill off the side and licked his thumb. "You own me more respect, you bitch. I pay for this by guarding the premises." The men nearby nodded. While quenching his thirst, George watched where she went in such a hurry. He glimpsed Harry's spiky hair between other customers. The man who sat opposite turned at her approach.

Under the slick hair, George recognized his namesake—the guy he'd left to fight Matt at Giant's Rock. Stomach clenching, George pulled his up collar and faced away.

Taking a few deep gulps of his drink, he chatted to an old codger who should know better than to spend all morning with a glass in front of him. He made a contact too. The soak's young neighbor needed a car.

Deal all but settled, George shoved his empty on the bar and took the opportunity to slide out the door hidden on the far side of a tourist couple.

Might be better to frequent the small pub on the hill until things died down. Or drive to another town in his old Volkswagen.

***

The murmur of masculine voices formed a strident beat for Van den Burg's thoughts while he kept an eye on the dark-haired man drinking at the bar.

"I've gotta get back to work." Harry peered in Hopkin's direction. "Some of us have to."

"Yeah, yeah. I'll let your snide remark sail over my head."

"He's slipped out the door behind some tourists," Harry said. "I'll leave now and let you know which way he goes."

"Right." Georg drained his drink and stood. From the exit, Harry pointed to the left. Georg nodded and headed outside.

On the busy street, a man with black jacket and dark hair walked away between two others. Georg dodged pedestrians and caught up, but discovered a strange face. With a silent curse, he stopped and glanced either way. His prey had escaped.

How could he trace the guy? Matt's car! His namesake probably drove home to St. Ives. *Start with parking stations.*

Georg headed for the closest one, entered the multi-story structure, and searched from top to bottom. Drat the man. Better check elsewhere before panic set in.

Outside again, shop fronts flashed by while Georg strode along the footpath. The second parking station loomed ahead and Georg hurried inside.

The man could have hidden the jewel anywhere. A business transaction with Hopkins seemed farfetched. Thoughts popped into Georg's mind about the heavy gold bracelet—the one under the loose floor-board in the cupboard at his digs. Could be an excellent bargaining device.

Exiting the place after a fruitless search, Georg caught sight of a dealer's yard at the top of the hill. *Better check.* The wily local probably had friends and acquaintances all over town.

A larger problem loomed. How would he temp the

thug to swap items? *Plan further ahead.* Find the car first, if possible. Then, head home to collect the box.

A good result depended on time and place.

Turning up his collar in the stiff hilltop breeze, Georg entered the premises which resembled a scrap yard rather than a dealership. A couple of half-decent cars lined the front. Further in, the place reeked of oil and rust. No prices on display. Probably have to make a deal with whoever occupied the ramshackle hut.

An idea formed while he ambled up and down the lines of cars. Sure enough, the gray Fiat sat at the rear. He checked the plate and breathed a sigh of relief. How long would the vehicle remain in the yard? Deciding to toss chance to the wind, he strolled toward the office sign. The sloppy man inside glanced up.

"Nothing here I'm interested in," Georg called. "Although I might be back if I don't see anything better." With a wave, he marched downhill to implement his plan. A fifteen minute drive to his pad—twenty tops. With any luck, he'd return with the box before anything changed.

***

On her saunter out of town with a few items for the evening meal, Liliha caught a flash of smooth silver hair amongst a few pedestrians walking uphill. "Yvonne. Wait."

Yvonne turned. A smile crinkled the edges of her eyes. "What have you been up to lately?"

"Where do I start?"

Yvonne touched her arm in a sympathetic manner. "Did you get your ring back?"

A swift blink removed the prick of tears. Liliha shook her head and focused ahead on a few shops clustered between houses.

"Life goes on regardless of our loss," Yvonne said.

"William and I are concentrating on work. It eases the pain."

"I know what you mean. I miss Oliver so much. And now, with the ring gone, I feel as if the whole purpose in my life has been whipped away from under me. I know, losing the ring isn't half as bad as . . . well, you understand." After Yvonne's nod, they strolled in companionable silence.

"Did you ever ask yourself what the visions were all about?" Yvonne asked.

Puzzled, Liliha gazed at her. "I whispered advice to the needy and prevented . . . well not always."

"You tried." Yvonne squeezed her shoulder. "What I'm getting at is a deeper meaning. Where did the ability come from? If the visions were something to do with the ring, how did that happen?"

"I don't know. Perhaps those Egyptian priestesses believed so much in whatever they were doing that the ring's role still lingers." Liliha shook her head and grunted. "Unlikely. A stone couldn't trap intentions. Anyway, it doesn't matter now. I've lost the ring." Lost Oliver, lost everything. She snagged loose hair from her mouth and inhaled the briny smell from a sudden gust.

"I'm so sorry." Yvonne paused outside a second-hand store window. "Isn't that what you were looking for?"

Among the display, a smooth brown stone cat sat beside a bright china one. But the brown statue drew Liliha's attention. "It must be old." Her mind jumped to the cat Georg had spoken about.

"I'd say it's the right size for your papyrus too."

Confused, Liliha glanced to where Yvonne pointed at the thin black frame and nodded.

"The early style should set the picture off really well.

331

Come on. Let's take a look." Yvonne strode to the doorway and swiveled to ask, "Have you got the measurements?"

"Not with me."

"We'll come back." Yvonne veered toward the street.

"Hold on. I want to look at this." Liliha entered the shop's protection and examined the speckled brown stone cat in the window. Unlike the statue she owned, the ears were intact in the sweet feline face. She slid one hand along the smooth neck to the muscular body.

A deep voice penetrated. "That's granite. Probably an artifact taken from a high-status Egyptian tomb."

Liliha turned to the assistant. "How much are you asking?"

"It's fresh on the market. I couldn't let the item go for under eighty pounds."

"I'll think about it." Liliha emerged with Yvonne into the wind. "Hard to consider a purchase at the moment." What use were possessions, without love or a semblance of her own importance in the grand scheme of things?

"Excuse me. I should get this."

When Yvonne turned aside to speak on her phone, a little voice whispered inside Liliha, *'Don't give up hope.'*

She tilted her head. Nobody close enough to hear. Maybe the person who stole the moonstone ring had taken over her former job of helping people in distress.

Or was the message a return of optimism caught in the sea breeze?

Chapter Forty-Nine

Alone in Liliha's cottage, Ellen fought growing despair. Life hadn't treated her to a party. Apart from quick flashes of pleasure from some of her clients, she'd been on a reckless ride without thinking of the future. Rather than taking control, she'd let men use her and they'd tossed her away when they'd finished.

Maybe she could accept the rules of proper society she'd ignored.

On the way to the kitchen sink to rinse out her mug, a longing for something she'd never known crawled in her stomach.

Did the past cause her flaw? Or a lack of basic character?

Why hadn't she tried to get away from her former life sooner? Wrapped up with the hassle of making money and finding enough distraction to endure each day, she'd taken no notice of where the lifestyle would lead. She'd end up just the same as the older women, with their pathetic pleading and sagging bodies—the women who'd worked on the streets all their lives. Some disappeared and she'd heard of their early death with a mounting horror. Yet, she'd carried on regardless.

Occasional chirps outside the kitchen window soothed her. She lifted her head at the sound of conversation. Liliha ambled past with a fashionable silver-haired woman.

Ellen padded over the soft carpet and opened the front door.

"Hello," Liliha called. "Come out and meet Yvonne."

Unsure, Ellen advanced toward the older woman.

"Hello, dear. Great to see Liliha's mysterious guest at last." Yvonne's eyes shone.

Ellen melted in the warmth of acceptance. A surge of hope eased her worries. Perhaps life offered more than she could see. Oh, how she longed for the idea to be true. She reached out, but drew her hand away just in time. Before they laughed at her. She didn't belong in their world.

The strange new desire churned her stomach. She felt like a giant bird, soaring in the wind over the cliffs close to Alana's house. This is what she wanted—to act the same way as the women beside her. Calm and gentle and expecting the best in everyone.

"We've been window shopping." Liliha's eyes sparkled, but when she leaned closer, the humor vanished. "What's wrong?"

Ellen rubbed her forehead and blurted, "The job—it's gone."

"Oh, darling," Liliha said. "I'm so sorry."

"How disappointing," Yvonne said. "Never mind. Keep looking and you'll find something."

Heart swelling with Liliha's endearment, Ellen believed the women until her mind settled on the problem again like a fly that refused to be chased away.

"Good things happen around Liliha," Yvonne said.

Liliha's eyebrows drew together. "Not so sure about that any more. Give her a quote from Desiderata, Yvonne. You always remember the words."

The older woman tilted her head and licked her lips. "'Exercise caution in your business affairs, for the world is full of trickery.'"

Ellen's mouth dropped open. She'd known plenty of trickery over the years. But the person on her mind was

Georg. The hard part was to decide if he was a cheat or a hero.

"You probably won't be interested in what comes next." Yvonne sucked in her lips, and then beamed. "This is the best one: 'Be yourself.'"

What would Liliha do? Question him? Charm him?

Neither would work for Ellen. How could she copy Liliha and still be herself?

***

With a smirk at his cunning, Hopkins sauntered into the car yard toward the spot he'd left the gray Fiat. He'd taken care of business and dodged every problem. No sign of Matt. Could be drowned in the sea, for all George cared.

He swung the car door open, eased inside, and started the engine. On the way past the hut serving as an office, he lowered the window, waved to old buggerlugs, and then eased the car onto the road toward the buyer he'd lined up.

"That's it." A deep accented voice came from behind. "Keep going to the park."

"What the—" Pressure on his throat choked off an expletive. George revved the engine. A sharp jerk on his neck from the South African convinced him to drive with care.

"This'll do. Pull over. I've got a proposal to make."

George parked the car outside a house. When the pressure released, he turned to face Georg van den Burg.

"Don't try anything silly," the fellow growled, "until you hear what I've got to say." A mane of hair like an African lion replaced his tied-back style.

George growled, "It'd better be good." Damm! His annoying squeak didn't sound very threatening.

"You're all bluster, you conniving rat."

George twisted so his body faced sideways. "Go on

then. Let me have it."

"Tempting." Lion Man held his hands ready. "I've got an item of great value, and I wonder if you'd be interested in shifting the thing for me."

Excitement stirred inside Hopkins. "What is it?"

"Jewelry. Pure gold by the look of it. Worth a fortune. Interested?"

"Could be. Let's see." George rubbed his hands. Might end up with two items.

"Not so fast," Lion Man blurted. "I need to know where you'll get the money."

"What? You want cash?" George pictured his wallet.

"You think I'd just let you walk away with my goods? Anyway, I hardly think you'd have much to swap."

"Maybe I have. But who's to say if your item is worth more than mine?" He had the bastard now.

The fellow reached inside his jacket and produced a wooden container about the size of a cigar box.

"Well. Open it. Why's the box sealed?"

"You'll see in a minute." Lion Man dug a coin into the red wax seal and flipped the lid.

George leaned forward to get a better view of the shimmering jewel inside.

The guy slammed the lid shut. "Satisfied? You can see it's heavy gold."

"Looks like it, but I'd need to check. Did you lift that from Truro? I read about the stolen Egyptian items in the local rag." George regarded Lion Man with more respect.

"How much will you give me?"

"Hold on." Hopkins' head whirled. "What about my cut? Perhaps you want to swap. I've got a ring." He could make a good deal without too much bother and gain a more valuable item.

"I might be interested. When I . . . acquired . . . the bracelet, I thought my mother might like it for her birthday. Trouble is, sissy told me she'd bought her one already. A ring would be better. You could make up the balance with cash."

"This ring is very valuable."

"Let me see the goods before I decide."

Hopkins reached into his jacket, and then slid two fingers into the coin pocket to produce the ring. With the item in his open palm, he waited for approval.

"Mmmm. Mother likes moonstones. I don't think she's got such a deep blue one," Lion Man said. "Not very big though."

"That's the proper goods." George tossed the ring and caught the weight in his left hand. "I heard a woman talking about it on the train. The Museum in London offered her good money in exchange."

"Got anything else?"

"Take it or leave it." Frantic about the chance slipping away, George slid his right hand along his jeans close to his sock where a knife lay ready.

"So," Lion Man asked, "where'd you get the ring?"

"As if I'd tell you."

The South African opened the lid again and studied the bracelet.

George leaned in. Gold sections sparkled. A scarab faced upwards, made of deep blue stones. "Why's the bracelet held by a seal?"

"The wax keeps the enamel decoration safe." The guy nodded. "Beautiful, isn't it? I don't really want to let it go. But ... well, you'll see. Now, as to the ring. I don't have much time to send the thing away for appraisal so let's settle the deal."

"Yours might be fools' gold. How do I know if I don't get it checked?"

"I didn't bother with questions at the exhibition. Took it on faith. You can see the quality."

George agreed, but didn't let the knowledge show on his face. "I want to think it over."

"No time. Up to you to make up your mind. I'm getting sick of this game." The South African reached toward the jewel but stopped before he touched the top. "Just for that, I'll take an extra hundred pounds for my trouble."

George narrowed his eyes while his thoughts raced. The treasure ship was hauling up anchor. He glanced down. Sell the ring in his pocket, or trade for something better? Darned if he'd hand over cash though.

When Lion Man grasped the door handle, George drew in a breath. *Think!*

Chapter Fifty

In the car seat behind George, the passenger leaned forward, eyes on the car-yard outside. From his awkward position of straining his neck to see what the man was up to, George panicked. Full on. He snapped out his counter-offer. "Fifty."

"Not so fast, Hopkins." The South African shook his mane of hair. "You've got away from me once already. I won't fall for your double dealing again. You hand me the money first. Then the ring."

George reached into his pocket, peeled off a fifty pound note, and shoved the money toward the guy before he changed his mind. "How do I know you won't do the same thing and snatch the ring?"

"You don't," the bastard said with a snigger. "You're a thief—I'm a thief. What do you expect?" His laugh exploded.

George opened his palm and bounced the ring. Of the two items, the bracelet must be more valuable. If he didn't go ahead, he'd lose a good profit.

"Tell you what," Lion Man said. "I'll pass you the box with one hand and accept the ring with the other. Then, neither of us will need to worry."

"Well, keep the lid open so I can check the bracelet's still inside. I'm not stupid."

"Right." True to his word, the South African handed over the box, contents revealed.

George let go of the ring. The parting hurt, but the exchange would be worthwhile.

The fellow climbed out of the car, slammed the door and walked away.

George secured the door locks front and rear. Deep breath. He flipped the box shut, and then raised his trophy like a boxer. With the prize resting on his knee, he started the motor, over-revved it, and then drove to the hut at the entrance. Although difficult to catch his breath, he managed to blurt out, "Thanks" to the man inside. The car pulled away from in a series of jerks.

"Want me to have a look at the engine?" old buggerlugs shouted.

Ah, shit! "No thanks."

Once he'd gained a sense of calm, the car settled. Wouldn't take long to reach somewhere safe for a look at his treasure.

***

Liliha sat with Sarah, Ellen, and Yvonne in her living room stroking Walnut's soft fur while they discussed Ellen's future job prospects. The buzz of conversation soothed her but she caught an undertone beneath her friends' words. When Sara shot a glance at Yvonne for the third time, Liliha asked, "What's up? I can tell there's something on your mind."

"I can't wait a moment longer," Sarah said. She reached into a roomy bag beside her feet and raised an item wrapped in brown paper. She planted the long parcel on the table, upright like a tree. It made a dull thud. "This is from us both." Sarah included Yvonne. "Open it."

Liliha tore the paper at the top and exposed an ear, and then a cat's head carved from granite. Warmth flooded her. "Aww! You went back for it. Thank you so much."

"Yvonne called me before I got here and asked me to collect it. I know the gift won't make up for the loss of your ring, but the cat will look good with the other one under the papyrus in the hall."

Tears welled up in Liliha's eyes. Friends cared about her. "So kind of you both." Once she'd ripped the paper off the little figure, she ran her hand over the smooth stone. "I love it." She lowered the statue to Walnut's eye level. "See."

Walnut reached out with a delicate nose, sniffed the top, rubbed his head against the stone image, and then purred like a well-tuned motorbike.

"Where'd you find it?" Ellen ran her finger over the statue, and then shot a puzzled look at Yvonne and Sarah.

"The second-hand shop at the far end of the main street," Sarah said. "They sell all sorts of household goods, luggage, jewelry—you name it."

"You give expensive things like this to your friends? Blood ...." Ellen sighed. "I'll probably need a suitcase soon. I can't stay here forever."

"Stay as long as you need to," Liliha said. "I know you won't take advantage of me now."

"Well," Sarah scooted forward on her chair, "I'd better pick up my husband. He'll be wondering where I am."

"I've got to get back, too," Yvonne said. "William will claim he does all the work in the pottery." She peered at Ellen. "You don't do office work, do you?"

"I've never learned how."

"Maybe you could enroll at the job center."

After a quick hug for her guests, Liliha allowed Ellen to accompany the guests to the door. Walnut rubbed against her leg before darting outside between them.

Liliha placed her stone cat on the hall table beside the rougher statue. She stepped away, examined them, and then adjusted their positions. Time to take charge instead of feeling sorry for herself. "I'll call in to the library tomorrow after work. Do you want to meet me there?"

"Sure." Ellen's cheeks flushed. "Are you going to get a romance?"

"You can borrow one if you like. I want to find a book about crystals." *Best to use this present state of mind to find out how the moonstone had produced such an amazing effect.* Might be easier to handle without the influence of the ring.

***

Van den Burg cleared his throat and frowned. Should have forced Hopkins to drive him home. While he trudged into the town, the historical buildings glowed in the final rays of the sun. A glance at his watch showed five o'clock. In the end, the swap had gone without a hitch and the ring bounced against his thigh with every step.

At the sound of raised voices, he paused. Staccato shouts. Threats. Must have come from the shop ahead. He hurried closer. Poised on the balls of his feet, he approached the door.

"Don't take it all, please, young sirs."

"As if I'm gunna' leave any behind."

"Shut up." Another voice said. "Shove everything in the bag."

A robbery in progress? Pricked by conscience, Georg waited behind a wall, out of view from inside the shop. He almost turned away but his inner lion flexed.

"Please, don't do this."

Scrapes and scuffs neared. Sloppy youths emerged and glanced either way.

Georg lunged, knocked the first one to the ground and landed on top. He flipped the kid over, raised his fist, and then resisted the weight pressing him down.

He jerked his elbow backward into the fellow riding

him, and slammed his knee into the groin underneath, leaving the kid doubled up. With a thump, the bag landed on the ground.

One of them lifted it by the handles. A thud. The other youth staggered and dropped to his knees.

Georg sprang to his feet.

A turbaned man holding the bag bent his head. "Thank you kindly, sir."

A thug clambered to his feet.

The head-wrapped man who must be the shopkeeper swung the bag again, and knocked the youth to the ground beside his groaning friend. "Let that be a lesson to you." He drew a breath and called, "Ring the police."

A woman dressed in a sari, standing beside two young girls, peered from the door. "I've done it, husband. They're on their way."

"Stay where you are." Georg placed his foot on the youth. The other kid remained curled up and gasping.

"You came at just the right time, sir. A blessing on you."

Georg gave a tight smile. This robbery didn't differ in intent from those he'd committed. Now, he'd have to face the police for his trouble. He dreaded their questions. He didn't have a record, but the guards had seen his face during his heist and he'd left his fingerprints on the van. *The road to hell is paved with good intentions.* He puzzled the meaning and came to a conclusion. Once you did something right, actions from the past returned to bite you.

After the police left with their charges, Georg picked up a newspaper. The light from the doorway dimmed as a wary customer left the shop. Deciding to plunge right in and keep the fire in his belly bright, he asked, "Do you ... ever had any trouble here?"

"No. No. My man keeps things running smoothly." The newsagent peered behind Georg, straightened slightly and focused on him again.

"Relax, man. I'm not here to cause trouble. I know about George."

"You mean Mr. Hopkins. Yes. Yes."

So his suspicions were true. "Are you happy to pay money to Mr. Hopkins for protection or would you rather operate on your own?"

"You know about this?"

"I've heard talk."

"How can I run my business on my own? This would cause big trouble."

"What sort of trouble would you expect?"

"I don't know sir, truly I don't. Mr. Hopkins said ..." The man shook his head. His brow puckered.

"Have you ever tried to stop him collecting your money?"

"Yes, sir. He threatened my wife and children."

"That's extortion," Georg said. "We can do something about that."

"Please. I don't want to take the risk."

"What if I got together a group of people to discuss what to do? Would you be willing to attend a meeting?"

The man's brow furrowed. "Where would be safe?"

"We'll need to think about that. Who else is under George Hopkins' so-called 'protection'?"

The shopkeeper lowered his voice. "Please, block the door. I wouldn't want you-know-who to overhear."

Georg strolled to the entrance and checked outside before he turned and leaned against the frame. "Go ahead. You can speak freely."

"Each one of the small shops along here. The baker,

the butcher, the launderette. You can see them all. With such people beside me, I'd be willing to speak to the authorities."

"Leave it with me. I'll contact them and arrange a safe place to meet. If you work together, you might be able to put him behind bars."

"Thank you, sir." The turban dipped forward. "But why are you doing this?"

"Let's just say I've seen how he works, and I don't like it." Georg swiveled on his heel and exited the shop. The library would be a good place to meet, or the pub. Once the shop-keepers aired their problems publicly, someone would take over and report Hopkins to the police.

The ring's weight inside his pocket reminded him of another loose end.

***

In his eagerness to examine his treasure, Hopkins parked the stolen gray Fiat in the street close to home. He'd shift it later. Found it a bit hard to breathe. Lion man must be mad swapping the dull little ring for the elaborate bracelet.

Once inside his flat, George carried the light wooden box into the living room. He released the bracelet from its wax embrace with the help of a screwdriver. The gold glinted under the slanted shafts of light penetrating from the window. A flash from the beetle decoration gave the impression of motion.

He raised the bracelet. At last.

An electric shock buzzed his hand. In an automatic response, he flicked the jewel toward the box. The metal wouldn't let go. He flailed his arms in an attempt to dislodge the beetle's pincers clinging to the fleshy part of his middle finger. The grip tightened.

345

Chapter Fifty-One

Panic blended with agitation while George attempted to dislodge the object causing such pain. His sight dimmed and stomach clenched as if he'd been transported by a tornado. Up and up he went—sucked in swirling wind. Why couldn't he see his living room? Breathing hard, he clenched his teeth.

This couldn't be happening. Must be dreaming.

To his horror, a giant tunnel opened at the top. The more he fought, the faster spiraling air sucked him toward the cavity.

He entered.

Inside the dark burrow, colors flashed at the edge of his sight. He was spinning. With the nausea came a childhood memory—recovery after the operation.

A sudden plunge left his stomach behind.

***

When the vertigo stops, I peer into the mist, unable to see properly, surrounded by murk. Dunno how I got here. Must be a new better-than-ever ride. The fog drifts away. I glance down.

What?

I'm in the air without a vehicle beneath me and my body's gone. I should be plunging. Holding my breath, I peer past the part where my legs should be. My scream makes no sound.

I close my eyes. When I open them, I expect I'll find myself in hospital as a little boy. Maybe I never grew up at all.

I crack my eyelids. Wish I hadn't. Much better when I couldn't pick out details of buildings below.

I drop like a bomb and tense for the impact but I don't explode. What's going on? It doesn't help to shake my head. I raise my hand to check if my head's there, but nothing happens. No hand. This can't be real. Am I dreaming? Hallucinating? Perhaps I overdosed on alcohol.

Bloody hell! Now I'm inside an enormous room full of echoing chatter and the smell of overcooked food. A school canteen?

Instead of sniffing dirt and grubby fingers, I choke on perfume —ghastly with the food odors.

Five ugly women face me at a table. What? Women? This needs a bit of thought. Get with it, Hopkins.

They don't wear uniforms. Bloody hell! I'm in a prison dining room. Now I've guessed, I should snap out of this daydream. I check the rest of the room. Where are the men?

A voice in my head says, 'Concentrate on the food. The other women might not notice me, Hope the guard doesn't call my name. Don't say Magda Stavinsky . . . don't draw attention to me.'

Where did those words come from? I can't think, can't reason with this scent drifting in the air and strange thoughts pounding in my head.

On the right, a soft arm lifts a forkful of mashed potato to my mouth. The smell sickens me. I try to hold my breath. A strange high, cough comes out of my throat. I'm ... no, that's not me. I look down slowly to prevent the dizzy sensation producing a heave.

Shapes rise out of my chest. Titties!

Mumbled conversation with occasional yells and clanks come from other women occupying the room. I try to drop the fork, but the hand keeps a strong grip and dives into a white glob for another scoop. Try as I might, I can't stop the food rising to my mouth, or the way I chew and swallow. The texture disgusts me, but I don't want to cause another coughing fit.

"Dolly," someone yells. "Over here, dopey." When I look up, a hard-faced woman of about fifty years stares at me from one end of the table. "That's your name from now on, newbie," she says. "Better get used to it. The other one's too hard to say."

"Dolly, Dolly." The chant starts up among the other women.

"She's a Pardon, no doubt about that," another woman says.

"Although she won't get one."

Strange thoughts grind inside this ... mind. Can't decide if I'm delirious or what.

I pick up another thought. 'Too many of them. Don't rise to the bait.' I'm forced to glance sideways. This body I seem to be inside is taking me with her to look at the communal dining hall.

I might as well provoke the taunting women and have some fun. Am I mad or what?

No. I might be locked inside Magda forever. I scream against the injustice of my fate, but no sound comes out.

I glance at the bullies. Better teach them a lesson now. Could be my pass out 'a jail. In the hope she'll hear, I sort of whisper in my thoughts, 'Flick some potato at them. Show you're not scared.' Nobody hears me. Let's hope Magda gets the message.

She swallows and thinks, 'I couldn't. I don't want to play their games.'

Yeah. I've got her under my control. 'You have to. It's flick or be flicked.'

The five women lean close to speak.

"The screws are busy at the other end of the room."

"Now's our chance for a little fun."

"If we're caught, we didn't do anything bad enough for punishment."

"Get her legs, Tracy. Hold her arms, Pat and Sue. Judy and I will jump her. I can't wait to find out if her blond hair is real. Go."

The three women stand and approach our side of the table.

'See what I mean,' I whisper. 'Now flick and get your fork ready to prick some skin. Play along. We'll win this game.'

She recoils and her thoughts reach me. 'Why am I confrontational all of a sudden?'

'You should change,' I whisper. 'Don't let them do this to you. Defend yourself.'

As they approach, our anger and frustration bubble up. We'll get the better of these women. 'Look out. Here they come.' I force her hand to grip the fork and dive for ammunition. The cannon might be plastic, but the stuff can cause damage. We flick.

Pat gets an eyeful of hot mashed potato and lets out a shout. Her bulky friend Sue yanks our hand, while someone grabs our legs. A distant whistle echoes.

We kick and struggle, and then prick the closest arms for all we're worth. They're not getting away with their treatment.

I've lost track of who's doing what while they punch, gouge and pull. The shocks jolt our body. The pain doesn't deter me from taking control of the fork hand and driving the weapon into every arm we can reach. It's amazing how much damage it can do, even when the plastic snaps.

"You bitch," someone screams. "Wait till I—"

Someone pulls our hair. The pain makes our eyes water. We break free of the arms holding us. Magda screams our joint fury and buries the weapon into more skin. We draw blood.

Women's voices yell and shout encouragement over loud whistles.

I lend strength to Magda's arms and legs while she slaps, kicks and dives away from retaliation.

Just when I start to enjoy the game, a closer whistle pierces the air. The room grows quiet. Uniformed screws secure women's hands behind. Inmates stand about, watching.

A loud voice with a northern accent says, "All right. All right. Who caused the fight this time?"

I yell into Magda's mind, 'Get them while they can't fight back. Kick and punch.'

But she's already summed up her chances. Her hands drop. Breath escapes her body and we slump.

The next thing I know, I'm hovering. I'm too hyped up to worry about floating. The women below fade.

***

George gasped in the sudden silence, rubbed his eyes and opened them in his living room. He took a quick glance at the box on his lap. The bracelet sat askew on the wax. He must have let go when Magda dropped her hands.

Hold on! That didn't happen. What a stupid dream.

The golden bracelet trapped his gaze. George gathered his legs to stand, but sank again and stared at the decoration on the top. Could have sworn the blue beetle moved. He held perfectly still.

A daydream replaced reality. He fought and won every battle, snatched treasure from under the people's noses, wore the latest clothes, and moved to a large house.

People clapped whenever he entered the pub. Everyone wanted to be his friend.

George shuddered. Where were these thoughts coming from? He should lay off the stuff.

The memory of how he couldn't drop the bracelet returned. Scary. He wasn't one to be frightened easily. All the same, whatever happened wasn't something he wanted to repeat. No siree, Hopkins.

He ignored the small voice calling him to experience the thrill of power again, and promised each time the game would be better. He slammed the lid shut and pushed the box to the other side of the sofa. The sooner he got rid of the bracelet the better. He didn't want to be a woman inside a prison again.

Maybe that's why the South African had wanted to trade down. Perhaps the same thing had happened to him. The fellow's words, *'You'll see,'* buzzed inside his head.

George preferred reality—a life where he called the shots. Small businesses in the town needed his protection from people who came up from the big city to take over. They were lucky to have him.

With a flick of his lighter, George melted the wax and resealed the lid. The beetle could thrash about inside the box for all he cared. He hoped Dickie-Big-Fence in London would take the jewel off his hands. If so, the guy would be in for a surprise.

Chapter Fifty-Two

On the half hour walk to town, the sharp morning air energized Georg Van den Burg. His meeting with Hopkins had been successful, and much to his relief, he wouldn't need to face the police. Not only that, but after his brush with thieves at the paper shop, an opportunity arose to mention the thug's activities. The locals might be interested in banding together if he arranged a time and place.

Georg slowed to check the number plate of a gray Fiat ahead. Hopkins must be mad to have left Matt's car in plain sight.

In one final game of switch-the-cars to teach the skulking creature a lesson, Georg hot-wired the engine and drove to another location, five minutes closer to town on a residential street. Some things had to be done. He didn't intend to let Hopkins get away free. This final shuffling act would ignite the veld's dry grass under the spotted hyena.

Georg chuckled, wishing he could watch the criminal's expression after he found the gray Fiat missing. The frustration vented in the creature's laugh would be spine-tingling.

On with staging an assembly to fan the flame.

***

Sunshine slanted from the library window onto the reference book on the table in front of Liliha. A shadow dulled the light.

"I've found a good romance," Ellen said, "about a man who rescues a woman from the clutches of the Taliban."

"On horseback?" Liliha's lips twitched.

Ellen glanced at the rear cover. "It doesn't say."

"I'm joking with you. I'm sure the story will be just

352

what you need at the moment."

"What's that one?" Ellen perched on a chair beside Liliha.

"This book explains body chemistry." Liliha read out loud. "'Four main parts form our fundamental needs: oxygen, carbon, hydrogen and nitrogen. The remaining tiny percentage comes from a sample of the periodic table of elements.'"

"Ah." Ellen flicked the cover of her book open.

"I won't be long here. Sarah will be calling in at home soon, and I don't want to worry her if I'm not there." Liliha gave a wry grin. "I guess you're hungry too."

Ellen nodded, eyes lowered, with her mouth pursed with slight frown creasing her smooth skin.

Liliha inhaled the smell of print and paper on the heavy book while she skimmed for more information. Nothing of interest. Her focus blurred. Had she possessed more of one rare micro-particle than other people? Was this how the crystal affected her in the past? She lowered the book, wondering why she'd bothered to look up the information. After all, she hadn't kept the world afloat all on her own. She, and everyone else, had a part to play, large or small.

Her thumb found the small indent on her finger in the ring's former position. Loss must be part of life. Trees dropped their leaves in winter. Parents died when they grew old.

Liliha gazed out the window.

What made her any different from Ellen? Nothing. They were both women, struggling to make a new life after a loss. Yvonne and William had helped her at a time of crisis. Now, she'd support Ellen with hers.

***

Restless after their evening meal, Ellen dried the dishes with quick swipes. Plates clinked against each other as she stacked them. Liliha showed her where each one belonged. She sure was finicky.

"I've got to get out of here," Ellen said. "I need to find a quiet place to do some thinking."

"Can't you do it here where you're safe?"

"Sure I can. But I don't want to hide."

"You're not going to—?"

"Don't worry. I won't go back to my former life. But what about my future?"

Liliha pulled the sink plug. "Up to you."

"It's not." Ellen's cheeks grew hot. "I don't know where I belong. What should I plan for?"

"I often do my best thinking on the beach." Liliha hung the dishcloth over the side of the sink.

"Great idea. I'll go for a walk beside the sea."

"Do you want company?"

Ellen paused and frowned. "Would you come?"

"Of course."

"Nobody's ever ... I'd love you to come with me. Let's go right now before it gets dark."

"Grab your coat. It'll be cold." At the hall cupboard, Liliha offered a scarf.

Ellen wrapped her neck in the perfumed softness and followed Liliha into the evening, feeling like a younger sister. A tingle of excitement filled her. The sort when you know something good's about to happen. It reminded her of the time she'd woken up in bed as a child, wondering if she'd get a really nice present for her birthday. And she did—a doll. But never again. When her mother died, her dad took over. Then everything changed.

Don't think about the past. But what should she do now?

***

While Liliha strode along the firm sand with Ellen, an unsettled peace filled her. The tranquility wouldn't last. Neither would the waves rising further out to sea—each swell a singular event which began many miles away with a storm, only to end by crashing on the shore.

The lesson she'd learned from her telepathic connections held her steady. Emotional variation was necessary for the flow of existence. Liliha nodded to herself. She and Ellen would adapt after the storm in their lives.

The regular pounding waves and the wind tugging at her hair, lulled Liliha. Nature invaded her senses. But no vision would follow. A quiet acceptance replaced her former rages against destiny while she followed her companion to a line of seaweed and shells left by the tide. Poor shattered shells. Once things of beauty, now unable to whisper secret possibilities—like her.

"Look at this plastic." Ellen lifted a piece of red material about the shape of a coin.

Liliha pulled her thoughts together. "Must have been a lid on a plastic bottle."

"Funny how the edges have gone."

"The constant pounding of the waves turns shells and rocks into sand. Even plastic might end up that way." While cool droplets of spume caught on her skin, Liliha drank in the view. Out to sea, the last rays of sunlight glinted on choppy water.

"Wouldn't it be great to have colored sand on the beach?"

"Everything changes over time." Liliha glanced at her bare finger. "You know I've lost my ring, Don't you?"

"I didn't take it. Honest."

"Don't worry. I never thought you did. I'm just talking things over, the way friends do. You see, I feel as if something's missing in my life. I got used to wearing it."

"Yeah. I guess you shouldn't count on things always being there," Ellen said. "Then it wouldn't hurt when you lose them."

"Sometimes, that's not possible." Liliha scooped up a rounded shell. "Press this close to your ear. You'll hear whispering."

While Ellen lifted the shell, Liliha caught the whiff of an approaching storm in the air. In every type of weather, the sea reminded her of Oliver. Yearning and sorrow stirred. Would she remain floating, never to end her journey, like a wave crashing on the sand?

Rather than dwell on her own loss, Liliha drew a breath and turned to Ellen. "Any messages about your future?" She didn't want to consider her own.

Chapter Fifty-Three

Georg van den Burg emerged from the bright beachfront pub, drew in a breath, and wrapped his jacket tighter. He strode to the sand at the bottom of the steps and waited. What luck to have spotted Ellen and Liliha walking by outside the window. He'd been over every possibility of how to return the ring to Liliha while he sipped a glass of bitter ahead of the meeting. He should have delivered it right after the swap. Having left it too late for the gesture to seem genuine, he struggled to find a solution.

In the fading light, female shapes approached. He strolled toward them. The little minx, Ellen, ran forward.

With a sudden flash of inspiration, he squatted over a line of smooth rocks and shells and lifted a long strand of seed pods.

"Hi, Georg." Ellen bent and searched the seaweed beside him. A crab scuttled out of reach and dug a new shelter under a rock.

"Only just enough light to see. But I spotted something here."

"I saw it too."

Now he'd test Ellen's reaction. A quickening in his breath showed how much he wanted her to pass his test.

He opened his hand and exposed the jewel.

"Wow! You found a ring right here? Can I have it?" Ellen strained forward.

"It's Liliha's ring."

"The one she lost? But how could it...? You didn't take it, did you? I thought it was those men who drugged her."

"I managed to find something to swap. A bit

357

complicated, but now I have it, I want to return it to her."

"I see what you're up to." One side of her mouth lifted in a grin. "I won't let on."

Liliha approached. With his left hand clenched, he used his right to move another piece of seaweed.

"Fancy seeing you here," Liliha said.

Georg's hands touched and he produced the ring, which he held cupped toward her.

"Did you just find that on the sand?"

"Caught up in seaweed, as you saw." He couldn't make out her features, although he suspected she frowned.

"You had it in your other hand."

"Why would I do that?"

"He's a magician," Ellen said.

"I don't know how you got it, but something's not right." Liliha bent closer. "You had to get the ring from somewhere. Did you send those two thugs to my door after you left?"

He shook his head, full of regret, and lowered his eyes. He deserved her suspicion. Never been strictly honorable with her—with anyone.

Ellen stood up. "He wouldn't, Liliha. Honest."

"How do you know?"

The minx frowned. "I just know. We're friends, aren't we? Well I've thought and thought and now I'm talking it over with you. He protected me when I needed help. You can trust him the way I did when he drove me to stay with you."

Liliha sighed and gazed out to sea in the gloom. At last, she faced him. "However it happened, I'd be glad to have my ring if you're offering." She said, "Seems a bit too easy though."

He rose from his cramped position and passed the

jewel to her. "My lady."

"See, I told you." Ellen's eyes flashed.

Liliha accepted his offer and slid the ring onto her finger. "I can hardly believe it. Thank you." She pecked him on the cheek. "I'm sorry. I shouldn't have accused you. You don't know how much this means to me."

Ellen jerked his arm and swung him toward her to brush his other cheek with soft lips. "Thank you from me, too."

Georg slid his arm along her spine to hold her waist and she melted into him like another part of his body.

She lowered her head although her gaze remained on him.

The crash of waves faded. His reality focused on Ellen. He couldn't let her slip away. Their meeting on the train must have been ordained.

Liliha murmured, "This is the best thing that's happened for a long time. Wish I . . . Well, maybe you two can celebrate for me."

He dragged his focus away from Ellen.

"Mark the occasion the way the Druids would."

He sighed, wishing he could concentrate on Ellen. "What do you mean?" he asked Liliha.

"The ancient Druids used fire in their rituals. Apparently they worked out the future by watching a flight of birds or the movements of clouds. They believed the soul . . ."

The words faded as Ellen grinned and extended slender arms toward him.

Lost in her kiss, a flame kindled inside him. Georg freed her warm lips and buried his face in her hair. Strands blew about his face. The smell reminded him of sunshine under a jacaranda tree in full bloom. Longing for summer, he released his breath into the sea breeze and glanced at Liliha. She stood apart, gazing out to sea.

He gazed into Ellen's eyes and inclined his head toward Liliha with his eyebrows raised. She nodded and one side of her mouth lifted in a sweet, crazy smile. He squeezed her waist and called, "It's going to rain soon. How about joining me at the pub? Quite a few of the local people are there at the moment. It should be lively."

Liliha rejoined them and they headed for the steps, reached the promenade and strolled to the Golden Lion. With a woman on either side, Georg hardly felt his feet touch the path. Ellen kept leaning forward to glance at Liliha.

Georg sighed in satisfaction at the completion of one task. Two challenges forthcoming: the meeting and a possible future with Ellen.

***

Inside the warm pub, they made their way to a table where a man already sat. Ellen slid along the bench seat to make room for Liliha, who introduced Harry. Ellen gazed up at Georg. Everything was working out at the end, the way it did in a fairytale. A nice kind of pain throbbed inside her chest. It made her happy. And his kiss—not demanding like the men who paid for sex—his was gentle, tender. Her cheeks flushed at the memory. She yearned for more. Was this the love that stories raved about?

Georg sat opposite with Harry—tall, good looking in a dark Italian way. She could tell Liliha liked him.

Without making her glances obvious, Ellen kept a close watch on the older woman's behavior. If she wanted to copy Liliha, she had to act in a different way—not flirty, not come-hither or sassy, but graceful and full of—. Ellen searched for the word. Poise. She straightened her shoulders and lifted her head.

The other people in the room concentrated on various men who stood and spoke in loud voices like teachers at an assembly.

"Listen to this," Georg said. "It's about George Hopkins. The man who was with Matt out at that rock."

"You mean Giant's Rock? The one who was after me with Matt? What slime-balls."

When Mary from the launderette climbed to her feet and cleared her throat, Ellen exchanged glances with Liliha.

"He calls in every day," Mary said in a voice loud enough for everyone to hear. "He gets all his laundry done free of charge, and takes a fee every week for looking after my business—he says. He can get nasty if things don't go his way. The other day he jabbed me hard in the stomach with his elbow."

"You should have reported that," someone yelled.

More voices joined in.

"Why do we need protection? Who from?"

"From him, I'd say."

"There's no threat to any of us. Just a few kids acting up."

"We've got a good police force if we need to call on them."

Georg pushed his chair back and stood. "If everyone's in agreement, we need a spokesperson to report Hopkins's activity to the authorities."

The group shuffled their feet, but nobody spoke.

A man wearing a turban rose to his feet. "I will do it. I made it my business to find out where he lives after he threatened my wife and children. I've been trying to figure out what to do."

Ellen glanced at Liliha, who wasn't paying much attention either. The way she was gazing at her ring, you'd think the thing was part of the royal collection in the Tower of London. The stone didn't even sparkle. But Liliha must attach sentimental value to the ring. Her mother probably gave it to her. Her mum must have been nice to have such a good daughter. Ellen swept a piece of fluff off the table, struggling to remember her own.

Georg spoke a few more words in a loud voice. Real business-like.

All very well to listen to other people's plans, but what about her future? Here in St. Ives, friends would help her get ahead. Perhaps she could have more. A partner. Not one for the night, but a real one, who'd stick by her and care about her. Of course, she'd have to do the same. Trouble was, she didn't know if she could be steady and true. She studied Liliha's calm face.

Chapter Fifty-Four

While people at the meeting aired their views about George Hopkins, Liliha remembered when she had shared the mind of the small-time thief during a vision, which had prompted the hunt for him. She added a few derogatory thoughts of her own. She wouldn't voice them though, not knowing the man in the flesh.

Finding her focus on the men standing at the bar on the other side of the room blurred, she blinked. Maybe she shouldn't have gulped the last few mouthfuls of gin.

A distinctive lily perfume swirled in the air, alerting her to the approach of a vision.

Liliha drew a shuddering breath. Heartfelt joy removed her lethargy. She took a quick glance at the people surrounding her. Luck worked in her favor. Everyone was looking at the speaker.

Elbow on the table she propped her jaw on her palm. Her relaxed body allowed her mind to surge into the tunnel of dreams. Smooth as a current below the surface of the sea, she tumbled amidst colors shifting between symmetrical shapes and patterns like an optical toy made from mirrors.

***

Below me in the darkness, solid soles pound over hard ground. Light rain falls. We approach an illuminated area. Judging by the masculine stride of the body I'm occupying, I've already merged with a man. I comprehend his thoughts.

'Boring. If Matt was here, there'd be more action.'

A familiar name.

'I should hire some help. We could patrol together like proper security guards. I'd have to be in charge

363

though. That partnership with Bertie didn't work.'

I'm stunned to recognize the thought-pattern of the local man, George from the previous vision. The George I'd hoped to contact. And the prime subject of discussion at the meeting.

Where are we? Too dark to know yet.

Hurrying past a couple of shops opposite the seafront, we approach a well-lit building nestled amongst several with darkened windows. We look up at the sign. The Golden Lion.

What? I'm sitting inside with my friends right now. This will be strange to see myself from his eyes.

We ease the door open. A subdued hum of voices comes from an area hidden from view.

A raised voice says, "Can I have your attention, please?"

We recognize van den Burg's heavy accent.

We step away. No sense in drawing attention. 'Something going on. A meeting. Better listen.'

"Nearly finished. Quieten down. Then you can get back to drinking."

Laughs and yells.

"Our friend here has offered to contact the police about your alleged protector, and I'm sure you'll all support him."

We stiffen and hold our breath.

Nothing I can advise him at the moment.

"I'll be leaving the area shortly," the speaker continues, "so I'll have to leave any action to you."

A few 'ahs' merge into the sudden silence.

We step outside. The door closes off the unwelcoming atmosphere. Voices dull to a murmur.

'The bastards.' He mutters, withholding his voice

because someone might hear him. 'After all I've done for them. How would they like outsiders to take over?' Our heart pounds faster. 'I'll give them plenty to think about.'

We head off along the street.

'I'll set fire to the newspaper shop. All the burning paper will be an inferno. While everyone's busy putting out the flames, I'll nip along to the launderette, the tearooms, and then double back here with a fire bomb.'

'Wait,' I yell over his plans. 'You could still earn the respect of the locals. What about becoming legit? The way you always wanted'? I've got to reach him this time.

'No chance.' His thoughts cut in. 'The coppers will lock me up and throw away the key. Nobody leaves the nick unscathed.'

I whisper in a comforting tone, 'You'll have time to study— work toward a proper job. If you changed your attitude, the locals might even accept you.' I hope he focuses on a need to change rather than the prison sentence.

With revenge firing inside, he shrugs off my suggestion. 'They want the coppers involved. I'll give them something real to worry about.'

Before I've had time to come up with anything else, a yell cuts the rain-soaked silence.

"Hey! You there." We stop and turn. Holding the door ajar, the customer swivels to face the interior. "It's George. He's here."

A voice from within the pub shouts, "Stop him."

We bristle and slink away in the shadows, planning to turn and whack whoever approaches.

I must try to change him this time. Before I've come up with another suggestion, fast footsteps approach from behind.

We slip on soggy rubbish, reel, but keep our balance. Before we can turn, an explosion of pain hits our head. The pavement rises up to meet us. A whoosh tells me I've disengaged.

***

Liliha returned to the table. Harry had come back and lifted his hand away from the glass he'd placed on the surface. No time for thought—take action.

"Quick, follow me." She stood and bounded toward the door.

"They'll take care of it, Liliha."

"They're too angry. They'll turn into a mob. Come on." She gestured for him to speed up before running out the exit.

Harry emerged after her. Ahead, two men stood over George. One held a solid, dark umbrella, the sort from the days of old. The other man kicked the prone man in the stomach.

Emboldened by the desire to intervene, Liliha called over the loud pounding in her head, "No need for that."

Harry gazed at her, his brows furrowed in puzzlement. "I'm here for you, Liliha."

"Bring him inside," she yelled, hoping to stop her shaking. "We can't resort to violence. That's not justice."

The man with the umbrella bristled. "He's taken our money for years."

His companion snarled, "Punish him now, I say."

Harry bent and grabbed the unconscious man's arms. "Give me a hand, you two."

"Blowed if I will," the first man said.

"She's right. My missus wouldn't approve of beating him to death."

"One last kick."

"Better not," Liliha said. "He looks unconscious. You don't want to be held for murder." She retraced her steps and held the door open.

"What the heck." The man grabbed George's legs. He and Harry lifted him.

Liliha calmed her ragged breath while everyone sitting inside the room strained to watch the two men carrying the prone man toward a sofa by the window. He sagged like a roll of soggy paper.

"Can we have some water, please?" Liliha called. The barmaid nodded.

"It's George," someone said. "Who knocked him out?"

"I did," a large man said. "Lucky I stood guard at the door."

"What now?" Harry stroked his chin and studied Liliha.

"Let him recover." Releasing a breath, Liliha glanced at her surroundings.

Several men approached, fists clenched and shouting angry words.

"Let's give him a good thrashing."

"Teach the bastard."

"We won't stand for any more of his shenanigans."

Harry stood beside her and beckoned to Georg van den Burg on the far side of the room.

"Hold on," Liliha said. She reached for the glass of water offered by the barmaid. "You've already decided on a lawful course of action." Strong in her belief, she kept her voice firm although she quivered inside.

"Let the police deal with him now," Harry said.

Liliha breathed silent thanks for his help.

"You're better than this," Liliha said to everyone. The

noise softened while she held the water to George's lips. Although his eyes remained closed, he swallowed a mouthful.

Good. At least he'd regained consciousness. A strange sensation filled her head and her hands shook with fatigue. Reality might vanish at any moment and she'd find herself inside the fog of the tunnel. She needed help now.

Van den Burg pushed his way to the front of the muttering crowd. "All right, Liliha?" He stood solid beside Harry.

She nodded and gathered strength. She didn't have to face anything alone. "Call the police now. You're all here. You can give your statements when they arrive." She met several of the surrounding people's gaze. "Please, see reason. This man is helpless." She'd meant to change George's life, never expecting she might have to save him.

George's lids fluttered. His eyes sprang open and he struggled, legs and arms working to gain an upright position on the sofa. "What the—"

"Stay quiet now, George," Harry said. "It'll go better for you in the long run. Or maybe you've got something to say."

"Now would be the best time," van den Burg said.

George's mouth dropped open. He licked his lips and swallowed a few times. "Should have listened to my own advice."

Liliha drew in a shuddering breath. He'd heard her visionary whisper.

"Can we have quiet, please?" Harry called in a voice loud enough to penetrate the clamor.

The noise hushed.

"You're going to hand me in?" George frowned and dropped his head. "I've made a proper mess for myself."

He raised his gaze. "I wanted to protect you all like a security guard. Guess I got it wrong." His mouth puckered and his eyes glazed.

"You assaulted me," Mary yelled.

Liliha wished she could be inside George's mind. Did he mean what he said?

"Get it over with," someone yelled. "Call the cops."

"They're on their way." The deep voice halted most of the murmurs. Everyone faced the direction of the bar, where the landlord stood with the barmaid. The room went quiet.

"Okay," George said. "I had it coming." His eyes narrowed to slits and he struggled to stand.

"Stay where you are." Harry pressed his shoulder to keep him down.

Chapter Fifty-Five

The meeting hubbub died away. Most people had left the pub. Surrounded by her friends, Liliha breathed a sigh of relief. George was safely in police custody and everyone had given statements.

Harry dropped into the seat opposite. The smile he flashed melted the protective coating over her heart.

"That went well." He gestured with his head at Georg van den Burg leaning close to Ellen. "The newcomers are getting on like two ducks in a pond."

Liliha nodded. She brushed away the image and reverted to the scene she'd left, stunned at arriving inside the same host for the second time and so close to her physical body. At least she hadn't faced the shock of seeing herself from another perspective. Although unsure of George Hopkins' remorse, she'd achieved her original aim of getting him to face his wrong-doing.

She tilted the ring's smooth moonstone to catch the light. Perhaps she did deserve to wear the ancient ring. Tears blurred her vision. After a few steady breaths, energy returned, along with surety. She could live a reasonable life without Oliver, although she'd always miss him.

"You're going to wear that out." Harry winked.

"I'm so glad to have it."

"It must have given you something extra. I didn't know you could handle a crowd."

"Had to."

"Remember this one?" He gestured toward the jukebox. Culture Club were singing, 'Do You Really Want To Hurt Me.' His eyes contained hidden depths.

Liliha nodded. What brought Harry such pain?

***

Georg sipped his bitter brew. Beside him, Ellen wriggled into her seat and straightened her shoulders. What drew him to her? Her small frame and sound mind? The way her mouth turned up at one side when she spoke? The acceptance in her eyes? All of them, but most of all, her vulnerability attracted him. She took whatever life threw her way and faced problems with courage, yet she could topple at any moment.

Murmurs in the old pub filled an awkward break in their conversation. With Harry and Liliha's attention elsewhere, Georg rubbed his sweaty palms on his jeans and leaned closer to Ellen. Former mistakes were tearing him apart.

"We've both done things in our past we'd rather not admit to," he murmured. "Let me tell you about mine, and then you can decide if you like me or not." He paused until she nodded. "My boss sent me to find things for him. I didn't have to. My choice entirely." He gazed at the old tobacco stains in one corner of the ceiling. "I stole goods for him. He said the arrangement was legit, but I have doubts. That's why Matt was in the area. To check the goods and report his findings to the boss." Georg looked Ellen straight in the eye although he struggled for breath.

"What if he asks you to steal again?"

"With the right incentive, I'd decline."

"What does that mean?" she asked.

"I might discuss things with a woman by my side. If she wasn't happy, we could always leave." His words came as a revelation. He must have planned this during the time he went over and over the situation. He didn't need Straten. He could make a new life on his own.

She murmured, "Thank you for telling me. But you should hear about what I've done with my life too. You

371

might not—"

"I already know. I've accepted your past. We both had lives before we met." He took her hand. The way her fingers snuggled into his palm felt so right. "Let's zip up the contents of that bag and leave it behind. We could make a new life together."

She paused and sat rocking, never speaking a work.

"You've made a start, and I admire you for adapting." he said. "I'll let you work out what you'll do from now on."

"It's nice here in St. Ives."

"I can't assure you about your future," Georg said. "All I can say is I like you ... a lot. We could go on from there." He wanted to win her love more than anything he'd ever set his mind on. Convincing her to leave with him would need time, and he didn't know if he had enough.

He glanced up. Harry and Liliha were listening in. With a grin tugging his mouth, Georg faced Ellen and blurted, "What I really want to know is whether you've decided to stay here."

"I've made some good friends." Ellen smiled at Liliha. "More than I've ever had."

"I can understand your reluctance. I left everyone I knew back in Jo'burg."

"Why did you come to live here?" Ellen asked.

"A tricky subject. I'll tell you about it when I get to know you better."

"Why wouldn't you? I want to ... I'd like to be your friend too."

"I'm getting around to that." Everything was so complicated. Georg raised his eyebrows at Harry, but the blighter just grinned.

Liliha stifled a yawn. "I moved into town to get away from the memories in my empty house in the country. How about you, Harry?"

"I went to uni with Audley and a couple of other guys in the area. He offered me a job at the music office as his accountant. After I left," he glanced at Liliha with a wary frown as if hoping she would keep a secret, "I stayed in the area."

"See," Liliha said. "None of us are locals, really."

"But I'm about to leave," Georg said.

"Why?" Liliha asked.

"The new job the boss has offered is close to London." Phew, slithered out of harm's way like a boomslang up a tree.

"Just when I think I know what I want," Ellen said, "everyone leaves."

"I'm staying," Liliha said.

"Exactly when are you going, Georg?" Ellen's cheeks flushed.

"I have to leave tomorrow." He leaned in. "I have room in my car if you want a lift."

"But where would I go when we get there?"

"I'll have accommodation next to my work—"

"What are you going to do, Georg?" Liliha asked.

"Chauffeur to a private house."

Harry laughed out loud. "Well done."

"I know it's early days, Ellen," Georg said, "but I could offer you some space with me until we work things out." Way too soon. What was he thinking?

Ellen flashed a glance at Liliha, then met his gaze. "It's happening so fast. I want to stay here, too." Ellen lowered her head.

Georg reached for his drink to prevent the shake in his hand and took a long gulp.

With her cheeks scrunched up, Ellen frowned in his

direction. "All right with you if I come?"

Georg choked, and tried to prevent spluttering while he nodded. He swallowed the urge to shout, *'yes.'*

Harry chuckled and Liliha glanced from one to the other.

"We could make things work," Georg said with more hope than certainty.

***

Ellen sipped her tequila cocktail. Harry leaned close to Liliha. A few of his whispered words reached her. .'.. young love. I'm glad I got to watch. It's . . .' The hiss overrode what came later. She faced away to stop her blush from showing.

Her future split ahead. A stab of worry caught her by surprise. She wanted to scream in frustration. She told herself not to forget about acting the part of a lady. Was she clinging to Liliha? She'd never been that type before, and anyway, she couldn't live with Liliha forever.

Liliha had been so ... what was the word ... forthright at the meeting. Ellen wondered whether she'd have the strength to stop a mob or even try.

She studied Georg. A strong feeling in her chest told her he was the one. The latest or the only? Too many questions and decisions.

"It's getting late. I must go," Liliha said. "Do you want to stay a while, Ellen?"

"I'll come. But—" She arched her eyebrows toward Georg. "Can I let you know later?"

"Sure." Georg's eyes flashed. "Don't leave it too late." A smile followed his words.

"What time are you going?"

"I'll have to make a move by eleven. I plan to drive this way, but I can't enter town with the driving restrictions in place. Now, I don't want to force you to do anything. But if you're willing, stand outside the new building on the top of the hill. Do you know the one?"

Ellen glanced at Liliha for advice.

"I know. I'll make sure she's there if she decides to go."

Once she'd gathered her bag, Ellen stood beside Liliha, the woman she wanted to copy. She gazed at the seated Georg, her rescuer like the one in the library book she'd read. She bent and planted a kiss on his cheek. Everything she'd ever wanted lay with these two people. How unfair to have to choose between them.

Chapter Fifty-Six

With his few possessions loaded into the boot, Georg headed toward London, excitement building at the prospect of Ellen waiting for him.

Caught up behind a tractor, he considered a future with Straten. Insurance scam or not, the man dealt in stolen goods despite his claim of making arrangements beforehand. Georg ran his fingers through his hair. Although the job sounded good, he might be asked to act as bodyguard at some time. And worse—take part in extortion, which would reduce him to the level of the slime-ball Hopkins.

After the slow-moving vehicle ahead pulled into a lane, Georg increased speed. *Ellen.* His stomach tightened. Who'd have known when love hit, he'd behave like a tourist on safari? He couldn't be sure if love caused this discomfort in his innards—too early to tell. But he wanted to protect Ellen from further mistreatment. She should be the one to say what she'd do with her life.

If he took her to London, she might not stay with him. He wouldn't stop her from leaving—would never force his will on a woman. But he needed her more than he'd ever thought possible. Up to him to ensure she appreciated him. Perhaps he could find a little job for her inside Straten's mansion. Or she might want to train for something better. A clerk or librarian. Up to her. She was smart enough.

He'd support her all the way. Commitment offered stability in an uncertain future. He hoped she felt the same way.

His thoughts jumped to keep up with the twisting

inside his stomach. Would he be good enough for her? Hard to say. Some women liked a rough diamond. From now on, he'd make sure his record remained clean. If Straten decided to direct him another way, he could always leave. He wouldn't share that way of life with Ellen.

Leaning forward, he spotted at a slight figure on the footpath ahead. He slowed the car's speed, his insides a giant wheel spinning.

***

Stomach quivering, Ellen stood beside the road. She took a quick glance downhill, wondering if she should change her mind. Too late. A car slowed and pulled off the road. Ellen held her breath until she picked out Georg inside. She waved.

Georg stepped out and strode toward her, hair drifting about in the wind. "Great. You're here."

"Yes," she whispered. More traffic whizzed by.

He leaned close to catch her words and she clutched his neck, reached up to meet his lips. She felt like a schoolgirl, kissing a boy for the first time. The quivering in his body surprised her, although his response filled her needs.

They pulled apart though she hungered for more. When she searched the expression in his eyes, she found sincerity.

With a smile hovering, he broke the magic moment. "Come on. Let's stash your things on the rear seat. The boot's full." He opened the door and heaved her luggage in. "Nice case."

"Liliha found it at a second-hand shop." Her voice sounded strange in her ears, husky, breathless, as if someone else had spoken.

"Lucky girl." He squeezed her hand. "Come on, let's

hit the road. We can talk in the car."

Once settled in the passenger seat, Ellen gazed outside. Was she ready to face the dangers of London? With a man she hardly knew? She glanced at Georg for reassurance.

He drew a deep breath. "Having second thoughts?"

"Yes," she squeezed out.

"About us?"

She shook her head. Tears threatened. "London." Big mistake to tell him. He'd leave her behind. She sniffed and hung her head.

"Ever been to Plymouth?"

"What?" Ellen blinked away sudden moisture. "I thought you had a job lined up in London."

He started the motor. A tender smile returned when he faced her. "Might not be the right one."

"Then we'd both need to look for work," she said.

"Want to give it a try?"

Ellen nodded, excitement firing. A fresh start?

With a deft shift of the gearstick, he drove the car onto the road and they sped away. "I want to know more about you. Not your past, but the things you enjoy doing. I want to do them with you."

His sincerity brought warmth to her cheeks. "Have you ever walked over the cliffs on a dark night?" The car's motion spun her toward a rosy future.

***

Alone in her cottage again, Liliha hurried to answer a knock. Before she opened the door, two police officers announced their presence.

"Mrs. Trevellyn. Sorry to bother you, but we're following up a report of a stolen item. May we come in?"

Liliha retreated to allow them entrance, heart

thudding. What now? Surely, not Ellen?

The smart female officer strode to the hall table and inspected the cat statues. "Do these belong to you?"

"Yes." Liliha held her breath.

"How long have you had them?"

"That one with the broken ear, I've had for years. A friend gave me the smooth one the other day."

The officers exchanged a nod, and then one of the policemen turned to the door and peered out. "Here she is now."

A shadow loomed in the doorway. Liliha resembled the innate Lilihaffertiti painted on the papyrus before she exhaled in relief. "Sarah."

"I'm so sorry, Liliha. I've given you stolen property." Sarah's frown and slight shake of the head stopped Liliha from mentioning Yvonne, who had been part of the conspiracy.

"We got your friend's name from the shopkeeper after following up a clue about certain articles for sale."

"I'm afraid we'll have to confiscate the statue." The male officer raised his chin. "Do you have proof of ownership for the other one? That looks ancient Egyptian too."

"Let me find the receipt." Liliha left the room shaken. Had she brought the paperwork with her? After a quick search upstairs, she returned to join them. "I must have left it at my other house."

The male officer slid the smooth cat into a plastic envelope. "Right. Where is this place?"

"Just outside town. By the Peters' farm."

The female officer looked at her watch. "You've had a tough time lately, Mrs. Trevellyn. We won't bother you now. Drop the receipt into the office at your earliest convenience."

Of course, they'd have a record of her assault. Liliha escorted them to the door and waited until they headed for their vehicle.

Sarah approached her. "I'm so sorry."

"You didn't know it was stolen." One hand nested the other to protect her precious item. "But Georg returned my ring last night, and I don't know where he got it. I hope that wasn't anything to do with their inquiries."

"They didn't mention a ring. They'd have a list of stolen property from that location. Anyway, they can check their files about the last time the ring went missing. Put it out of your mind."

Liliha swallowed, and then released a sigh. "I should have told them I got it back. I'll do that when I take the receipt to the station." Her stomach churned at the prospect of her ring being taken into custody so soon after its return.

Chapter Fifty-Seven

Liliha held three Romaine lettuce leaves under running water, her thumb sliding up the curl to remove dots of soil. The leaves would form the base for her salad of chick peas, spring onion and steamed broccoli coated in olive oil, thyme and balsamic vinegar.

Strange how she, Ellen and even Georg van den Burg had arrived in St. Ives on the train just a few weeks ago. So much had happened in that short time.

The flow of water brought thoughts of the sea, tides, the moonstone ring caught among shells and growth on the shore. Seaweed, torn from its roots, to spread seed to another part of the ocean bed. A death of sorts, but a necessary part of the endless circle of life and regeneration.

A fresh gust of wind from the open window produced a dizzy sensation. The ozone tang changed to familiar sweet perfume. Alerted to an approaching vision, Liliha clutched the edge of the sink and toppled inside the aperture toward the unknown.

***

Exhilarating freedom washes over my mind. At last, the tumbling journey ends and I gain balance.

In the early dawn, I concentrate to pick out details below. Houses spread along suburban streets. Occasional lights resembling stars in the night sky twinkle behind swaying branches.

I must be in an overseas country, separated by half a revolution of the Earth. Will I prevent a crime? Assist a child?

In an overwhelming rush, I'm sucked down.

My psyche heads for a solid roof, slips between particles the way sunshine penetrates glass, and hovers inside a kitchen. Overhead electric light bounces off the shiny table. The smell of dust battles with the scent of air freshener in the stifling atmosphere.

I pop into a woman's mind, grasp her name which echoes from her husband's voice after he leaves the room.

Now I observe with Mora's eyes. She doesn't feel my presence. Her elbows lean on the table, her head resting in her hands. Emerging from a nightgown, the skin of her inner arms hangs loose, cratered like the surface of the moon.

I absorb her sorrow and regret over the recent loss of her daughter in another part of the country. Unable to travel because of her disability, she wonders if she could have made more effort.

No use joining her in grief although I'm tempted. I must remain impassive if I'm to work with her. This is why I'm here. My empathy rises with the softness of a gentle breeze lifting damp locks from the neck on a hot day.

Her husband James re-enters the room clad in pajama pants and wiping his forehead with a handkerchief. We straighten to face him, quivering hands smoothing tousled hair.

He adds milk to the mugs on the bench and carries them over. "Here you go." His Australian accent soothes us. The bitter aroma of tea rises in the steam and emphasizes his apartness —sympathetic, but the loss is not of his own flesh. His hesitant hand strokes our shoulder. With a sigh, he sits opposite.

James is the perfect person with whom to discuss her self-blame. But she needs a nudge. I whisper, 'Look at his caring manner. He considers your feelings.'

We sip our drink. Memories flood our mind —raising

Laura, teaching her to talk, and welcoming her home after school before she set out on a life of her own. Time passed faster. An indrawn breath. Seventy years old next birthday. Already her child has died before her.

I ease a suggestion into her mind. 'Those who remain must go on.'

A cloud of regret drags us down. She'd lost touch because of the distance and hadn't discovered what was happening during brief contacts. We swallow tears.

Mora retreats into memories. Her daughter drank so much she damaged her liver. Oh, the wicked waste of a precious life. What did she do to cause this flaw in her child?

'Each person takes responsibility for their own life,' I whisper, soft as a feather.

We nod, unable to let go of the past.

How can I help Mora stop this endless remorse? There's no turning back time, but can she go forward? That's what I must achieve. 'Your husband needs you. If you retreat into self-judgment, and lose the joy in your life, he'll follow your lead and give up too.'

A smile flicks over his face. Unwilling to respond, we sink into a numb state.

'He loves you, right here, right now. Nobody lives forever. True love is hard to replace. Don't take him for granted.' We glance up to study him. Hunched shoulders, neck leaning to one side in the grip of advancing age, fragility replaces his once proud strength.

Shock at his potential loss jolts us.

'He's waiting for you to make the first move.'

Releasing a soft breath, we return his smile and blink away self-accusation.

I read the depth of her emotion. She loves him, needs

him, now more than ever.

A rush of warmth rises into our cheeks and filters into every part of our body. We reach out.

I withdraw from her mind and drift up.

***

Liliha turned off the tap, shook excess water off the leaves and placed them in a colander while she considered the lesson learned. Appreciate each moment. Anything could be snatched away.

But more—let go of the past. She'd always love Oliver. Time for her to move on with life, as his message had conveyed. Her loneliness didn't come from a lack of support and understanding. She had those in plenty. Now, she must live her life and strengthen her soul.

Renewed by the simple joy of helping someone out of their separation without interfering or bossing them, she stroked the smooth cabochon moonstone on her ring. She thanked the creator for returning her treasure. Sure, Georg van den Burg had done the work, but who had directed him?

When she'd tried to influence Georg, charming in his own way, her efforts didn't achieve the result she'd hoped for. However, in the long run, he'd been the one to find and return her ring.

Would she ever work out why her mind-shift occurred? Perhaps some events were meant to happen. Maybe the theft of her ring brought out the best in Georg— enough to make him take risks to return it.

He'd never told her how he'd acquired the ring. In no way could she imagine him stealing it from her while she lay unconscious. With his integrity established, she admired his honor in not blaming someone else.

All mankind's experts couldn't provide answers to the most basic questions of creation. The human race had developed an ability to plan and second-guess. They'd become strong enough to dominate all the other species. Was their increase in numbers meant to happen? Their actions had weakened the planet. She hoped mankind would understand and change before they caused irreparable harm.

At the sound of approaching footsteps, she let go of her thoughts. Outside on the cobbled street, Sarah approached the gate clutching a large parcel.

Liliha hurried to open the door, appreciating how her good friend had called in every day as promised. "What have you got there?"

"I've brought my finished painting."

"I'm dying to see. The table's clear."

In the kitchen, Sarah removed the wrapping. "I smell vinegar."

"I'm making salad. There is enough for two if you would like to stay." When Sarah shook her head, Liliha said, "Come on, open it."

Sarah lifted out a canvas filled with wonderful colors, and then stepped away.

"Wow," Liliha said. A gleaming maroon Rolls Royce swished a spray of mud from the gutter onto a shelter made from cartons beside the road. Inside the car, the satisfied smirk of a tubby man and an overdressed scowling woman faced the street ahead. From the hovel, a gaunt face smiled at a small scruffy dog shaking moisture from his coat. Her mouth opened in wonder. "You've captured the difference between wealth and poverty perfectly."

"Did you like my choice of car?"

Liliha nodded, involved in the story so skillfully

captured on the board. "Who do you think is happier with their lot?"

"I hope the painting will make people think." Sarah glanced at Liliha's face. "Everything okay?"

"Ellen's gone. She left with Georg for London."

"Funny kid." Sarah sat on a straight-backed chair. "I admire the way you helped her, but it's not always safe with a stranger."

"I know." Easing onto a chair, Liliha joined Sarah in a wry smile. "I must have reached her in a roundabout way." Liliha touched her forehead. "Or did she change because she had to hide from Matt?"

"Lucky Alana could take her."

Liliha sighed. "Well, everything worked out in the end."

"Will you miss her?"

"To tell you the truth, I'm looking forward to a rest." Plenty of diversions during her visions. Satisfaction too. "My job at the tearooms finishes soon."

"That's my cue." Sarah stood. "I'm off to collect my man."

***

At eight thirty in the evening, Liliha settled in her comfortable chair in the living room and waited for Kaelyn to answer the phone in Australia. After high voices and the occasional hollow call, a scrape indicated a presence on the phone.

"Hello, Mum."

"Hi, darling. How's everything?"

"Okay. I'm settling into my job and I get on well with the people there. Eddie's got a job too. And, before you ask, I haven't heard about my medical tests. I'm a bit anxious, but the doctor assures me the condition is controllable if the results are positive. So don't worry. What have you been doing lately?"

Liliha swallowed her concerns. "I had a guest staying here. A young woman. She's gone now."

"Why? Was she a friend of Yvonne's?"

"She needed somewhere to stay and I felt sorry for her."

"Are you coping alright?" Kaelyn's voice wavered.

"I'm fine. Of course, I still miss Oliver."

"How's ... you know...?"

Liliha's heart thumped loud in her ears. "You mean my visions? Everything's okay." The opportunity to mention Kaelyn's worry had arrived at last. "I think the bracelet's been hidden away. No more of those horrible contacts from the scarab lately."

"What a relief."

"Oh. Another thing. I lost my ring for a few days too."

"Your wedding ring?"

"The other one ... the star moonstone," Liliha said.

An intake of breath. "But ..."

"The ring turned up on the sand surrounded by seaweed."

"As if I'd believe that. Mum, you tell stories."

Liliha chuckled. "I live them too, as you well know. Let's talk about you. Are you doing anything special tonight?"

"Eddie and I are going out." Kaelyn's voice held a quiver. "Dad bought me a new dress."

Pain shot into Liliha's heart. Life went on. No use feeling left out. "I hope you have a great time."

"Thanks, Mum. Well. Gotta go."

"I love you."

"Me too. Speak to you soon." The phone went dead.

Liliha took a moment before calling Alissa. When her daughters visited again, life would return to normal and she'd welcome them with open arms.

A sudden swirl of air raised the hairs on her neck.

The candle on the mantelpiece fluttered.

Smoke formed the shape of a face. Between one blink and the next, she caught the impression of lips forming words. *'Well done.'* The apparition dissolved.

Liliha leaned back, gripped her hands behind her neck and sighed.

-The End-

About the Author:

Francene Stanley found initial inspiration in poetry and songwriting but later turned to writing novels. Like her main characters, she expresses optimism, determination to succeed, and illustrates the principle of positive thinking combined with the trust that things will work out. You can see how this works in the Moonstone series novels: Still Rock Water, Tidal Surge & Shattered Shells.
Born in South Australia, Francene married young. Retreating to the small fishing village of Robe, she ran a craft shop and tea room, welcoming tourists to the area. In the nineteen seventies, she and her husband travelled in a caravan with three children around Australia looking at various ways of alternative living.
After her divorce, Francene left Australia and moved to England, where she worked as a nanny, travelling around the world with the family she worked for. She met her present husband in London, worked in the catering business for 12 years, and travelled extensively.

Acknowledgements:

I consider myself lucky to have worked with a talented group of novelists in the Internet Writers Workshop. There is so much to learn through association with like-minded word-smiths. Similarly, contact with my publisher, Solstice Publishing, and their group of authors has given me support in a field which is crammed with new books.

Social media links:

Facebook author page:
https://www.facebook.com/Authfs

Twitter:
https://twitter.com/FranceneStanley

Amazon author page:
http://www.amazon.co.uk/Francene-Stanley/e/B007XP8D7C/ref=ntt_dp_epwbk_0

Daily blog: http://511580395457358476.weebly.com/

Author website:
http://francene--wordstitcher.weebly.com/